CHILDREN OF DISOBEDIENCE

by
A. Findlay Johnson

ANDRE DEUTSCH

First published 1989 by
André Deutsch Limited
105-106 Great Russell Street
London WC1B 3LJ

This is a work of fiction. The island of Boreray is
imaginary and bears no relation to any island of that
name. The people and events described are fictitious and
any resemblance to anyone alive or dead is entirely
coincidental.

The quotations from *Four Quartets* by T.S. Eliot are reprinted
by permission of Faber and Faber Ltd.

British Library Cataloguing in Publication Data

Johnson, A. Findlay, 1947-
Children of disobedience
I. Title
823'.914 [F]

ISBN 0 233 98368 6

Phototypeset by Falcon Graphic Art Ltd
Wallington, Surrey
Printed in Great Britain by
Ebenezer Baylis & Son Limited, Worcester

PRELUDE

Gille nan caorachan, gille nan caorachan, gille nan caorachan, gaolach thu.

— Uist, Traditional.
Boy of the sheep, you are my darling.

Chapter 1

Mairi had a little lamb. One morning very early crows came and pecked out its eyes and tongue. Mairi's father found it. He cursed the crows and threw the dead lamb on the shore. The crows guffawed.

When he had done the round of his ewes and drunk a cup of tea (he was a quiet man) he said to his wife, 'The crows took the wee one's lamb.'

'Oh no! She'll break her heart, she's playing with it all day. You'll have to bring her another one.'

Mairi came down with her sisters and ran out to see her pet. In whispers her mother informed the older girls.

Mairi called, 'Snowy, Snowy!'

She ran in again. 'Where's Snowy?'

But no one would tell her. They fussed her and brushed her hair, gave her chocolate biscuits for breakfast, carried her out to see the chickens. The mother hen was in a coop of her own, so the crows had not got her brood yet.

Mairi asked again after her sisters and brothers had gone to school, 'Where's Snowy, Mammy?'

'You'll see her later. Da's taken her up the hill.'

Later Da came down the hill. Donnie was watching for him. He ran in to tell Mairi, 'Da's coming. He's got Snowy.'

All the girls came out to see. The weary man set down the lamb, and Effie set down Mairi.

'There's Snowy back now!'

But Mairi recoiled, first silent, then wailing, 'No! no! Not Snowy! Not Snowy!'

The mother hurried out when she heard the commotion. 'Look, now, it's a lovely wee lamb Da's brought you. You'll give it its bottle just like Snowy.'

3

Mairi ran away howling, followed by sisters and mother clucking and cajoling. Chrissann smirked. She was only eight, but she knew a pair of balls when she saw them: how was Da thinking a ram lamb would pass for Snowy?

The man was left staring glumly down at the tottery lamb, which nuzzled his gumboot hopefully.

'Ach, I might as well have left you for the bloody crows.'

He became aware of Donnie, watching him with round shining eyes.

'I'll look after him, Da. I'll give him his bottle.'

He looked the little boy over doubtfully. None of his other three sons, the big important ones, had ever wanted to nurse an orphan lamb. It was the girls who took them on.

Donnie stared back, with anxious eyes and reddening cheeks.

'Och well, there's no harm in it. Take it to the shed tonight, and get a bottle from your Mammy.'

He stuffed the lamb into the child's arms and trudged in to the kitchen.

Donnie fed his lamb and loved him. He called him Billy. Billy grew fat and lusty, jumping on the backs of later orphans, and butting them away from the bottle. He butted Donnie too, and sucked his fingers, and bleated loudly whenever he appeared, bouncing up and down the length of the fence in excitement. After some weeks, they put a castration band on him. Donnie cried, but they told him it didn't hurt sheep. Later he lay full length in the buttercups to inspect it. It looked very tight. Donnie squeezed himself as hard as he could and it hurt like anything. He whimpered, with his face in the flowers. Mammy shouted it was tea-time, and he got up, snivelling. Billy was bucking round the field, chasing the other lambs. Perhaps lambs were different.

When Billy got bigger and was let out on the croft, he followed Donnie everywhere, into the shed on wet days, down to the shore, up the hill and under the old upturned boat at the mouth of the burn. Donnie was proud and pleased. His older brothers and sisters had their own concerns, Mairi was timid and clung to house and mother; he had not had such a playmate before. He got new

4

courage for forays off home ground, wandering along the shoreline peering into rock pools, or scrambling to the base of the high crags which rose behind Nanan's house. His adventuring went well, till one day he and Billy visited Uncle Ewan, two miles round the coast. Uncle Ewan said nothing, but walked home with him, holding his hand tightly. Later there was a big scolding from Mammy, and Mammy got a big scolding from Da, and Auntie Effie said, 'That boy needs a hot bottom. You're too soft, too soft.' Everyone was grumpy, and Donnie was banned beyond the croft boundary.

But not Billy. He was a raider. He jumped out onto Nanan's croft, and onto Lal's and Roddy's, and out across the common grazing. He visited Uncle Ewan, who chuckled toothlessly and fed him potatoes when his wife wasn't looking. Billy didn't stay away long: nearly every morning he was at the back door, bleating for scraps and attention. Sometimes he stayed around all day, sometimes he wandered.

By the time he was a year old, he came less often. He went up on the high crags to find green patches of new lush grass, sheltered by overhangs, and uncropped by less agile sheep. There were other orphan lambs on the croft that summer, but Donnie still watched out for Billy, scanning the crags each morning if he wasn't at the door waiting for his toast and jam.

Donnie started school. He didn't like it. The room was hot and noisy and once someone was sick in it and it smelt so bad he thought he might be sick too, and he did not want to be sick in front of all the big boys and girls. The teacher was trying to teach him to read and he could not remember the words except 'dog' and 'cat'. School dinner was horrible.

As autumn drew on, Billy was at the door more often. He was in everyone's potatoes too. He ate Roddy's cabbages. They threw stones at him, but his fleece was thick and he didn't move far. Murdo shot him with the air gun. Donnie flew at Murdo, punching, kicking and biting. Murdo would have thumped him, but Ewan said he'd better not or Mam would catch him.

One sleety October day Billy wasn't there for his breakfast. Donnie went to school reluctantly. Billy would be cold and hungry. When he came home, he asked, 'Where's Billy?'

Mammy was tying up the black puddings she had been making. 'I didn't see him.'

Next morning there was still no Billy. There was no school either: it was Thursday of the autumn communion time. Donnie wandered round the croft, shouting for Billy, down to the shore, up the hill, and under the upturned boat by the burn.

The church bus came and everyone went off in it, except the old great aunt, the two little children, and Effie who was to mind them. Effie was slicing vegetables for soup, with the radio blaring. Mairi was under the table, putting a kitten to bed in her doll's cot. Donnie watched quietly for a while, then as quietly, he spread two slices of bread with jam from the breakfast things still on the table, and stuffed them into his pocket. He went out the front, so that Effie wouldn't see him from the kitchen window. He followed the burn till he was above Nanan's fence, where the hill grew steep and slippery, with boggy rivulets seeping between tumbled boulders. Panting, he looked up at the cliffs, where he would see Billy.

There were many sheep grazing the narrow ledges and steep slopes. Fine rain was sifting from a dull sky, and the top of the escarpment was lost in cloud. One sheep looked much like another in the mist, but Donnie was not disheartened. He would climb on up the cliff, and when he was safe away from Nanan's he would start shouting. Billy would bound down to him and take his bread and jam. They would be home before the people came from church.

Climbing was harder work than it looked. Sometimes he slipped back down water-smoothed slides of rock. Sometimes patches of small scree began to trickle under his feet and hands, slowly at first, then faster and faster, till he scrambled sideways onto firm rock, with pounding heart. He swung himself upwards clinging to clumps of heather and fern, which often gave way, dropping him on his knees.

When he was completely breathless, he stopped climbing and looked around. An old ewe just above him stared at him disapprovingly.

'Baa-aa-aah!' she said, in a hoarse voice. She turned her back and picked her way along a narrow terrace of rock.

Billy wasn't there. The sheep in the mist looked no nearer. But Nanan's house was definitely smaller. Donnie shouted: 'Billy!' Being out of breath, he began to cough, but he hung on to the rock, and didn't fall. After a bit he shouted again, louder and louder, peering up at the misty white blobs on the highest ledges.

At last, one raised a head.

'Billy, Billy, come on!'

The head stayed up.

Joyfully, Donnie scrabbled and clawed his way upwards, shouting while he still had enough wind. He came to a boggy flat place below the last crag. It hung over: he could no longer see the sheep on top of it, but he knew it was the right ledge because of the stunted rowan tree sprouting beneath the lip of the rock, brave with fire-red berries.

He frowned at the wet black outthrust. Water dripped on his face and trickled silently into the deep sphagnum, so that his feet soon stood each in a cold brown pool. There was no way up the rock. But Billy had got up: even Billy couldn't jump the height of a house straight up in the air.

Donnie squelched to the limit of his ledge. A fallen boulder higher than himself blocked his way, with cliff above and steep scree below. He pulled himself up until he could see over it, and there was the way: a narrow grassy slope curving out of sight beyond the top of the ledge. He tumbled over on to it, and clawed and crawled up the slippery wet grass to Billy's platform.

There was a big wedder there, but it was not Billy. It bounded past him, and slithered down the way he had come.

Donnie squatted on the ledge, too tired to think, too tired even to cry. Slowly it came into his mind that he could not get down. He saw Nanan's house, tiny and grey with the red shed roof next to it. If he went off the ledge, he would fall all that long, long way.

The wedder had gone down without falling. Billy could go down.

If Billy came, he could go down with him.

Billy would come soon.

Donnie stood up, on shaking legs, and shouted.

'Billy! Billy!'

His voice echoed back from a dozen faces of rock. There was a raven kronking above him: his voice echoed too.

Donnie was cold. A misty drizzle cut out Nanan's house, cleared and formed and cleared again. He crouched down under a big boulder, where sheep had worn a hollow in the ground. It was dry and maybe the wedder had made the rock warm. He felt better at once.

His cold hand in his wet pocket encountered the forgotten jam sandwich. Suddenly ravenous, he thrust a fistful of soggy bread into his mouth. Then he remembered it was for Billy. Frowning, he scraped it carefully out of his pocket with one hand, placing it in the palm of the other. He squeezed it into a ball to keep it all together, and put it down on a flat stone.

After a minute or so he got up and put it on another stone farther off. He did not want to smell it, because he was so hungry. He hoped Billy would come for it soon. Back in his shelter, he shouted again.

The ravens swooped by, curious to know what was going on. They banked along the cliff face and dropped like falling black rags into the mist. Donnie was pleased to see them, and listened to their conversation before his next shout. One of them soared into view and banked again, very close – too close to Billy's bread and jam. Then Donnie jumped up, and yelled, 'No, no, go away!' Hastily he fetched the titbit back to its former position.

It began to grow dark. Donnie shouted a few times, and dozed, and woke and shouted, and dozed again. He was cold and hungry, but not frightened. He knew Billy would come, and lead him down from the cliffs, and they would go home together.

Flustered, Effie glanced round the kitchen when she heard the bus on the road. Plates, bread, juice for the wee ones, mustard for Dad.

'That's them back,' she called through to Auntie Effie.

'Oh well, well, they didn't take long,' muttered Auntie Effie, disapprovingly. Church in her young day took longer than that – three, four hours at a communion season.

Young Effie poured the potatoes and transferred the last slices of black pudding from the frying pan to a big tin plate in the oven. She took the lid off the soup pot, and dredged out slippery oblongs of mutton flank into a bowl, mashing the residue with the back of a ladle to break up the vegetables. She was a bit anxious about it: had she remembered salt? She tried to taste it from the ladle, but the hot greasy metal burnt her lip.

Voices and footsteps distracted her. The boys crowded in, elbowing each other and complaining about the length of the service. The girls looked consciously improved, and primly hung up their hats, straws with ribbons, one pink, one blue. Dad drew rapturously on his second smoke.

'Did you remember salt?' asked Mam. She tasted, adding 'No,' as she salted.

Effie put the plates round while the family tussled for the bathroom and paid their respects to Auntie Effie.

Dad stubbed out his cigarette and cleared his throat, ready to say grace.

'Shush you boys,' said Mam, as usual, and then, 'Where's wee Donnie?'

'Oh!' Effie flushed. She hadn't been watching. 'He must've went out to play.'

'But it's pouring! Well, maybe in the shed. Have a look, boys.'

Dad lit up again. Johane looked in the bedroom while the brothers checked the shed and then the croft. They returned dripping and grumbling. Auntie Effie muttered under her breath. The soup was getting cold.

'Not there?' Mam had started washing up the cooking things, but now she stopped. 'Then where is he?'

A small voice spoke from under the table. 'He's gone to find Billy.'

Mairi crawled out from her housie-place.

'What? When? Which way?'

But the little sibyl knew no more. She shook her head, reddening, and hid her face against her mother's skirt.

'Oh Angus! What if he's gone out on the cliffs?'

'Ach no! He'll have gone down the shore to Roddy. I'll go out after dinner and see.'

'No!' The mother's face was grey. 'I'll go now.'

'Sit down, woman.' Dad got up and went to his boots by the back door. 'You boys go round the place when you've had your dinner. I'll go as far along as Uncle Ewan's.'

No one spoke after he went out. Effie and Mam were very white. They had both noticed the muddy boots and oilskins go on recklessly over the Sunday suit.

Murdo helped himself to black pudding.

'Aye, aye,' muttered Auntie Effie, mumbling her soup, slowly.

Angus reached Roddy's back door. He could hear Chrissie and her sisters laughing and talking and clattering dishes.

It was his own cousin's house but he did not want to go in. He knocked like a stranger. By good luck it was Roddy that came to the door.

'Is wee Donnie with you?'

He knew he was not.

When the story was out and the women were crowded round exclaiming, Roddy put on his boots over his Sunday suit. Together the two men trudged on up the path. The slope to the sea grew steeper. Heather gave way to bare rock, hillside to low cliffs and then to higher. They peered over the edge. The sea was quiet, but deep, sucking at the black shore. At the top of the pass, the path turned away inland down a shallow valley. Roddy clambered up to the cairn on the seaward side. He had brought his spying-glass. He steadied it on the cairn, and scanned all round.

'No sign,' he said.

They carried on down the valley and over the moor to the coast again. Uncle Ewan's house was at the head of a gentle inlet, where the path wound up and down among russet bracken and the shore was shingle and coloured seaweed, but no child was playing there.

The old man was outside having a smoke. His wife would not let him smoke inside. His smooth-haired sheepdog Nell sat pressed against his knee.

Ewan beamed toothlessly when he saw his son and nephew. They shouted their questions several times, for he was deaf. When he understood, his face turned ashen. 'Oh well well!' he said, shaking his head, and folding his lips in on each other in dismay. 'Oh well well well.'

'He'll most likely be home by now,' said Roddy, loudly.

Nobody believed it. Old Morag came to the door with Ewan's working jacket. 'Take your Sunday one off,' she said.

Her face was impassive, Ewan's creased with distress, but there was one mind between them. When Angus saw it impotent anger filled him.

'Ye old fool,' he stuttered, 'you can't come — you can't come.'

10

But it was no use. He fell silent, and the three men started back across the moor. Nell slunk behind, unreprimanded. At the cairn, Roddy set up his spying-glass again.

He folded it away slowly. 'No sign.'

Angus said, 'We'll try the cliffs above Mam's house.'

Uncle Ewan twisted his shaking hands in and out, in and out before his chest. 'Oh well, oh well,' he whispered.

Angus turned violently down the slope, swearing. The others followed.

From the croft gate they could see Mairi Anna waiting by the door. When she saw the three men with no child she crouched down on her doorstep with her apron to her face. Her daughters crowded round her, howling.

The eldest son shuffled out miserably from the shed.

'We've looked everywhere, Dad. He's no here. He must have gone on the cliffs.'

Angus said slowly, 'Go to Lal's and ring the police.'

The boy stared at him, shocked.

'Go on!' his father shouted, hoarsely.

He went. Uncle Ewan sat down on the wall, speechless now.

Chrissie and her sisters and daughters came, wide-eyed and whispering. Lal's wife Katie came back with Alex Angus, and other neighbours followed. Old Morag strode in silent and dry-eyed, but the others were all weeping, and soon the house was as full of women and tears and whispers as at a funeral. The men hunched outside in the slow rain, silent.

When Donnie's mother saw that they all thought her child was dead, she sank down with her head on the kitchen table and stayed there not moving or speaking. Chrissie cleared the remnants of the meal gently away from her, congealed black pudding and crumbs of bread. But her arm was in a puddle of the wee one's juice, sickly orange seeping into the mauve Sunday dress. Chrissie mopped it with a paper hankie, gulping and crying.

The church bus crawled along the road in the dusk, for the evening service. It was half empty, but the faces of the next township peered down at the Morrison croft. Everyone had heard the news.

The policeman came. He had brought the doctor's young assistant, wearing knee-breeches and a back pack.

11

'Just in case,' said the policeman, steadily, 'we hope he won't be needed.'

Uncle Ewan began to cry too. Nell shoved her nose into his face.

The policeman noticed them. He knew old Ewan, because he had often had to pretend to be unaware of his salmon net. He had seen it clearly all summer as he passed on a distant loop of the road; sometimes with the small green boat in attendance, and the black and white dog at the bow.

'Do you have dogs too, Mr Morrison?' he asked.

'Ay.' They were decently shut in the shed for communion.

'Bring them then. They might get the scent of the wee fellow.'

Out came Moss and Fly. The searchers set off in a long horizontal line beyond the croft boundary, Roddy at one end and the doctor's assistant at the other. It was almost dark, and the mist had changed to thick low cloud and steady driving rain from the south-west. Even with torches and shouting it was difficult for each man to keep track of the next; but everyone knew they had to keep in contact, if they were not to miss the small body huddled below a crag or face-down in a peat pool. Very slowly, they made their way up, sending the dogs through each gully and out on every ledge.

Uncle Ewan stumbled at Angus's heels. He couldn't manage to carry a torch and drag himself up, so he dropped his torch. It rolled away and bounced down, down to old Johane's house. Uncle Ewan couldn't shout: he was breathing too hard. He couldn't hear the others shouting, because he was deaf and the blood pounded in his ears. No one noticed he had followed, till with a sudden hoarse cry he grabbed Angus's ankle on a ledge above him.

'Listen you! Listen you!' he gasped.

Angus and Murdo and the policeman listened, but heard only, 'Away there, Fly,' 'Hi Neil!' 'Up here, Lal.'

'There's nothing. Get back,' said Angus, savagely.

'It's wee Donnie. Listen now!'

'He's as deaf, he'll never . . .' began Murdo, but then in an instant between shouting they all heard it: a high distant voice calling 'Billy!'

The father flung himself upwards in the direction of the sound. Uncle Ewan couldn't move. He summoned enough breath to shout in a cracked voice, 'Away to Donnie, Nell' and sat down suddenly on a boulder.

Donnie was dreaming Nell was licking his face.

'Hello Nell,' he said, and kissed her in return. Then he woke up with a start, terrified of the wet, hairy panting thing he could not see. He gave a sharp wail of fear. Nell whimpered and licked his ears and eyes and squirmed against his chest and he knew it was her.

'Oh Nell, where's Billy? Is he down at you?'

Nell whined with love and relief but he was not sure what she meant about Billy. Her whines grew to a volley of excited barks.

There was a faint shout – more shouting and closer – lights bobbing.

Donnie crouched very still, sick, cold and frightened. They would be angry, very angry. And they wouldn't look for Billy now it was dark.

His father was calling him, hoarsely, between oaths. A torch flashed above the rim of the ledge, and the man heaved up after it, gasping. Donnie was grabbed and crushed roughly against wet oilskin. His father was making funny noises. Donnie had never seen a man crying so he did not know that was what it was.

Men and dogs yelled and barked and piled onto the ledge, grinning faces peering up between the great boots when there was no more standing room. Everyone was shouting and joking and Alex Angus kept thumping him on the back and laughing and laughing.

'Did you find Billy?' asked Donnie at last. Maybe that was why they were so happy? His heart jumped.

His voice was lost in the clamour.

He was suddenly utterly weary, battered and hemmed in by the noise and the big boots and the smell of men who work with sheep. Hands passed him down the crag and set him on his father's shoulder. He lurched half-asleep, making nonsense of the talk, aware only of the torches which flashed and bobbed, gleaming on wet rock and splintering in the falling rain. There was something he wanted but he did not remember what it was. It gleamed and he nearly caught it, it splintered and drifted away.

They reached the gate in the fence by Nanan's house and saw the lighted doorway. There were figures running down to it, Ewan and Alex Angus, racing each other. People came out, and there was more noise, women this time, shrieking and then laughing.

Da swung him down and delivered him to his weeping mother.

'There's your wee lamb!' He was laughing and said it again and again.

Donnie struggled out of his mother's arms, but he was pulled and tousled by his sisters and Nanan and Chrissie. Everyone was pushing and exclaiming and they smelt of talcum powder and Sunday clothes.

He saw Uncle Ewan, toothless and beaming, and Nell, and remembered. He thrust the women away as hard as he could and spoke as loud as he could: 'Where's Billy?'

There was quiet for a moment, then his mother made to snatch him up. He darted away, through the open door, across the living room and into the kitchen, blinking and staring in the bright light at the homely scene now foreboding as a nightmare, the scattered toys and thrown-down coats, the half-empty soup pan, the platter of fat-stuck black pudding.

They followed him in and he opened his mouth and screamed. His screams rose and joined together till he no longer saw anyone or anything.

The doctor's assistant gave him an injection. He was glad to do something. It had really been meant for the mother when they broke the news of her child's death, but half of it did nicely for Donnie.

'That will make him sleep for twenty-four hours,' he told her, 'and we'll be in to see him tomorrow afternoon. Don't hesitate to ring if you're worried, now.'

They thanked him with deference and escorted him to the gate, and he went away feeling warm and jaunty, pleased to have been of use.

Donnie's question got no answer. He woke up next day, and was quiet and petted and visited all weekend. On Monday he went back to school and was just his old self, Mammy said, and he never mentioned Billy and neither did anyone else.

But love and grief sank in his heart like a stone in deep water, lying there so still he forgot what he carried around with him. Yet it would drag him away at last from everything he knew, to anchor in a strange sea.

PART ONE

How but in custom and in ceremony
Are innocence and beauty born?

— 'Prayer for my Daughter', W.B. Yeats

chunna' mi long steach'sa bhàghan,
co bh'air an stiuìr ach mo leannan?
ògannach ciùin, foinnidh, fearail,
mo run Ailean . . .

— Uist, Traditional

I saw a boat in the bay: who was at the helm but my sweetheart? A young man calm, handsome, brave – my love Alan.

Chapter 2

Alan loved boats. His passion was promiscuous: any boat would do, every boat was lovable. Recent experiences crewing a racing thoroughbred between Auckland and Portsmouth did not detract at all from his delight in the tubby, grubby little ferry with the fat red funnel now rolling gracelessly out into the rainy Minch. On the contrary, he felt like running up the mast from sheer joie de vivre. There were footholds, but a covert glance at the massive bosun grimly coiling warps amidships convinced him the behaviour would not be acceptable. He stuck his knuckles hard down in his pockets, quivering with pleasure, and bounded down the companionway. A small group of men in bonnets waiting for the purser's office to open stared at him curiously and he took the next flight less impetuously. This brought him to the car-deck. He had two boats down there, one precariously crowning the other, trailed by a beaten-up Transit van. The vehicle was borrowed but the boats were his, though they might have seemed a doubtful asset to anyone but Alan. The top one was recognisably a Fireball, not young, but intact, only lacking sails; a month's pay in the new job would remedy that deficiency, hopefully before winter set in. The underneath craft was more distressed. She was (perhaps) an Inellan-class sloop, Largs-built in the 1890s. The shape and dimensions of her clinker hull convinced him of her decent ancestry, but she bore marks of bastardisation. Her ballast keel had been supplemented by a grotesque iron fin, and her mast had taken two hops backwards before disappearing altogether. Someone had squeezed a tiny cabin out of her seventeen feet, reducing the deep cockpit to barrel-size. A taste for the grandiose was evident in the elaborate panels and mouldings lining the cabin, and in the now broken scroll-work adorning the corners of the coachroof. Flourishes worthy of the Great Harry surrounded the bowsprit and the letters

16

of her name: but the letters themselves were almost illegible, and the bowsprit was reduced to a jagged filthy stump, protruding now igno-miniously from under the tarpaulin. She was scabby with generations of barnacles, spilt paint and seagull shit. Her transom was holed and her planks gaped. Alan gazed at her with love: *Selena*, or so he had romantically deduced from the faded letters SE which were all that was left of her name.

He had found her during a summer of dinghy instructing in Argyll, in a sheltered inlet which was the favoured venue for new parties. She might still have been lying there forlorn, if the third Tuesday had not been windy, and his pupils untalented. At the end of an exasperating afternoon, he had said (thinking now or never), 'Head for that cluster of floats by the old jetty and we'll go about.'

'Yes,' agreed the middle-aged lady on the helm, but without enthusiasm.

'Now, perhaps?' suggested Alan, encouragingly: he had a tendency to increased politeness under duress.

'Ready about – Lee-ho – ' whispered the poor pupil, hope-lessly; and then clutching the tiller as if frozen to it she squeaked, 'Which way?'

A sudden gust pushed the boat on her ear and the lady on her bottom, and the tangle of floats and ropes and broken slats surged up on the bow. Alan swore and leapt from side to side, bewildering the erstwhile helmswoman and delighting her teenage daughter, who was crew. When they were safely on the other tack he retrieved her spectacles from the bilge with a charming smile and apologies for his language. He was excited. He had noticed a fluid sheerline among the broken rectangles of the jetty: barely more, but that was as enticing as a girl's nipples under a tee-shirt.

Weather and his pupil's nervous disintegration allowed him to finish early. He began the pursuit at once. Since the way to find things out in a strange land is to go to the pub, he was there by opening time. The barman was surly, however. Hates the English, thought Alan, who was Scottish but used to this sort of rebuff, being tall, blondish, ex-public school and therefore unrecognisable to his countrymen. There was a frizzy-haired girl sitting in the corner eating a sandwich, whom he had seen kayaking around in the loch of the collapsing jetty. Judging that she was very unlikely to share the barman's prejudices, he treated her to his most disarming smile. She was disarmed. Her name was Frances. He soon learnt that the jetty lay in the grounds of a derelict neo-baronial hotel, bypassed since the decline of railways and pleasure steamers. There were plans for redevelopment, including a small marina.

'I'll give you a run out there, if you like,' said Frances, with transparent cunning and flushing cheeks, which were freckled.

Alan was accustomed to such useful effects of his lithe good looks. He felt distantly sorry for her confusion but not to the extent of refusing the offer of a lift. Vagrant instructors, however attractive, were not permitted to borrow boats outside working hours, since one had demolished a brand new craft on a return trip from the rival pub across the loch.

They were very soon winding round the shore road in Frances's van. It was a large vehicle, she explained, because she used so much equipment. She was researching on survival rates of larval shallow-water crustacea, and carried an assortment of nets, tanks, pumps and cameras. Alan expressed an interest in larval crustacea, to conceal his greater interest in her vehicle; he was rather ashamed that he had already noticed it had a towing hitch.

A bottle of whisky to the contractor's boys had proved enough to release the boat from her dreary prison: so that three months later she lay hopefully in the ferry hold, attached to Frances's tow bar. He repositioned the blocks under the trailer wheels, checked the handbrake, and squirmed as far aft as was possible on the crowded car-deck to inspect the web of knots securing the huge untidy bundle. The ferry was by now both pitching and rolling, and the gleaming roof of the new BMW parked next to Selena looked in danger as she jarred on the overloaded trailer springs. Alan watched for a few minutes, but she didn't actually rub. He thought if he met someone who obviously belonged to a BMW he might mention it: three inches forward would clear it. Selena on her trailer was impossible to reverse.

He left his boat rather reluctantly, but the car-deck was hot and clangorous. He glanced cautiously into the bar. It was occupied by more of the quiet men in bonnets, drinking decorously but with purple faces. The air was foul with smoke and stale whisky, but not with oaths. Alan was surprised by this, being familiar with the drinking habits of more southern Scots. Boreray people must be a different breed.

The swing doors of the cafeteria spewed forth a panicking mother and two green-faced children. He flattened himself to the wall as they surged into the ladies. He could see father abandoned in a corner amidst rolling plastic cups and scattered crisps, stoically spoon-feeding a fat-faced infant and wiping away its regurgitations with an inadequate paper napkin.

Family life, thought Alan, happily.

The only other occupants were two surreal figures in black, poised in silent eyeball-to-eyeball confrontation, each shading his brow with a pallid hand. Alan was so fascinated he opened the door, though he didn't in fact have the money even for a cup of coffee. The black characters simultaneously replaced their black homburgs on their pale pink pates, and as they raised their heads, the grace being over, their white dog-collars identified them. They stirred sugary tea and stuck knives into sausages.

Alan wrinkled his nostrils, feeling queasy, not from the movement of the boat but from the heavy odour of rancid cooking oil, frying burgers and stale bacon. He didn't eat meat unless he was quite exceptionally hungry. The solemn twins had chips and bright green peas as well as sausages.

In the observation lounge rain and spray rattled on the windows and the horizon lurched beyond the foredeck. The huge bosun was stolidly sorting his coils of this and that down there. Alan made his way out between benches occupied by tall German girls supine and prone, with pale faces and large rucksacks.

The ship churned a soapsuds wake through a foam-streaked sea. Black waves rose glassily quiet to starboard, and broke with a slap and a long hiss on her side. The rigging sang and jangled. Silent gulls banked and steadied round the stern, sleek and wàry-eyed. Relays of them perched on the rail for a free ride, the adults flying off when importuned by unwieldy speckled youngsters drawing in their necks in hopes of appearing smaller: family life in the gull world. Suddenly one plummeted and then there were none at all: they were all squabbling on the water for the cafeteria waste.

The gulls grew tiny and distant and beyond them the mainland sank into an irresolute grey of low clouds, spray and rain. Alan

19

went forward and leant out to see if Boreray was visible yet, but ahead was only an uneasy horizon and scudding spume. The wind tore at his hair and filled his lungs to aching. He retreated to a sheltered bench, very happy, licking salt from his lips. One of the German girls walked by, glancing at him in surprise, and he realised that *soave sia il vento* had not remained inside his head and anyway must seem a very inappropriate ditty to anyone feeling as seasick as this girl obviously was. She turned and walked back and he smiled at her in the usual way. But this time he really meant it. He had not felt so free and light-hearted since returning to Britain. He was at sea, on a plump Russian doll of a boat with more boats in her belly; and going to live on an island that was only forty square miles of land in a large quantity of ocean. Also, by removing to Boreray, he was putting a good stretch of water between himself and his mother, thus indirectly furthering two important negative aims: not to get married and not to have a career. Recent escapes had been painful, if not particularly narrow. Argyll had not been safe enough; she had even telephoned him to say she would be shooting on a friend's estate near Fort William, and wouldn't he like to join her for a weekend so that they could really talk? He had only got out of that one by referring to the absentee laird in question, distastefully but accurately, as 'one of your boyfriends'. That made her go quiet: she was prudish, though loose. But the conversation had left him feeling so guilty for not being nicer to her that it had hardly been worth being nasty in the first place. He usually avoided making vicious remarks for that reason. The recollection of the two letters in his pocket bothered him, too. He had taken care not to look at the handwriting, but one of them was certain to be a follow-up to that telephone call. He had met the post van while negotiating a tricky downhill bend that morning, and had grabbed the envelopes through the open window as he became aware that the brakes were inadequate to the occasion. Since no further excuse for forgetting about them presented itself, he pulled them out. One from Mother and the other from Sally, even worse than expected. He extracted both letters and glanced quickly to see which looked more threatening.

'Darling Alan,' his mother began, and 'Darling Alan,' Sally wrote.

He stared gloomily out to sea for a few minutes before going any further.

20

'I was *so* disappointed not to see you last weekend,' his mother continued. 'I knew it would be our last chance before you went off to that dreadful island, but really after what you said about Robert I simply couldn't bear to call on you. It makes me so miserable darling to think that you are my only son and I was within an hour's drive of you and didn't dare come to you because I knew I wouldn't be welcome. It would have been perfectly lovely if you had come, Robert's daughters were both there on Saturday night and you would really like them now – I know you remember them as podgy little girls with pigtails but they are both *gorgeous* now and Emma is into absolutely *everything* you are, she is just back from whalewatching in California or somewhere . . . '

Here Alan broke off, swearing under his breath on behalf of poor pestered whales.

'Anyway, that brings me to one of the things I wanted to talk about . . . '

Alan cursed again, aloud.

'I *have* to say this darling, please forgive me – you have been perfectly beastly to Sally. As I tried to tell you when you were with us (briefly!) the poor girl imagined all the time you were away that you were going to marry her. Her mother says she went into her room unexpectedly and found her with a pile of *Brides* magazines crying her heart out, now don't you see how pathetic that is? I know when we were all in Madeira just before you came home she bought *yards* of antique lace and I'm sure she was thinking of her dress. (Darling, I do hope you don't think that's funny 'cause I know how awful you are about clothes.) Sally is incredibly pretty and I can't believe you really don't care for her. You *must* grow up! It is putting such a strain on Harold – you know how indebted he is to Sally's father and so far, I must say, the Clements have been very understanding but I do feel a coolness growing. It could be very awkward for all of us.

'Well, you do know what I think about it sweetie. I know you have always had lots and lots of girlfriends or should I say partners but you *will* have to settle down like everyone else in the end.'

So twenty-three is the end. Partners indeed! Poor Sally, he thought, as the implications sank in.

'I do realise you have never got on with Harold (but that is so stubborn – he only wants you to act sensibly darling and especially he doesn't like all these silly rumours. It was really naughty of you to bring that French boy here, and *I* know it was just a joke but Harold was so embarrassed . . . '

Alan's mouth twitched. It had been the best joke ever at his stepfather's expense, worth a weekend in the company of the appalling Jean-Jacques. He grinned, wondering if Harold had found the three copies of *Gay Times* concealed under the cushions by the swimming pool.

' . . . and quite furious.) Anyway, supposing you don't want to work with Harold, surely you could let him help you to find your feet. We would both be so relieved. John Clement would I'm sure be as helpful to you as he has been to Harold. It's simply childish to go on telling us how bored you would be making money – what about spending it?? You *must not* end up like your father – such a waste of talent and of everything. Did I tell you the Fowlers met Torquil in NY last month? He has taken up with a girl of *nineteen* can you imagine? And absolutely blotto half the time. Apparently several of his papers have dropped him – he never sits through a performance now, which isn't much good for a music critic is it?'

Alan's grin faded as he read this. There wasn't much more, though what there was did not improve.

'I do hope you enjoy your new job, but really I think it sounds perfectly frightful. There can't be *any* money in teaching boatbuilding and whatever else it is to a handful of bumpkins. Please please think about all I have said – you really must get your head out of the clouds.

With lots and lots of love darling,

Mummy xxx.

P.S. Sally's birthday is on the 20th. It would help if you were to send her something.'

Alan crumpled the three pages into a ball and aimed it over the rail, then changed his mind in reverence for the sea and thrust it forcefully into his pocket. His mouth was dry with anger. He focussed on a group of gannets crossing the bows. They headed out to sea and plunged in disciplined succession, with a knife-thrust accuracy which went some way to calming his nerves for the second letter. It was written on some sort of self-consciously recycled paper, with a shadow picture of an elm tree. Sally was no greenie: presumably she had bought it to please him.

'You said not to write but your mother told me about your teaching job on a small island, it sounds quite exciting and romantic. I couldn't let you go without wishing you all the very best. Don't be cross because I am just writing as a friend, I know there is nothing between us now and I really do realise that you meant it was all over.

'I just wish Mummy would realise it too, she is such a pain, and it doesn't make things any easier because I am very unhappy, I can't help telling you that. I wish you had let me know how you felt before you went abroad, everything is such a mess now.

'Anyway that is not what I am writing to say, I only want to wish you good luck. I expect I'll hear how you are enjoying it from your mother, she has been very nice to me.

'Hope to see you at Christmas – don't be nervous, I really *do* know it's over!

Best love,
Sally.'

Poor dumb Sally. Three of her vapid ill-punctuated letters had awaited him in Punta del Este, and he had been touched, but quite unaware of the yards of antique lace. If the restaurant of the celebration dinner hadn't supplied free postcards, she wouldn't even have got one. Only the champagne had inspired him to scrawl generously over four of them, ending, untypically, 'Love you!' He had certainly never spoken the words to her.

The seasick German girl walked aft, looking at him sideways. He caught himself in mid-smile. Hell, why do I do that? He wandered to the rail, and leant forward into the wind, but there was nothing in view yet but ragged grey clouds and ragged grey sea. He slumped down in his corner, still holding Sally's letter, uncomfortably conscious of increasing agitation. He would always go a long way round to avoid being either author or victim of recriminations. It seemed to him incredible and unfair that he was being pursued across the Minch by his mother and Sally, when he had made such efforts to take himself off where they wouldn't trip over him. He would buy peace at any price, short of going anywhere near them. He had a great disinclination for emotional scenes, and even for memories or

23

threats of emotional scenes. The present symptoms of raised emotion, to which he was far from immune, were alarming indications of loss of peace to come. He dreaded the tight throat, hot ears and raised pulse as the queasy consumer of suspect shellfish dreads the onset of food poisoning.

He watched hopefully for more gannets to suppress these manifestations, but it was no use. His mother's disingenuous pleas thumped in his veins. The crafty bitch. 'Very nice to me,' said Sally. Yes, for a purpose. 'My only son,' said the upright matron. Harold this and Harold that – what about Robert and half a dozen others, what about Torquil rotting in New York? Shallow self-dramatising whore. Grotesque repulsive old bag.

Suddenly his anger collapsed. She would hate to be called old. At fifty she still bore a valiant resemblance to a leggy blonde. Her repair work was discreet and effective, and her backview in tight faded jeans remained exhilarating. But he remembered that last time he had seen her in a bikini there were wrinkles on the tops of her breasts. That seemed a pathetic pointer: twenty years on she would be part of the tortoise-necked *vieillesse dorée* he had seen laid out in rows in Florida, blue lips smeared with scarlet lipstick, brains addled by slimmer's malnutrition and gin. And doubtless Robert would be fucking his secretary, if he could still get it up.

Well, there wasn't much left in her head, except the increasingly desperate pursuit of her own reflection. Perhaps there never had been. He remembered sprawling on her bedroom floor in the childhood house in Atholl, counting the spokes and flourishes of the plaster ceiling-rose in a warm sleepy miasma of scent and nail-polish, while she sat in her underslip painting her eyelids and trying her hair this way and the other. They must have spent hours like that, days and weeks. That was what home meant: Torquil coming in laughing, with a glass in each hand, a martini for her and a double whisky for himself.

'Celia, aren't you ready yet, darling?'

'Very nearly, darling.'

He would set down the glasses and kiss her neck, then roll Alan over and pull him along by the arms, saying, 'Time for bed, boy!'

He was always easier after a whisky or two, but at that time he never drank during the day. When Harold replaced him Alan hadn't waited to be told it was time for bed. No more scent and lacy lingerie: he had begun to understand their uses.

And now she lived in mock-Tudor glory in Surrey, with hunters in the paddock and Harold in the City. She was a star in the local firmament, with the status and confidence that accrues to women when they are both seducers of husbands and respectable matriarchs. Inevitably, the second category must rise in importance as the first falls with age. She longed, she had begun to claim, for grandchildren: she could imagine them playing in the knot-garden talking to the stone cherub – wouldn't it be divine?

Alan had thought it would be more miraculous than divine. He was not interested in propagation.

'Darling, you're such a cynic!'

'You seemed quite bored by it yourself, Mummy.' He said it lightly enough, but she was irritated by the truth of it.

'That *is* unfair, Alan. Things were very difficult with Torquil – he really was impossible, and so stingy! And that great barn of a house in the country. I was desperate to get out – sometimes I could have screamed—'

'You did. But I meant, you and Harold could have produced if you'd felt inclined.'

'I should have loved to darling, of course. But how could I? You were such a miserable little thing at the time – so jealous – you'd have hated me for it.'

Alan had wandered uneasily off round the knots, kicking the cherub with covert savagery. There had been a man called Enrico for several years who was oily and dark. Harold was pasty and fair: even he might have remarked on a swarthy infant, though he did not notice much that happened outside the pages of the *Financial Times*, which matched his complexion.

That conversation had taken place just after his return to England, before he had realised Sally had been laid as bait in the respectability trap. The plotting behind it was so crude he hadn't even suspected it. He knew, of course, that he was a prime personal asset to Celia, a bargaining piece in the incessant game of one-up played at bridge, cocktails and dinner, at weddings and christenings and, he suspected, in the bedrooms of men with less gratifying sons. She could lay to her credit his brilliant, if flighty, school career, Oxford successes social

25

and academic, dashing exploits on the Himalayas or high seas, hints of affairs with beautiful people of both sexes. Even Harold made good capital out of all this, as long as the offspring of anyone who mattered were plugging away at cramming college, failing secretarial courses, and eloping with stable-boys. But at twenty-one local custom decreed a change of lifestyle.

'I'm *very* surprised Alan hasn't gone in with Harold.'

'I say, is Alan really working in a boatyard?'

'Is Alan still at that Findhorn place? How odd!'

'Patrick's wedding was *such fun*. What a pity for you darling that Alan has other ideas.'

Harold in particular disliked other ideas. He had never found the suspicion of boyfriends remotely amusing: and with AIDS in the ascendant no one else was likely to either. Hadn't Celia noticed the vicar wiping the chalice these days?

The vicar could have spared himself the trouble for Alan, who was not to be found in his congregation. That was another grievance: forays in Katmandu festooned with incense and bells were to be expected in undergraduate days, but a speedy return to Anglicanism, jacket and tie, was a test of mature worth.

Sally went to church, in a Victorian squirrel-fur muff in winter and designer hats in summer. She had a boyfriend called George who sometimes accompanied her in his old school tie and hand-made shoes. George was an accomplished bridge player. Sally's mother described his prowess in glowing terms to Celia. Celia was nettled. Alan had once ruined a bridge evening by playing stretched full-length on a sofa.

Alan was a little nettled too. He had played tennis and gone hacking with Sally off and on for years. She was agreeably pretty in the approved leggy blonde manner, and intellectually undemanding.

Celia asked the Clements to dinner – 'Nothing formal, just the two families.'

Alan suggested a hack on Saturday afternoon. George played war games with his friends most Saturdays. Sometimes Sally went too. 'But I'd rather go for a ride,' she said placidly. 'I do think these games are childish, and you get covered in paint.'

Celia sang Sally's praises. Alan saw how her mind was moving, but didn't feel inclined to resist. He was appallingly bored, at home

26

for a spell after climbing in Nepal. He would have quickly found some other interest if he hadn't been hanging on the hope of racing round at least the second half of the world; he had the promise of a place if some more seasoned crew member dropped out. Sally was a pleasant enough diversion. She was at a loose end too, waiting for a friend to finish at college so that they could start a cordon bleu course in Paris together.

They rode Celia's hunters and went for woodland walks with the Clements' dog. George disappeared, after a row overheard by Mrs Clement and reported to Celia, leaving Sally with a tranquil smile. Celia held another dinner party to review progress. With his place secured, his ticket paid for, and the last of Torquil's allowance to him looking as if it needed spending, Alan took her to a few expensive restaurants, where there was scarcely anything he considered fit to eat. But she loved it. She was happy with lots of noise and people to comment on, without the strain of too much conversation.

'I shall get so fat!' she said each time, as she must have said to dozens of expensive men in expensive places. 'But I do adore sweet things.'

She was willowy slim, but Mrs Clement was of regal proportions, and watching Sally attack Gâteau St Honoré he could see the family likeness.

They went to theatres, and to the opera twice: *Traviata* and *The Magic Flute*.

'Wonderful – really moving,' Sally proclaimed the first, without tears; and the other, 'magical,' but she had yawned through Pamina's agony. Alan felt obscurely angry as he hailed a taxi, but once sitting beside her, complacent in her longline wild-silk jacket, he pitied her, and took her hand affectionately. She was an incredibly stupid girl, but quite without ill feeling.

With only two weeks left, he made love to her one evening in a romantic woodland clearing. The dog was scandalised. So was Alan, when she told him it was her first time.

'I don't think people should before they're engaged, do you? Not really properly.'

Alan missed the hint, if it was one, being preoccupied with the horrible possibility of pregnancy. But no, she had been on the pill with George: it seemed that there were ways of not really properly having intercourse which presented as great a risk as the act itself. The puzzling morality of the distinction amused Alan greatly.

In any case, she was not averse to doing it again. Mrs Clement pursued charitable work some afternoons, leaving them conveniently in possession of Sally's befrilled white bedroom. Sally seemed gratified, though not ecstatic. He leafed through her reading material while she was in the shower: women's magazines, two types. The first had children's knitting patterns and recipes for cakes and pies, the second articles on rape and finance and recipes for orgasm. In the one the male appeared as a disembodied head, in the other as a disassociated phallus. What on earth did a girl like Sally make of the dichotomy? Alan stretched lazily, caught sight of his reflection in the long mirror, and regarded it thoughtfully: a fine-boned blue-eyed head set on a spare bronzed torso, strong thighs, nice tight balls, and hair only in the right places. Perhaps the dichotomy was resolved for her. He laughed, admiring his even white teeth, then turned away sheepishly. He was not really vain, most of the time.

All the same, he could not help feeling he had done her rather a favour.

On the day of his departure, she drove him to the airport. They talked about her trip to Paris.

'I'm so looking forward to it!' she said, bright-eyed as a child anticipating Christmas. 'I know I'll spend every penny on clothes.'

Every penny was quite a sum, but Alan didn't doubt it.

She kissed him goodbye affectionately. 'Lucky you – all that sunshine! Wish I were going too.'

'Have a lovely time in Paris.'

'I shall! 'Bye!'

That was all. No tears, promises or reproaches. So on his return to England, he was at first perplexed, then dismayed, to discover what the mothers had been up to in his absence. Celia's reasoning was simple: if he married, that would save her humiliation and Harold ill-temper; if he married a girl used to luxury, he would have to take up a responsible career a once; if he married Sally, her father would enhance the money-making capacity of both generations. The plot was as economical and as monumentally unfeeling as a work of Nature. Docile Sally would bend with the wind.

He had counted on that docility to save her pain when at length, after furious scenes with his mother, he had gone to see her. She had seemed to take things quite well at first, agreeing that she had rather thought he was going to marry her; agreeing also that he had never suggested it, it was just something she sort of thought; but of course she didn't want to marry him if he didn't love her.

'I don't,' said Alan, relieved, holding her hands.

'That's all right, then.' She smiled with only a slight tremble.

It seemed the worst was over without the expected agony. He got up to go, and she went with him to the door. But when he announced that he was leaving for Scotland to escape from his mother, she turned pale and asked 'When?'

'This afternoon, actually.'

There was a dreadful moment during which she bit at her thumb, with tears streaming down her cheeks.

'Oh Alan, Alan!' she sobbed.

Undoubtedly he should have stayed to comfort her, but self-preservation took over, and he left her crying.

Her letter was the only contact since. He folded it slowly and replaced it in its envelope. Poor old Sally. Miserably, he fidgeted with the familiar shapes of a wampum necklace he wore, under the pullover Frances had made for him. The action offered no reassurance, only double bad memories. Why did he still wear those blasted beads of Richard's anyway? Why on earth had he let Frances knit for him?

He thought about throwing the necklace in the sea. The thought had occurred to him a hundred times before, but he had never carried it out, and he didn't now. Thoroughly displeased with himself and the world, he wandered aft and round the other side, passing the seasick German with a slight scowl.

The north end of Boreray was coming into view on the port bow, a low dark hump featureless except for the white waves breaking round its base. As the ferry altered course for the harbour entrance, a small lighthouse appeared on a long promontory, above a greedy salivating sea pierced by jagged black fangs. There were more skerries to either side of the lighthouse. They were passing very close to them. On the highest one, two cormorants perched facing each other in a welter of spray, solemnly trying to dry their outstretched wings. They reminded Alan of the two ministers in the cafeteria. There was more rock and ominous white turbulence on both sides of the ship now. The passage was obviously narrow and tricky. Alan strolled from side to side, back-seat navigating as far as was possible with the ship's bows in the way. The two lines of shallows diverged again, joining up with a low headland on either side. Port Long harbour was almost a lagoon, a sheltered elliptical basin of empty dark water, calm enough to show the pockmarking of incessant rain and hail. The village was coming into sight – a few straggling rows of small grey houses and three or four groups of windowless box-like buildings seemingly randomly sited. The one on the pier with the red double doors was presumably a freight depot. The others might be anything – fish-curing sheds, hospital, slaughterhouse? What sort of institutions did Boreray need? One of them was presumably a school, probably the one to the right. It was the correct shade of yellowish cream for an educational establishment, and the colour was somehow in relationship with the council houses dominating the low hill behind the village: these were the same tint of pale pink as Japanese canned salmon, or for that matter the *Financial Times*. Everything else was grey or brown, or some indeterminate mixture of the two. The close-packed main street straggled off on the outskirts of the village into single cottages, some facing the sea, some sideways on. 'Cottages' was scarcely the word: they were mostly either corrugated-iron shacks or new bungalows. Some were a combination of the two modes. Each of them sat in a long fenced strip of poor rusty grass, identical to the neighbouring strip. Inside and outside the fences, up the main road and along the shore, small dingy sheep were grazing as if their lives depended on it – as indeed they probably did. They were sprinkled the length of the island, till distance and rain merged them into the moorland. At the south end of the island the ground rose steeply, but what might have been a picturesque summit was blotted out by steel-grey cloud. The mountain fell off sharply into the sea. Fladday and Rona were presumably out there somewhere in the shifting mist and water.

A dozen or so people were standing on the pier in the wind and rain, impassive as film-set Red Indians. Alan, pushing his wet hair back from his freezing forehead, admired their fortitude. A certain macabre relish began to repair his fallen spirits. Boreray was certainly no beauty spot – what a climate.

He went below to rejoin Selena. She looked grotesquely bulky and dirty next to the BMW, causing him a slight tremor in confidence. A man who looked every inch a BMW driver was slouched behind the wheel. He glared at Alan slithering past his bumper and did not respond to a friendly smile.

'Bugger you, then,' muttered Alan, bending to pull out the blocks. He patted Selena's broken nose and squeezed with difficulty into the driving seat. Suddenly he felt quite jaunty again.

Chapter 3

The Children Crossing sign had been knocked sideways in some recent collision, or perhaps not recent, or perhaps in the gale: at any rate it was pointing up a narrow alley between two shops, obscured by mud. But though there were no children crossing at 6 p.m. on a Friday, the pus-coloured complex was undoubtedly a school. A drift of chocolate wrappers skittered around gateposts well cemented with blobs of chewing gum. A janitorial-looking person emerged from a distant door carrying a bucket and mop. Mindful of Selena looming behind, Alan halted cautiously to have a better look. A black-stockinged sheep appeared surprisingly from the playground, glared at him, stamped her foot, and flounced down the road with an exclamation of disgust. Alan recognised the authentic voice of establishment disapproval.

He scanned his new work-place with a mixture of terror and amusement. Selena was to blame: he had really intended to spend the winter as a ski-instructor in the Cairngorms, but Aviemore was patently not a sympathetic home for an elderly boat. He had worked in the past for a boatyard near Dartmouth, and had thought of taking her there, but preferred on the whole to keep a few more hundred miles between himself and his mother. Then Frances had shown him an advertisement in the *Oban Times*: 'Teacher of Technical Subjects, Islands of Boreray and Fladday (temporary post).' After the incomprehensible details of qualifications and salary scales, it

31

was divulged that 'some knowledge of boatbuilding (traditional construction) would be an advantage' and further, that 'a candidate with suitable Instructor's qualifications might be considered'. Alan possessed Instructor's qualifications in quite a few subjects: they were the effects of a morally fibrous education on a twin natural disinclination for doing nothing and for doing the same thing for very long. He had to ponder whether the piece of paper received after a couple of spells teaching carpentry to old age pensioners was the right sort.

'I might have that one,' he said to Frances. 'I seem to remember there were boring lectures I didn't go to. Unless I'm thinking of Mountain Rescue.'

For a few days, the prospect of an island home for Selena struggled in the balance with a humbling telephone call to his mother asking her to look for the necessary certificate. Selena won, the job was applied for, and nothing more heard of the matter till after the start of the new school session, when a letter arrived offering him the post, 'consequent on the withdrawal of the previously appointed successful candidate for personal reasons'.

Perhaps the previously appointed one had found the wind-blasted tarmac agoraphobic, or had been tossed down the furnace-house steps by the horny-headed sheep now threatening the janitor, who waved it away with his mop, and approached Alan with even more lowering looks than its.

Alan drove off, with misgivings. He hoped there would be some sort of textbook on technical drawing. His imagination quailed before a year in a dingy classroom full of grubby little boys, and began to run wistfully on sun and wind and blown-out spinnakers in the southern ocean.

He braked suddenly, wincing at the complaints from the trailer. He had left the village without noticing and was heading out across a featureless moor to the north, away from the sea. A few fenced crofts skirted the road on his left. An orange windsock about half a mile away presumably marked the airstrip. There were several hundred sheep visible, tails to wind and jaws to ground, but no sign of human life. On his right, a rutted track led to the shore. He was looking for somewhere to pitch a tent: that would do.

Selena provided good shelter from the horizontal rain. He

tightened her tarpaulin and checked the knots again, then, since he could think of nothing else to do for her, got back into the van and investigated the box of food Frances had thrust in there that morning. He had been ungracious then about lack of space, but hunger put a different complexion on it. He spread oatcakes with honey gratefully, and reminded himself to remember to thank her. His chequebook and credit cards were under the box: that was welcome, too, as failure to find them at the ferry office had meant parting with all the cash from his pockets except for sixteen pence. The trailer had cost a formidable sum to transport. He hoped the place would be worth it.

Next morning he woke feeling improbably cold for the first of September. The tent and sleeping bag were the same as he had used in Nepal. He wondered vaguely how it could possibly be chillier on Boreray than halfway up Annapurna. The answer, as he realised when he wriggled out, was damp. The wind had changed during the night, and a fine mist was now swirling in to the mouth of the tent from the north. The rain had stopped, but the grass was white with moisture, icy on his bare feet. The only way to get warm was to run, so he ran, down to the shore, along a shingle beach and out onto a low rocky headland. A group of oystercatchers rose from the tideline, calling anxiously, their pied plumage and brilliant beaks vivid in the soft misty air. His eyes followed them with pleasure, and he crouched down quietly to see what else was to be seen. Ringed plover were piping, but try as he might he could not spot their plump little clockwork bodies against the grey and brown shingle. Then a black gorget stood out plainly in front of a lump of white quartz, and suddenly five or six more resolved from their background; and dunlin, winter-grey already, flittering over the grey water. Beyond them, unidentifiable ducks bobbed and upended between the waves, one or two, and then a few more, and further little clusters of dark dots as far as the lighthouse. The low cloud on the horizon was dispersing. A mainland peak appeared, and another, touched with sunlight. The clouds closed over, then swirled apart to reveal a window of limpid blue sky. The water caught and dappled the colour, tossing it from wave to wave. The rushing clouds flared silver and the sun was out. Boreray was blue and green and white, pristine, sweet and salt.

Alan gazed, forgetting time and his freezing toes, till an incoming wave splashed his ankle. He straightened and walked slowly back, shivering as much with delight as with cold. The grass under his feet was unseasonably shrivelled at the tips with salt winds, but here and there a daisy was spreading its petals to the sun, and harebells fluttered on slender stems, pure as the sky. The grazing sheep were unalarmed by his barefoot tread. One stopped champing to come a few steps nearer, regarding him with peaceful amber eyes in a soot-black face.

'Hallo, sheep,' he said, but she bounded off when he stretched out his hand.

He wondered if he had really said hallo sheep to a sheep. It would have been nice to scratch the thick wool between her horns.

It was something of an effort to turn his thoughts to his appointment with the headmaster in Port Long at ten o'clock. It would take perhaps fifteen minutes to get there: that gave him half an hour to improve his appearance as near as possible to interview standards. He decided against breakfast as Frances's box would have to last till the bank opened on Monday. He rooted amongst the jumble of sailing gear, tools and loose bits of boat for a clean shirt and trousers, dank and chill to the skin. It proved possible to shave with the aid of puddle-water and the driving mirror. He combed the wind and salt tangle out of his hair with vigour, but the effect wasn't really as good as it might have been. It was too long: he realised he had been pushing it out of his eyes for days or perhaps weeks. He tried combing it down, like the toffee-coloured forelock of a Highland cow; and back, revealing an odd white stripe above his tan. Having himself attended a rather bracing school with a low tolerance for shagginess, he was well aware that neither style was likely to appeal to a headmaster. He doubted he could improve it with a pocket knife, so resolved to do something about it on Monday, or possibly Tuesday.

Mr Carnegie noticed Alan's unruly hair before he had even shaken hands, and the barely-visible wampum beads had made an unfavourable impression before their wearer sat down. That much could be deduced from the glint behind his horn-rimmed glasses. He was a thin dark man, very neatly dressed, even to a white handkerchief in his breast pocket. He addressed Alan as Mr Cameron, and handed him a sheaf of timetables, school rules, and instructions in case of fire. Each page had 'Mr Cameron' printed on it, in neat black fountain-pen letters.

'I would like you to check these now, Mr Cameron, and make sure everything is clear.'

Alan opened his mouth to say 'for God's sake call me Alan' and said instead, 'Yes, everything seems perfectly clear.' It seemed very clear indeed that he was expected to teach a hell of a lot of technical drawing.

Mr Carnegie eyed him beadily. 'I hope so,' he said, in a precise Lothian accent indicative of doubt. He leant forward slightly with fingertips together. 'To be frank, Mr Cameron, we have never had an Instructor in this school before. There has been a certain amount of union trouble because of your appointment. The feeling was that it could be a precedent.'

Since he paused as if expecting a contribution, Alan said gravely, 'Yes, I see.'

'However, objections were waived on the grounds that the post is only a temporary one, coterminous with Mr MacDonald's absence for health reasons.'

Alan was so astonished at anyone using a word like coterminous in conversation that he said nothing. Mr Carnegie's gleaming spectacles indicated a black mark, but he continued. 'However – I take it we can assume you are fully familiar with the syllabus you will be using?'

'Well – not terribly familiar actually. I haven't taught in a school before.'

Mr Carnegie's fingertips whitened against each other and parted. 'I am aware of that, but it is very unfortunate.'

'My boatbuilding is pretty good,' said Alan, genially. 'Where does that come in?'

Mr Carnegie had opened a drawer and was inspecting the contents. 'Mr MacDonald was constructing a fibreglass hull, which I believe is almost completed. I think there is another one on Fladday.'

He shut the drawer with controlled emphasis.

'Boatbuilding is an excellent thing, Mr Cameron – very useful out of school – but it won't get boys through their exams. No O grade pass, no training. There's thirty per cent unemployment on these islands, Mr Cameron. Those boys need all the qualifications they can get.'

'Thirty per cent!' Alan was appalled.

35

'Well, I'm not claiming thirty per cent are actually seeking employment,' said Mr Carnegie rather less briskly. He handed Alan another bundle of papers. 'Look over these carefully before Monday, Mr Cameron. The syllabus is the thing.'

'Thanks!' said Alan, sincerely, leafing through.

Mr Carnegie eyed him for a moment or so. 'By the way, I am right in thinking you were yourself educated in Scotland?'

'Yes – yes, of course.' Alan hoped guiltily that he would assume a Strathclyde comprehensive.

'You must excuse me if I'm not very well up on your c.v., but as you know I was expecting someone different for the post.'

'Yes, of course. What happened to the other chap?'

Mr Carnegie clearly did not think the question well formulated, and waited.

'The one I'm here instead of.'

'He withdrew at a late stage,' Mr Carnegie leant forward as if to deliver a major indiscretion, 'for personal reasons.'

Alan began to laugh. Mr Carnegie added reprovingly, 'I believe it may have had to do with the council's failure to provide housing.'

'Oh – that reminds me. Have you any suggestions about renting accommodation?'

Mr Carnegie considered. 'I take it you would want to board somewhere where the lady would cook for you.'

'No!' Alan was most alarmed. He had suffered a week of white sliced bread and cornflakes at a landlady's hands in June. 'No, anything but. The only thing is I must have a large shed or outhouse.'

'A shed?' Mr Carnegie waited for elucidation.

'I've got a boat – two boats. One is quite a size and it will have to be under cover for repairs.'

'I see.' Mr Carnegie straightened his blotter carefully and stared at it hard. Then he placed a sheet of paper on it and picked up his fountain pen. His actions stirred unpleasant memories of another headmaster writing a tight-lipped letter to Mother, but in fact the sheet contained nothing about outrageous conduct or lamentable lack of responsibility.

'These are the addresses of people who normally rent accommodation to tourists. But I have no information about the size of their sheds.' Mr Carnegie capped his pen. 'May I ask where you are

36

staying at present?'

'I've got a tent.'

'A tent!' Unexpectedly, he laughed, a sharp, barking laugh, wuff – wuff – wuff. 'Mr Cameron, when you came in this morning, I confess I thought your appearance a little untidy. If you spent a night like last night under canvas, I'm not at all surprised.'

'I thought I'd done pretty well managing a shave,' Alan agreed.

'Indeed!' Mr Carnegie wuffed again, and stood up, looking quite good-humoured. 'All the same, I'd prefer to see a tie on Monday, Mr Cameron.'

'I've got one.' He had thought about it on the journey, and dashed into Woolworth's last mainland outpost to remedy the deficiency.

'Very good. Now let me show you where you will be working.'

Chapter 4

Alan tried the Port Long addresses first. Mrs MacDonald had no shed on offer, there was no one in at Mrs Morrison's, and the second Mrs MacDonald's half-dozen children didn't know where Mam was or when she'd be back. The next two on his list were further MacDonalds at 4 and 15 Garve. His map indicated a pleasant moorland walk from Port Long, to a village called Garve near a long sandy beach on the north-west of the island. In fact the single-track road never reached open ground, but ran between fences with scattered houses on either side. About a mile out of Port Long, a road sign appeared with 'Garve' on it. On the back it said 'Port Long'. The latter was still visible, made picturesque by distance around its blue harbour, with the white-flecked sea and mountains beyond. But between it and the open water on the west of the island there was no other village to be seen, just a succession of single houses a few hundred yards apart, each separated from its neighbours and the road by a post-and-wire fence. There were no crops in these fields; in fact the mixture of stones, bitten grass and rushes looked incapable of producing any. There were sheep in most of them, and one had a tethered black cow and a few hens. Every dwelling had at least one shed, but small and tumbledown for the

37

most part, dwarfed by enormous chocolate-brown peat stacks which were the neatest things to be seen. The tapered sides of the stacks were arranged herring-bone fashion, and some were thatched with tarpaulin. There was no one about, though the sweet reek of peat surely suggested human presence. Alan walked on, puzzled about number 4 and number 15.

When he reached the highest point on the road, a man with a crook and a black and white dog were walking towards him. The man greeted him with 'Fine day,' and the dog circled him twice and flattened itself behind his legs.

'Can you tell me where Garve is?'

'Ay.' The shepherd leant on his crook as if considering for a moment, then raised it and pointed with solemn emphasis east and west. 'That's Garve.'

'What, all this? Where's number 4 then?'

'Ye're past it. The second croft behind you now is number 4.'

'Oh – so is 15 just eleven on from 4?'

'No.' His guide leant once more on his crook, while Alan mentally checked his own subtraction. 'It is that one down there with all the sheep.'

Alan did not find this a helpful distinction. All the sheep were everywhere, to his eyes.

'There is a new fence and a new gate to it,' added his informant.

'Yes . . . there are a lot of new fences, aren't there?'

'Ay. The grants for the fencing are very good just now.'

'I see. Can you grow much on these crofts then?'

'Och no. Not on the crofts. The potatoes are growing very good on the machair.' The shepherd had taken out cigarettes. He offered one to Alan, who declined it, and lit up deliberately.

'You are a stranger here yourself?'

'Yes.' Alan realised he should probably have stated his credentials before asking questions, to be in line with local etiquette. 'I've come to teach woodwork and so on at the school. I'm looking for a cottage to rent.'

'Och ay.' The shepherd sounded as if he knew all of that anyway. Alan was just about to thank him and go when he volunteered. 'Norman has the family at home. You will be better to try Hector.'

'Is that number 15?'

'Ay.'

'Is it the house with the green roof?'

The man gazed down the hill. 'It might be,' he allowed.

His voice was quiet and civil, but Alan, thanking him, noticed a sardonic something lurking in his eye. He was suddenly aware that he had asked too many questions too loudly, and that his English diphthongs were outlandish. He smiled as ingratiatingly as possible and went on his way.

Number 15 did indeed have a green roof, but Hector was not at home. Mrs Hector agreed that there was a cottage to let 'over the way', but she would have to ask Himself.

'When will Him – your husband be home?'

'Oh well, I couldn't say.'

The last address was 3 Achmore. He took the right fork indicated. Number 3 must surely be the third house after the village sign. The woman who came to the door shook her head gravely. 'No. This is number 17.'

'Where is number 3, then?'

She shook her head again. 'Oh well, I couldn't say.'

Alan turned to go, but she called after him, 'I think it is Jessie you are wanting.'

He had no idea whether Jessie came into it. Mr Carnegie's list indicated a Mr N. Mackinnon.

'Jessie has the bungalow to rent. She is living next to the post office.'

With that she closed the door. Alan walked on, totally befogged by this uncanny Celtic perception of his requirements. Rather nervously, he knocked on Jessie's door. It was opened at once: he had a fleeting impression of a children's game, the players huddling in excitement. 'Knock, knock, who's there?' A white-haired chuckling old lady looked up at him, guileless blue eyes in a rose-petal face. She took his hand in both hers, which were gnarled with arthritis, the skin white and thin as tissue paper.

'Well, well, come in – come in.'

She led him in unresisting and dazed. 'Sit now there!' she exclaimed, in the dark little sitting room, pushing him with surprising force into the only armchair. As his eyes adjusted to the gloom, he became aware of another smiling old face and another knobbly hand outstretched towards him. He started up to shake it, but was firmly repositioned by his hostess.

'Sit now!' she said, with authority, adding, 'Neilie's legs are not so good,' in explanation for her husband's failure to rise.

Alan introduced himself; though the process seemed quite unnecessary to him by now, it gave apparent enormous pleasure to his hosts, or perhaps captors. There was more chuckling and handshaking, a large whisky was thrust into his hand, toasts in Gaelic and English spoken.

'What a pity, what a pity,' sighed Jessie.

'Och yes. The bungalow is all right, but it has no shed,' explained Neilie.

Alan laughed incredulously. He hadn't had a chance to mention the purpose of his visit.

'It is a good boat you have there.' Neilie leant forward, eager-eyed as a child.

'Did you see her?' Alan was surprised.

'Och well no! I am not moving from this chair in ten years!' Both old people shook with mirth.

'My son is telling me. He has the *Maid of Rona* himself. That is a nice boat too.'

Since the conversation had turned to boats and the whisky had hit his empty stomach, Alan subsided in the best chair and talked, vaguely aware, as the whisky bottle reappeared above his glass, that the episode bore some extraordinary inside-out relationship to 'Hansel and Gretel'.

'No – really, I must go.'

'No, no, sit you there! Jessie will be bringing the tea.'

The tea was milky and sugary, and accompanied by a large plate of buttered oatcake, homemade scones with syrup, and sandwiches containing thick slices of corned beef which would have been alarming on any other occasion, but he was by that time so hungry, so inebriated and so charmed by his hosts' hospitality that the experience of eating dead cow passed almost unnoticed. Jessie refilled his plate approvingly, Neilie talked of rounding the Horn in his youth. Eventually the food blotted the whisky sufficiently for the import of the picture-clock above the mantelpiece to sink in. It said 3 p.m. and probably meant it, and he hadn't found anywhere to live. Jessie had some advice.

'Try you down at Skalanish,' she said. 'There is my own cousin's house there empty.'

Neilie chuckled, 'Ay, Ewan was a great man for building boats. There will be a shed there right enough.'

'Oh, there will be a shed.'

'Maybe it will be no big enough, but then maybe it will.'

Jessie handed him a scrap of paper with an address on it, and with thanks and promises to call again he reeled out into the brilliant afternoon. Once out of sight, he leant rather unsteadily against a fence post and unfolded his map. Skalanish wasn't to be seen. He consulted Jessie's note: 'Roderick MacDonald, 4 Gnipadale.' Gnipadale was there, at the south of the island under its only steep contours, with a few houses marked. Skalanish, in small letters, appeared as a little headland on the low ground to the south-west of the mountains. It was some ten miles by road. There was just about enough petrol left in Frances's van to make it, if he didn't put the thing in the ditch.

The drive sobered him. There were few other cars, but the sheep required concentration. He assumed the first one he approached as it rested in mid-road would move. It did not. The bump was slight, but sickening. He jumped out expecting the worst, but his victim merely bleated reprovingly and picked her way with dignity over the ditch. After that he was more careful.

As he headed south, the monotonous poor grass and the strung-out houses changed to heather moorland, richly purple, and climbing towards the bare steep summit of Càrn Bàn. The other islands came into view, Rona forbidding with steep escarpments, and Fladday lower and green. The sea was increasingly sprinkled with skerries and islets, long stone fingers pushing out from the mountainside. A few small fishing boats were working between the seething rocks, pulling and dropping lobster pots. They looked fragile to the point of unlikeliness, against Rona's distant black cliffs. The road wound on perilously under the grim southern crags of Càrn Bàn, furrowed and fissured, glowering across at Rona's equally unfriendly face. Squinting up at clefts and waterfalls, Alan could see sheep up to the skyline, walking on air and grazing on nothing. Below, the afternoon sun dazzled on the water, striped closely with the black and white of many skerries. A fierce tide was ripping through the narrows. Alan was jubilant: it was the most exciting place possible for sailing the dinghy, at least if the wind ever moderated sufficiently to take it out single-handed. He must look for a crew. He must order sails at once. He wondered how much he had in the bank still.

A road sign announced 'Gnipadale', but the only visible building was a concrete sheep pen. It contained a man and a dog as well as a few sheep. Alan asked for directions.

The man straightened up. He was a fine-looking figure, light-eyed and hawk-nosed.

'It is my cousin's house you will be wanting,' he declared, gesturing biblically with his crook.

The cousin's house was third below the road. He passed a smiling old woman in a floral apron and her cow, both timelessly placid. At the second house, a boy was sickling a small patch of green oats between ribs of rock. The slope became gentler and in a wide fan of grassy ground appeared the house he was looking for. It seemed incongruously modern, with a glass porch and ugly dormers.

A woman came to the door, and he realised with a rather sinking feeling that Himself was probably not in. Mrs MacDonald, however, was made of decisive stuff.

'The key is with us, but the house is my brother-in-law's. You would have to telephone him in Glasgow. But I will send the girls over with you and you can look at the place. Mind you,' she continued, as she led him into the living room, 'it's not much of a house. You will be bumping your head on the ceilings there.' She went out to fetch the key, leaving him with the girls. They clustered round the television, pretending to ignore him, till she returned and introduced them.

'This is Morag Ann and Kirsty and Dina, they are my girls, and this is Mairi their cousin.'

They were astoundingly pretty, creamy-skinned and raven-haired, with high cheekbones and firm round chins. They wore the same clothes as any other teenagers, yet in manner they were as exotic as girls from Kashmir or Isfahan. They looked away from him with conscious modesty, casting sideways glances. Morag Ann and Kirsty were pretty, but Mairi was beautiful, with wide grey eyes framed in superlative lashes. Only little Dina was unremarkable, nine and podgy with a tight black ponytail. It was amusing to think such a duckling would soon be a swan like her sisters.

Morag Ann protested in whispers as her mother handed her the key, and ushered them all out firmly.

'You would be best to walk over,' she said. 'They are driving sheep along the road from the fank.'

Alan followed his bevy of guides, greatly entertained. They tripped through the mud and heather in pastel-coloured shoes, leaving a wake of strong perfume. They linked arms and giggled, careful not to turn around. After a short distance Dina fell back, holding up a bag of violently coloured boiled sweets. Alan accepted one rather doubtfully, and she ran back to the others, butting her way into the giggling phalanx. Over a stile they came unstuck. There were shrieks: a too-tight skirt, wobbly high heels. Alan lent a manly arm. Abruptly the tittering and head-tossing stopped. They regrouped quietly around him, not speaking, but curious as young heifers. Still-eyed Mairi gazed full in his face past Kirsty's straight profile. Conversation was evidently expected.

Not that they joined in. Alan asked questions, and Morag Ann, as eldest, answered monosyllabically. The path climbed then dipped into a wide shallow glen, out to the seashore again, and up a short steep rise.

'This is Uncle Ewan's house,' Mairi volunteered. A little ferny valley with a cascading stream led down to a shingle beach, and on a flat green just above the shore was a small low cottage. Alan hardly noticed it. It had a shed: that was the important thing. It was, in fact, larger than the house. He paced it out: twenty-six feet.

'Can I have a look inside – no, the shed I mean.'

The girls giggled again.

'I've got a boat,' said Alan, defensively.

Uncle Ewan had had boats too, by the look of it. The shed contained stocks and a ladder, coils of rope and wire, rusted tins of antifouling and green paint, old lemonade bottles full of nameless fluids and jamjars with brushes stuck in them. There was a sturdy bench with a vice, a bundle of clamps and a rusty adze. From the door, a gentle slope improved here and there with concrete led down to the beach, where the boulders had been cleared to make room for a boat. A track led away up the hill, presumably towards the road.

43

'Can you get a vehicle and trailer down that?' he asked. The girls stared silently, but a quick run up the first rise persuaded him that you could, just.

Morag Ann had opened the cottage door and his escort was waiting. Entering, he cracked his head hard on the lintel. That seemed to bring out the bacchante in them. Dina jumped up and down shrieking with mirth. Morag Ann told her to shut up and chased her up the loft ladder. Mairi took his arm and pulled him away from the kitchen doorway, with peals of laughter. Suddenly they were all wild-eyed and bubbling.

'Here's the kitchen. What do you think of that stove, eh? Been here since the Flood.'

'That's the pantry — there's beetles in it.'

'Ooh help, there's a dead mouse under the cushion!'

Shrieks and squeals. The nymphs fled into the parlour, bounced on the rickety armchairs, plastered each other with spider's webs, fled back to the kitchen.

'Look in here,' Kirsty danced before him, throwing open a door in the corner. 'This is the bedroom. There is a bed — of sorts.'

Dina jumped on it. The older girls whooped with delight, hands over their faces. Mairi's eyes gleamed between her fingers.

The atmosphere was uncomfortably Orphic. Alan made for the fresh air.

'Mind your head!' shrieked the bassanids, pealing with glee.

Dina skipped in front of him up the path. 'How tall are you? You're awful tall!'

'Shut up, Dina.' Morag Ann had collected herself slightly.

'Six-two or so.'

'Shut up yourself. Have another sweetie?' The child showed alarming green juice on her tongue and teeth. Alan put her offering in his pocket. They all clamoured round him, noisy as they had been quiet before, full of questions and exclamations.

'Will you stay there by yourself?'

'It's lonely — I wouldn't stay.'

'Ooh, not near the *sidhean*!'

'Shee-an?' Alan attempted curiously. 'What's that?'

'It's haunted. It's—' She was shouted down at once.

'Rubbish girl!'

44

'Who told you that? It's fairy tales.'

'He'll think we're savages here.'

Dina hopped in for another round. 'Are you really a teacher?'

'Yes – as from Monday.'

'You don't look like one then.'

'Good!'

'Shut up, Dina!'

'What are you teaching?'

'Woodwork and things. Shall I be teaching any of you?'

Squeals of laughter.

'It's only *boys* does woodwork!' Dina shouted gleefully. 'Girls does cooking and sewing.' Her mouth was blood-red this time. The setting sun touched the heather with flame and four long black shadows danced before them. Alan began to hope the boys would be less uncanny than their sisters. They babbled about school, laughed breathlessly, leapt the stile with the grace of valkyries. But as they drew near the house, they fell silent, walking decorously with downcast eyes. Mairi went on along the shore path without so much as a backward look. The others filed in to their own house in order of size. Alan followed. Morag Ann handed the keys to her mother and sat down in front of the television without a word. Kirsty followed suit and Dina knelt on the floor.

Exotic was an inadequate description.

Roddy MacDonald came in and shook hands, a stocky weather-beaten man recognisably like his cousin at the sheep pen. He had telephoned his brother in Glasgow. All was well if Alan wanted the cottage.

Chrissie brought tea, with more whisky and fresh crowdie on the scones. Alan stayed talking till it was dark, and all that time the three girls sat before the television, silent as sphinxes.

Chapter 5

The warm glow faded from the heather, and Mairi quickened her steps past the looming bulk of Holm rock. The lights of home and the familiar milky scent of cut corn drew her on. She stopped suddenly with a squeal: she had almost bumped into Donnie, crouched motionless on a boulder by the path.

'Oh, the fright you gave me! What are you doing here?'

'Just looking.'

Mairi scanned the glimmering water with its drifts of weed and hunching black rocks. 'Och, you're daft.' But she sat down beside him anyway.

'The otter was there.'

'Where?'

'By that float. She's went now. She didn't like your noise.'

'Was she at Murdo's net?'

'She might be. Don't you go and tell him.'

'No.'

They sat quiet, but the otter didn't reappear. Mairi nudged her brother. 'I been talking to your new teacher.'

'Who's that?'

'The one is taking Clap's place. Didn't you hear? – och, you never hear anything, you're half asleep, boy! Well, I can tell you I wish girls got woodwork.'

'Is he nice then?'

'He's great! Fantastic looking – young – real good fun. You'll get a laugh with him. Well, Kirsty's a brat. You should have seen her showing him the bed at Uncle Ewan's house. What a laugh!'

Donnie looked at her enquiringly. 'What was you doing down at Uncle Ewan's?'

'He's going to stay there. We took him over.'

Donnie was silent, considering this. After a minute Mairi said in a low voice, 'Donnie, is it true what Dina was saying about that place? She said it's haunted.'

Donnie looked down, scraping small shingle with his fingers. 'I don't know.' He tossed a pebble into the water. Black and silver rings spread on the evening calm. 'Uncle Ewan said he seen something. A wee man was looking in his workshop one day. When he went out there was nobody there.'

'Och, he was old. He didn't see too good.' Mairi had heard the story before, but she drew closer to Donnie, with her arm in his like when they were little.

'Well then, what about the music he was hearing?'

46

'Uncle Ewan was that deaf, he'd not have heard a foghorn.'

'Well, he was hearing that music. I seen him one night. He was smiling and nodding his head.'

'It's nonsense that!'

Donnie threw another pebble and watched the ripples. 'I'll bet you wouldn't go there at night. Would you go on the *sidhean*?'

Mairi hugged his arm, trembling. 'Ooh, no, not on your life!'

'Well, you don't think it's nonsense then. Do you? There is places like that. No one knows.'

They huddled small together in the dusk. When Mairi spoke again it was in a whisper.

'Have you seen anything, Donnie?'

'There?'

'Ay.'

He hesitated. 'Will you not tell if I tell you? You promise?'

'Promise! What was it?'

'I . . . ' he paused, shivering, turning his head from side to side.

'Come on you!' She shook his elbow.

'I seen a light. It wasn't a light either – on the house. Like flames, running all over the roof, in the windows too.'

'When did you see that?'

'Not long past. A week, maybe ten days: prayer-meeting night.'

'Was it dark?' Mairi was impressed. 'Were you scared?'

'There was a moon. I wasn't scared. I was . . . ' He couldn't express the inexpressible. 'It isn't like being scared.'

'Donnie! Mairi!' A shout from the house made them jump violently. They crouched again in silence, conscious of the guilt of their forbidden stories.

'Now Mairi. Don't you tell anyone, not anyone, right? They will all be saying I am daft. I seen that thing.'

'I won't tell.' She was halfway up the bank.

Donnie picked up his sickle, and stood a moment gazing at the silver ripples before following her home.

'Come in you two, it's late enough.' Mam's voice was sharp. It was the eve of the Sabbath and she was getting everyone ready for it. The floor was newly swept and the cushions plumped up, and Auntie Effie's hair was just out of rollers. Dad's collar was red with blood from a shaving nick.

Mairi switched the television on.

'Turn that off, girl!'

'Oh Mam, but you're still ironing yourself. I only want to watch—'

'Cut that out, Mairi.' Her father seldom bothered to cross her. Silenced, she made a face at Donnie. They both knew what was wrong: Murdo was out at the pub, and couldn't be counted on to be home and dry by midnight. Not that their parents were very strict, but Auntie Effie would have had her say.

Sabbath gloom descended on them. Mairi looked at a magazine and Donnie scratched the cat's ears. Angus stared into the fire, smoking and coughing alternately. His wife thumped quickly through the ironing, while old Effie tutted not quite under her breath, sometimes at her, sometimes at Mairi's magazine.

Donnie lifted the cat on to his shoulder and turned his cheek against her soft fur. Her purring filled his ears and teeth and surged in and out of his fingers as he stroked her. She was just one big purr. The noise she made and how happy she was feeling were all the same to her. It was cat music she was making. He stroked her in long firm sweeps. His mind drifted to how smooth beech felt and the powerful strokes of the plane, the scrape and swish as the shavings fell away. He could make a good job of it, of anything with wood. Even Clap was saying that: a first-class craftsman, he said, and that was something coming from him, usually he wasn't bothered what anyone did.

'Take this, Donnie.' Mairi was pushing a cup and plate into his hand. The cat jumped down and the cup went flying. Mairi ran for a cloth and Auntie Effie tutted.

'You're in a dream again,' snapped his mother.

'He's never awake.' Mairi pushed the cloth in his face.

His father glared at him. 'You're a disaster, boy. Your mind's not on things at all. When I was your age I was running the croft. All this bloody school. What you need is a job.'

'There won't be one for him anyway,' observed his mother, tartly.

'Ach well, what a world, eh?' Angus threw his cigarette butt into the fire, speaking half to himself. 'No work at sixteen, and at sixty you're finished. Finished.'

He said it louder the second time. He had had two heart attacks in the past three years. Auntie Effie muttered something about the will of the Lord.

'Say the grace now, Angus,' his wife cut in quickly.

He did so. After it he relented a bit.

'Ach well, the others are all doing good enough. You're bound more or less to have one daftie in a family, eh?'

Donnie hung his head.

'Ay ay, Murdo. How's yourself, Shonny? Home again, eh? How's the deep sea?'

Donald Alex Mackinnon was a big fresh-faced man with a barrel chest and a voice to match. When he crashed cheerfully into the bar of the Port Long Hotel the glasses jingled and a chair fell over. Do'l Alex waved it on high to attract the barman's attention, shouted his order, thumped the chair down and sat on it.

'Ay lads! What's doing tonight, eh? Eh, Shonny?'

'Nothing much.'

'Same as usual in this bloody place.'

'Ach, Murdo! It's no such a bad place. Here's a dram to cheer you up. *Slainte*! How's your dad?'

Murdo drained his glass. He intended to get drunk as quickly as possible.

'He's no doing much.'

'Lucky for him he's got you at home.'

'Lucky for him, eh? You tell him that, Do'l Alex. You tell him. I'm doing every bloody thing in that place and they still treat me like a kid. Fuckin' hell, I been dipping all day and they tried to keep me in tonight. "Don't you know it's the Sabbath tomorrow?" Don't I know too bloody well.'

Shonny grinned unpleasantly. 'Good God, man! Why do you stand for it, eh? Get yourself a job, get away.'

Murdo lapsed into silence.

'Ach, that's no so easy,' Do'l Alex put in for him.

'No easy! It's fuckin' impossible.'

'Your dad needs you at home.'

Shonny leant over the table. He was one of those who turn yellowish, not red, with drink. He was beginning to point belligerently. He pointed at Murdo.

49

'You get away, leave them to it. You got a brother at home, haven't you? You leave them to it.'

'Fuckin' rotten little bastard. He's useless.'

Do'l Alex scratched his head, embarrassed. 'He's just a wee lad. A year or two on, you'll get away Murdo. You got the ability – join the army, maybe, see the world.'

Shonny sniggered. 'Better than shooting crows, take it from me.'

'Or go on the tankers like Shonny.' Do'l Alex was doing his best to keep the peace. 'Shonny's looking wealthy on it. Jacket and tie, eh Shonny? Got a new girlfriend?'

'There's no talent round here, I'm telling you. I been looking for it. No bloody talent.'

Do'l Alex guffawed, slapping his thighs. 'You don't speak to them nice enough, boy.' He rolled a cigarette. 'Anyway, you got competition now, lads. Did you hear about the Englishman?'

'Who's that?' Murdo had returned with fresh glasses. He spoke indistinctly, and as if threatened.

'The one got old Clap's job while he's drying out. He been to see my old mother today – you should hear her! Tall, fair and handsome, speaks like a gentleman. Best thing she's seen for months. Just as well she's not fifty years younger, I was saying to the Da. That's what the women like!' He chortled and downed his drink, pushing his chair back noisily. 'So look out lads. The Englishmen have got it, eh?' He slapped each of them on the back with good-natured emphasis. 'Lock up your daughters!' He had five. ' 'Night then, boys. I'm off home before the wife will catch me.' He strode out, bellowing to other acquaintances and slamming doors.

Murdo and Shonny glowered at the table, drinking silently, a dram and a pint together every round.

'Fuckin' English,' mumbled Murdo at length. The drink was warming his entrails, so that hatred was a pleasure. 'Fuckin' English. Got all the jobs, all the money, all the girls.'

Shonny stabbed the air with his finger. 'Shut up you. You got yourself to blame. You get out any time you like. Any time. You got yourself to blame, right?'

'I hate the English.'

'God, they're fuckin' bastards.'

'They get all the jobs.'

50

'All the money, all the jobs.'

The litany of resentment tailed into silence. Shonny lurched to the bar, and returning slammed the drinks down on the table.

'You get out of here any time. Get off your arse, can't you? Tell the old bastard you've had enough. Knock him on the head – he's no use anyway.'

Murdo lunged forward. 'You mind what you say about my father!' His fists were up.

Shonny was on his feet, suddenly quick and dangerous. The table was over and they were both down in smashed glass and spilt liquor, pummelling and grappling amongst the chair legs. They were grabbed and separated in seconds by Shonny's relatives. Other men formed a restraining barrier round Murdo, but they were wary of his opponent: he had trained for a time with the SAS, and though common rumour was that he had been expelled for drunken indiscipline, his own account hinted at something more glamorously violent. No one liked to attract his unfavourable attention, just in case. His brother and uncles frogmarched him home, and the barman thrust Murdo out to the carpark.

He slumped in his driving seat. 'Fuckin' English,' he muttered. 'Fuckin' Shonny. Fuckin' English.' His head lolled back and he fell asleep.

In the mission house at Ardbuie the windows were misting and the mist disintegrating into small rivulets of condensation. Mr MacNeil's sermon had been going on for a long time. His voice had swelled through rising and falling waves of passion, and now it pounded full tide upon his listeners. His subject, as most weeks, was Sunday observance.

'I am telling you, my friends, there are those among us and those about to come among us who are heedless of the commandment of the Lord regarding His Sabbath. Oh, there are some who come from far away, who come from places where there is no knowledge of the ways of the Lord and no instruction in the Word of the Lord – poor benighted Catholics and others. Those men are to be pitied – yes, pitied. And God may yet pity them, He may yet turn and quicken them to a knowledge of His holy Word and a knowledge that the fear of the Lord is the beginning of wisdom!'

Here Mr MacNeil paused briefly to wipe his glasses. He recommenced with an upflung arm and a shout of 'Oooh!' that made some of his congregation jump, although they were used to his preaching manner. An old man dropped a bag of pan drops on the floor and whispered 'Oh Jesus!' loudly and a girl tittered.

'Ooooh!' wailed Mr MacNeil, in increased agony. 'Oh, dearly beloved brothers and sisters, far worse – *far worse* – is the case of some among us – of one who is not here today – who is not here today because of the excesses of his *sins*.' The preacher's voice rose to a shriek. 'This man who is guilty of drunkenness – of drunkenness and violence on the very eve of the Sabbath – this man has been instructed in the Word of the Lord, he knows full well – full well, my friends – that he is dependent on the Grace of the Lord. It is not ignorance with this young man! No! It is sin, *sin* my friends. And I say unto you, if he does not turn from his wickedness – oh, my friends! If we do not all turn from our wickedness unto the Lord of all Grace and Mercy and Truth – then, brothers and sisters, we shall not live – oh no, eternal life shall not be ours – we shall go our ways into eternal damnation, to the place of wailing and gnashing of teeth!'

Mr MacNeil finished on a triumphant howl, with an audible clash of dentures.

Mairi giggled and shook under her hat. Her mother, white-faced and tight-lipped, quelled her with a glance. Angus sat hunched with bowed head and crimson face, his less deaf ear tilted to the pulpit so that he should not be thought guilty of sparing himself humiliation. Donnie looked down at his own clasped hands, waiting for the ordeal to be over. Sweat prickled behind his ears. Kirsty pressed against him, trying to catch Mairi's eye. He shifted away from the oppressive warmth of her thigh. It was difficult to breathe and impossible to look up.

The precentor gave out the psalm. Usually the Morrison family sang lustily, for they had good voices, but today they were mute with shame. At last it was over. The door was opened and cool air flooded in.

Outside Mr MacNeil waited to shake hands. When not inspired, he was a small meek man with a kindly expression.

'How is Murdo's eye today?' he asked Angus solicitously.

'No too bad.' Angus's voice was thick.

'He will need to look after it. The eye is a bad place – a very bad place.'

The congregation drifted towards the road, separating into knots according to age and sex. The women, with much head-shaking, sympathised with Mrs Morrison; the girls chattered about the charms of the latest benighted incomer; the men lit up cigarettes and arranged the sheep-dipping programme for the week; the boys scuffed their toes in the dust and jostled wordlessly.

Once in the bus, the excuse for light conversation was over, and families reassembled. The Morrisons were a cowed group. Angus's face was still crimson, and he rubbed his chest now and again.

Dinner was a silent meal. Everything that could be said had been said, or shouted, at three in the morning. Only Auntie Effie was still grumbling, maliciously but mostly inaudibly. Murdo ate nothing and looked at no one. Donnie felt sick when he saw his face. One eye was completely closed and purple, and one cheek split in a blood-blackened groove. The other cheek was grazed fiery red. His left hand and wrist were swollen till no joints showed. Thinking about the pain he must be in, Donnie found it difficult to swallow. His father's face was growing redder by the minute: he must be working himself up to say something. At last it came out.

'You were preached against.'

Murdo said nothing. Everyone else stopped eating. His mother put in sharply, 'Go and see to the cow, Murdo.'

Murdo got up then.

'I'll come and help,' said Donnie, sorry.

His brother turned to him with a speechless curl of the lip. He shrank back in his chair. The father left the room, and his wife followed, telling him to take his pills. Mairi began to clear the table. Aunt Effie heaved herself into her armchair with much groaning and whispered lamentation. Soon she was nodding half asleep.

Donnie went out quietly, keeping to the shore to avoid Murdo. If it had been any day but Sunday he would have gone to see his grandmother, but on the Sabbath she would ask a visitor to read the bible to her, as the print was too small for her own eyes; that was all right if he could find verses he knew by heart, but if not, it was torment. Instead he followed his usual Sunday route: along the shore till he was past Roddy's house, then up the flank of Gormul. In fine weather he often went to the top, and lay on his back watching the ravens rolling and spiralling: then he would have to run all the way down to be in time for evening church. But this Sunday hung like a weight on him. The heather dragged at his knees and a grey wind pushed against his throat. His stomach was in knots. He came down above Uncle Ewan's house, and dropped full length on the grass, with his chin in his hands and unfocussed eyes. Murdo's ugly look and the raised voices of the past twenty-four hours floated in and out of his head, unquiet as the white foam flickering on the skerries beyond the narrow beach. Uncle Ewan came into his mind, an old bent figure pottering on the shingle or standing in the low doorway watching the sea. He longed intensely to see him again, to be among the wood shavings and the smell of resin and tar in his workshop. 'Good boy, Donnie – good work, Donnie.' He remembered hammering his first nails with a small hammer and planing with Uncle Ewan's arms behind his own, and later the praise for his first dovetails, though they gaped. The chill of longing melted in the warmth of the old man's approval, and images came and went of the workshop and the boats, things he had seen and things he had not seen. His head sank slowly on his arms. There was a boat there, and everything in a golden glow and music.

Suddenly he looked up sharply. The grey sea washed the shingle as before and white foam licked the skerries endlessly. He jumped to his feet, knowing it was late, and ran with the wind behind him and the weight gone from his limbs.

Chapter 6

Alan arrived early at the school on Monday, intending to spend half an hour initiating himself into the mysteries of technical drawing before Class 2 assembled to put him to the test. He had noticed an untidy heap of books and leaflets in a corner of the wood-store when Mr Carnegie was showing him round.

Unfortunately for his good intentions, the first item he picked up was a timber merchant's list. It had struck him on Sunday, as he wandered round a completely treeless island separated by twenty miles of sea from the equally treeless Highland mountains, that he could scarcely have chosen a crazier place to bring an old wooden boat in need of much patching. The catalogue was a gospel of salvation. He read it from end to end, revelling in the attributes of Oak, English, plain, kiln-dried, and Oregon Pine, selects and better. He began to tick things and squiggle calculations beside the terms of payment and conditions of carriage.

The bell made him jump. Clattering feet and shrill voices were drawing near, sinking to scuffles and whispers. Class 2 filed in, and stood watching him in expectant silence, fifteen small identical figures with thick black hair and round rosy-brown faces. It was very like being in charge of a pack of garden gnomes. However did one tell them apart?

Alan had a bright idea. He handed out sheets of squared paper.

'Write your names at the top, and then repeat whatever the final drawing was that you completed last session. That way I'll be able to see how much you know.'

After a few minutes he looked over shoulders to judge the result of this ingenious plan. Most of them had written their names, except for a few who had forgotten their pencils. He handed out pencils, leafed covertly through the timber list, and tried again. The names were now completed. There were three: Morrison, MacDonald and Mackinnon. Some of the little creatures had heroic praenomina, Hector, Alexander and Archibald. The rest were divided between Angus and Donald.

Alan soon realised that it would be more difficult to keep up with his pupils' nomenclature than with their skills. Most of them did seem to know how to use a ruler, although five hadn't brought one. He found rulers and handed them out. Further investigation revealed that at least two didn't know the difference between a centimetre and a millimetre and that less than half of them could draw a right angle. Forty minutes passed without anyone in the room having the least idea what the final drawing of the previous session had represented.

Gnomes of graded sizes passed in and out of his room all day. Some used their chisels back to front and others pointed them at their own entrails. One hammered its thumb and wept copiously. Alan was at a loss: should he tell it to shut up or put his arms round it? The rest of the class seemed to expect some reaction. Fortunately one of them piped up helpfully, 'Send him to Miss Mackinnon, sir. He'll get a plaster there.'

In the lunch hour he went to the bank and thence shopping. The shopkeepers were all benign ladies in blue nylon overalls who smiled at him discreetly. He had the impression there was not much they didn't know about him. Numerous unidentifiable gnomes greeted him politely on his way down the main street. How would he ever sort out Mackinnon from Morrison or Angus from Donald? Perhaps by individual preferences for ice-lollies, chocolate bars or bubble gum, for every pair of jaws seemed to be champing on something, and all afternoon E320 and E330 reigned in unnatural supremacy over the homelier odours of pine shavings and boys' sweat. The windows on the seaward side of the classroom seemed to be wired up; by four o' clock he was glad to gulp fresh air.

When he reached Selena, he found an antique Land Rover and a huge man in seaboots waiting.

'Oh well, that's a nice boat you have there,' bellowed this individual, shaking his hand in a powerful grip, and adding as an afterthought that he was Do'l Alex Mackinnon.

Naturally Alan warmed to him at once.

'She's lovely, but there's a couple of years' work there,' he agreed. It seemed an absurd statement of the obvious to introduce himself, so he didn't.

'You will be wanting a hand to get her down to Skalanish my father tells me,' pursued Do'l Alex.

Alan added the surname to the seaboots. 'Oh, you're the skipper of the *Maid of Rona*. She's a beauty. I was watching her in the harbour yesterday. Is it lobsters you fish?'

'Anything that's going – usually not much them days!' Do'l Alex laughed, showing a piratical lack of front teeth. 'If you're all loaded up we better get down the road – catch Roddy before he's at his tea. We'll need a few hands to get this down that track.'

Do'l Alex's vehicle pulled away with the roar and rattle of a hole-peppered silencer. Roddy was banging in fence posts. With him were his cousin Lal, whom Alan recognised as the man he

56

had spoken to at the sheep pen on his previous visit, and Lal's two sons. The younger of them might have been one of the bigger lads he had been teaching that day, but as they did not join in the conversation or look him in the eye he was not sure. The whole group downed tools at once and set off with Do'l Alex. Alan was embarrassed by this unsolicited assistance from total strangers, but in fact the project would have been impossible on his own. Even with the trailer rehitched to Do'l Alex's more robust vehicle and the van taking the rear with a fearsome array of bracing ropes in case anything slewed, the half-mile of narrow up-and-down track, little more than a footpath, took almost an hour to negotiate, and it was more than one man's work, in the confined space in front of the cottage, to reposition Selena straight on to the shed door. Alan expected to leave her there until he could lay hands on suitable timber to brace her up, but his helpers had other ideas.

'There is a big heap of old fence posts by the road,' Roddy volunteered. 'You will have a saw with you?'

'Yes, but please don't bother—' Alan had private doubts about the strength of old fence posts.

'Ach, no bother!' bellowed Do'l Alex. 'Lal will drive up there now and bring them down in the Land Rover. Is there pulleys somewhere, Roddy?'

'Well, there is somewhere. Go you and look in the loft, Sandy.'

'Everything out of here now!' Do'l Alex shouted cheerfully, swinging himself up on Selena. Alan jumped up quickly to rescue the dinghy, which Do'l Alex was heaving onto his broad shoulders, trolley and all. They got it safely down to soft grass. Do'l Alex regarded it with amazement.

'You'll no take that piece of flotsam out on these waters?'

'As soon as I get sails for it.'

Do'l Alex shook his head, but approvingly. 'By God, you've got some nerve, lad, eh?'

Alan felt absurdly proud of himself; it was something to be complimented for nerve by such a weatherbeaten mass of confident muscle as Do'l Alex.

Young Sandy returned dragging a weighty bundle tied up in sacking, hooks, blocks and chain, all carefully greased. Old Ewan had obviously been about similar work in his time; and he had built his workshop with beams to take it. Lal arrived with the fence posts, which were by no means in bad condition.

'Don't you need these?' Alan asked Roddy.

'Och no. The grants for fencing are very good just now. You are welcome to them. And there is some heavier stuff in under the bench here.'

Do'l Alex produced a second saw from his vehicle, and everyone set to work. Daylight was almost gone by the time they had her in and safely buttressed. Even so, Do'l Alex was not fully satisfied with the result.

'She is not quite level, Alan. You will need another wee chock in here and there.'

But nothing further could be done in the gloom inside the shed. As they gathered outside in the luminous twilight, Alan realised with considerable embarrassment that he couldn't even offer them a cup of coffee: the stove was unlit and the power disconnected. He stammered apologies and thanks, but Do'l Alex roared with laughter.

'Be quiet now! I've got something better than coffee.'

With that he produced a bottle of whisky from the Land Rover. The boys were sent in to find cups and then left to stand by in silence while the bottle was shared out between their elders. The three Boreray men tossed the ferocious liquor back with no more apparent effect than a cup of weak tea, and departed into the dusk leaving Alan incoherent and unco-ordinated. He made some attempt to unload the van, but having hit his head on three different doorways and fallen over the kitchen table, he decided on an early night. The bed looked rather doubtful by torchlight. He didn't mind that it had obviously sheltered mice, which were pretty little animals anyway, and woodlice were not too bad, but he hoped there were no cockroaches. He picked up a pillow and suppressed a shudder at the fleeing family of earwigs. It came into his intoxicated head that since everyone had been so kind to him that evening, he perhaps owed a reciprocal duty to earwigs. He studied one solemnly as it lay in a dark fold of blanket, doggo, bead-black and minding its own business. When he could regard it with just affection, he replaced the pillow carefully, lay down flinching only slightly, and was asleep in seconds.

In the morning someone had left a sack of peats and a bag of potatoes outside his door.

The next few weeks established a tranquil routine, in which Boreray shone forth as the most beautiful place on earth and her people as the best of neighbours. The children were docile and quiet, rather too quiet, but their very shyness was disarming, and their life fascinatingly different from his own childhood. When the school bus stopped above Ardbuie to wait for the little orange foot-ferry from Fladday, as it braved the gale to offload its dozen or so boys and girls, matter-of-fact with their school books under their arms, he felt oddly stirred; and again when he noticed, at every house it seemed, a shapeless aproned mother with two or three little ones waving their older sisters and brothers off. They really were families, large, close and interrelated into one community. Against the near-barren ground, the uncertain sky and wild sea, their everyday lives appeared touched with a scriptural dignity, a balance of fragility and continuance, which the ugly modern houses, the post-and-wire fences and beat-up vehicles could not quite dispel.

Even the ramshackle cottage at Skalanish seemed included in it. Its thick walls tapered outwards to the ground, end-on to the sea, hunched patiently against the wind. It must have stood there for generations under thatch, but that had rotted long ago, and it was capped now with rusty corrugated iron. That was decaying too, but just holding its own. One chimney pot was short and black, the other a tall octagon pierced at the top with a fancy design, salvaged no doubt from some more imposing building. Two deepset windows looked out under the sagging gutter with modest pride, as if to say, 'Look, I'm surviving.'

In the first few days, as he cleaned it up inside, he kept coming across reminders of its past. There were, of course, a few beautiful and simple pieces that old Ewan had made: a big sea-chest at the foot of the bed, a low slat-backed chair, a milking stool. But more haunting were the unobtrusive ingenuities of a man who had always been poor and always made the best of things: the collapsing settee webbed underneath with an old trawl-net, the rotten floor patched with boards sawn from a stout baulk of driftwood, the hand-gouged wooden draining board over the chipped sink, the curious metal skirting round the kitchen which turned out to be cut from many flattened beer cans, rat-proof and rot-proof. Most idiosyncratic, perhaps, was the bathroom. Alan hadn't even realised there was one on his first night in the house, but discovered it when he investigated a cupboard opposite the bedroom the following day. The door opened only halfway: behind it was an enormous washbasin with brass taps and no waste-pipe, which saved on space, with admirable simplicity, by draining into the massive club-footed bath. This had itself been fitted in beside the handsome WC pedestal by trimming off most of one side of the mahogany seat. Roddy told him about its installation, laughing half shamefacedly. 'Dad held out against a bathroom most of his life. But my mother would have one – everyone else had got one long ago, she said, and there was her friends coming in at communions and that, and gone were the days when they would go to the outhouse – they was too shy. So when they got a new suite at the manse, Dad took away the old one, and there it is. Many a good man's bum sat on that seat, Alan, before it came to Skalanish.'

After that Alan never sidled round the impossible door without a flicker of affection for Ewan. He had good reason to be grateful to him. Not only the workshop, but the loft and various drawers and shelves, were full of boat-lover's bric-à-brac, from mooring buoys and several-sized oars to waxed thread and brass shackles. As he rummaged happily through these late in the evenings, the old man's benevolent presence was almost palpable. In fact, he found himself increasingly reluctant to disturb or alter anything in that house which was still Ewan's. He had intended to dismantle the bed, as it was an oldfashioned double-ended one of thrifty Scottish proportions, less than his own length. He would undoubtedly have slept more comfortably with the mattress on the floor, but in the end he left it and put up with lying diagonally. He could not quite come to terms with the little dark sitting room, though; the rexine-covered armchairs swelled threateningly there, the shiny rayon cushions were balefully overstuffed. He shut the door on them. He couldn't imagine that Ewan had spent much time there either, in front of the slime-green fireplace with its row of spiky Venetian glass ornaments. His wife had probably kept him in the kitchen, and that was where Alan lived too. It was shabby, and the cream-painted woodstrip lining was startlingly yellow with age, but it had the tranquillity of use about it. It was warm too, when he remembered to fuel the Rayburn stove – a delicate operation, as it was disintegrating with rust. It heated water, choking and belching over the task so that the room shuddered, would boil a kettle, and could be cooked on if the wind was in the right quarter, at least enough for Alan's unambitious requirements. There had, apparently, once been a cooker as well: its outline on the wall near the door appeared in pallor edged by tarry brown, like a Hiroshima shadow. The propane cylinder which had served it still stood inflammably red and cheerful on the lobby side of the wooden partition wall; Ewan had presumably decoded the warning 'for outside installation only' somewhat eccentrically. Alan thought about removing it, but in the end it stayed, because of the neat wooden cradle with hinged gate the old man had built round it. Initially, too, he cleared the kitchen of such unpleasing articles as the orange sunburst rug, the pink and yellow floral cushions (one stained with dead mouse juice) and the plaque informing him that Christ was an invisible witness to all his profanities; but after a few days, contrite, he reinstated them, and lived as Ewan's guest.

Each day after work, he spent most of the time till nightfall outside. The much-indented shoreline demanded exploration. At first he walked back towards Gnipadale, but he was always apprehended by Roddy or Chrissie, who insisted that he come in out of the rain and have tea. An alternative higher route brought him into the smiling orbit of Johane, Lal's mother and old Ewan's sister, who kept him there till after dark and sent him away with eggs and homemade butter. Alan was immensely touched by their warmth, but all the same he was not easy with it. He got into the habit of wandering westwards from the cottage. The road curved north under the hills, leaving the whole south-west end of Boreray uninhabited. Old Ewan's was the only dwelling there still intact; but on the other side of the stream which ran out into the shingle cove, there were remnants of farther habitations. All that was left of them was the low soft-cornered outlines of the walls, unfaced boulders held together with earth. A few of the more substantial ones contained broken bedsprings, cracked iron pots, fragments of china, all grown over with nettles. But the older ruins sported nothing but emerald green grass, inside, outside and over the walls.

There had been other settlements by some of the many small bays around the coast, wherever a friendly stream had worn shelter from the moor. Each group of ruins was marked by a brilliant splash of turf in the brown and tawny heather. To come down to these green places from the massive flank of Gormul was to enter another world, where the vast sombre spaces of sky and moor gave way to the tiny, the fragile, and the many-coloured. The soft bright turf was still starred with tormentil where the tumbled walls provided shelter. Lichens, grey-green on egg-yolk yellow and black on green, scaled the stone with their various whorls and arabesques: all just stone, all just lichen, all minutely and differently beautiful. In the protected hollows of the stream-beds, fresh sprays of green and purple heather overhung six-inch-high waterfalls, the tiny mauve cups trembling in the vibrations of the plunge. The water was clear and amber, always full of bubbles, forming and following and disappearing in the smooth lip of the cascade. Every little pool had its beach of striped and spotted pebbles and its tuft of stiff, pale green ferns. These streams ran out into sheltered inlets, not actual harbours, merely indentations between ribs of rock where the slope of the shore had been found gentle enough to launch or beach boats. Now they were totally lonely, with not so much as an iron ring on a rock to show where the fishermen had once tied up. Yet to look out of these little havens between their containing rocks was curiously homely, as if the particular pattern of reefs and islets thus framed had been so familiar to human eyes that it had become forever relevant. In these windows little things crystallised: a secretive wren searching in and out of the boulders on the upper beach; sea-anemones, closed and glistening, under the black overhang of a half-tide rock; an otter's rounded back, just slightly darker and slightly less shiny than the tangleweed it dived among. The crash and rumble of the sea and the bewildering torrent of wind were occluded by these hollows, and small, individual sounds rose to the surface: the repeated gurgle and drag of small waves coming and going on shingle, the wing-beat of a passing rock dove, the tick-tick-tick of bladder-wrack draining as the tide withdrew.

Out of the little sheltered valleys, the perspective altered. Startling distances opened in the racing clouds and shadow-raked moorland, and closed again in a squall of hail or a blinding shaft of evening light. The low hump of Fladday and the summits of Càrn Bàn and Gormul were murky uncertainties one moment and graven images the next. In the swift-running sea between Boreray and Fladday, the fangs and skerries were so many and so foam-weltered that it was difficult to see how they joined or where the channels were. Only the thick black line of Langasker retained definition, pointing southwards at Fladday, the chaos of broken rock and water contained within it, and the slow leap and fall of Atlantic surf flaring behind. Beyond it there were no more reefs or islands, but limitless sea and a charging line of breakers pounding scoured sand the whole western length of the island: Tràigh Mhór, the great beach.

Returning from his forays, Alan often found himself walking towards a rainbow. He had never seen such rainbows. They sprang up sudden, brilliant, double-arched, and on the underside of the lower arch the colours appeared a third time. Beneath those great glowing bows, the wide solitudes of moor and sea shrank to the intimacy of a garden, feathered with golden light. He would reach the cottage giddy and heavy-limbed, incapable of concentrating sufficiently to get his boots off or towel his dripping hair. As his wits regathered, he mused whether this disorientation was an effect of the sublime, or merely of Boreray's atrocious autumn weather. From inside the warm kitchen, with hail battering the small cracked window, it looked, on the whole, more like the latter.

By the end of his first week on Boreray, Alan felt happier than he had ever done except at sea. The wild beauty of the place spelt freedom; the community smiled on him, and he smiled on his pupils. Old responsibilities were satisfactorily buried, and new ones had not had time to become irksome. It was therefore an unpleasant shock to be intercepted by Mr Carnegie on his way in to work on Friday with the news that his mother had telephoned, and would ring again at the start of the afternoon session, if he could be in the staffroom to receive the call.

'I judged that to be the most convenient time, as I see you have a free period then,' Mr Carnegie declared. 'She seemed anxious to speak to you. Most anxious.'

There was the merest impression of a smirk on his face. Alan went to his room squirming inwardly. What might she have said to the wretched man, and how, anyway, had she managed to track him down? He had been carefully vague. The maternal re-emergence prompted unwilling recognition of something else he had been trying to forget: Frances was due to arrive the next day to collect her vehicle. She had done without it for a week and her journey would be long and rushed. He would have to be decently grateful and terribly nice to her all weekend. In consequence he was uncharacteristically nasty to his pupils. He precipitated a messy nosebleed in Class 1 by shaking someone too hard, made all fourteen pairs of jaws in Class 3 surrender their chewing gum to the waste-bin, and nonplussed Class 2 into total paralysis merely by remarking that he supposed they were all their mothers' little darlings. The morning passed in an irritating sequence of forgotten textbooks, spilt solder, misapplied glue and misdirected screws.

The staffroom was not empty, either. Alan gritted his teeth to find someone else in occupation after the lunch hour. He hadn't seen the girl before, but she had a large pile of exercise books and did not look up from them when he entered. He introduced himself.

'Eleanor Brown,' she countered crossly, still without looking at him. The voice was Dundee.

Ill-mannered bitch, thought Alan. But not bad looking, he could not help allowing. She was small and russety-haired, with slender legs and arms. Her red pen flickered across the pages with vibrant ill-temper.

'I hear you play the clarinet,' she snapped, suddenly.

'Oh – yes. How on earth does anyone here know that?'

She shrugged impatiently. 'Word gets around.' Her hand scattered ticks pizzicato. 'Anything else?' she demanded.

At a loss to know what else was required Alan didn't answer. She sighed in exasperation, glaring at him with fierce tawny-flecked eyes.

'Any other musical instrument?'

'Flute – piano, well, if pushed.'

'I'm a competent pianist myself anyway,' she said dismissively, eyes flicking the pages again.

Alan was silenced. The telephone rang. He looked at his watch, but without hope.

'Hello—' He choked on 'Mummy'. It was quite impossible with Eleanor sitting there.

'Darling, you sound so distant! You're not cross that I rang are you sweetie?'

'No, of course not,' he lied. The more filial he sounded, the sooner he might get rid of her. 'I would have rung you earlier, but I'm living absolutely miles from a 'phone'.

'Oh darling, is it dreadful? Terribly primitive?'

'No, it's lovely.'

'But I'm sure it must be awful. Harold says they're the poorest peasants in Europe – worse than Greece or Sicily or anywhere. Look darling, what I really rang to say is, there's absolutely no need for you to stay. I know you went off in a huff because you felt I was trying to run your life for you, but I shan't say anything more about it, I promise.'

'Please don't worry. I like it here. I don't want to go anywhere else.'

There was a silence, very brief, but for Celia rare. Alan dreaded what was coming.

'Did you get my letter?'

'Yes – thanks.'

He knew what her next line would be: then-darling-surely-you-realise-how-I-feel. It was exactly that. For the next quarter of an hour she coursed backwards and forwards over the old ground. Alan's replies dwindled to monosyllables, then to grunts, and eventually to furious silence.

'Darling, are you still there?'

'Yes.'

'You are cross. It's so offensive of you.'

'Sorry.'

'Please, please, darling, try to understand— '

'Look, I'm sorry, but I shall have to go now. I'm working.'

'But keep in touch. Promise you'll ring me when you're not so angry.'

'Yes, I shall.'

'Make it soon darling – won't you?'

'Yes, of course – I must go now.'

'Don't forget. I do need you, Alan.'

The appalling thing about that was the suspicion that it was actually true.

'Goodbye – look after yourself,' he said, putting down the receiver hastily.

Eleanor had obviously enjoyed the entertainment.

'Anxious Mummy?' she asked, with relish.

Alan detested her. For a moment he even felt protectively fond of Celia.

Suddenly, Eleanor laughed, showing very pointed canines. 'They get like that, don't they? Mine keeps sending me woolly vests and knickers.'

'God, mine hasn't thought of that yet!'

The ice was broken. Eleanor scanned his face with frank, if qualified, liking.

'Now, when can we have a play?'

Alan gasped, gulped and tried not to snigger.

'I'm violin, by the way. I can get by with quite a few other things too – depends on what's available.'

'You teach music, then?'

'Yes. What about this weekend?'

'No – I've got a friend coming.'

'Girlfriend?'

'No – yes, a girl.'

'Make up your mind. I take an evening class on Monday. How about Tuesday evening? At your place. You haven't got a car, have you?'

'No. That's fine.'

'Bell!' She got up briskly. Her full skirt swung about well-defined hips.

Alan made to hold the door for her, but she had already kicked it back with one foot. She marched off along the corridor without a goodbye, straight-backed and purposeful.

There was one more class to go. It must be Class 4, he decided, hearing their almost-deep voices and exaggeratedly heavy tread. He got them in and quietened down, big flushed jostling boys just off the football pitch, each as awkward and gangling as the next, and just as likely to be called Angus.

'Now, which lot are you?' He scuffled for his list of names. 'Oh, yes. You're the class with four Donalds.'

'Five today, sir,' corrected a large grinning boy who was one of them.

'Oh, not another one! Right, hands up everyone called Donald.'

He counted four rough red paws, and as he turned, one slim golden hand. The fifth Donald was standing at a bench just behind him, watching him with wide grey eyes under a fringe of dark hair.

66

Alan stared. For a strange moment the room and the voices withdrew, leaving nothing but those brilliant eyes, silver-grey irises ringed with a darker line. With difficulty he looked away.

'How am I going to sort you out, then?' he asked. He had to say something.

'Easy sir!' that was the stout spokesman. 'There's Donnie Mór – that means Big Donnie, sir – over there is Crabbit, he's crabbit – that's Panda, some kind of animal I think – and that thing in the corner is Donnie Beag, that's Wee Donnie sir, he's a bit undersized.'

The boy scowled beneath black brows, a faint flush creeping along his cheekbone.

'You're Mairi's brother,' said Alan. But Mairi's eyes were mudpools to those.

Mairi's name was greeted enthusiastically by the remaining Donald, who was drawing hour-glass figures in the air, with guttural noises of appreciation.

'And what's he called?' Alan asked the room at large. A universal howl of 'Porky!' drowned out Porky's protestation that he was called Donald.

'Very apt!' For Porky was indeed of porcine appearance, with small eyes set close to a wide-nostrilled snout. Crabbit was a lanky boy with a surly narrow face, but Panda was puzzling.

'His Dad's the polis-man,' elucidated Porky, telepathically.

Alan thanked him, deciding he had better keep a tight hold on his own thoughts for the rest of the afternoon.

'Well, at least I've learnt something today.'

He had learnt something. He was not sure what it was, still less that he liked it.

'What about the rest of you? Do you remember anything at all about morticing?'

Several voices declared that they did not, and the next hour proved this to be no lie. Alan went from bench to bench, though with flagging concentration, inwardly stifling eclogic lines, in case Porky should turn out to be clairvoyant in tongues as well. He succeeded in running out of time before he could get round to the bench in the corner.

Chapter 7

Frances had come and gone. Alan leant against the lighthouse wall watching the ferry grow small. He had expected to feel relieved, but instead he was dejected. She had looked very wistful saying goodbye. In fact she was obviously going to cry. Perhaps a fraternal kiss would have been kind at that point. He had tried quite hard not to entangle her, he thought, gloomily, but it had turned out the same bloody mess as usual. He became unwillingly conscious of Sally's letter, still in his pocket, unanswered and likely to remain so: and of other reproaches from the past, also unanswered and unanswerable. He fingered Richard's beads, wondering yet again why he wore something that carried such discreditable memories. He considered Daphne, and wished he hadn't. However things started, they all seemed to end in the same way, wallowing in a horrible porridge of emotion. Porridge laced with syrup. He loathed porridge.

The sea was heaving only gently, full of shifting light, making no promises. He watched it with longing. It was the safest place to be. Turning to walk back to the village, he saw Do'l Alex and a mate making the *Maid of Rona* ready, and wished he were going too. It seemed a more probable way of spending the day than school and the nine o' clock bell, and wired-up windows. And there was that girl Eleanor. She didn't look as if she would cling, but no one could be trusted.

Do'l Alex was tying his lobster pots together in fleets, and attaching orange marking-floats. The other man was baiting them. He was using mackerel, salted stiff but still recognisable from its bold black markings. His hands dripped brownish oil as he slashed each fish in half with a quick knife stroke, thrust it into the bait-hanger and laced the creel. He was a dour-faced man, unpleasantly sallow against his yellow oilskins. He did not look up as Alan approached, but Do'l Alex hailed him cheerfully.

'Hallo there – grand day!'

'Yes, isn't it? I wish I had your job, Do'l Alex.'

'Och, maybe today.' He gave a bellow of laughter. 'No every day. I lost eighty creels last Thursday.'

'That's a big loss.'

'Ay! We'll put out another eighty today and lose them next Thursday likely enough.' This seemed to amuse him enormously. He continued, with great good humour, 'You'll need to come out with me some day. I can do with an extra hand. Murdo's only with me off and on.'

'Oh, that would be great— ' began Alan enthusiastically. Then in an instant he saw it differently. He was following Murdo's quick vicious knife and the rough thrust of his arm into the black net of the creels, and suddenly he was aware of cornered creatures and terror. Each of these eighty pots was a death trap. Each of the eighty lost might have had its prisoners. He had never thought about it that way before. Fishing boats had seemed picturesque and jaunty: now there was the *Maid of Rona* a reeking engine of death. He blinked at her smart green, white and brown paintwork and the yellow letters of her name, and his stomach crawled.

Do'l Alex had finished with the tackle, and disappeared into the doghouse with a shout and a wave. Alan turned up towards the school, shaking slightly. A scraggy sheep ambled in front of him, looking back every few steps with wary cairngorm eyes. Two roast gigots and a bag of rather lean chops. He loped past her, occasioning a bleat and a scramble, and vaulted the school fence. There were shrieks of delight from a group of little girls at the gate. One of them was Dina.

'Hi, Dina,' he said, feeling rather silly.

'Look out – here's Jock,' warned Dina confidentially, and fled.

He looked round. Mr Carnegie was approaching briskly across the road, spectacles gleaming in the morning sun. Alan was at once quite certain that fence-vaulting was forbidden, and reached his room by a hasty detour round the back of the school canteen. It smelt like mutton for lunch. He wondered if the sheep could smell it too.

One session with Eleanor was enough to dispel any doubts about her. She had come to play music, and that was what they did. She quickly told him his fingering was clumsy and his breath control abysmal: but added, without rancour, 'I suppose you're out of practice. You'd better give it an hour a day for a while.' She leant on his shoulder about as languorously as a hod of bricks to point out his mistakes, and nudged him with unaffectionate emphasis in the middle of a duet attempt at the Mozart clarinet quintet.

'Look, this may be larghetto, but you're making it sound like a commercial for a new brand of toilet paper.'

This tetchy remark reduced Alan to helpless laughter, but she snorted something about schoolboy humour, and what it showed about his education. He felt this was a dangerous subject, and applied himself to a severer rendering.

She herself played very well. Alan was curious to know why she had come as a music teacher to a place like Boreray, but he didn't have the courage to ask. He offered her coffee, hoping she might relax and become more expansive.

'Tea, please,' she said, firmly.

He rather disliked tea, but would no more have dared drink an independent mug of coffee than put a hand up her skirt. During tea, she sorted her sheet music into piles, one for each of them, and gave out his homework.

'We can have another go on Friday after school,' she said, 'at my place this time. The piano will widen our range a bit, as you're not up to anything very advanced. I suppose I can give you a lift home afterwards.' She lived in one of the pale pink council houses in Port Long.

'I certainly don't want to walk ten miles,' Alan ventured. She looked as if she thought he was being cheeky.

After she had gone, he realised that he had enjoyed the evening immensely. It was well over a year since he had had much chance to play, and her criticism was fully justified. It was even invigorating: he had not felt so inspired to improve his technique since the days when Richard had taken his training in hand, with equally blistering honesty and a similar adamantine resistance to sentiment. Richard was a rigorous formalist, always insistent that the performer must not use the music, but the other way about; and he could detect the seeping of gratuitous emotion as a shark smells blood. Alan flicked through Eleanor's music. He wanted to try the larghetto again, but hesitated, abashed by Richard's voice from the past, hissing such remarks as 'soggy cardboard' and 'candy floss'. He smiled, reflecting that Eleanor and Richard might have enjoyed insulting each other: on second thoughts, probably not, for Richard was such an inveterate snob he could scarcely bring himself to speak to anyone with a regional accent, even to be rude. After two nervous false starts, he began to play, forgetting everything but the music; but at the piercing moment when the instrument soars from its lowest to its highest, he found himself contemplating lambent grey eyes, and realised they had been there from the beginning. He stopped playing at once. Richard would call that prostitution. The shattered tranquillity of the music trembled uneasily just out of hearing. He told himself that he did not like being haunted by the eyes of a grimy little schoolboy; but that categorisation was so crassly untruthful that it was no help in laying the ghost. He fixed his attention on cleaning his instruments and tidying up. That was Richard's training too. He recalled many asperities about undergraduate slovenliness, which at nineteen he had ascribed confidently to the onset of old age in one approaching thirty. Richard's remark as he fastened the wampum string had been characteristic: 'These are for decoration. I hope they won't stop you washing your neck occasionally.'

Yet it was Richard, the contemptuous, the despiser of sentiment, who had been left devastated. He himself had taken a bosomy girl called Charlotte to the college ball, and enjoyed it thoroughly.

At that moment, not for the first time but with more pity than before, he felt ashamed of that enjoyment.

Eleanor established a strict routine of music practice, alternately at his house and hers. They would review the situation at Christmas, she said, adding threateningly, 'And if we're not getting anywhere we'll think again': from which Alan inferred that his progress would then be subject to examination. But though he had some inner regrets for time that might have been spent out of doors or working on Selena, he acquiesced. He was used to obeying irascible skippers, and Eleanor seemed more likely to keelhaul naysayers than any of them.

After one of their sessions he asked her respectfully if she had any interest in sailing.

'Why?'

'I could do with a crew for my dinghy.' He added hastily, 'Or I could crew,' realising the indecency of giving Eleanor orders.

She glared at him: 'Is it one of these horrible things where you hang over the side?'

He admitted that it was.

Her nostrils twitched. 'I hate boats. I absolutely loathe the sea.'

'Why on earth did you come to a place like this then?'

Her face told him that he had been both obtuse and impertinent. Perhaps the one excused the other; at any rate, she replied quite patiently, 'A place isn't just the sea around it, you know. A place is the people who live in it.'

'Oh yes.' Alan considered this slightly alien notion. 'Yes, people are very nice here.'

'Very *nice*!'

'Well, neighbourly, I mean.' He paused in alarm. Perhaps she meant she loathed them as well.

'Neighbourly. That's a pretty wet term, isn't it?'

'Is it?'

'Of course it is. Don't you recognise a real community when you see one? Real families – not your rotten little mainland nuclear group, proper extended families, the whole lot, babies and idiots and incontinent great-grannies. Society isn't an artificial construct here, it's an organism – no one's left out, everyone is part of it and fits in with everyone else. Even criminals – what would be called criminals on the mainland. Do you know there's a murderer living in Garve? No one bothers – they just accommodate him.'

'Really?' Alan found this more amusing than inspiring, but tried to look serious.

Eleanor scowled. 'You don't like that, do you? You're too law-and-order minded— '

'I certainly am not!' Alan was stung. 'I believe in living and letting live. More than you do – you're the bossiest person I've ever met.'

She drew herself up to an indignant five-foot-two and then suddenly relaxed. 'Well, at last I've made you say something that isn't charmingly polite. Good!'

'But why do you want to be so bloody rude all the time?'

'Not rude – frank. If you don't say what you think, you end up thinking you think something else. I expect it happens to you all the time.'

72

Alan worked this out carefully. 'Yes, I suppose it does. But I might want to change my mind, so why not?'

'It's a let-out, that's why not. Slipshod and lazy, like not keeping up your music when you obviously have a talent for it.'

'Look, I was racing halfway round the world with nine other people on a fifty-foot yacht. Do you think they would have wanted to listen? I'd have been chucked overboard.'

Eleanor tossed her head impatiently. 'Nine other people just like you. Over-privileged overgrown kids playing at running away to sea.'

'Yes, that's exactly it!' He couldn't help laughing. 'I'd do it again tomorrow.'

She looked severe, but not as furious as he expected. 'It's time you grew up, then.'

'So my mother keeps telling me.'

'She's dead right. It's not all your world, you know: not all your toys.'

'I'll keep the sea. You can have the rest of it.'

'Don't be so idiotic. You can't run away from things. If you have any wit at all, you should at least learn that here, looking at the way people co-operate.'

Alan thought of a flippant answer, but then of his kind Gnipadale neighbours, and said instead, 'But most people here haven't got much chance to run away. Perhaps they would if they could. Some things about the place are pretty awful – what about unemployment?'

'That's the system!' she replied angrily. 'Nothing to do with the islanders. If it weren't for that sort of squeeze from outside, I don't believe anyone would want to leave.'

'But there must be a lot of pressure on individuals – all this living in the bosom of the family— '

'Individuals! Individuals aren't anything. It's relationships that count, in any real society. People are willing to give up their own little preferences for that sort of security.'

'Not everyone, surely— '

'Oh, not people like you. You're a leftover from the Romantic era. Properly socialised people I mean. Look at all these neighbours who have done you so many good turns. You don't think it's because they *like* you, do you?'

'Well – no, I suppose it's not.'

Eleanor gave him a withering look. 'That's exactly what you did think. Well, you're wrong. It's because they recognise an obligation to you as a stranger and as a neighbour. They would treat you well whatever they thought of you personally. And what do you think they *do* think of you? You've taken a job a local might have had, you're an atheist— '

'I'm not— '

'Church of England, just as bad— '

'I'm— '

'A Sabbath-breaker, anyway; historically you're one of the oppressors – rich, English— '

'I'm actually completely broke and I'm Scottish.'

Eleanor paused to draw breath. 'Well, I don't want to get involved in politics today.'

He gathered she was saving politics for another occasion.

'If I have to give you a lift we'd better get going,' she continued, looking at her watch.

'I'll walk. I could do with it.'

'Sure? Oh well, someone will probably pick you up on the road.'

'If so, should I apologise for being English, rich and oppressive?'

She merely snorted. But her prediction was accurate; he had only reached the far side of Port Long when a car stopped, with its front-seat passenger already scrambling into a back seat full of smiling old women and infants with chocolaty faces. He demurred, but the driver was insistent; the old ladies even more so.

'We are going to Ardbuie. It is no bother, no bother at all. Get you in now.'

There was nothing else for it. The oldest grandmother patted his hair, cooing and chuckling. The smallest child shrieked with glee and the biggest offered him a bite of a well-slobbered ice cream, as inescapable a courtesy as a sheep's eyeball. The man in the driving seat made a grave speech of welcome which intimated that Boreray was the fairer for the presence of the stranger, adding more prosaically, 'And ye've taught that idiot of a boy of mine how to use a screwdriver at last!'

There were no detectable signs of oppression. They drove him all the way to Skalanish, and the benevolent granny thrust a packet of chocolate biscuits into his pocket as he got out.

Eleanor did not sweeten as he got to know her better. When his playing improved, she shifted her more virulent criticisms to his background and character, both of which were an affront to her principles. Alan did not object: indeed, he was greatly entertained by her edgy intelligence, her alert, wiry looks, her abrasive east-coast voice. He felt rather like a large peaceful dog fascinated by a yapping little terrier bitch. He tried not to seem too indulgent, because it made her so angry to be looked down on; often she spent most of an evening standing while he sprawled, so that physically at least that would be impossible. Because of his objectionable upbringing, it came hard to him to sit while a woman was standing, but he soon learned that if he got to his feet he would presently be indicted of sexism on some chance remark.

'I can't help being a foot taller than you,' he said, subsiding again.

Eleanor glared, obviously suspecting a failure of will. She did not believe that anyone could not help anything, particularly anyone upper-middle class and male. She was a doctrinaire socialist and a doctrinaire feminist, and belied both doctrines by being splendidly in love with Boreray society, which was intensely conformist and patriarchal.

'What about these village headmen, then?' Alan asked once, to tease her.

'Headmen?' She bristled, arms folded tensely.

'Everyone has to do what the oldest inhabitant says. It's crazy. Roddy told me the other day he's been planting potatoes in the same mud-patch for fifteen years. They've got every disease under the sun – or rain – but some old uncle comes along and glowers at them every year, just to make sure tradition is upheld. Roddy knows he'll never get a crop out of that land, but he has to go through with it just because that's how things were done in the past.'

'That's a total misinterpretation. Haven't you thought about what humanity to the aged means? It means making them feel

75

needed – showing them their advice is valuable, not putting them on the scrap heap.'

'This old uncle used to get drunk and beat his wife, till she gave up and died.'

Eleanor frowned. 'Some things have got to change, obviously. But you don't understand the constraints of local custom. It doesn't mean the same as it does in Surrey, you know.'

'What about female circumcision in Mali? Stoning adulteresses in Afghanistan? Are these harmless local customs?'

'That's beside the point.' Her hair was standing on end: it did when she was particularly irate. 'You can cut out the cheap jibes. The people on this island are about as non-violent as you'll find anywhere. All right, they may get drunk occasionally, but it's a safety valve: it's bound to happen with the pressure of obligations and responsibilities. But the community is so healthy, it can deal with it. It's a wonderful place.'

And so on. Her arguments were coherent, forceful and blithely inconsistent. Yet the strength of her loyalty to Boreray was so disarming that it was difficult to doubt or dislike her. Her passion was not only for speeches, either. She spent much time recording old Gaelic songs and stories, ran an adults' evening class free because there was no money to provide one, and made an unpaid trip to Fladday each Saturday to teach *clarsach*, the Gaelic harp. She shopped for several elderly neighbours and babysat for younger ones. She was extremely fond of babies: the cooing and cuddling Eleanor who accosted every passing pushchair in the main street was not recognisable as the critic who suspected every rallentando of vicarious sentimentality. She was popular with the schoolchildren too, and did her utmost to instil music into their unpromising souls. She even kept open house for them in the lunch hour twice a week. 'Just sitting in the room with them isn't an activity,' she told the staffroom firmly, justifying her apparent breach of union rules: she was, of course, a strict unionist. So there she sat, munching a sandwich or an apple, conducting, pointing, shouting as necessary – but inactive, in her own terms, as long as she didn't rise from her chair. The children loved it. It was an astonishing sight to see Porky delicately tapping a xylophone and Crabbit rapt with a multi-coloured panpipe, when they might have been smoking in the lavatories instead.

'How on earth do you keep it up?' Alan asked her, impressed by her good works.

She cast him a fierce glance, which led him to expect an attack on his own lack of self-discipline, but instead she said, 'I'd find it a lot more difficult if there wasn't someone like you around to be nasty to.'

'Thank you,' he said, meaning it: it was the nearest thing to a compliment she had ever paid him.

She moved in swiftly on her advantage.

'It's time *you* did something for somebody round here.'

'Any suggestions?'

'Yes. You've got a lot of tools and things in that shed of yours, haven't you?'

He admitted warily that he had.

'Well, there's quite a number of the older boys live down your way. You could have them in on Saturdays and let them bash around.'

'What do you mean, bash around? With my tools?'

'There you go. You don't really want to help anyone.'

'Yes I do, but—'

'Look, these kids need something constructive to do. Saturday's the day they all take to drink. You've got that dreadful old hulk down there, they could really have fun hammering away at that.'

'She's not a hulk. She's – they'd wreck her!'

'It's a wreck anyway. You just couldn't care less, could you?'

'That's unfair.'

'And you've got that other boat thing. You could teach some of them to sail in that. But I don't expect you'll bother.'

With that, she snatched up her bag and whirled out of the staffroom.

Alan had an uneasy feeling that her challenge could not be ignored. It was Class 4's post-football Friday woodwork again. Their normal end-of-the-week restiveness was aggravated by the rain which had cancelled their game.

'Gym instead!' Porky informed him glumly. 'Physical jerks.' He did a few, hit his head on a vice, and swore loudly and distinctly, to cries of 'Sir, sir, did you hear that sir?'

'I heard. To your sty, Porky,' he replied grimly, assisting with a prod from a metre rule. He was reflecting that Porky certainly lived within walking distance of Skalanish and was certainly in danger of taking to drink on Saturdays. In the next hour, he considered his other young neighbours, with misgivings. There was Porky's cousin Donnie Mór. He was a patient, cheerful lad who merely grinned when the stool he had been painfully assembling for six weeks collapsed under Porky's sitting test. Alan swore.

'You swore, sir,' Porky pointed out.

Alan moved on to contemplation of Crump. He had presumably earned his nickname from a tendency to fall flat on his face. In the first ten minutes he had already tripped over Donnie Mór's hapless wreckage and Crabbit's less innocent outstretched leg, scattering screws like confetti.

'If you want anything else, I'll fetch it. Don't move from that bench.' Alan found that he was clenching his teeth as he said it. He could envisage Crump in a confined space with Selena.

He considered next Lal's boy Sandy. Sandy had never uttered a word in his hearing, though since no one had mentioned that he was dumb Alan assumed he could talk. Sandy was staring silently at the jagged end of a broken-off tenon protruding from the leg of his stool.

'How on earth did you do that, Sandy?'

Silence. Then, 'It broke.'

'You can speak after all!'

Sandy looked offended.

And then there was Donnie Beag. Alan had got used to his presence in the room, but took care to pay him as little attention as possible; not much was required, since he was invariably well behaved and his work was impeccable. Amongst his clumsy rawboned classmates with their various slouches and swaggers, he was small, quiet and self-effacing, and to that extent easy to ignore; his likeness to his pretty sister was not in itself unnerving; but he had speaking eyes, like Andersen's voiceless mermaid. When he was listening to instructions or studying a blackboard diagram, his gaze was luminous and intent, out of all proportion to its object. When he was actually addressed directly, the eyes quivered with exquisite life, transfiguring his face. When he was working at the bench, his rapt concentration flowed through eyes and hands and into the wood, in a hallowing rhythm of innocent integrity. Those eyes were disturbing, even uncanny. He was reputed to be illiterate and very stupid.

Alan inspected the piece the boy was working on. He had finished that term's project well in advance of the others, and had been handed a book of designs for useless decorative objects, with instructions to make what he could out of hardwood scrap. He had scrutinised every piece of wood in the pile, and by scaling down his design he had contrived to find sufficient iroko to start a small box with compartments and a fitted lid. He had just finished cutting. Alan picked up an end and a side. The dovetails were immaculate and the pins fitted to a hair's-breadth.

Certainly Selena wouldn't suffer from that standard of craftsmanship, he thought, smiling.

'You really are very talented,' he said.

Donnie looked up, eyes brilliant with wondering gratitude.

Alan, shaken, betook himself to Porky's bench, to remove a commando comic from its incumbent. He was quite sure he did not want to pass his Saturdays with Donnie Beag. Rather a dozen Porkies.

Chapter 8

Alan spent the weekend closeted with Selena. He was dismantling the cockpit to get at the rotten sternpost and discovered more rot, not unsuspected, in several ribs too. By Sunday evening most of her top layers were arranged round her or balanced on the rafters above, all marked for easy recognition when it came to reassembly. He picked his way out at bedtime, reflecting with relief that it really would be impossible to let a group of clumsy boys loose in the workshop.

His decision was reinforced by the sight of them on Monday afternoon, falling over their own and each other's feet and jostling for room. He had discovered a cache of test papers at the back of the store, and handed them out. He wanted peace to compose a second timber order following his weekend investigations. Since they were supposed to take a written examination at the end of the session anyway, he told them it was good practice, waited till the groans subsided and settled down with the timber list.

After a while he noticed that the smallest Donnie was writing nothing and had gone very white.

'Are you feeling sick or something?' he asked, with unpleasant memories of a first-year boy who had thrown up on the floor.

'He can't write, sir,' Porky volunteered. 'Can't write, can't read, can't— '

'Shut up you!' Alan threw a piece of chalk at him.

Porky continued his list of 'can'ts' sotto voce. His neighbours stifled guffaws. Donnie cringed.

It was obviously true. Even if the boy could read, he certainly couldn't spell with sufficient confidence to convey his meaning in writing, and in any case after half an hour of the torment his hands were shaking so much he could hardly hold pen to paper. Alan called him back as they were leaving.

'You're for it now, boy,' gloated Porky, with rolling eyes. Donnie looked as if he couldn't be for anything worse than he had already suffered. He cowered like a half-grown puppy caught widdling on the carpet. Alan had no idea what to say. 'I'm sorry I put you through this,' was all he intended, but obviously inappropriate.

'I didn't realise you had so much trouble with written work.'

Silence.

'Your practical work is brilliant, but I suppose you have to pass this wretched exam to stand a chance of any sort of training, do you?'

'Yes sir.'

'That's crazy.' He wondered if it were really true. Perhaps it was just something put about by teachers and headmasters. 'Are you sure?'

'Yes sir. Mr Carnegie says, sir. So did Cla— Mr MacDonald.'

That sounded suspicious, but whatever the ins and outs of the matter, the effect on the victim was all too apparent. Alan was at a loss how to help, but he had to offer something.

'Well – let's see if we can improve matters at all. Try that paper at home again – as slowly as you like, and look things up if you need to.'

It struck him that the boy was probably incapable of looking things up. He tried another tack.

'Take home this book you got the box out of. Don't just look at the diagrams – I know you can do that. Read it and fit the text to the pictures.'

Reaching for the book, Donnie brightened a little, faintly touched with confidence in his craft, the only confidence he knew.

'You can borrow any of the big picture books from the store – and look, couldn't you practise writing a bit? Have you anyone you could write letters to – any brothers or sisters away from home?'

Donnie looked horrified. Alan realised at once this wasn't the local idiom: letter writing, for a Boreray youth, was presumably rather like taking a teddy bear to bed.

'Well, what about keeping a diary? No one would have to see that, but it would get you used to writing every day, even just a line or so.'

This suggestion could hardly have appeared less grotesque than the previous one, but Donnie nodded, and gave him a grateful look, even a shy smile.

'You'd better get along to your next class – who is it?'

'Miss Brown, sir.'

'Tell her I kept you. She can thrash me later.'

Donnie's smile widened into a soft laugh, leaving Alan with a warm feeling which he interpreted as an indication that he had actually been of some use. But on reflection, of course, he knew he hadn't. He asked in the staffroom about the boy. Comments ranged from 'a nice lad but nothing up top' to 'half-witted'. Everyone seemed agreed that that sort of boy never got anywhere.

He mentioned it to Eleanor. 'The boy's a really skilled woodworker already. He can't be no good for anything.'

Eleanor shrugged. 'Well, that's the system. There are no local employers for boys like that, and no one will take them on without the right bits of paper. These kids get a raw deal.'

She picked up her bow. 'Hurry up! I'm going out later. And by the way, have you thought about what I was saying?'

'What about?'

'These boys, of course.'

'Oh – yes. That's fine. I'll organise something for the Saturday after the holiday.'

Alan was surprised and dismayed to hear himself say it. Eleanor merely nodded and told him to get a move on.

*   *   *

The first morning of the October holiday dawned still and frosty. Alan stood on the little hill above the cottage, watching the steel-blue air turn milky and the silver hoar golden as the sun swung clear of the mainland mountains. They were misty pink below and capped with white. The sea was at peace, just foaming lazily on the black edge of Rona, caressing the nearer skerries with a light pulse of blue.

It was the only calm day of his six weeks in Boreray. In the absence of a usable boat, he spent it wandering around the places he had come to know in wind and rain. Everything was enticingly changed. Against the limpid sky the summits were clear, still and benign as vast sleeping animals, flanks softly furred with russet and fawn. The black sucking bogs were paved with ice, the small footprints of sheep set firm and neat, and dusted with silver. The sea barely lapped on the little beaches of the deserted clachans. Even on the wild expanse of Tràigh Mhór the thundering surf had died to a soft swish and hiss. The upper beach shimmered with frost, but the withdrawing tide had left the lower sand deep ochre yellow, drifted with shells of many colours. He stooped to pick them up as he walked, then knelt, then crouched, as his eye caught smaller and smaller delights, purple, yellow, pink, and blue. There were hardly any he could name. There was one delicate horn-yellow type with thin sky-blue rays, and others like scallops, but tiny, and patched with orange or crimson; and some fragile and coral-pink, like a girl's painted fingernail. The sand itself was shells, each grain an iridescent fragment, or a tiny perfect whole, unbelievably small and fine. He gathered handfuls of them, dropping the dulled or broken ones as more beauties appeared. But when he stood up, he let them all fall back gently on the sand. He could not have said why he should not carry them away: in any case he had ceased thinking; senses were enough.

He climbed Gormul, and lay for a long time on its bare summit, conscious of nothing but blue sky. A noise grew out of it, eager and joyful. It was a long skein of greylags with sunlight on their wings, heading perhaps for pasture on Fladday. He jumped up to watch them pass, and saw that though they flew low over the green island they carried on southwards. His eyes followed them with love till they were lost in the brilliance of sun and water. He ran down to the saddle and started up the final ridge of Càrn Bàn. He came to the fence which partitioned its summit, one of these utterly incongruous

Boreray fences dividing nothing from nothing. On either side was bare rock and blue air, and in the middle a futile cobweb of skewed posts and rusty strands. It ended in a rickety crucifix of angle-iron, trailing a tangle of wire over the crag on the seaward side.

He followed it down and looked over, then drew back with a grimace of pity. There was a dead sheep hanging in the wire, neck crooked and hind legs limply bent. Unwillingly he looked again. He couldn't turn away without knowing the worst about its suffering: how long it had hung there, how agonised its twisted limbs.

His heart lurched. The animal was alive. Its eyes rolled and its sides heaved painfully in the cruel web of wire. He slithered down beside it and it flailed impotently, jerking and jangling the fence above. Then it hung still again, head drooping further back. He wedged it between the rock wall and his own body, feeling for the wires buried deep in its heavy fleece. They were tight and invisible and entangled in the wool, an impossible conundrum. Thinking he would go home for wire-cutters, he let go his hold. The animal hung helpless, one foot scraping the ground with a feeble sound. The rock was piled with dung. It must have been dangling there for days.

'I can't leave you,' he said aloud, and felt again for the wires. At first he could make nothing of it. There was no slack anywhere, and his fingers cringed from the barbs. Then he found that by crouching he could take the animal's weight against his thigh and chest, lessening the strain on the wires above. He worked first on an isolated loop round one foreleg. Gradually, he prised it up through the wool, till he could bend the leg back through it. That gave sufficient play to start on the throttling criss-cross round its neck and belly. 'We're getting somewhere now,' he muttered to the black head lolling against his shoulder. Loop by loop he dragged and jerked and twisted, bringing the top fleece away with the wire. He tried to keep the under-hair pressed to its body, to cause less pain, but even so the work made him wince. The sheep hung silent in its agony, only pawing the air weakly with its free forefoot. When it was at last disentangled, it lay inert, not even kicking.

He scrambled up and down, twisting the loose wires back around the fence above, to save further casualties. When he had finished, the sheep still lay where he had placed it. It was almost certainly dying. Or perhaps it was just weak with hunger. He did not know enough about sheep to tell. He wondered about carrying it down the hill. It had a red mark on its back, like the sheep around his house, so it was probably Roddy's. Roddy would have some idea what to do for it, if anything. He slid down from the narrow ledge, and pulled the animal off onto his shoulders. It was not heavy, but awkward: the descent was steep and slippery. He had stopped for breath at the first flat place, when suddenly the animal began to struggle and kick. He set it down, hoping it would run off. It lay on its side with jerking legs, its yellow eyes full of fear. When he bent to pick it up, it staggered to its feet, running and falling and running again. He could have caught it, but shrank from causing it further terror. He left it backed against a rock, and continued downwards to find Roddy. His clothing stank of sheep's urine. It stung his torn hands. The creature's pain crept along his sinews.

There was shouting and whistling from the road below. A knot of sheep was penned in the fank and another group was streaming down the hill, herded by three men and a low swift dog. He recognised Roddy and Angus's sons. They were splitting off the rams from a mixed flock the dog had brought down, turning the great curly-horned beasts in to the pen and dispersing the others back up the hill. The dog streaked to and fro, crouching and circling. Donnie was running ahead of the stream of sheep, to halt them at the gate, while Murdo and Roddy were dodging among the press, waving the ewes aside. They had almost sorted out the two groups when three rams bolted after the ewes. The dog separated them again, but the rams charged on uphill and out along a narrow terrace just below Alan. Donnie raced after them, bounding from rock to rock, fleet and careless as his quarry. The dog reappeared and crouched ahead of the rams. They turned and thundered back along the ledge. Donnie met them with an Apache yell, scrambling to get above them, slipping and leaping. The bewildered beasts turned again, and bolted for a steep scree between the dog and Alan. Seeing what was required, he leapt up ahead of them, with a moment of unexpected terror as the huge horned heads surged upwards in the narrow treacherous gap. But they turned and dropped six feet to the next ribbon of grass, the dog circling to Donnie's shouts, 'Come by! Away here! Come by!' Alan jumped down, and the boy cannoned into him, a sudden shock of hard bone and warm flesh and a wild-eyed laughing face,

84

and then leapt over the edge, with a long yell that might have meant anything or nothing. Alan's pulse was racing; he followed, running ahead and above the still recalcitrant rams, with Donnie below and the dog in the rear. He jumped the roadside ditch with blood singing in his ears, and with it the thought, now I know what it feels like to be a wolf. Donnie was panting beside him.

'Well done there, Alan!' Roddy greeted him. 'You were our second dog today. The old one is lame.'

'The bitch has puppies,' added Donnie.

His brother gave him a grim look and he fell silent, eyes to ground. Alan knew it was not considered modest for a Boreray boy to speak in the company of grown men but still he disliked Murdo for that look. It sobered his own exhilaration too: he remembered the pathetic victim of the wire. He told Roddy about it.

'It's in a poor way,' he finished. 'Maybe one of you could look at it? I'll go back to show where it is.'

'Och no. We'd find it easy enough.'

'Well, it's just to the right of the bottom of that crevice with the scrubby rowan trees.'

Roddy looked oddly embarrassed. At length he said, 'Ach well, there's no much profit in them. Plenty work but no much profit.'

It took a minute for Alan to realise that this meant he would not go to look at the animal. There was another short silence, then friendly conversation about the weather and the weather forecast and the weather of the week past. Alan got away as soon as decently possible.

He walked home by the shore path, feeling sick and angry, and yet he could not say why. Roddy had doubtless been working all day, mostly with his cousin's stock. He was a kind and industrious man, very family-minded. The sheep was obviously dying anyway, he would know that from the description. As Alan passed above Roddy's neat modernised house, his anger turned to bitter sadness for that chill and lonely death. He remembered the proud-headed rams encircled by human wolves and the geese crossing Fladday in the bright noon. He tried connections, but they would not be made: the terms stood alone and mysterious; there was no sum. Back at the cottage, he worked late on the boat, but without enthusiasm.

Towards early morning, he dreamt about the trapped sheep. He had got it down on the ground, but more wires kept growing round it. He wrestled with them, and it stared with dreadful eyes. Then it was no longer a sheep lying there, but Donnie, looking up at him with a tremulous smile; but as he bent to touch him, the boy's head twisted back, his back arched in death, and he slid from the narrow ledge. Alan woke moaning, with a distant scream sounding in his head. The room shuddered with it: it was in the house, it filled the whole darkness. He lay shaking, knowing alien presence with nightmare certainty. It passed, and the window was blue with the first faint light. He got up and dressed, still shivering with worse than cold, and set off up the hill as day was breaking. As he drew near the place where he had left the sheep, two ravens flew up with relishing croaks. He did not have to go close to see it was dead, lying by the rock wall where he had left it; perhaps it had not taken long. Fresh blood reddened its tattered fleece. He looked up at the soaring ravens, mate and mate, strong and alive, and was glad they would enjoy a good breakfast.

As he neared home, he realised it was raining. He would spend the day working on Selena.

Chapter 9

'Interfering bastard,' said Murdo with a black sneer as Alan left them.

'Ach, he's all right.' That was Roddy.

Donnie scratched the dog's ears, head bent. He had had a quick look up at the crevice with the rowan trees to mark the place, in case it got dark on him later. He would not have gone up there, probably, just for the sheep, but he would have to do it for Mr Cameron. It was clouding over. It would rain in the night, and the crows would come at dawn. Mr Cameron would not know about that, but if he knew he would be sick at what they did.

After tea Murdo was watching television. He might be there about an hour, maybe more. Donnie realised it was the best chance he would have. He hesitated in the porch, wondering whether to take one of Murdo's rifles which were hanging there, but it would be too easily missed; it was going to have to be the knife. He took it from its block of wood in the byre and stuck it in his belt. A soft movement in the corner made him jump. There were two of Roddy's wedders tethered there: Murdo must be going to slaughter for him later. Donnie filched a couple of handfuls of sheep pellets and held them out, and the soft noses whiffled against his palms. 'Poor things,' he said. He hoped Murdo would not want help.

There wasn't much time. He covered the ground as fast as possible, stopping just short of the scrubby trees to get back his breath. In the fading light, the ewe was a dingy white blob against the dark rock. She had grown small, as things do when they are at the point of death. He dropped quietly beside her and pulled her head onto his knee. Her eyes were still bright but she couldn't move any longer. He parted the wool under her jaw, talking to her gently. When he was sure he had the right spot in mind, he rolled her quickly on her back between his knees and cut her throat. After the kicking and jerking was over, he turned her as much on her belly as possible, to conceal the wound, so that Mr Cameron wouldn't see it when he went back next day: he knew he would go back.

He washed his hands in a puddle and wiped the knife carefully on damp moss. It was back in its block before Murdo had stirred from the house.

It was in play again later, though. Murdo wanted help. The beasts were too heavy to hoist on his own, he said. Angus turned in his chair.

'Go you, Donnie,' he said. Two years ago he would have done it himself, and every year before that back to the age of his youngest son. It was not a job he had ever liked, but that he could no longer do it made him less of a man. Now there was one lad there who liked it too much, and the other who was too soft to hurt a fly.

He remembered something else, but said, 'Och no, I'll do the pups myself.'

'Donnie can do that. There's time before I need him.'

'Ach well. All right then.' Angus had never liked that job either. 'We'll keep the black one.'

Donnie, his time thus disposed of, stood by the shed door in the blankness of despair, in one hand a plate of scraps, in the other a torch and an old stocking weighted with stones.

Murdo was on his way to the byre. 'Hurry up, boy,' he said, jeering.

Donnie opened the door. He heard Tess's growl in the dark, changing to an anxious whine when she recognised him. In the torchlight he saw her shining eyes and her ears moving between warning and affection. She hadn't been fed, and it was not difficult to get her outside with the dish of meat. Picking up the puppies was the worst bit. They were warm and their blind pug faces searched hopefully for the teat. Once they were in the stocking and held away from his body they had ceased to exist already. He knotted the top and threw it as far out in the water as possible. It was the first time they had made him do it. The certainty that it would not be the last lay like lead on his soul. Tess was whimpering to get back in the shed. He opened it and shut it quickly behind her.

After that he hardly felt the other thing. Usually he retched and heaved cleaning out the warm innards and flaying the still trembling muscles, but this time he was numb. Murdo watched him as usual for signs of weakness, but seeing none, said spitefully, 'We'll do plenty of these this week, seeing you're at home.' He was good at the job, and often killed for neighbours in return for other favours.

Donnie went in and scrubbed himself clean, then straight to the bedroom. He had the woodwork book hidden under his bed. He pulled it out and opened it at random. It would have been difficult for him to read at any time; with that night's drained mind impossible: but he eyed it hungrily, running his fingers over the pages, trying to fill his terrible emptiness of heart.

He had never killed anything. You could tell that just by looking at him. If he knew . . .

There was still blood under his nails. The warm puppies wriggled in his hands.

If he knew . . .

Donnie thrust the book away violently and flattened himself to the bed, sobbing.

Murdo kept his promise. There was plenty killing that week. Donnie didn't look at the book again, except to leaf through it in case it bore

88

bloody fingerprints. The pages were clean, but still he felt it could tell tales against him.

But he was thinking about the diary. Not that he believed it would help him: it was purely a matter of trust. It would be difficult, as he shared a room with Murdo, and keeping anything hidden was risky. And he would have to get hold of a notebook. He asked Mairi if she had one, but she wanted to know what for, and he didn't know what to say.

Any other boy would have 'lost' a school jotter, but Donnie lacked guile. He went to buy one in the lunch hour. There were other children in the shop: he hadn't reckoned with the possibility of being questioned by them, perhaps found out. He hid nervously behind the postcard stand till everyone else had gone, and raced back to school with his guilty purchase feeling as if he had robbed a bank.

The next problem was where to write it. He tried the bedroom, but Mairi and Kirsty were playing a noisy cassette next door, so that he couldn't be sure of hearing anyone coming. He tried the byre, but as that was Murdo's preserve, he was jumpy. Down on the shore was the safest place. He curled up in a hollow of the rocks, out of sight of the house and the path.

He had no idea what to write. The blank lined page brought back bad memories. He chewed his pencil till the end splintered, and fidgeted with the fragments. He remembered you should put the date, and tried. 'monday 15eth octobir.' He looked at it for a bit and it was encouraging. His handwriting was round and neat. He missed a line and wrote carefully.

I am going to writ this diery. Mr Cameron said to rite it it will help my speling i will not get th exam so I migt as wel try.

That was four lines. He looked at it with surprise and pride. He would have liked to write more. There was more in his head but he could not put it into words. He stuck the book inside his sweater, pinioned by his arm, and got it safely back to the bedroom. He had another look at what he had written, and pushed it as far under the bed as he could reach.

The next day it was dark and raining by the time he was left to his own devices. The diary travelled inside his shirt to the bathroom. He leant against the door for extra security and wrote:

Tuesday OCT 16 Woodwork mr cameron sade my dovetals are superb he is a grate techer Clap was terribl he count car les evryone rasing hel al the tim you coudnt get anthing don.

And the next day, crouched behind the remains of the old boat by the mouth of the burn:

Wedesday 17t october not much doing i dug tates and helpd Murdo geting the bote up ther is gale forcast.

He began to look forward to writing in his book. He spent much time in school gazing dreamily out of windows, thinking what he would say. Most of it was never written down, because the effort of even a few lines was exhausting. But he remembered the things he had missed out when he reread it. It focussed his thoughts: he felt he knew what he meant. 'I' had a new solidity, even when he forgot to write a capital letter.

Creased and folded and rain-splashed from its many concealments, the diary went on:

Thursda 18 OCT Mr Cameron said we can go to his plase on Satiday me Porky crump and sandy and Donnie Mor he got an old woodn bote ther it shuld be good he livs at uncl ewens hous it a good work shop

Fri October ninteenth Mr cameron got a book of shiprigts joints he show me what he is using i wil lik to work on that bote I got the book home to much reding but the drawngs is very good.

Sat 20 OCT it is gret the boat abowt 90 yeres old SELENA. He got cabn top of in bits ther are som carvd bits rel prety he sai you could mach that up Donnie I could to if i got desent Gowges we going agen nex weke he migt let me try he has gret tools. She is clinkre som of the planks is sprung roten ribs too that wil tak steming and a lot of work he says 2 yeres mabe, and a lot of mony he says he hasnt got any jus now.

90

Sunday Octobir 21est Church twise Mairi fel aslepe and we both gigling Mam was wild Da dint notise he so def.

Monda OCT 22 Jock sent for me mrs macphersn was ther she is going to giv me extra english Jock said ther is no way you get that exam without boy This is terribl she takes the litel kids i went with her on primry they wil al lagh whe they here i am not teling any on it is no good anywa I cant rite I cant spel it is hopeles but whe they tel you to do something lik that you hav to you cant get out of it I feel rele sik Porky wil giv me hel. I am not riting this any mor it is no use it is hopeles.

For the next three days the notebook lay untouched under the bed, where for some hours its owner moped with feigned stomach-ache. That didn't have to last long. Angus was having a poor week and could do very little, and Murdo was glad enough to leave the monotonous chores to Donnie while he went fishing with Do'l Alex; he would have some money at the weekend, for once.

But by Friday, though the dread of Mrs Macpherson had not faded, other influences were proving stronger.

'Mr Cameron was asking where you were,' Mairi volunteered on Thursday evening. 'He said would you be all right by Saturday.'

Donnie's heart jumped. He hadn't thought of that. 'What did you say?'

'I said I didn't know.'

Teachers could be very funny about you not going to school. He would have to put up with Mrs Macpherson.

Friday 26 OCT Mr C. ask me why i was not on scool this weke Porky start to sai about mrs macphersn but he jus saide shut up fatfase i felt a fool I hardly did any work whe we going he caled me bak I thogt that was al becaus of the mes I made but he was asking me abowt wha Jock sade and Mrs macpherson and I told him and I sai it was no use i will nevir get that exam but he said dont giv up he is rel kind it is no good I am just thik Jock thinks so so dose evryon but mr C is nise I hope he stays I hope Clap is of a long time. I am going to cary on this diery sometims I look up a word in dictonry at scool it miht help you never kno

Sat Oct 27h he let me hav a go on a peece of scrap to mach that Carving I markd out and got startid it is mor difficilt than looks I dint relise it was late til Porky paked up and mr C. said I coud have stayd but he had to go out. I wish I askd to go bak tomorow but i dint like to

Sunday 28eth octobir sermns was about how kids shuld not be going out on Haloeen It is only a game Mairi stil gose Sunda is rel boring I nipd out whe Antie effy droped of i seen 2 oters 1 had a crab, theyr nise.

Mon 29 oct Porky mak me mad he is caling me Wee Donnie al the time in mr C's leson he says that is becaus you don understan the Galich sir being a sasunach Mr cameron said you idiot where do you think I com from with a name lik cameron, I was born in perth. So he is not English man but he talks lik one Crabit sas he dosent beleve it he seen him riting a leter to his mother in sury that is in england but Crabit dosent lik him evryon els does.

Tusday Oct 30th I finishd the box mr C sade do what I lik I am going to make a toy for Johanes wee one ther is a book on toy making it is a hen that peks grane I wuld rathir the toy boat but he wont go in the boat he scremed at it but he liks the hens.

Wed Oct 31 Mairi went trik or treting antie Efie was wild whe she seen them dressd up Kirsty said they wer going to mr Camerons al the girls think he is gret the litel kids wuld hav gon but Kirsty and Mairi went al sily you coud here the gigling and shriking along the rode antie Effie was raving about the fere of the Lord she was mad I had a good lagh at her.

Thursday Nov first Murdo said a fank on Saterday and I got to go out and I got to go tomorow insted of scool that is terribl i wantd to work on selena

Fri novenber 2 Hil al day hope it ranes tomorw and they cant do it I do not want to mis Selena

Saturday Nov 3 I went down ther in the afternoon I got a coupel of ours work don anway he got me making new peeces for the front now I think its cald the forfoot. Whe the othirs went he showing me how to set the old molding planes one very old it says 1894 he says it was uncle Ewens the blad is very short now but it makes a lovly job.

Sun Novembr 4 Murdo was mad at me for being out last nigt he was kiling he did 4 weders I am glad I was out I hate that job

Monday nov 5eth the hen toy is cut I am going to carv som fethers on it that is not in the boke

tuseday 6 Nov We had Mr C for R E the Scart is of I had to go early to mrs macphersn Porky lookd at his wach and sai 10 past 2 sir time wee Donnie went to remedeal to hav his smalnes remeded I was wild but mr cameron just made one dive for him and turn him upsid down over his desk shouting over the top you gadreen swin, it was rely funy Porkys fags fel out of his poket and evryon chering, wel then we wer hering Jocks dore slaming and Mr C hoped bak to his desk we were al quite he is good fun evryon likes him but Crabit he hates the english so do al that famly

Wed 7 nov Murdo is a b he told Mam and Mairi after tea we going kiling tonigh it was a pet lam 2 yer ago it nevr took to the ram Mairi was crying like anthing I wount go with him he got wild swering at me Da told him be quite with that lanugage but he sad you bette go boy Da was al red Mam sai go on you got to help your Dad but she was cring to I went then anway I dont trust Murdo in a bad mood hed nock the poor thin abowt it was over more quik it was horribl I went awa and was sik, he coud hav left poor Betsy she was that tame. Mairi is crying al nigt she is cryng in bed i hate this killng Murdo went out he drinking you bet.

Thursday 8 Nov Chrissann is home for comuinions paint al over her fase Dad told her go and wash it of she got a pink hat with net for church it looks daft she has died her hare red Antie effie says she is a hore like Johane that is not fair Johane is not a hore she only had one boyfren it was a mistak the baby I think mabe she dint know Chrissann knows al rigt porky says she went with him after a danse

93

once but I dont belive that Porky fances Mairi but she sas he is a gret fat lump.

friday Nov 9eth Ther was truble Murdo was going out aftir his diner whe Mairi and Chrissann was coming in from church he told them it was Betsy for diner Mairi woudnt et any I dint ete any more Mam was teling us to but she only had tates herself Mairi was cryng agane Chrissann says that is daft you got to ete. It was rele roten about Betsy Murdo is roten he woud kil anthing he shoots the seaguls on the croft.

satday nov 10 Not alowed to work on Selena comunions.

That circumstance of November 10th cast such a desperate gloom on Donnie that he could think of nothing else to write. He crouched behind the shed sucking his pencil mournfully till he was called for church.

Later he was back in position, scribbling by torchlight.

Aftr church I went to put out the cow for Nanan and I went round the ard I met mr cameron he was watching birds throu binoclars it was raning he told me come in we wer talking a long tim he done a lot of intresting things saling and climing in the himlayas he is very fit

He paused, frowning. The words did not seem to say what he meant. He tried again, 'he can do anything. I was teling him about Betsy he says he does not et mete.'

He stopped again, shining the torch close to the page to see if it looked any better. It was not right. He hesitated and wrote, 'I am glad I told him about Betsy.'

That was not all but it was as much as he could piece together. He folded the notebook more slowly than usual and held it carefully against his chest. Before he went back to the house, he went into the shed and fondled Tess for the first time since he had taken her puppies. She licked his face. The fat black survivor squeaked and chewed his fingers. He picked it up and it squirmed ecstatically against his cheek, combing his hair with needle teeth and claws.

'Hallo, Ben,' he said, kissing it. Mairi was calling it Ben. Ben was a big strong puppy and he would work well. Already he was rounding up the hens when he got out. He would be safe, surely.

All the same Donnie stood for a long moment staring into the darkness, his arms tightening on the warm little body.

Chapter 10

Alan would much rather not have heard about Betsy, or about the other crimes in Donnie's catalogue of murder. There was a macabre disparity between the soft gentle voice and the bloody deeds it confided.

'The heart is still all moving when you take it out, sir. It is like when you take fish off the hook.'

Alan had darkened his maternal grandfather's declining years by refusing with tears and screams to take fish off the hook. He said, 'How horrible,' rather faintly.

'It is horrible. My brother Murdo doesn't mind. He is always shooting things. I pretend I can't shoot straight or he would be making me go after the rabbits. He made me shoot a seal once.'

'Why?'

'He was saying it was chasing the fish away. He had a net out, like. But it was just a wee thing.'

Donnie gazed into his face with earnest appeal. Alan looked away, repelled and angry. Yet the grotesque incongruity of that innocent expression was funny too. He half-smiled at him, and was consternated to see that the boy's eyes were filling with tears.

'Can't you— ' he began, hastily; but no, of course he couldn't refuse: not only the elder brother but the parents, the community, the whole weight of tradition leant on Donnie. He said instead, 'When you're a bit older you won't have to do as they say all the time.'

Donnie smiled, apparently feeling himself forgiven. He slid off Uncle Ewan's slat-backed chair and sat cross-legged on the rug. 'Well, I won't do any of that killing when I don't have to. I hate it.'

Alan disliked the drift of this conversation. He felt Eleanor breathing down his neck: they had had recent words about what she called his fancy ideas. 'I don't know,' he said, doubtfully. 'It's got to be done, I suppose, to a certain extent. After all, what would you and your family eat if Murdo was like you? It's not as if you can really grow crops here. You can grow sheep, you might as well eat them.' Or so Eleanor says, he qualified inwardly, aware that he was perjuring himself in one direction or another.

Donnie was not silenced as easily as he had expected. 'But you said you don't eat meat.'

Alan cursed himself for having said anything of the kind. 'Yes, but that's sheer squeamishness. It doesn't actually make sense here – it's just that I can't stand the thought—' he floundered, unable to make that positive acknowledgement of the virtues of local norms which Eleanor considered appropriate to conversations with youth. 'Anyway, I don't recommend it,' he finished rather desperately.

'Well, I think it's great,' insisted Donnie. He was sprawling with his chin in his hands. His eyes expressed unswerving hero-worship.

Alan began to wish very fervently that the boy would go away, but the hope was somewhat confused by a sudden perception of the extraordinary length of his eyelashes at the outer corner. The negative message must have been the clearer, though, for Donnie jumped up looking uneasy and crestfallen, muttering, 'I better go home now.'

Alan felt sorry then, not entirely because of the eyelashes.

'Come and have a look at Selena first,' he offered. 'I've got the forefoot repair finished at last.'

That restored harmony, and Donnie went away happy.

Alan fidgeted in the workshop, unable to settle at any task: drowned puppies and eviscerated sheep made his hands nervous. He started planing, but the blade baulked and tore. He tried pinching rusty panel pins out of the reusable coamings, but they broke off. Eventually he crawled under the keel to scrape at the old layers of varnish, paint and antifouling. It was a mindless and endless task usually reserved for Crump on the grounds that if he were lying down anyway he would be unable to fall over. For once, he would have welcomed his cheerful disaster-prone presence and the clatter and horseplay of Saturday mornings. The workshop seemed grimly silent, and it was difficult to put Donnie out of his mind. It was all very well having him there with the other boys and giving him a chance to use his skills, but Alan had no wish to be involved further by becoming a confidant for his dissatisfactions, or a source of imitation: confidences might be binding, and he did not intend to be bound. Nevertheless, he could not stop thinking about the boy's unease with the routine and necessary brutalities of life, his outward docility belying a pathetic inward revulsion. So that conflict was what was included in the community bargain, what Eleanor had touched on when she said individuals weren't important, only relationships. Donnie was his father's son and his brother's brother before he was himself: never could be himself, but always part of the group. There would never be a choice for him, no chance of running away, no other niche was available to him. He would have to adjust; inevitably he would toughen, and should not be encouraged to do otherwise.

It was a relief to decide that his own influence could be nothing but malign, and that the boy was best left alone. The theory was satisfactory; but only till a vivid image of his face shifted the ground. Grown up and hardened, he would not look like that. The eyes would no longer speak, the gentle mouth would have set fast over the nuances of joy and sorrow, hope and fear.

Alan stopped scraping, blinking paint debris from his eyes.

So to gain the only world open to him, Donnie would have to lose his soul.

Eleanor, who called him an atheist, did not believe in the soul.

For some time, Alan lay in silence under the keel, considering, but concluding nothing.

'Alan!' An angry shout made him jump, banging head and knees. He had forgotten about Eleanor. She bounced in on a gust of wind and rain.

'What on earth are you doing?'

'Sorry. I forgot you were coming.'

'I could have saved myself a walk down your abominable path in the rain, then. It's tipping down.'

She did look very wet, as well as cross. They went into the house, and he put his hands on her shoulders to take her coat; she shrugged it and him away quickly, and bent to pull off her boots. He was pleased she had come. She had broken in on a nasty moment of metaphysical loneliness. He would have liked to touch her, but didn't dare.

97

'What are you looming over me for?' she asked suspiciously, as she straightened up.

'Nothing! – I'm glad to see you,' said Alan, retreating.

She snorted. 'You might have put the light on, then. I fell in that horrible puddle outside the door. I don't know why you don't fill it in.'

They played Bach sonatas and some Brahms. Eleanor complained that he was inattentive.

'What's the matter with you tonight?' she demanded, as they were packing up.

'Oh, nothing. Maybe the weather. It seems to rain a lot here.'

'I thought you were tough about that sort of thing.'

'I don't make any claims to be tough about anything.' He wanted her to talk, if only to castigate him. He put his neck on the block with his next remark. 'It's the animals that depress me. These poor cows squelching around in the bog with nothing to eat but rushes, and the sheep, all sodden and half of them limping. And it seems to be the time of year for stringing things up and killing them.'

'Oh, that's what you don't like, is it?'

'I know you'll say that's a fact of life here and so it is – look, sit down, won't you?'

She remained standing.

'*Please*, Eleanor. I wish you'd sit down.'

To his surprise, she did.

He went on, 'It just seems such a rotten deal, that's all. A miserable life and a miserable death. Depressing to watch.'

'It's the only life they know. And they're people's livelihood. You're nothing round here if you don't have sheep, they're everyone's pride and joy.'

He thought of the biblical figures with crooks, of flocks coming down from the hill, of the dosing and dipping and driving to and fro that made up so much of his neighbours' lives, and said, 'Yes, they are.'

'Of course they can't afford to be sentimental about animals. Life is hard here for people as well, you know.'

'Yes.' But he was remembering the sheep he had freed on top of Càrn Bàn. 'It's just that when people are such good neighbours, you might expect a bit more – well, fellow-feeling for other creatures. It doesn't seem in character, really. It's a – disharmony.'

She jumped up in exasperation and marched round the room. 'You're soft, Alan! Where will fellow-feeling get crofters? If that's what you want, go and keep a poodle.' She stopped in front of him with tightly folded arms. 'You can afford the luxury of fine sentiments, but you're a parasite. You've never had to work – you've never had to do a damn thing you didn't want. If you had to feed a family off five acres of miserable land, you'd soon forget your scruples.' She tossed her head. 'Or take to drink. You might be one of that sort.'

Every family seemed to have one of that sort. Alan's heart sank; he had been afraid of hearing something like that. His talk about the sheep had been to an extent disingenuous: that discussion had all been covered before and he accepted her judgements. He had reopened it searching for some assurance that there was a chink of hope for Donnie.

Eleanor sighed heavily. 'You're not good company this evening. I'm going home now.'

Alan shook himself and rose. 'I'll come up to the road with you.'

'I don't need an escort.'

'But I need a walk. Right?'

'Right!' She had an attractively sly Primavera smile, but didn't often favour him with it. He was surprised to see it now.

'I don't like this awful path of yours,' she said as they set out.

Alan had stopped, and was listening. 'Did you hear that?'

'What?'

'Music – very faint. It must be on the wind from next door, that's amazing— ' Even as he said it he realised that could not be the case: the wind was blowing from the desolate reaches of Tràigh Mhór, not from Gnipadale.

'Come on!' Eleanor was shivering and impatient. She hurried ahead of him, but tripped so often that he kept bumping into her. He realised her night-vision must be poor, and caught her arm several times when she stumbled. The last time, uncharacteristically, she did not pull it away. He could feel that she was still shivering, and something about her posture told him she was not cold, but frightened. This was an astonishing revelation. Eleanor afraid of

99

the dark? Her head bobbed close to his shoulder. He could hear her teeth chattering and smell newly-washed hair. He was still wondering whether he dared put his arm round her when they reached the car.

'I really hate that path,' she said. Her voice was more subdued than usual.

'I like it,' said Alan, 'all ups and downs.'

'All potholes and puddles,' she sniffed, apparently recovering her spirits.

She drove off. Alan wandered home, enjoying a brief spell of clear moonlight. The moon, three-quarters full, swung above Fladday, calm and white in a deep blue sky. The sea heaved silver, regular as a pulse-beat. He climbed the small hill under which the track wound to widen his view. As he reached the top, streaming black clouds with sleet in their breath poured in again from the north-west; the moon was caught and veiled, tossed between great black pillars, then obliterated completely, the sea darkened, except for a faint pallor of breaking water around the blacker skerries. The sensation of inexorable flux was awesome and liberating. Alan stood with his back to the sleety wind and let himself be awed and liberated. It was a frame of mind he was used to at sea. But as he picked his way downhill in the murk, a huddle of sheep bolted from their scanty shelter in a hollow by the path. That sobered him. There was no liberation in that night for them: only cold, wet and fear.

He thought about the Morrison family consuming Betsy in honour of religion, and wondered what Donnie was doing. Then he noticed his own front door was open, spilling light onto the grass. The boy must have come back for something. He was more than half glad. He quickened his steps, jumped the stream and went into the kitchen, already opening his mouth to greet him. Donnie wasn't there. Alan looked round in surprise, and even spoke his name. In the silence after it, his scalp prickled. He was not in the house: it was impossible that he could have been, at ten o'clock on a wild night, and the eve of the Sabbath. No one was there, yet the certainty had been so compelling that he went to look in the other rooms, and even out in the workshop. When he returned to the house, he closed the door behind him slowly, and smiled to himself and shrugged. There was something slightly uncanny about the house. It played tricks; it had a memory, perhaps, maybe forwards as well as backwards. He pulled himself up short thinking that, and decided it seemed meaningless. He went into the kitchen, yawning, and patted the pleasing slat-backed chair. If anything haunted the house, surely it must be the spirit of nice old Uncle Ewan. He leant back in the old man's chair and smiled once again at his eccentric skirting board. He had found one of Ewan's shopping lists the other day:

3lb copar nals
1 bag siment
20 fete 2 x 1

He had probably had no more brains than his great-nephew. But he had made a life for himself: perhaps it was not impossible.

Chapter 11

The year drew towards the solstice darker, wilder and wetter. Alan had always rather liked rough weather, but he found his enthusiasm modified by this relentless succession of storms. Boreray winter weather seemed to blow in from the Atlantic carrying half the sea with it, and then swirl back carrying it out again. Daylight was very short, and what there was of it dim, so that the only time left for tramping around was Sunday. It was exciting to watch heavy seas thundering over Langasker while Fladday disappeared behind spirals of fuming spray, but once he had noticed the continual parties of cormorants scouting anxiously to and fro over the churning sea, he felt less exhilarated by the sight. There were dead birds washed up with the piles of kelp in Tràigh Mhór, and a couple of young seals. They kept the blackbacks happy; but nothing else got much joy out of the weather. Back at the cottage, a line of starlings filled the roof-ridge, waiting hopefully for his reappearance. He had taken to throwing out food for them on the grass by the stream. He felt vaguely guilty about it: his mother had always (or at least when she remembered) put scraps out for the birds, in a variety of expensive terra cotta feeding devices, and he had been in the habit of regarding it as a gross interference with Nature. He did not even have the excuse that Nature was providing poorly for his starlings, since they did well

101

enough off the remains of the numerous sheep which had succumbed to bad weather; though they seemed enthusiastic about stale bread and peanuts as well. A few sparrows and a robin soon found out about it. He scattered food for them as he left in the half dark for work. One day, looking back, he realised that he was also feeding several hoody crows and a pair of herring gulls. A day or so later, they were joined by three wise old ewes. He brought them home a present of carrots for the pleasure of having them feed from his hand. They did so with alacrity, and would have followed him into the house if he hadn't hardened his heart.

'They're poor old things,' said Donnie. It was the last Saturday in term time and he was leaving Selena reluctantly and by degrees. 'That one's teeth are bad, sir,' he went on. 'Look, she's dropped her carrot, it's too big.' To Alan's amusement, he picked up the rejected root and crunched it into smaller pieces between his own white teeth. He spat the modified offering into his palm and presented it.

'You got a robin,' he said, with interest. 'We had one coming round the back door and we was feeding it, but the cat got it.'

'Cats do.' His mother had two cats, who wore collars and bells but still caught bluetits.

'Would you like a cat, sir? Our cat's going to have kittens.'

More drownings, thought Alan. 'No,' he said rather shortly. 'I don't like the way they go for birds.'

'They'd go for mice too,' pursued Donnie, hopefully, but with a slight quaver.

My God, he'll have to drown them, Alan realised. He gritted his teeth. 'I like mice,' he said.

'So do I.'

Alan suspected favour-currying, but if so it must have been unconscious. His eyes were as candid as usual.

Eleanor appeared on the path above as he was trying to think of something kinder to say.

'You shouldn't be doing that,' she reprimanded him, eyeing the sheep severely.

'I know,' he replied, hastily tossing them the last carrot. Then he rebelled. 'Why not? I expect you've only come to cadge some tea. These brutes feel the same about carrots.'

She smiled. 'Quite right! It was a cold rough ride today.' She had just got back from her trip to Fladday.

As they turned to go in, Alan looked around for Donnie, but he had disappeared.

'That boy's avoiding me,' said Eleanor.

'Why?'

'He's quite musical, but he won't come near me at lunchtimes.' This combination was an arch crime in Eleanor's eyes. 'He had a lovely voice a couple of years ago, and it will be good again when it settles, but he won't open his mouth in class.'

She clapped her hands emphatically on the warm enamel of the stove. Alan secretly congratulated Donnie on courageous resistance.

'Anyway,' she went on, 'he thinks I'm a spy. I've been going out with his brother, and they don't see eye to eye.'

That was news indeed. Alan experienced a quick shock of jealousy. He told himself at once it was absurd: he had known she had a local boyfriend, but had taken care not to find out who. She might have done better than surly Murdo, he thought, remembering the thrusting arm among the lobster pots with unpleasant vividness.

She turned suddenly with her back to the stove. 'Well, what about that tea?'

'Oh, yes.' He rooted rather hazily in the pantry while she shouted to him that the floor looked as if it hadn't been swept for a week and that the mice had been eating the rug: didn't he have a mousetrap?

'Yes.' There was one in the loft.

'Use it, then!'

'No.'

'Oh, really!'

He handed her a mug, hoping she wouldn't notice it was chipped.

'This mug's chipped.'

'I know. Sorry I don't seem to have anything to eat.'

'I suppose you've fed it all to those sheep?'

'Would you have eaten stale treacle scones and raw carrots?'

'I'd eat anything. I'm ravenous.' She looked at her watch. 'Anyway, I'm just popping along to see Chrissie, I've got some wool for her from her sister. I might as well come back for you later and we can have another go at that Brahms sonata. It's our last chance this term.'

'All right.' He was unenthusiastic.

Eleanor buttoned her jacket. 'For God's sake sweep that floor before I come back.'

For the first time he resented her interference. Why didn't she save her bossiness for Murdo? He sulked while she was away, but swept the floor nevertheless. He was still sulking as they drove to Port Long, but Eleanor didn't seem to notice. She was in an unusually friendly mood, and even insisted on feeding him when they arrived. Chrissie had given her a bag of fresh oatcakes and a bowl of crowdie to take home.

'It's not often I have anything in the house you're actually prepared to eat,' she said. Alan waited for the expected jibe but it didn't come. Furthermore, she even made him coffee, though she stuck to tea herself. He was touched but rather perplexed. Perhaps the affair with Murdo was giving her a leaning towards domesticity.

The evening progressed from the unusual to the astonishing. When Alan suggested a second run-through of the duo, she closed the piano decisively.

'No, stuff music for tonight.' She twirled round on the stool to face him. 'It's nearly Christmas. Why don't we go to bed to celebrate?'

Alan failed at first to reply to this extraordinary suggestion, or even to decode it.

She jumped up, biting her lip. 'Don't you want to? You can say so, you know. I don't get offended about that sort of thing.'

'No! – I mean yes – sorry, I thought you said – what about Murdo?'

'Oh, I wouldn't sleep with *him*,' she said impatiently, adding, before Alan had time to feel flattered, 'it isn't done round here till you're engaged at least.'

Alan remembered Sally, and began to laugh. 'Oh, Eleanor, you are funny!'

She looked distinctly unamused. He grabbed her then quickly before he missed his chance.

Bed with Eleanor was invigorating but rather nerve-wracking, in fact very like music with Eleanor. She was practised, energetic and critical. It made a change to hear her snapping 'Slow down!' rather than 'Hurry up!' On the whole she seemed satisfied with his performance.

She got up very early to have a bath. He lay in bed wakening slowly, and observing her bedroom. It didn't give much away. There were no ornaments or pictures and few books, in fact little sign of occupation. She had even placed their clothes tidily on a chair. His eye fell on a pile of magazines, neatly stacked under the alarm clock. He was entertained to find history incongruously repeating itself: they were exactly the same selection as Sally's. Perhaps every woman in the country read them.

'What's this?' he asked, waving *Woman's Realm* at her as she came in. 'It doesn't look very liberated.'

'Nosy!' she snatched it from him. 'I happen to be knitting a jumper out of it.'

She sat on the edge of the bed to dry her toes. Her skin was milky white and her breasts apple-round and firm. He crooked an elbow round her waist to pull her back into bed. She slapped his face, not particularly gently.

'Not just now. I've got myself all nice and clean.' She looked at him disapprovingly. 'You'd better get up and have a bath too. And a shave. There's a razor in the cabinet.'

Alan knew her too well to argue. When he rejoined her, she was frying bacon in the kitchen.

'I don't suppose you eat this?'

'Certainly not.'

'Very silly too. There's some cornflakes in the cupboard over there.' She sandwiched the rashers between two slices of bread and bit with relish. 'I'm going to have mutton chops for dinner too,' she added gratuitously.

'You seem more like your old self this morning,' said Alan, reading the cereal packet intently.

'What do you mean?' She stopped chewing.

'Full of essential vitamins and good humour.' He smiled at her blandly. Her mouth twitched in answer. She relented sufficiently to pass him the milk.

After breakfast Eleanor announced that she had a busy day ahead, as she was leaving on the ferry early in the morning.

'That means you want rid of me?'

'Yes.' She picked up her car keys from the mantelpiece.

'I'd rather walk. It's actually not raining.'

'Are you sure?' Relief made her quite polite.

They were each increasingly anxious to get away from the other. All the same, Alan suffered a slight pang looking at her, standing back to the wall, slender, tense and upright. He pulled her close and kissed her.

'I don't like slobbery kisses,' she protested, pushing him away.

'You wouldn't,' he said, with feeling.

He enjoyed the walk home. It was still early and Sunday, and Boreray was asleep. The wind had died to a manageable breeze, and a soft golden light suffused the bleached winter grass and faded heather. The sheep had come out of their corners and hollows, and were grazing peacefully, though there looked to be nothing worth eating. All down the coast groups of gannets were diving; the sea had calmed sufficiently to give them some chance of success. Mostly he walked without thinking at all, with nothing in his head but the shapes of hills and skerries and the noise of waves, but intermittently he considered Eleanor, first with amazement and then with misgiving. What if she turned clinging? She hadn't shown much sign of it, but it could still happen. He had once had a girlfriend called Daphne, a fierce classicist, who beat him at squash, always made him make the coffee, and wouldn't sleep with him. Yet one day she had put her hands to his face and said dreamily that his eye-sockets resembled Alexander the Great's. He had hastily dropped out of her life, but he still felt bad about it, off and on. She had gone and got a job at GCHQ.

But in spite of fears for and about Eleanor, he felt very jaunty walking past Murdo's croft. He whistled the rest of the way home. An indignant whirr of unfed starlings greeted his return. Inside, the mice had been eating the rug again.

Chapter 12

On Christmas Eve Alan went home to Mother, feeling rather sheepish about it. She had written begging him to come, and he had stalled, but acquiesced in the end for the inglorious reason that he had nothing better to do. He had a climbing trip arranged for the second week of the holiday, and had intended to spend the first week at Skalanish as a matter of pride. But pride was not very well developed in Alan, being too much trouble to maintain. It turned out that Boreray spurned Christmas on the ground that it was a Popish festival; he was sick of the rain; and though family Christmases were invariably ghastly, the residue of childhood expectations still had potency. Anyway, she hadn't mentioned Sally for at least two letters, and everyone had had 'flu including the gardener and one of the cats.

Celia met him at the station. She seemed overwhelmed to see him, so much so that after a few embarrassing public embraces she began to sniff and wipe her eyes. He was perturbed: though she often wailed and pouted, he had rarely seen her cry.

'It's this nasty 'flu that's left me weepy,' she said. 'I expect I look dreadful now.'

She did. She was grey and haggard and her make-up was too heavy.

In the car she talked incessantly, paying little attention to the traffic.

'You should have let me drive,' said Alan, as they provoked furious hooting at a roundabout. She leant over to kiss him, laughing rather wildly. She did smell of gin, but only a bit.

As they got out of the car, she said, 'Please darling, you will come to the midnight service with me, won't you? It's terribly important to me.'

Alan had been thinking more in terms of a bath and bed, but he agreed with a fairly good grace.

'I used to so *love* that when you were home from school, sweetie, a little bit taller every year—'

When you weren't out at some bloody party, he interposed silently.

'D'you know, I cried the year your voice broke?'

'But you— ' Alan told himself to shut up. It wasn't really necessary to remind her that she had been in the Bahamas that year. She hadn't heard him: she was prattling about the potted Christmas trees on either side of the front door.

'I took red lights, darling. I hope that was right? Perhaps you prefer white? I thought red was more festive – a bit vulgar really – '

'Red every time,' agreed Alan firmly.

'Oh, I'm *so* glad you like them.' She squeezed his arm.

Harold met them in the hall. He was on his best behaviour. He shook hands dutifully, and remarked without enthusiasm that Alan looked well. Alan reciprocated in similarly lukewarm terms. In fact, his stepfather looked as pasty and dull-eyed as usual, although he tried hard to be agreeable. He poured drinks, and made his wife sit down while he waddled heavily to the kitchen to fetch the stuffed mushrooms and mince pies she had left warming in the oven.

'Harold's such a sweetie!' she exclaimed, obviously hoping Alan would agree. He couldn't quite summon up yes, but he managed a vaguely affirmative noise. He was suffering unexpected culture shock. Harold's parquet flooring, washed-silk rugs, and mother-of-pearl inlaid satinwood were not consonant with his own grubby jeans and frayed fisherman's sweater. Really it was quite decent of the man to put up with it. The Burmese cat, the non-invalid, jumped on to his knee. He was surprised he fancied the perch.

Celia talked non-stop. Her eyes darted from her son to her husband and round the room, restless and slightly glittering. She looked disconcertingly strained and unwell. After a while she went to dress for the service, leaving Alan and Harold in uncomfortable conversation. As soon as seemed decent, Alan rose with the excuse that he would have to change too.

Harold looked less relieved than he had expected.

'I shall go to bed, then,' he said, in his usual dull weighty manner.

'Aren't you coming too?'

'No. It would spoil your mother's pleasure.'

'I'm sure it wouldn't.'

'I'm tired.' His voice was suddenly pettish.

Alan shrugged angrily, as he had done for the past sixteen years. As he strode towards the door, he almost collided with Harold who was shambling across to draw the spark-guard. Something in his unco-ordinated movements made Alan hesitate.

'Wait there, will you Harold? I've got something for you.'

He had done some hasty Christmas shopping in Glasgow, including a bottle of an unusual single malt whisky. He dug it out of his sailbag in the hall, and thrust it into Harold's pudgy hands with the nearest to a friendly smile he had ever managed for him; but past habit caught up with him before he could hear out his stepfather's thanks. He bounded upstairs, thinking, My God, what a pair of wrecks, and almost trod on the other cat. It looked pretty seedy too, he thought.

'If only it would snow!' murmured Celia, hanging on his arm at the churchyard gate. 'It's *so* pretty.'

It did indeed look very like a Christmas card, with ancient yews and coloured light streaming through the stained glass. It only lacked crinolines and frock-coats and, as Celia said, snow. Alan had a fleeting image of huddled sheep in a black gale, and realised he had better decide, at once, to go through the correct performance. He would genuflect to the altar, cross himself when she did, and take communion. It was like practising Man Overboard before it happened: if he left it to the whim of the moment, he would be distracted by the outrage of someone's crocodile handbag or the vicar's chummy anticipations of roast turkey. Even as they entered the porch, he noticed a girl in front wearing a jacket of clouded leopard. He recognised the fur before its illegitimate wearer: it was Sally. His disgust was somewhat modified by relief that the figure next to her was George.

'D'you want to speak to her, lovie?' whispered Celia.

'Not just now.'

Inside, the aisle was entirely candlelit, and a competent organist was playing a discreet French pastorale. The stout columns were garlanded with slenderising spirals of holly and ivy. The perpendicular apse was softly floodlit. Wafts of expensive scent mingled with the odours of stale incense and candle smoke. The women's faces were flattered by the warm light, and their rings gleamed in stupendous size and genuineness among the prayer books. He observed that Sally was engaged, with a diamond as big as a smallish hazelnut. He knelt with closed eyes, emptying his mind as far as possible until the surrounding anomalies ceased to grate. After that, by concentrating only on the singing he succeeded in behaving himself to his mother's satisfaction.

She was dabbing her eyes again as they came out.

'Wasn't that divine? I do so love that service.' She took his arm and hurried towards the gate. She seemed unusually disinclined to talk to any of her acquaintances.

'Thank you, darling, for coming with me. I – I thought we might never go together again.'

This was followed by a full-scale sob. Alan patted her hand awkwardly. Either he had really overdone the quarrel in the summer, or else she had some new plot up her sleeve.

'I see Sally and George are engaged,' he said, to test which way the wind blew.

'Yes – do you mind?'

'No, I'm delighted.'

'Oh, I'm so glad. I didn't dare write to tell you – just in case.'

He noted that she had, as usual, rearranged the known facts of the affair so that her part in it was less discreditable. By now she really believed he had been in love with Sally.

'You've gone all quiet. Sweetie, are you sure you don't mind? Not at all?'

'Not in the least. I – was just hoping it hadn't made too much unpleasantness for Harold with her father.'

'Oh, that. No, I think it's all smoothed over. Nice of you to worry, darling.'

He felt bad for never having given it a thought.

'Actually,' she went on, 'we're all invited to the Clements' on Boxing Day morning. Obviously I couldn't refuse, but I've been in absolute agonies about it. Is it really and truly all right, darling?'

'Lovely.'

At the Clements' party Sally kissed him on both cheeks and they talked like strangers in the window bay, about her ring and the flat George had bought in Marylebone and what the weather was like in Scotland. She was slightly glassy-eyed. Their lack of contact was quickly approaching hostility. He didn't want it to end like that.

'I'm glad everything turned out so well, Sally,' he said determinedly. 'I hope you'll be really happy.'

She laughed. 'I look it, don't I?'

'You look wonderful.' That was true. Her beautiful hair swung round dazzling shoulders; she was wearing a slinky black garment, backless and strapless; but she did not look happy.

She took his hand and pulled him through the crowd. 'Come and speak to George. He gets so jealous.'

He had an affable conversation with George, and escaped. It was not Alan's impression that George was in the least jealous. It was unlikely he saw any reason to be so: he had bought Sally for a fair price, after all. His arm encircled her waist with proprietorial care-lessness. She was wearing a Fabergé belt of gilt mesh and enamel.

Mrs Clement sailed towards him with outstretched arms. He had an impulse to bolt for the lavatory, but stifled it. She was a matron of old-fashioned habits and dimensions, genuinely kind. He succumbed to a bosomy embrace, and congratulated her on her daughter's good fortune. After a few minutes, the lady led him to her two presentable nieces, to show there was no ill-feeling. He overheard her whispering to her husband.

'You must talk to him, for Celia's sake.'

But Mr Clement was sulking, and confined himself to a frigid nod. Alan suspected his wife would make him pay for it later.

Back at home Celia complained of a headache. 'I think I shall go and lie down. I really shouldn't drink at midday.'

'Oh damn!' she added, passing the patio doors. 'I forgot to feed the birds.'

'I'll do it.'

'Oh, that *would* be sweet of you.'

He distributed birdseed, Stilton crust and ham rind equitably between the various tables, bells and trays. He wondered how his starlings were surviving without him. As he turned, he noticed Harold shuffling miserably just inside the glass door.

'I'll get lunch, shall I?' said Alan, scooping up the Burmese cat.

At Skalanish, Donnie squatted patiently in the biting wind, with the first snowflakes clinging to his dark hair. He crouched very still, a few yards away from the squabbling mêlée of birds and sheep, holding out secret crumbs to the clever bright-eyed robin. Even in three days it had grown much tamer. By the end of the holiday he hoped it would eat from his hand.

The last crumbs gone, the robin flew off. The oldest ewe came nudging up to him. He opened his hands to show he had no more. She bleated, a hoarse elderly sound, and walked off along the path. Her fleece looked yellow under the powdering of snow.

Donnie leant against the cottage wall and watched the flakes falling, more and more of them from the lead-grey sky, fast, soft and silent. They vanished in the bubbling stream and tented the

111

clumps of dead heather and the lumpy lichens on the rocks. The wind was rising, so that the steady slanting streams began to swirl and thicken, blotting out the sea and mountains. The smooth hump of the sidhean was soon all white, with the old ruins sharply outlined in front of it. The light was fading and he grew very cold, but he did not want to leave the quiet and the beauty of the snow. He knew he could not stay much longer, or they would be asking where he had been. It would be difficult getting food out there every day. His mother was already wondering why he was so much hungrier than usual, and Murdo might notice the sheep pellets were going.

Reluctantly, he turned to leave, with a last look at the friendly house and Selena's shed and the soft white drifts turning blue in the twilight. As he walked with the snow blowing endlessly in front of him, he wondered what Mr Cameron was doing in England. He knew they made a big thing about Christmas there. It looked nice there on Christmas cards, huge churches with coloured windows, and Christmas trees outside. Roddy's girls had a tinsel tree with lights, but Chrissie made them keep it in the kitchen, in case the missionary would call, or Roddy's uncle Kenny, who was very strict. Mairi had always wanted a Christmas tree, but they couldn't because of Auntie Effie. She grumbled about cards too, but people away sent them, and they had to go up. She didn't like Mam making a special dinner, either. Johane had brought a big iced cake home, but they were keeping that out of her sight. The robin was enjoying the raisins from it.

Outside the door he knocked the snow off his boots and jacket, and shook his hair before going in. In the kitchen the table was set with the best china, and big plates of fresh baking covered with clean cloths stood at the side. Ewan was coming home: Murdo must have taken Mam and Dad up to bring him from the ferry.

There was lovely singing coming from the sitting room. It distracted Donnie from his purpose of stealing scones for tomorrow's birds' dinner. He went in, drawn by the music. Mairi was sitting on the sofa with Johane's wee one asleep on her lap. She made faces at him to be quiet, pointing at Auntie Effie, who was snoring faintly with her chin on her chest. She wouldn't have liked what was on the television screen. It was one of these big English churches like on the cards, with beautiful windows and a Christmas tree. Donnie

112

sank down on the floor, totally absorbed. It would be a church like that where Mr Cameron was. There were young boys singing, so high and sweet it didn't seem human, and the church was lit with candles. It went up and up, great stone pillars carrying a vast shadowy roof, and all the wood and stone was carved and decorated beyond belief. The organ filled the church and the screen filled the sitting room and drew him into it in an ecstasy of form and sound.

There were noises at the door and Ewan's deep seaman's voice. The wee one woke up with a wail and Auntie Effie groaned and muttered. Mairi jumped up quickly and switched off.

Donnie sighed. He had missed his chance with the birds' dinner, and he knew what Ewan's first words would be.

Ewan came in, big and swaggering.

'Good God, when's the boy going to start growing?' he said.

Chapter 13

Mon Febrary 11 Ther is going to be a Valntines day disco in the hall Crabbits brother Shonny is orgnising it hes a big head. Mairi is keen on that she is going but Im not non of the girls woud danse with me anway Porky is a brat he sai try Annie on first yere she may be 4 fete short but she got a good pare of tities she has too I sene her crosing the playgroud bounsing I laghed in mr morrisons clas and got 100 lins

Tue feb 12 Porky was making sure Mairi is going to that disco he was whispring me in Tec draing what sise bra dose she ware I coudnt stop laghing Mr C grabed me by the colar and said if I want to talk to Porky hed mak me sit biside him no one wil sit with him becaus he pokes you al the tim Porky sai no sir giv me his sister to poke Ill have Mairi insted evryone started yeling and lauhing Mr C mad us run round the plaground 3 tims but he was laghing to

wedsday Feb 13eth Angs Shaw is bak from sea he was on the pich toda its al frozin but he was trying a few shots he was grete at the games last yer with the hevy hamer he is some waight but he looks flaby ther was fat shaking undr his arm but stil it is fantastic how he throws Crabbit is not bad and Porky and Donnie mor I dint try I sneked of befor Porky had a lauh at me he is a b somtimes

Thurs Feb 14 we were going in for woodwork som of the girls Kirsty and a few more rushd in gigling the had a huge card for Mr C whe he came in he opned it he was saing not from anyone here is it. We was laughing he dose not get angry he said he hoped we al got one to. The girls had al sined with funy nams like Hary Mary that was mairi and Snoopy they al think he is fantastic he is rely good looking with bright blue eyes he looks at you very straigt he is sort of taned but not red he must be nerly 24 but you wount think he so old yesteday he raced me and Porky down the felde bete us of cours and then up the fense like a monky Porky was yeling Jock will giv you the sak for that sir but he sai not likly hed hav to take you lot himself for woodwork then

While Donnie was puzzling over the correct way to spell 'bright' (it seemed important to his intentions that it should not be wrong) Eleanor was casting a less admiring eye over the events of the day.

'I see you have fans,' she said, picking up the girls' candy-pink offering from amongst the sheet music.

'Yes – someone might speak up for me come the revolution.'

She had just delivered a harangue on the subject of class privilege, as instanced by people who thought it was quaint to live in a hovel, and didn't bother applying to have it condemned as substandard, even though such anti-social laziness would undoubtedly imperil the health of future tenants and more particularly of their children. She was in an exceptionally bad temper, even for her.

She perused the card with grim zeal.

'You shouldn't encourage these poor girls.'

'For God's sake, it's a completely harmless bit of fun.'

'It's bad enough all this plastic pop culture they're exposed to, without men like you coming along for them to fantasise about. It gives them entirely unreal expectations.'

114

'That sounds like a very paternalistic analysis to me,' said Alan, slyly.

'Rubbish! It's just common sense.'

Eleanor's doctrinal inconsistencies were usually attributable to common sense. She snapped her violin case shut and squared her pile of music.

'You're not staying, then.'

'No. I'm going out tonight.'

'With Murdo?'

'Yes, but that's none of your business, is it?'

'To the festival of plastic pop culture in the village hall?'

'There will be a perfectly authentic ceilidh after it,' she answered, haughtily. 'If you weren't so standoffish, you could come and learn something about local tradition.'

'And walk home at three in the morning? No thanks.'

She tripped crossly to the door, switching on her torch before she reached it. Alan opened his mouth to offer to walk to the road with her, but closed it again. He had had enough for one evening. He stretched out on the offensively coloured hearth rug, scowling.

Yet he felt, as usual, wistful when she had gone. Greater intimacy had not made her any more affectionate: in fact she was increasingly acerbic, and plainly regarded as recidivist such liking as she had for him. They went to bed together only when she felt inclined. In itself that didn't bother him: sex, like food, was something to be grabbed with good appetite if offered and forgotten if not. But it hurt somewhat that she would never spend a whole night with him, after the first time. Possibly she was trying to keep the affair secret, more likely she was avoiding any opportunity for affection to develop. Wide awake and in full control of the mechanisms of pleasure she would enjoy herself, and would take some trouble to ensure that he did too; but she never lay half asleep in trusting animal warmth beside him. If she slept at all, she would turn her back and lie at the edge of the bed, as angered by his touch on her hair or skin as if he had been a complete stranger. He did not want her to cling, but he would have welcomed the occasional hug. Yet he had to conclude wryly that he deserved the treatment. In every previous affair, he had taken it as his right to enjoy all the intimacies of love and still shake free when he felt like it. Though he did not love Eleanor, he was sufficiently fond of her to wish her less assertively free of him. He had to admit to himself that he resented Murdo: what could she see in him, he wondered, as he often did – a sour-faced, hard, uncouth fellow, suspicious of everyone and, given the chance, drunk and violent as well.

But then, as Eleanor had frequently told him, he himself was vain, selfish, immature, a half-baked greenie and a mother's pet.

Perhaps there was not much to choose. He flicked mouse droppings out of the orange sunbursts and considered it.

Murdo's brother had no such doubts. The following evening in the uncertain privacy of his bedroom he wrote:

> Feb 15 Friday Murdo is in good mood for onse he was with miss Brown las night he is going out with her somtimes she is at Mr Camerons a lot to I don know why shed bothir with Murdo if she coud get him. Porky was fed up today Mairi was not dansing with him last nigt he is realy quite and sad i nevir sene him lik that usualy he is real hard it is funy geting lik that about a girl.

He sucked his pencil, considering the oddness of it, then wrote: 'I suppose Mairi is prety she got big eyes and a nise smile'.

A thought struck him. He crossed to the mirror on Murdo's side of the room and looked at his own reflection. It was something he rarely did and he was disappointed, as usual, with what he saw. He picked up his pencil and finished the day's entry somewhat despondently: 'Evryone used to think Mairi and me was twins we are so like, wel that is al rigt for Mairi but not for me i wish id grow a bit and look more tuogh.'

Murdo's tread in the hall sent the notebook spinning under the bed; but the front door slammed and the footsteps continued up the path, accompanied by whistling, a most unusually cheerful sound. Presently the car started up. Donnie reflected on these noises with wonder: they must indicate that Murdo had somehow persuaded Miss Brown to meet him two nights running.

'Ay, ay,' said Shonny in the bar, taking in Murdo's tie and aftershave, 'seeing her again tonight?'

'I been going with her for months, man.'

'Uh-huh.' Shonny regarded the other's reddening face sardonically. 'Hotting up then, is it?'

Murdo grunted.

Shonny considered the implications of the grunt. 'She's a good looker,' he volunteered ingratiatingly, suppressing coarse detail.

'Ay.' He kept darting glances at the door.

'Here she is now. Isn't that nice.' Shonny narrowed his pouchy eyes inscrutably.

Eleanor turned heads. No Boreray girl would have walked into the public bar alone, but she marched through it with as much propriety as a hospital matron through her wards. Shonny stood up with exaggerated politeness.

'What are you drinking, Eleanor? This one's on me.'

'Thank you. A dram, just a single.'

'Lemonade in it?'

'No. Spoils it completely.'

Shonny raised an eyebrow and went over to the bar. When he came back she was saying very definitely, 'You shouldn't let it go. All it needs is a bit of practice.'

'What's that now?' asked Shonny, with the blandest of leers.

'The pipes. I've just been with Jessie and Neilie. They say he's a grand piper — or was when he kept it up. A silver medallist, I believe.'

'Ach, I haven't the time these days, Eleanor.' There was a conciliatory note in Murdo's voice which was not lost on Shonny.

'You're keen on music, then, Eleanor?' Shonny was relishing his friend's embarrassment.

'It's my profession.'

'You have to practise a lot, eh?'

'Yes, every day, or you soon get rusty.'

'Every day?' Shonny spoke with a slow emphasis, enjoying the stiffening of Murdo's jaw. 'You have to practise with other people too, eh?'

Murdo's breath hissed. The glasses rattled as his knees tensed under the table.

Eleanor was quite up to him. 'I only play with Alan Cameron,' she said, fixing Shonny with a falcon-tawny stare.

'Oh, ay, the Englishman.'

Eleanor turned her back on him, so that his smirk was wasted. 'He's not English. Murdo, I'd like to learn the pipes. I've done a bit of chanter. Could you teach me?'

The glasses stopped jingling.

'I could, maybe,' replied Murdo, with such a fatuous look that Shonny abandoned his baiting with a shrug and went off in search of more congenial company. 'Fuckin' idiot,' he muttered as he went; but if Murdo heard he gave no sign of it.

'Hi there, Mairi.' Porky, with an atrocious leer and a flourish, leapt the stream at Skalanish an hour earlier than usual.

Mairi jumped up sniffing, with pink cheeks. She had come along with Donnie to give the puppy a walk, or so she had said. The three of them and Alan had been cavorting on all fours on the frosty grass in front of the cottage. Ben yapped and ran at the intruder gleefully. Mairi called him, pulling her dignity round her with her blue blouson jacket, and set off down the path, head held consciously high.

'Can't let her go all that way alone, sir,' declared her admirer, following with twitching fingers and crossing eyes.

Alan grabbed him by the scruff. 'This is for your own protection. Her dog might savage you.' He was frogmarched into the workshop protesting. Crump and Donnie Mór arrived.

'Just sit on him for ten minutes while I see what's going on up here,' Alan instructed them. Donnie Beag was complaining about a gap in a half-beam joint he had assembled the previous Saturday.

'I'd beat you up if I wasn't such a gentleman,' hollered Porky from his ignominious position.

'Nothing wrong with that, Donnie. You're too fussy.' Alan dropped down again and gave Porky a friendly kick in passing. 'You're too fat. You couldn't beat me up.'

'Wanna bet? You tell him lads — you seen how far I got that heavy hammer last week.'

'Ay, he did sir. Must be some muscle in there somewhere.'

'What's this?'

'Angus Shaw's been training on the pitch, him that won all the heavy events at the games last year. We was having a go too.'

'You should come down next week, sir, have a shot at it yourself,' Crump advised.

'Ten minutes is up.' Alan felt more than usually accommodating towards them. He had suffered a lot at Eleanor's hands that week, and their cheerful good nature was in welcome contrast. 'I'd like to give it a try, if you let me know when it's happening. I've never done anything like that before, though.'

Porky was making exaggerated feints. 'Allow me to demonstrate by throwing Wee Donnie, sir. He's about half the weight.'

Alan felt the other boy's embarrassment welling from his silent perch above head level.

'How come he sawed down that big pile of boards last Saturday, then, when the big Strongman gave up after one?'

'Ach, I was thinking about Mairi. It got the wrong muscles going.'

'Oh, someone stuff a rag in his mouth!'

Alan turned quickly, and encountered Donnie's look of worshipping gratitude. He should have regretted it, but instead he smiled, reflecting that it was a pleasant change not to be glared at.

Feb 21 thursda Angus was on the pich toda at diner time Mr Cameron to they had there shirts of wel he is fantastic looking flat stomac and al hard musle Angus has a grete hary bere gut on him and a big behind. He can throw rel wel Angs was surprisd he said I never thoght a ligtweght lik you would do so wel you got good sholders man. The bel rang we had to go angus said to him see you tomorow i hope it is not raning a lot of people was watching

Friday Feb 22 A lot of the girls were on the pich after diner Porky says they come to see you with your shirt of sir so Mr C says Ill keep it on then first shot he riped it al round the arm Porky says Mairi got her sowing stuff sir Mairi was whispring shut up but he said no shed stick a needel in me Porkys a cheeky brat he shouts no the other way round sir wel Mairi went as red but he just swiped Porky and knoked him flying then piked up the hamer agen Porky was

119

swering lik anthing Mairi dint know wher to look I wonder if he thinks shes prety. We dint here the bel we were al late Mr Cameron to.

Sat 23 Feb A realy great day, it was suny and not much wind Mr C said he take us out in the Firebal I went first no one els woud go after the seen it heling over it is real scary but it the best thing I ever don so whe no one els woud go he took me out al morning it is gret on the trapese I was frigtened at first but he knows what hes doing he semed realy pleased with me said your a natural Donnie. We can go again when the wether is good.

sun 24 feb Murdo is a buger I hate him he was teling Dad I was saling yesterday i was not saying anthing i new he woud go mad becaus his father was drownd in a saling boat. He got wild he looked rely ill Mam got frigtened he had the docter i am in dead truble and no more saling

Mon Feb 25 I told Mr Cameron no more saling he just said wel I migt see your father about it I dont supose he will it wont mater to him. He was asking about Alex Angus in Glasgow he is teling me I shoud do a YTS ther and then id get an apprenticeship easier I know that but I dont fansy it. he looked quite angry he has never been angry with me befor I felt roten but I dont want to go to Glasgow

Tue Feb 26 Angus was practsing agen Porky was asking Mr C if he coming down but he said no, I got into truble for exposing myself on Thursday he said 1000 lines for being a bad boy. he was in at Jocks just befor woodwork yesteday mabe thats why he was angry not at me.

Feb 27th Wednsday Mairi says it was Croaker that told on Mr Cameron. The girls wer late for sowing and she was mad she cant stand anyon having fun I bet she nevr seen a man with his shirt of anyway shes a rinkled old stick.

Thur 28 feb I had a figt and I won I bete Crabit but I got a blak eye. We wer geting ready for woodwork Crabit hates Mr C he was snering and saying hes a poofter with that neklace he is wearing he seen that on the pich last week I was mad I said what you think you are with 3 earings in one ear he come at me swinging his fists I was rely wild I dont rember much but I got him down I was hamring his head on the flore when Mr

120

c come in and puled me of him I was cryng i wish i hadnt but crabit was worse blubering away Mr C pushed me out told me go and wash my face whe i got bak evryone very quite he was bandaging Crabbits rist it spraned and his lip is split i wish I choked him. I felt sik I thoght hed ask what we wer fighting for but he didnt after a while Porky sai like to here wha these bad boys was having a punch up for sir, but he just said shut up real savige and Porky did no one said anthing. if he reports it to Jock we are al in truble spesialy me Jock cant stand figting, he wil ask what it was for

This appalling possibility made him whimper. Ben lolloped up to see what was wrong, sticking a friendly nose into his bruised face. Donnie yelped, then crouched dumb, fearing discovery. It was a fine evening, and his father was out on the croft. He wound his arms round the wriggling puppy, rubbing his unhurt cheek against the furry head. But Ben was growing too big to cuddle; he bounced away down the shore barking at small waders on the water's edge. They flew off crying in their strange sad voices. Donnie cowered from the noise and movement in his narrow refuge between two rocks. His head ached and his whole body jangled. Dread knotted his innards and throbbed in all his bruises. It did not occur to him that by his own lights he should have been happy: it was the first fight he had ever won, and against the toughest boy in the school. All he knew was that he wanted to hide.

'That boy's not right in the head anyway,' concluded Eleanor. She had had the infamous details of the fight from Murdo, who had heard of it from the victim's brother, threatening reciprocation over his lunchtime drams.

Alan had been half asleep, intent on burying his face against her bare, apricot-fragrant shoulder while she was absorbed in relating the day's gossip. As her story sank in he sat up with a jerk.

'My God! The poor child.'

'He's a little pest.' She sat up too. She was indignant on Murdo's behalf. 'Just making trouble for his family. What a thing to get into a fight about anyway!' She was even more indignant that

Boreray blood should have been split on Alan's behalf. Usually her outrage would have amused him, but not on this occasion, with the recollection of Donnie's bruised face and quivering lip.

'Time I went home anyway.' He had never been the first to suggest it before, but Eleanor agreed quickly that it was. She lay back with her arms behind her head. It was a posture that showed her breasts to irresistible advantage, and any other night he would have pleaded to stay, but he was already occupied with plans for averting retribution from Donnie the following morning.

'Why do you wear that silly string of beads anyway?' she asked at last.

'Habit.'

'Isn't it time you grew out of it?'

'Probably is.'

Frida 1st march Mr C caled me into his room this morning he said you have to go to Mr Carneges ofise Crabits fathir complaned about you I was going to go but he shut the door then and says look, Ive been in ther teling a lot of lies on your behaf you say as littl as posible and it wil be al rigt. i said thanks sir, but i felt sik in case Jock would ask what the figt was for but he didnt. I dont know what he said to him but it did the trick Jock just sai not to get into any mor figts then he was asking me how Im geting on with Mrs Macpherson and if I am thinking of going to Alex Angus in Glasgow i hope mr Cameron wil not find out why we wer figting.

He was staring at this sentence out of his good eye and hoping as hard as possible when he heard Mairi and Ben outside. He thrust the book under Tess's blanket and jumped up.

'He peed on the cushions. They made me take him out.' Mairi sat down on an upturned orange box. 'What you doing in here?'

'Keeping out of Murdo's way.' That was partly true. Murdo had been bitter about the trouble he had made with Crabbit's family.

'Ach, he's just a grump. It's not so long since he broke Shonny's nose himself anyway.'

'Da's mad about it too.'

'Anything for a quiet life with Dad. Well, I think good for

122

you. I bet your face hurts.'

She looked at him with unaccustomed admiration. He bent his head in embarrassment, letting Ben gnaw his wrist.

'Serve Crabbit right,' she went on. 'That's rubbish what he said anyway.'

Donnie straightened up so suddenly that Ben flew across the floor with a yelp.

'You know what he said?'

'Course – everyone does.' Mairi laughed. 'You're daft. You never know what's going on! Well, you should hear Kirsty. She thinks that necklace is the sexiest thing out. She nearly widdled herself when she seen it last week on the pitch.'

Donnie laughed too. A load was lifting from his shoulders.

'He's really good-looking,' sighed Mairi, 'wish we got him instead of Croaker.' She slipped off her perch. 'It's dark out here. I'm going in.'

Donnie gazed after her thoughtfully. He pulled his book out, crouching over it in the fading light, and wrote, 'Mairi says evryone knows what hapned wel if Murdo says anything to me about it I wil fill him in too.'

He shut the dogs up for the night and went in. His knees had stopped shaking for the first time in two days.

Eleanor appeared as Alan was tidying up after the boys on Saturday. She climbed up on Selena and sat swinging her legs. She was in good spirits. Being above the level of his head made her quite genial.

'Lovely day!' she said. 'Spring's almost in the air. I actually didn't feel cold on the ferry.'

'I was thinking of going for a walk. Will you come?'

'I might.' She slipped her toe under the debatable necklace. 'You're still wearing that horrible thing. I wish you'd get rid of it.'

'You're throttling me.' He ducked away from her foot. It was not lost on him that the expression of a wish that he could grant denoted a new and hopeful kind of intimacy: she was no wheedler. He considered it.

'Well?' She kicked his ear, unusually gently.

'Well what?'

'I'll come for a walk if you take off that nasty string of beads.'

He looked up at her. Her lips were parted in a Primavera smile, showing just the tips of her teeth. There were many secluded hollows along the shore where it would be delightful to make love to her. He intended to agree, but to his own annoyance he said, 'No.'

She closed her lips and crossed her ankles. 'No walk then.'

'Well, I'm going anyway.'

'Right.' She jumped down looking much less good-humoured.

'See you on Tuesday.'

'Probably.'

Alan tramped along the coast with mixed feelings. She was absurdly touchy, but he regretted the lost opportunity: spring, as she had said, was almost in the air. A few courting lapwings were calling and wheeling in the luminous evening sky, and out on the water unseen eiders were in fulsome uxorious conversation. He grinned ruefully to himself, running his fingers under the despised beads. The beastly things had caused about as much trouble as the necklace of the Brisings. But for once he had absolutely no inclination to get rid of it: it had been too dearly paid for by Donnie's black eye.

Mon 4 Mar I never thoght he woud realy go to see dad about me going saling but he did and it is al rigt I dont know what he was saying to them Mam sent me of to milk the cow for Nanan when I came down he was leving he said see you Donnie, smiling so I knew then it was al rigt Dad was standing at the door he was looking cherier than he is usualy looking thes days, I think he had a dram. He said mabe you got a futuere after al boy I dint know what he was mening but Mairi was teling me later, she did the tea for Mam the were al talking about me going to Glasgow and he was saying I had to get the chanse becaus I got the talent I wish they woud give that up I dont want to go but anway it is gret about the saling, he got round Mam and Dad al riht they were saying how nice he is. He woud get round anyon exept mabe Murdo probly not antie Effie either.

Donnie switched off his torch and sat back on his heels. The moon reflected on the water, shimmering like fish scales between the dark ribs of rock. His eyes were full of moonlight and his mind of wordless hopes and images as shy of capture as half-heard music. If anyone had asked him what he was thinking about, he would probably have said, 'I'll be sixteen tomorrow.' That was true, but irrelevant. It expressed, perhaps, a dividing line crossed, and a future from which he could not look back.

PART TWO

Tempus transit gelidum,
mundus renovatur,
verque redit floridum,
forma rebus datur,
avis modulatur,
modulans letatur,
lucidior
et lenior
aer iam serenatur.

— *Carmina Burana*

Only through time time is conquered.

— 'Burnt Norton', T.S. Eliot

Chapter 14

The northern spring was grudging and hesitant. The courting lapwings of early March were washed out in April. Some of their chicks succumbed at the beginning of May to the same deadly sleet which reduced the first primroses to slime. The blackbirds' nest in the old corrugated-iron privy behind Selena's shed was blown to pieces twice. Three times on his lengthening evening walks Alan rescued winter-weakened ewes from slippery pot-holes among the sodden heather. Yet spring did come, a slow ineluctable progression, with the first daisies opening in the trodden turf outside the door, and a week later the first lark, invisible in a soft morning mist; then every day a new sign, the blackbird singing in the evenings from his perch on the chimney, snipe drumming in the dusk, a sudden stain of new green round the ruins, a clump of vivid blue violets amongst the dead brown heather. Bright white lambs appeared beside their dingy ewes. Suddenly the redwings had gone; as suddenly, midnight was luminous, with an opal afterglow creeping up on the dawn.

Alan had never been so conscious of the seasons. The many English springs of daffodils and fresh green beech, of fluffy baby bluetits and apple blossom, had passed him virtually unnoticed. Yet at Skalanish he ran outside to hear whimbrel flying over at night, and rehearsed every new flower he passed on his way up to the road in the morning: daisy, dog-violet, celandine, primrose, milkwort, tormentil. Some of them he had never known or even noticed before. They seemed inviolably precious and distinct now, raising audacious heads wherever a rock or a bush of old heather gave a little shelter from blustering winds. He spent more time than he ever intended just standing on the doorstep of the cottage, looking, listening and scenting for the latest delicious portents of approaching summer. After a while, he would come to with a start, remembering that he had meant to haul and cut driftwood, or finish some piece of work on Selena, or climb the craggier side of Càrn Bàn to get the frustrations of a day in the classroom out of his system; but even so he would linger, waiting for an unseen bumbling bee to appear, or for the scent of primroses in the little valley to come again on the breeze.

Roddy caught him at it one day, as he did his round of the lambs. 'Ay, my father was always stood there like that. It's a grand way to pass the time.'

Alan was pleased to think that the old man had watched the slow change of seasons from the same tranquil post: or perhaps that tranquillity had flowed from him into the very stones of his dwelling. Roddy was plainly busy, though: his time was not to be passed in looking around.

'Can I give you a hand?' he offered, feeling guilty, but unwilling. He had already abandoned some desultory cultivation in favour of doing nothing.

Roddy laughed. 'Ach no, not on this job. It's a midwife I need. Come and help us with peats when the lambing's over, and I'll see you get some yourself.'

Roddy doubled back along the shore, and Alan wandered up the stream, aimless, and glad to be so. It was a still placid evening of blue sky and blue water, full of living voices. There was a constant conversation of sheep, the hoarse-voiced ewes answering the high whickering 'me-eh-eh' of the young lambs. A corn bunting jingled cheerfully on a fence-post. Scolding redshanks followed Roddy's progress along the shore, and when they fell silent, more distant song welled out of the quiet, larks in joyful competition and the unearthly sweet spring call of golden plover. The elemental *dies irae* of storm and winter had lulled to a flute-breath, to a fluttering rhythm of ephemeral wing-beats. He stopped to watch a newly born lamb by the roadside fence, with wool just drying into curls, and frail sides pumping quick moist breaths. It stretched its neck in a nearly soundless bleat, showing a pink tongue under busily respiring nostrils, and staggered on two black legs and two white to the ewe. She was cropping ravenously to make good the strength that had gone out of her. The birth membranes still trailed from her faded and bloodied skirts. She stamped her forefoot at Alan, nudged the lamb gently towards the right end, then raised her head to stare at him calmly. Her face was dignified and peaceful: if it had been a human face, he would have said proud. So this was the happiness of sheep. She had starved and huddled in the meagre hollows of the rocks all winter, and would for all her winters, nourishing new life in her belly. It would be taken from her soon and one autumn she would end her days hauled roughly to the knife or drowning in a peat hag; but for this short space each spring she had what she wanted, and was herself.

He moved away quietly so as not to break her calm, puzzling unanswerable questions, remembering Roddy's dying sheep in the wire, in which there was no profit; but there was only doubtful profit in the chilled starving orphan Roddy had brought the previous day into his kitchen to beg a little milk for it. He had warmed it in his own mouth and squirted it carefully into the lamb's, his weatherbeaten face intent and tender as the dribbling little creature began to swallow. He left with it tucked inside his jacket. And it was the same on all the crofts: however foul the weather, whatever time of day, there would be figures patrolling among the ewes. Some of them he had never seen before except reeling drunk outside the bar, men whose neglected stock had lain dying by the roadside in winter. Others were bent old men tottering on sticks, or young women with an infant on each arm. There was no doubt that in this season of hope his neighbours loved their sheep. Perhaps it was the hostility of barren ground and black weather, the hopeless struggle against an overwhelming environment, that accounted for seeming indifference to the beasts' sufferings in the winter. Eleanor had told him so often enough, anyway. Her explication, though, did not include how you could love what you were going to have to make into mutton chops; not surprising that people did not dare to look on the full-grown animals with the affection bestowed on the new creatures as yet innocent of any resemblance to Sunday dinner.

Alan wandered along the steep side of Càrn Bàn, touching budded honeysuckle in the clefts of the rock, and reflecting on the pastoral fields below. The older lambs were big enough to play, skipping and chasing among the rocky outcrops. The smallest lay folded neatly in the grass, or suckled with wagging tails. Roddy had almost reached home, surrounded by a press of ewes hopeful for sheep pellets. Old Johane was toddling slowly along the road, nodding her head approvingly at the pretty creatures frisking by the fence. Donnie was at the top of her croft, crook in hand, heading out on to the hill in pursuit of a strayed lamb, all on its own and bleating plaintively among the tumbled rocks. It bolted when he was within a few yards, and an agile chase began around the boulders. He got his crook round it at last, flinging himself headlong on it before it could struggle to its feet again. He rose lightly, stooping for the crook, with the lamb in his other arm.

Alan had started downhill as soon as he noticed him. He had seen very little of him even in school over the lambing season, and had missed him surprisingly, more than was comfortable. He called, and Donnie turned and scrambled up to him, smiling and brilliant-eyed, but when he drew near, he looked down, suddenly shy. Alan was no less so: it was unusual for them to meet except over some specific piece of boat or woodwork business, and faced with this Arcadian figure he was unexpectedly tongue-tied. He looked down too, and noticed that the boy's feet were bare, strong and fine like his hands, and as grimy. He looked up again, seeing the warmth of the day's sun on the curves of his cheek and brow, and quailed, but said, 'You had quite a chase with this one,' touching the lamb's head. Another few inches and he could have plunged his hand into Donnie's thick black hair instead: his heart pounded. Then the lamb seized his fingers in its hard little mouth, sucking with comical determination, and the crazy moment passed. Donnie laughed, restraining the struggling lamb with a hand round its chest.

'He's hungry. He's been lost all day, I was looking for him earlier. Lucky the wind's gone down, or I wouldn't have heard him.'

'Is he an orphan?'

'No – the mother's down there.' He jerked his head towards the road. 'She hasn't much milk, so she's no very interested.' He hesitated, shy again, and as Alan didn't speak, said, 'I'd better take him back.'

Alan went with him. The many and well-considered reasons for avoiding him had dropped from his mind without a trace, wiped out by the straight soot-black lashes framing his clear light eyes, the upcurved lip just faintly darkening with first down, the unconscious grace of wrist and hand encircling the lamb. All his

131

customary reservations, the barriers he had constructed for their mutual defence, flowed away as easily as water in the soft spring evening and vanished in the scent of primroses and the call of the plovers. Oblivious of everything else, he studied Donnie's face with the same concentrated attention he had given each newly-appearing flower. And as, in looking at a flower, the longer he looked the less it could be categorised by so many sepals, so many petals, such and such a tint, but seemed to contain in its minute particularity all symmetry and the whole spectrum; so with this face, individual beauties of colour and form dazzled and refracted till he could not have described so much as the shape of his nose or the tilt of his head.

Perturbed by this intense scrutiny, Donnie looked up timidly, and Alan perceived at once that his nose was straight and rather short, and that his head had been most poignantly bowed, showing enchanting shadows at the nape of his neck. He couldn't meet the boy's eyes, not from shame, since he had forgotten even the possibility of it, but from ecstasy. Turn away thine eyes from me, for they have overcome me. But the heady magic thinned as he sensed the other's confusion and anxiety: he would have divined criticism, perhaps anger, in silence and a suddenly averted gaze.

Alan struggled for self-possession, realised that he was scowling, and assumed a more normally friendly expression. With his features under control, he dared to look at the boy again, this time with a determination not to let things get out of hand: he was still sufficiently dazzled to realise that survival depended on that for both of them.

'Lambing's nearly over, is it?' he ventured, as they climbed the fence. It was an effort to speak: he was not sure what words would come out, or, when he had spoken, what they had been.

'Yes, only ten to go now.'

'We'll get some sailing next week, then.'

'Yes.' Donnie tried another experimental glance, which opened into a smile when it was not rebuffed. 'It'll be great if the weather stays like this. I was thinking you would be out tonight.'

'So I should have been if I hadn't been too lazy to launch the thing myself.'

Donnie looked wistful. 'Wish I could have got away.' He set the lamb down near its mother. It gave a few frenzied bleats, then cut itself off in mid-voice to suckle frantically. The ewe sniffed it with mild surprise and continued cropping.

'It'll need some extra,' said Donnie, half to himself, then turning to Alan with admiring eyes, 'I seen you out on Saturday. You were going some lick. I thought you'd go over coming past Vatasgeir.'

Alan laughed. 'So did I. Glad I didn't though, there was a nasty rip out there.'

'I was thinking there would be. I was really frightened.'

His guileless candour inspired a flutter in Alan's throat. 'Where were you, anyway?'

'Over on Rona. I was there for ten days.'

The Gnipadale crofters had grazing shares and a bothy on Rona. This explained why Donnie had been so totally absent from school since the day of the odious examination paper. Alan was glad to learn that he hadn't been moping over it, as he had feared.

'It's great on Rona, very peaceful. There's more birds than here,' said Donnie, adding shyly, 'I thought you might land that day.'

'I would have done if I'd known you were there.' That was out before he could stop it, followed with mischievous haste by, 'Were you there alone?'

After that Alan was making such an enormous effort at self-control that he hardly heard the answer.

'Some o' the time.' Donnie looked at him enquiringly, because Alan was staring at him again. He shifted nervously, curling one bare foot round the other ankle. 'I better get that lamb a bottle,' he muttered, glancing towards the house, but not quite going.

Alan has succeeded meanwhile in reducing him to a shockheaded urchin in a torn buttonless shirt and filthy trousers, smelling of sheep and sweat and with a streak of mud or worse along one cheekbone. If he could keep him fixed like that they were safe.

The ewe had wandered away, and the lamb stood with hunched back, bleating despondently.

'I better go,' said Donnie, anxious-eyed, but still not going.

The contrived image faltered, but it had lasted long enough to cool Alan's senses. He could see the boy now in his familiar form, sweet-faced, healthy-limbed and innocent as one of his own lambs, as pleasing to contemplate, and as unsuitable an object of passion. Nevertheless he was still reluctant to leave him.

133

'You'll come along on Saturday, won't you?'

There was really no need to ask: he knew Donnie would be there if he possibly could.

'Yes – I hope I can, anyway.'

Alan heard, or thought he did, the slight edge of weariness in his voice, and then noticed for the first time faint smudges of tiredness under his eyes.

'You look exhausted,' he said, 'you probably need to spend any free time asleep.'

Donnie shook his head. 'I'll be round if I'm not sent to Rona again on Saturday morning.' He pushed back his hair, and Alan saw his forehead was marked where there had been an ugly graze after the fight with Crabbit.

'You still— ' he began, and stopped, because he had just noticed a fresh gash from the barbed wire fence on his instep, and realised with desperation that if he didn't tear himself away at once he would find so many instances in which the boy required protection and pity that he would never extricate himself at all.

'I'd better let you get on,' he said, thinking wryly, not before time. 'See you soon, anyway.'

He set off quickly towards the shore-path. Resting lambs jumped up as he passed, bleating this way and that till the mothers' deeper voices sent them bounding across the field in the right direction. That was enough to start the redshanks. He heard Mairi shouting to her brother, and his answer. The girl was calling the cow home. Boreray cows did not speak English.

'*Trobhad, trobhad, trobhad,*' she called, and then sang a bit, softly, but her voice carried in the still clear air. '*Trobhad, trobhad, trobhad,*' again, and another few bars. The cow mooed in answer, a deep strong peaceful sound as she swayed slowly down the hill. Mairi kept calling her high quick '*Trobhad-trobhad-trobhad.*' Donnie had taken up her song, and was whistling it on his way down to the house, a lilting tranquil melody with many grace notes.

Alan stopped where the path dipped to the stony beach, till the human voices ceased, and the cow's lowing sank to a friendly murmur. He was intensely happy. It came into his mind that he should instead be wretchedly worried, but this theory seemed so foreign and out of place that it lacked any reality: he considered it briefly with

134

surprise and forgot it. For the time being he had lost the power of analysis. Mind and body were flooded with the sensations of spring, birdsong, flowers, lambs, milky blue water, limpid light on the fresh green islets, and every sensation led directly and simply to Donnie. He no longer thought or cared about the future, at least not beyond their next meeting. The present was illimitable, a golden present of manifold and interconnecting beauty. A grace lay on everything, on the curves of the hills ready to tremble into sentience, on the soft promises of the little waves losing themselves in the shingle. His fingertips brushing the rocks caressed living warmth. He ran some of the way home, and then lay still in the grass, while dunlin trilled overhead and time ceased to move. The sun had set when he reached the gentle bay at Skalanish. The light above the horizon was rosy, but the sea reflected the pale blue of the upper sky. He stopped to swim. Even the shock of the icy water could not cure his delirium, but when he had dressed again and reached the cottage, still shivering, he stood outside blinking, while his giddiness subsided slightly. He could not remember exactly what he had been doing or thinking before he left the house, but he realised with astonishment that, whatever it was, Donnie had not been in his mind then at all. He noticed the patch of bare earth and the hoe, and the packet of lettuce seeds, with two fat rabbits sitting on the warm soil nibbling silverweed roots. He looked at it all rather puzzled, trying to put things in order, and then said, 'Oh my God!' aloud. Startled, the rabbits bounded away.

He picked up the seed packet and scattered the contents at random over the bare ground. All of a sudden, the whole business seemed incredibly funny. He grinned and then laughed, remembering from schooldays:

a Corydon Corydon quae te dementia cepit?
semiputata tibi frondosa vitis in ulmo est

What a secret and exquisite disquiet it had been, in all the sniggering and nudging, to wonder if there might be any truth in it.

Water was dripping icily down his neck. He wrung his hair out with an unsteady hand. He caught the scent of primroses from the stream bank as he turned his head. 'Oh Christ!' he muttered.

He went in, leaving the door open to the spring night, threw off his clothes and dropped into bed, suddenly exhausted. As soon as he

135

closed his eyes, the boy's face was before him. It was impossible to sleep: the whole situation was impossible. What on earth would old Uncle Ewan have thought of it? A breath of wind from the open door chilled his damp hair, bringing with it a faint recall of Mairi's song. Before his ear could catch what he was listening for, he was asleep.

Donnie had finished his last round of the ewes and lambs. He lay on the grass at the top corner of Johane's croft, safely invisible in the dusk, with his diary in front of him. He had written:

Wed. May 16 Only about 10 lams to go now Im glad to say I hav to go out evry tim this year becaus Murdos hands too big if he had not got them cheeviot rams it woud hav been al rigt the lams are too big, most of our ews is smal I told him but he wont listen he says they got to be hevy to sell now We losing so many it not worth it and the poor beests are sufering it is horible murdo is a fool al he wil do is shoot the crows. i wish mairi woud go out but she says cant stand blood.

He was uneasy, and not only with the clinging stench of birth blood on his forearms, though that was pungent enough when he put his head down to think. He had neglected his diary for the three weeks of lambing, and he had not resumed it to write about sheep, but because the meeting on the hillside needed to be set down and considered. He did not know why he had been so intently scrutinised. Perhaps it was because he had got bigger and stronger with all the work. He felt as if he had, anyway. Or maybe it was the lamb: he always seemed to like animals. But if it was the lamb he wouldn't have been so friendly about Saturday. Donnie gave up on words and let his mind drift in images, in happy anticipation of the next week. He tensed at the memory of the nasty moment off Vatasgeir, and thought, I'd not have been scared if I'd been there with him, but maybe that wasn't true. He hoped it was. He picked up his pencil and wrote, 'The wether is beter I migt get some sailing next week', then hastily changed 'I' to 'we' and stared at it, agitated, with a faint coolness of sweat forming on his lip and brow.

He turned over on his back, questioning the indistinct evening sky. Of all that was teeming in his mind, there was nothing more he could set down, or even think about clearly. There was a barrier that seemed to him to be insurmountable: he no longer had a name for Alan. 'Mr Cameron' had become impossible; but to call him by his first name without permission was equally impossible. Every islander used Christian names with every other islander, regardless of age or status: but incomers were 'Mr' until they indicated otherwise. He couldn't write, or even think, 'Alan', without cringing at his own forwardness. As there was nothing else in the world he wanted to think about, he was torn. He folded his arms over his eyes, to see if darkness would make things clearer. Porky wouldn't care, he thought, he'd say what he liked, and get off with it. He'd only laugh. But Donnie didn't want to be like Porky, and he didn't want to be laughed at, and anyway, what if he really thought it was cheeky? He sighed and sat up. A chill dew was falling. He rubbed his hands against his rough jersey to warm them, and yawned and shivered, too tired to think any longer. He would have to be up again at five. He walked quietly down through the flock, stopping to check the newest lambs and the rescued stray. It was resting peacefully enough against the ewe's back, but he stayed there for a little, leaning on his crook and dreaming open-eyed, till the back door slammed, indicating that Murdo was coming. In an instant, Donnie was over the fence and bolting down the burn, noiseless and unseen in the steep dark hollows.

Chapter 15

Alan half woke to the sensation of diffuse dread associated with undergraduate hangovers, and the uneasy certainty that there was some embarrassing misdemeanour to be paid for. His immediate defence was to go back to sleep, but the blackbird's vigorous song made that impossible. Since an unwilling review of the previous evening revealed no public indiscretions, he dared to wake up further, stretched, and relaxed. After all, he had done and said nothing that could not easily be glossed over.

While he congratulated himself on this, he began to feel unaccountably depressed. Of course the whole thing was a lot of nonsense. He had never lost his head over anyone and to imagine he had over a boy of sixteen was ludicrous and distasteful: unprofitable, hadn't Plato said? He had not been in the habit of seducing boys, except for a flagrant diversion in his last year at school undertaken mainly out of anti-establishment zeal, because the place prided itself on a wholesome proportion of girl pupils. He had instituted a poetry magazine expressly to fill it with rather explicit verses in praise of a pretty blond a few years younger than himself, but the intention had been more mischievous than amorous. The main object of attraction at the time had actually been an Indian princess in his own form, whose slender neck and incredibly long and thick black pigtail in front of him had lost him many hundred lines of Homer. But she never got any poems: and in fact he enjoyed silky-skinned Mark, when they got the chance. The Indian girl certainly wouldn't play.

He hadn't thought about them for years and the recollection of happy irresponsibilities brightened his mood considerably. He got out of bed grinning about the time he had bribed the ducks into the swimming pool. But while he was shaving it occurred to him that chlorine was probably bad for ducks, and he was immediately plunged into an uncharacteristic excess of self-recrimination which spread inevitably from ducks to Donnie. He should never have shown any interest in him. It had been bad enough letting him come on Saturdays with the others, but far worse taking him sailing on his own. The boy expected it now, there was no getting out of it; but nothing could be crazier. Alan paced round the kitchen, poured his coffee down the sink, threw himself back on the bed and got up again hastily, bedevilled by wild imaginings of seduction on deserted offshore islands. Or even if it didn't come to that, what if people gossiped, what if it ended in the boy being ridiculed and despised by his friends? Poor Donnie had enough of a bad start to growing up without that.

Alan went out, slamming the front door behind him furiously. The doorknob fell off, as it often did. He swore and stuck it back, hearing the inner knob clatter on the floor inside. This time he was too angry even to curse at it. He scowled moodily at the path. He had an enormous disinclination to go to work. The thought of spending

138

the day surrounded by pestering boys and stuffy teachers was intolerable. He wouldn't go. He would play truant, and damn old Jock. He had hurled his bundle of books and papers on the ground and was already pulling off his tie before the absurd childishness of it struck him. Feeling very foolish, he adjusted his tie, his face and his books and started up the path; reflecting tenderly that while he was behaving like a child of ten, Donnie would have been occupied since dawn in responsible care of his flock. He remembered him standing shyly before him with the lamb in one hand and the crook in the other, and the previous evening flooded back in heady waves, every word and gesture clear, the inarticulate devotion in the boy's eyes and voice inestimably sweet, his smile the ultimate treasure. Nothing else mattered. Uncontrollable lust on lonely islands was unthinkable. He couldn't ever want to hurt him in any way, even if it meant never seeing him again. But impetuous new love assured him that it need not mean that, could not possibly mean that. The summer stretched ahead in chaste and dazzling promise; they could be together as much as Donnie chose, he wouldn't cajole or push him: just wait and be glad of his presence. That he had already passed five minutes thinking about him without expiring from his absence made this well-intentioned resolve seem almost credible, till the school bus drew up and the desert of time between Thursday and Saturday obtruded itself: two whole days at work, two evenings to fill, two nights – what if he were sent off to Rona for another week? The agitation produced by this possibility was aggravated by Mairi getting in with Kirsty and Dina. Dina smiled at him and the older girls looked down as they passed with conscious modesty. Mairi's profile was so like her brother's that he followed her with an incautious stare. She giggled and whispered behind her hand to her cousin.

At once he was miserably aware that he would have considered it incongruous and disgusting to fall in love with Mairi or Kirsty. They were mere children. How could it be different then with Donnie, who was more ignorant and more innocent than any girl? The idea was a revolting aberration, and dressing it up in a lot of fine sentiment only made it more untrustworthy, the sort of thing that got vicars and scoutmasters into trouble. Sweating with confusion, he opened a jotter and placed a few random ticks, struggling to scrape some shreds of reason together. Since he had managed to survive as long

139

as he had without falling for any of his previous attractive, intelligent, compatible partners, it was extremely unlikely that he was in love with a half-grown, probably half-witted little rustic. 'Unlikely' changed to 'impossible' before the charging wave of male adolescence at Ardbuie – Crump, Porky and Donnie Mór, shouldering, jostling, swearing as loud as they dared and ostentatiously hiding their cigarette packets. They were a salutary warning. Alan gave up trying to make sense of things and concentrated grimly on marking Class 3's technical drawing.

That day and the next passed somehow, in continuous rapid cycles of elation, despondency, revulsion. It was like steering through a whirlpool, never sure where the next shock was coming from. By Friday afternoon he was so tormented that he took the boat out, although the tide was ebbing strongly against a freshening westerly wind and ominous scarves of cloud were streaming from the hilltops. The real eddies were a welcome distraction from their emotional equivalent, but predictably he capsized in a sudden smack of wind from the north. He had been watching for it in the vicious kicking water between the skerries, aware that his weight was nothing like enough for a two-man dinghy in such conditions, but his attention lapsed as soon as he was back in the bay. It was a cold and sobering task getting the hull upright in the increasing surge, which threatened damage to the mast from the inshore rocks. The waterlogged main pulled her over a second time before he could get to wading depth and drag her in bodily, in the wind now funnelling offshore and hurling sleety rain in his face. He cursed the weather as he unrigged and dismasted her with clumsy fingers. Even taken to bits as far as possible, she was still heavy to heave up on the rickety trolley and the effect on her underside was atrocious. He wished for a single-hander: or a crew. He wished for Donnie, and swore at wet knots aloud and querulously. By the time he had the hull tied down with a couple of extra lines for security, his teeth were chattering. The sleet had cleared to brilliant shafts of flying sunshine. It looked like another gale on the way.

Eleanor was waiting for him in the house. She was unsympathetic, but as he pulled off his wet clothes she watched him with the tilted chin and gleaming eye he had come to know, and suggested with one of her rare touches of dry humour that they might as well go to bed now to save him the trouble of undressing twice. He had been alternating between the view that making love to Eleanor would be absolutely meaningless, if not impossible, and the contrary conclusion that since he would certainly still grab Eleanor whenever he could, the business about Donnie was rarefied nonsense. She launched a merciless attack on his privates while he was struggling free of inside-out wet-suit, before he had a chance to decide which frame of mind he was in at the moment. It proved perfectly possible to acquiesce. Nevertheless, half an hour later he was already listening with relief to the wind roaring on the roof: no chance of sending a boat to Rona if that kept up.

It seemed as if it would.

'Filthy night,' remarked Eleanor disapprovingly as they walked to her car. 'One of these days that leaky shack of yours will blow into the sea.'

Alan was used to her dislike of the house, and ignored it. 'Does the weather ever improve?' he asked, hoping it wouldn't for the next twelve hours or so.

'It's always foul during lambing. It usually gets better just after. I predict summer next week.'

'Wonderful,' said Alan, gazing dreamily out to sea.

She gave him a sharp look. 'Don't drown yourself – or anyone else.'

He started at this. What did she know?

'You're taking Murdo's brother out, aren't you? I don't suppose he can swim. Hardly anyone here can.'

'Really?' That had never occurred to him. He had made him wear a lifejacket anyway, but it was still disconcerting.

'It's traditional in most fishing communities. They reckon you drown less painfully if you don't resist. I must say I think that's rather defeatist.'

Alan left her at the top of the track, and walked back worrying about drowning Donnie, looking forward to teaching him to swim, longing to understand his foreign background, warning himself against involvement with someone who would bore him to death in a week. By the time he reached the cottage he had been through the whole maze several times and felt thoroughly disgruntled. He wished the wind would drop so that the wretched boy would disappear to Rona. He wondered how he could possibly have wished such a thing. He wished, as so many times before, that Eleanor had stayed the night; but then when he went into the bedroom it smelt of girl and he didn't like it. He spent half the night awake hoping the wind would go down, and the rest of it jolting out of an uneasy doze panicking in case it had.

Donnie usually arrived earlier than the other boys, but Alan reassured himself that he wouldn't get away easily from the lambs, with such bad weather. Porky appeared with Crump and Sandy.

'Just us today, sir – bet you're glad,' said Crump cheerfully, falling over the sawhorse.

'Donnie Mór got a hangover and big trouble from his daddy,' Porky explained, crossing his eyes expressively. 'Donnie Beag got drowned on his way to Rona.'

Alan's heart stopped, but as Porky immediately donned a plastic bucket for a hat with unfunereal levity he concluded that this was merely another instance of the horrible boy's telepathic short-circuitry. He was fairly used to it, and assumed it was usually unconscious. All the same he hid behind Selena for a few minutes to recover composure, until Porky's unprovoked assault on Sandy with the flat of a saw forced him out.

'If you bugger that saw up I'll wring your neck!'

'Ooh! language, sir!'

There wasn't much chance to moon around if he wanted to save Selena and his tools. He begged Sandy to turn up his cassette recorder as loudly as possible to drown out Porky, found them all something to do, and hovered over them to make sure they didn't do anything else too vandalistic instead. He told himself firmly that Donnie couldn't be coming: but when he entered quietly a little later, he was aware of it, though his back was to the open door and the noise in the shed was overpowering. He didn't turn. He realised he was giving Sandy completely false measurements for the hatch cover he was working on, but couldn't find words to correct himself. Donnie appeared at his elbow. He looked astonishingly much as usual, equally free of angelic iridescence and doltish rusticity; Alan blinked at him hazily, as amazed by his completely normal appearance as he would have been by any metamorphosis.

'What will I start on, sir?'

Alan flinched at 'sir', but it brought him back to earth.

'I've got the toerail on since you were here. Can you match up plugs for the screwheads? The mahogany offcuts are under the bench.'

'I dunno, but I'll try.' He was always pleased to be entrusted with his own bit of work.

'You'll make a better job of it than I should, anyway.'

That was it for the rest of the morning. Donnie was immediately absorbed in his project, and Alan had plenty to do keeping the other three from inflicting damage on his boat. He felt remarkably cheerful and well adjusted, and didn't even climb up to see how Donnie was progressing till the others were allegedly tidying, ready to leave.

'How are you getting on?' he asked, expecting a sweet smile.

Donnie scowled and said indignantly, 'That old wood you've put back in. It's much closer-grained than the new bits. I can't match it right at all.'

'It's not that different, is it? Those you've done look pretty good.'

Donnie grunted. 'Only the ones in the new wood. You didn't keep any scraps of the old stuff?'

'No, except what I re-used. I've burnt everything I wasn't counting on.'

Porky's ugly chin appeared resting on the gunwale. 'Coming, Beag?'

'No, I'm finishing something off.'

The other boys left on a receding wave of shouts and heavy rock. Alan took a screwdriver from his belt and handed it over.

'Take up one of the old sections and use that, if it will make you happy.' He was amused, if rather taken aback, by Donnie's disapproval of his methods.

'Thanks.' He cast an eye and a hand over suitable victims and attacked the strip of his choice intently.

Alan sat back on his heels watching him in besotted silence. He would have been quite content to sit thus admiring his quick, assured movements while he took up the whole rail and relaid it, if that was what he wanted. In fact Donnie had only got one screw half out when he sat up with an audible gasp, and consternation in his face. The screwdriver fell with a clatter.

'What's wrong?'

'I'm sorry!'

'What about, then?'

143

Donnie twisted his hands together, blushing with embarrassment. 'I been giving you a lot of cheek. I forgot – I'll put this back.'

'No you won't! You were quite right – you carry on. I'm far too lazy about details.' He jumped down to save the boy further squirming. 'I'm going to improve on Crump's execrable planing.'

The board was still in the vice and the improvement required was considerable.

Donnie joined him after a few minutes.

'I took that up and marked it, but I better be going now. Murdo will give me hell if I'm not back.'

Alan straightened up, flicking shavings from the mouth of the plane. 'Have the lambs all arrived yet?'

'Last one this morning. It was a difficult one too, it got the cord round its neck. That's why I was so late getting here.' He leant on the bench curling shavings round his forefinger pensively. His eyes spoke reluctance to go.

'Has it been a good year?' Alan asked, unfairly encouraging him not to.

'Och no. The weather was bad to start, and there's no much grass even now. We lost quite a few.' He ran his hand over the half-planed board. 'The crows are bad this time. They got a lamb last night, took its eyes out. They're horrible things.'

The judgemental human assumption behind his words upset Alan, as always. 'Crows have got to eat too.' He shot the plane forward suddenly. Donnie pulled his hand away, startled, and looked down, mutely accepting reproof. Alan was at once disgusted by his own insensitivity: he hadn't had to deal with the tortured animal, which had doubtless been Donnie's first discovery that morning. Even thinking about it made his skin twitch.

'It is horrible, though.' He put the plane down. The sound of wood on wood lingered in an awkward silence.

'You'd better go, hadn't you?'

'Yes,' said Donnie, miserably, not looking up, still leaning on the bench.

'I'm not trying to get rid of you.' Alan was distressed by his unhappiness. 'I don't want you to get into trouble, that's all.'

Donnie sighed, his head so bent that his face was almost hidden by his forward falling hair.

144

'Stay if you like – if you can.' Alan moved involuntarily towards him, and half-heartedly away again, and after a moment's indecision, thrust his hands nervously in his pockets.

Donnie shook his head, but looked up. 'No, I'll have to get back.'

Sadness as well as silence fell between them. They gazed at each other mournfully, Alan wanting to say, 'I love you', and realising that it was not only impossible now, but always would be; and Donnie wanting to ask, 'Can I call you Alan?' which came to the same thing.

Donnie was the braver: he almost got it out.

'Can I—' he began, faltered, and changed it to, 'Can I come round tomorrow afternoon?' which to his own mind was almost as forward. He flushed and averted his face, appalled by his own temerity.

Alan cheered up at once. 'Yes, of course – come any time you like.'

Donnie turned to him, smiling with the full brilliance of his eyes. 'You'll never get rid of me, then.'

'I don't want to. I – look, you really ought to get back.' Alan retreated to the far end of the bench and got his hands safely busy removing the board from the vice.

'That's not finished. It's not flat on this corner yet.' Donnie's palm brushed the other end of the wood.

'Go on! Go home!' Alan nudged him off the bench with the plank, laughing.

'Right, I'm going,' agreed Donnie, laughing too. His laugh was still rather high and girlish. They were both as absurdly light-hearted as they had been downcast five minutes earlier.

'See you tomorrow,' said Alan, for the delight of being assured he would.

'Sure you don't mind?' Donnie asked, for the pleasure of hearing he didn't.

Chapter 16

Alan was up early on Sunday. A fine rain was falling, but he was too restless to stay indoors. The air was mild and smelt of growing things. The rain-flattened water looked warmer than it was: he dived in and came out shuddering, reflecting that it was no wonder Borerayans didn't learn to swim. As he reached the grass he noticed something white flapping beside a boulder. It was a gull with a trailing wing. He approached it quietly, but it ran in panic, making several attempts to take off, falling headlong each time. He tried to corner it, but gave up after a few minutes, as the concerted voices of Roddy's sheep warned him that someone was around inspecting the lambs; it would certainly be regarded as highly indecent to race up and down the shore stark naked on a Sunday morning. He dressed and went back to look for the injured bird. He had no idea what could be done for it, but he knew enough to realise that a broken wing could not heal in the wild; perhaps he could splint it, and feed it till it recovered.

It had taken refuge in a lush patch of sorrel between two rocks, or perhaps it had fallen there in trying to take off. At any rate, it was easy enough to creep up behind it and make a quick grab. He caught it, but he was unprepared for the harsh screech and threshing, and dropped it again. It lurched pathetically off-balance among the stones, the broken and bloody wing flopping at a sickening angle. He just caught it by the other wing-tip before it could regain its footing, and this time held it immobilised in the crook of his left arm. It pecked his wrist, but feebly. Its beak glanced off the bone, and slid along his thumb without a further attempt. It was a common gull, with a pale yellow beak and dark eye, lacking the fierce predatory look of a herring gull. Alan moved his arm cautiously to reveal the broken point in the wing, grimacing in sympathy as he caught sight of the jagged ends of bone protruding through blood-matted feathers above the joint. As he held the wing out gently to have a closer look, his fingers encountered bare slimy skin under it. The bird jerked away from the touch, with another weak attempt to peck. He flinched himself, and the good wing got free, flapping wildly. He carried the captive up to the workshop, to continue the examination under the window at the bench. It took a few wincing attempts before he could bring himself to push the mangled wing out of the way in order to look at the wound underneath. When he succeeded his throat constricted with anger: the skin was torn back to darkened bloody edges, revealing a patch of raw flesh studded with shotgun pellets. Filled with loathing for the perpetrator, he rummaged with one hand for tweezers in the bench drawer. He clutched the gull awkwardly against his body with the broken wing flopping excruciatingly back and extracted the three most obvious pieces of shot. Purple marks indicated that others were more deeply embedded, but his hands were trembling and the bird looked so weak and exhausted that the task seemed pointless. Its beak was parted and the nictitating membrane flicked to and fro over its dark eye. He remembered reading somewhere that the best first aid for injured birds was rest in a darkened box. With his free hand, he tipped rigging accessories out of a carton and gathered up wood-shavings to make it more comfortable. He settled the gull as well as possible, but he could not imagine it was anything but agonised. He knew he should kill it, but couldn't force himself to do it; he told himself that if it was no better by evening he would finish it off then. Perhaps it would die anyway. Perhaps Donnie would know if anything could be done for it. He was filled with a sudden longing for his gentle presence, but it was only ten o' clock. He looked at the box for a moment, biting his lip, and went back to the house.

Donnie arrived about three, looking as if he had been out in the rain for hours, as indeed he had.

'How on earth did you get so wet just walking here?' Alan asked, throwing him a towel from the rail in front of the stove.

He didn't answer, and when his face was visible, it was apparent that he was dispirited and anxious as well as damp.

'Did you lose more lambs with this rain?'

Donnie hung up the towel. 'No. Will if this goes on though.' He seemed to have difficulty in answering. His lower lip was twitching downwards. He went to the door, poured a considerable amount of water out of each wellington boot, and came back leaving a trail of wet footprints.

Alan followed his movements with growing concern. Perhaps he was in trouble at home for insisting on going out on Sunday. He should never have encouraged it.

'What's wrong?'

Donnie leant on the stove rail and sniffed and said nothing. Eventually he brought out huskily, 'You know what I was telling you about the crows.'

'Yes.'

147

'I wouldn't touch them whatever they did.' For the first time that day he met Alan's eyes. 'I wouldn't. Not now.'

'All right. What's happened?'

He was silent again, then suddenly dropped on the floor cross-legged, speaking very fast.

'I got home yesterday, Murdo was shooting, I thought it was the crows he was after. Well, it wasn't just them. I was out at the lambs after church, down along the shore. He's been at the gulls. They nest there every year. They're harmless, the small ones, not blackbacks. He got fifteen, twenty maybe. There was eggs in most of the nests, all cold. Some of the birds are still flying around, all quiet like, I think maybe the mates of the ones that are dead. It's terrible.'

'Oh, God.' Alan could think of nothing more helpful to say.

'I hate Murdo. I hate him.'

'Don't say that, you look like him when you do.' It was the first time he had ever seen a resemblance, and it was sickening.

'I'm not like him. Don't say I am.' He jumped up with fury in his eyes and clenched fists, increasing the likeness.

Alan rose too, towering over him. He was bitterly angry for the injured gull. 'You have a touch of the same evil temper, then.'

Donnie huddled on the floor again with an audible whimper. His moods were as instant and unconcealed as a dog's. Alan found himself looking down at his drooped shoulders and the back of his neck, and his anger drained away at once.

'I'm sorry. I don't like your brother much either. I think I've got one of his victims in the workshop. Come and tell me if there's anything can be done for it.'

The box was silent. Alan had a fleeting hope that the occupant was dead, but as soon as he opened the flap there was a rustle and the bird lunged at his hand. He lifted it out carefully, gritting his teeth as the smashed wing flopped across his wrist.

Donnie shot a keen glance at his face before turning his attention to the wing. His fingers moved gently enough under the bloodstained primaries, but with more assurance than Alan's. He pinched the jagged ends of bone together, and the bird struggled with silently opening beak.

'You'd never get that to mend. There's a bit missing.'

Alan averted his eyes, feeling sick. 'There's a wound in its body, too. I picked out a few pellets, but there might be more.' He supported the trailing wing on his outspread hand to reveal the other injury.

Donnie shook his head. 'Och no, that's hopeless. That wound smells bad already. It would be better to kill the poor thing.'

Alan put the bird slowly back in the door, holding the flaps closed under his hand. It went quiet at once in the dark. 'What's the quickest way to do it?' he asked, hoping he sounded casual.

'Just pull its neck.'

Alan hesitated, his palm flattening on the lid as he contemplated the prospect. If it really had to be done, compassion demanded that it should be at once. He swallowed, and pushed the flaps apart again.

'You never killed anything, have you?' asked Donnie, softly.

'No.' Unwillingly, Alan met his eyes, and encountered an unexpected look of shining tenderness.

'I'll do it for you.' His voice was as eager as his eyes.

Alan resisted, but foundering. 'No, that's rotten. Why should you have to do it?'

'I'm used to it.' His gaze never left Alan's face. The dilation of his pupils had turned his light eyes dark.

Alan strove for normalcy. 'Well, if I watch what you do, I can do it myself next time.'

'No!' The change in his voice and features was so violent that Alan jumped. 'I don't want you to see.'

'All right – I'm sorry. I'll go away.'

Outside the rain had stopped, and the grass was sparkling in widening shafts of sunlight. He crossed the stream and wandered up the slope above the ruins. He was preoccupied by embarrassment at his own inadequacy and confusion over Donnie's intensity of feeling. The boy seemed to lack a self-protective skin: his moods were as quick and raw as the poor gull's wound. Alan slumped against a boulder, shaking slightly from unaccustomed emotional exertion. He had a distinct desire to escape. He began to consider what other engagements might prevent him taking Donnie sailing in the forthcoming week, and whether any of his old contacts might possibly still want crew members for the latter part of the season. The ease with which these treacherous thoughts presented themselves astonished him. He looked round guiltily, and found Donnie standing silent beside him. His air of apologetic chagrin gave Alan an uneasy sense that he knew what he had been thinking.

'I just left it on the shore, sir,' he said timidly, and then, noting Alan's slight frown, 'wasn't that right?'

'Yes – thank you, I'm very grateful. Look, can't you stop calling me "sir"? You know my name.'

Donnie's eyes brightened. 'Alan,' he said, with a shy smile coming and going.

'That's better.' How much better had to remain unsaid. He had never heard his name spoken so caressingly. Donnie sat down beside him. He wanted badly to take the boy's hand, but even that simple impulse had to be denied. The shadow this realisation cast must have shown in his face, for Donnie asked, with an anxious look, 'You're not thinking I'm always killing things, are you? Do you really think I'm like Murdo?'

'No, of course not.' There was no longer even a capability for the resemblance in his upturned face. 'I've never met two brothers less alike. There, will that do?'

He smiled, and nodded, and with manifestly lightened heart, sprawled on his back on the damp turf, shading his eyes with one hand while he searched the clearing sky for larks. At least three were singing. Alan sat enchanted to stillness by the ends of Donnie's hair flicking across his fingertips in the grass, and the air quivered with passionate sound.

Donnie jumped up. 'Have you found their nests, Alan?'

'No.'

'Come and see.'

Alan followed, enthralled, not up the green hillside behind them, where he had assumed they nested, but west of the old ruins. Here the slope of Gormul levelled out towards the shore in a featureless region of ancient cultivation, with neglected grassy ridges snaking downhill between uncleared drains which held water in wet weather and mud in dry. Donnie bounded from ridge to ridge towards a slightly flatter and less marshy area behind a long boulder beach. They had flushed a couple of snipe and several twites and pipits on the way down, but the only birds alerted as they neared the shore were worried oystercatchers, whose loud calls drowned out even the song of the larks. Donnie stood still for a moment or so, then turned without hesitation to a tussock identical to all the others, parting the grass carefully. There was a nest, with four eggs. Alan was impressed; he had spent hours as a child annoying larks in the hope of such a discovery, but had never once made it.

'How on earth did you spot that? Did the bird get up?'

'No.' Donnie withdrew his hand gently, the grass sprang together, and the nest was invisible at once. 'There's more.' He walked on, glanced perfunctorily to either side, and again unerringly chose an occupied tussock. He found five nests thus in as many minutes, but only once did a bird fly out.

Alan followed him with growing fascination.

'How do you do it? Can you see through grass?'

Donnie smiled and shrugged, looked at him and then quickly away under his dark lashes.

'Them black and white birds – what's the English for them, Alan? The ones is making all the noise.'

'Oystercatchers?'

'Oystercatchers. But it's mussels and limpets they eat.' He seemed put out by this.

'All right, musselcatchers. What about them?'

'They got nests too, down on the beach.'

He leapt from one smooth round boulder to the next, gripping with strong bare toes, till they came to a place of smaller stones between two ribs of rock.

'There and there,' he said, pointing right and left.

'Where?'

He went forward to the first site. The mottled eggs lay in a shallow depression lined with fragments of blue and white shell. The breaking of tone and colour dissolved the telltale shapes of nest and eggs into their background. Even from a distance of a few feet, Alan found he lost the place if he looked away.

'Where's the other?' he asked, curiously.

'Over by that old fishbox.'

But Alan had to walk across and look carefully: even so he almost trod on it before he saw it. He came back shaking his head incredulously.

'You're uncanny. What else can you do? Ever tried dowsing for water?'

Donnie looked puzzled. 'What's that?'

Alan explained as well as he could. Donnie considered his reply silently. He was jumping on and off a weathered log of driftwood with disconcerting animal concentration; if he had had a tail he might have been chasing it. 'Why do they need a forked stick?' he wanted to know.

Alan laughed. 'Well, you might not. Come on, these birds are worried.'

Donnie slithered from his log, yelped, and twisted up his foot in a childishly slack-jointed contortion to inspect the damage.

'Hurt yourself?'

'Just a splinter.'

A sudden thought struck Alan. 'Don't you have to get back for church?'

'Oh, ay.' He stooped to examine a patch of soft mud, glowing with kingcups between two ridges. 'There's an otter been here. She's got two young ones, very small too.'

Alan looked at the prints with interest. 'I'd have thought that was a dog.'

'No, much rounder, and shaped more like a foot.' And indeed, as he stepped up on the grass, his own print, with the splayed toes characteristic of barefoot walkers, was not dissimilar. His preference for going unshod was presumably some relic of childhood: Alan had seen no other Boreray male over the age of twelve who was not firmly socked and booted.

Donnie was heading towards Traìgh Mhór. Alan looked at his watch. 'Come back, it's nearly quarter to five. If you're late for church they'll never let you out again on Sunday.'

Donnie turned unwillingly. A limp became evident. Alan waited for him to catch up. 'Is that foot hurting, or is it just the thought of Mr MacNeil's sermon?'

'Och, both.' He scowled at his foot, then looked up smiling at Alan. 'Better try and get the splinter out.'

He sat on the ground and bent his foot lotus-wise on to his thigh, then crooked it out to one side and twisted it up in his hand, with the comical vitality of a preening starling in search of an elusive

152

flea, but the splinter was in the outer side of his left foot, and could not be reached. Alan looked at his watch again, suspecting delaying tactics. Donnie's youthful disregard for the possible distressing future consequences of present delights was similar enough to his own habit of mind to make him apprehensive. If they both forgot about church there would undoubtedly be wrath in the Morrison household.

'Lean against that rock and I'll see if I can get it out for you,' he offered, exasperated.

It didn't seem likely. He was extremely squeamish about such things, and the way Donnie balanced himself with a hand on his shoulder made it difficult to focus and too easy to tell when he was hurting, because the fingers tightened. The splinter was in fact of impressive size and thus comparatively easy to remove, but it left a bruise and a hole.

'Not much wonder that hurt. It wasn't just the sermon after all. Now, come on.' He got up, disengaging himself with reluctance from the proximity of Donnie's hand and thigh, and began to walk quickly back along the shore. Donnie followed obediently, turning aside sometimes to point out this and that. 'That plant catches wee flies,' he said, indicating the pale rosettes of butterwort in damp hollows, and, 'these flowers got honey in them,' thrusting a blossom of lousewort into Alan's hand and sucking another between his teeth. Then he scrambled down to the shore, and came back with two smooth white stones: 'These shine in the dark if you rub them together,' and he bounded up the hill, returning with a piece of lumpy grey lichen, black underneath. 'That's crotal. It makes brown dye. You don't wear anything with it in if you're going to sea, it will pull you back to the land.'

'Do you believe that?'

'I dunno.'

And he was off again, darting ahead with the grace of Ariel and the earth knowledge of Caliban. He lingered on the rocky point at Skalanish, turning over fragments of sea-urchin tests. 'The blackbacks drop these here to break them. Have you seen them?'

'No. They do sit here to feed, though.'

'You have to watch them at low tide, that's when they catch these. Look, Alan!' He handed over an empty urchin, perfect except for a neat hole top and bottom.

Alan took it, smiling. His pockets were already full of stones and feathers. He turned the delicate pink and mauve shell gently to avoid brushing away the spines.

'I've learned more about this place in an hour with you than in nine months by myself,' he said, wistfully. It was true, but the sentiment behind the statement was as independent of fact as the comparison of one's love to a red, red rose.

'Me? I don't know anything.' But his unaffected surprise changed to wondering delight as their eyes met. 'There's a lot on Rona,' he said, excited. 'Can we go there in the boat?'

'Yes.' Alan turned with an effort towards the house, glancing at his watch again. In a few minutes Donnie would be gone. It seemed as unthinkable as losing his shadow.

Donnie reclaimed his jacket, which had dried, and his boots, which had not. 'The sky looks good,' he said hopefully. 'We'll get out in the boat tomorrow.' And he set off home at a run.

Alan watched him out of sight with that obscure sense of exquisite yearning which had hitherto in his life been elicited only by sails and blue sea.

Chapter 17

Eleanor's prediction proved correct. Summer began that Monday. Alan spent the morning invalidating the ingenious closing devices which had accrued over the years to his classroom windows. He had slept very little the previous night and incongruities hovered about his mind in dreamlike irresolution. It was inexplicably odd that he should be balancing on the hot radiator pressed against this smeary glass which deadened the shimmering sea and sky. It was quite extra-ordinary that a dozen other overheated people were confined in that stifling room, who addressed him as sir and did more or less what he told them to. Most strange, Donnie was one of them: no different – quieter – a bit smaller.

'Sandy says could I finish off his box, sir,' had been his only words that day.

154

Alan glanced at the dark head bent over Sandy's box. It was totally unremarkable. Every head in the room was similarly thatched, except for Crabbit's which was mohawked. How had it happened? What on earth *had* happened? His hammer screeched unpleasantly on the glass. He turned his attention back to the three floor brads which were the last security of the rickety casement. Pincers would be better. The handles were cool for a moment and then slippery with sweat. A gull banked close to the window, dark eye and tucked-in feet. He remembered. Was that true, or this? The back of Donnie's head was still indistinguishable from Sandy's. The last rusty brad sheared. He wrenched the catch and thrust with his shoulder. The casement gave, trailing dingy webs of classroom detritus, and sweet blue air flooded in with the clamour of courting gulls and the freshness of tangle at low tide. The cool draught lifted Donnie's hair and he looked round, smiling. Only when Alan turned from the sea to answer his smile did he realise that he had perceived the cat's-paw ruffling of glossy black and the sudden beauty of his eyes without use of sight.

The day passed slowly then. How could the hands of a clock, the dazzling sun, the clumsy fingers and thick heads move so leadenly? But the last lesson in the afternoon he had free. He thought he would sneak down to the shore (a forbidden diversion) and leant out of the window to see if Jock was about. He got no further. The morning had enchanted the dirty glass and ravaged paint: time tumbled over itself and the final bell rang.

Donnie followed Mairi down the path. Their friends teased them if they walked it together. She waited for him once the bus was out of sight.

'You'll catch it, boy,' she said, shaking her head. She had a new haircut, all spiky on top, with long bits at the back.

'Ay.' Donnie tried to sound as if he didn't care, but he couldn't help a glance at the house.

'Where were you this morning anyway?'

'Round the lambs.'

'How did you not come in?'

'No bloody likely. I'd have got sent to Rona for the week.'

'I thought you liked it there.'

'It's all right.' His eyes flickered westwards to Skalanish. 'I wonder did Murdo go.'

'I'm sure. Someone would have to. He'll skin you when he gets back, I'm telling you. He was fair raving this morning.'

'Ach, he's always raving about something.'

By unspoken agreement, they took a roundabout path along the burn, to prolong talking time. They did not speak to each other in front of other members of the family.

'He won't like leaving the girlfriend for a week,' Mairi said, adding with a giggle, 'scared Cameron gets his hands on her.'

Donnie scowled. 'She was going with him first anyway. What she doing with Murdo?'

'Playing the pipes.' Mairi exploded with mirth. 'You should hear Kirsty about it!'

Donnie's scowl deepened.

'You don't like her, do you?'

'No.'

'Why no?'

He looked at the ground, and at the sea. There was no reason. The first time she came into the classroom he had turned cold.

'Well, I like her,' said Mairi, decisively. 'She got a smashing figure. Hope he marries her.'

Donnie snorted, though the prospect of a terrifying sister-in-law was hardly borne in on him: it was her disloyalty to Alan that filled him with indignation.

They were almost at the back door. Ben and Tess bounded up to them. Donnie looked uneasily for his father and retribution. He caught Mairi's arm.

'I'm off,' he said.

'What, again? You better not, boy.'

'You tell them. I'll be back to do the lambs last thing.'

Mairi eyed him curiously. 'Where you going then?'

'Sailing.'

'What about peat? Mam's been out all day – she'll be mad.'

'I'll do it tomorrow – the rest of the week.'

'Oh, will you now! They'll be glad to hear it.'

'I'm going anyway. I said to Alan.'

156

Mairi laughed. 'Alan, eh? You've got very friendly!' She sounded surprised: and envious.

Donnie blushed, and fled, with such speed that he almost didn't hear his father shouting after him.

'Let's go over to Stac an Fladday,' said Alan.

Conditions were perfect. The steady breeze was bowing a gentle five knots on the beam, from just south of east, and they had half an hour or so of fairly slack water to negotiate the fearsome reefs between Skalanish Island and the Fladday channel. On the way home the falling tide would have made that region too perilous. They would tack back along the channel to Kilmory Bay, and make a dead run to Skalanish Point. There was a narrow but clear passage marked on the chart, and Alan had tested it out returning from Vatasgeir. The triangulation point on Gormul lined up nicely with an ogre-headed boulder on the pass between Gnipadale and Skalanish. Alan explained all this to Donnie as they were getting the boat ready. His eyes widened in consternation.

'Never mind,' said Alan hastily, 'it'll all be perfectly clear when we do it. I'm going back to get an anchor from the loft in case we want it. You finish rigging her.'

He had forgotten that for Donnie a chart might as well be written in Sanskrit, and that triangulation probably sounded like some humiliating ordeal invented by Mr Morrison the tight-lipped maths teacher. But as for rigging, it was done and correctly in the couple of minutes it took to go up to the house and back. He had had it explained only once: but because the demonstration of hanking the luff to the forestay and shackling the sheet to the clew cringle had been patient he would never forget either the terms or the actions. Alan had noticed in the classroom that his memory was incredibly retentive if things were done peacefully, but if snapped at he became as stupid as people generally took him for.

'Well done!' Alan rummaged in the sail bags, divided between delighted surprise at the boy's engaging keenness and tantalising preoccupation with the new and unused spinnaker. He scanned the just-emerging litter of rocks, considering potential broaches.

'I think we'd better leave it till the way back,' he said, regretfully.

Still it was a fine sail. Donnie had not been out for six weeks, but he had forgotten nothing.

'You hardly need to be taught. You've got it in your bones,' said Alan, happy to see him slither inboard unprompted as they entered the lee of Skalanish Island. It was true. His instinct was perfect: he moved and thought with the boat, alert to every tilt and tremor.

Once through the skerries, the breeze freshened slightly. They headed down for Stac an Fladday, a crooked black thumb of rock standing free of the cliffs at the north tip of the parent island. A snow of white bird bodies drifted round it. The distant quarrels and lovesongs of the nesting ledges came and went between the soft regular hisses of the low swells, each falling from the blunt scow hull in a sparkling rhythm of bubbles wisping the glass-green water. The white main with its red emblem dipped and breathed against the blue sky, as vital and nonchalant as the soaring birds. The boat had come alive. They looked at each other once in silent recognition of her life which they shared, and had no need to look or speak again.

The dark bulk of the stac grew with every surge, and the confusion of bird-sound resolved into identifiable voices. Kittiwakes shouted vigorously from their guano-splashed ledges. Jostling razorbills growled and churred under the shady overhangs on the landward side. As they neared, a few black guillemots scattered from the water with whirring wings and frantic scarlet feet, and shags flipped over, bobbed up again, and took off with a reptilian creak and rattle. Fulmars coasted by on straight silent wings, observing them with intelligent eyes. The stac was a small one, unimpressive by ornithological standards, less than a hundred feet high; but it reverberated with such intense and urgent life, with such sounds and movements of triumph and longing, that a wordless awe fell on them. There was nowhere to land, but a steep slide of gigantic boulders falling off into the glassy water on the lee side indicated possible holding ground. And a possible reef: they were moving too fast. Alan intended to say, 'Get the jib down' and found he hadn't, so intrusive did it seem to speak; but a glance was enough. Donnie had it down and they turned up into what was left of the wind. The great squared blocks were visible beneath, emerald-green and many-faceted till the dusk of the bottom engulfed them. The light anchor dropped fish-bright, trailing bubbles.

The sloping brow of the cliff above was home to the fulmars. A dozen or so sat on their nests, patient and proud, turning their gentle heads to preen or to adjust the sparse tussocks of campion and sea pink to better effect. They had odalisque dark eyes, soft and beautiful. Their mates flew in and out, touching bills and bowing heads with affectionate courtesy. One pair nestled side by side, making love with infinite tenderness, their white necks arching in balletic grace, but with such joy that their very beauty seemed an expression of mutual giving. Alan had watched the blackbacks and herring gulls mating on Skalanish Point, and had smiled and yet been touched by their wholeheartedness. But these birds were different. He felt that if he had been alone he would have wept: or perhaps he would not have noticed. Being with Donnie, he sat still and shaken, blinking at half-remembered fragments: in a mutual flame, single nature's double name – he grinned at himself for being such an idiot. In a boat in a screaming sea bird colony – the white spouses laid bill to bill in an arcane gesture of offering and acceptance. If this be magic, let it be an art lawful as eating. Total irrelevance! Mere visual association: that bit of regurgitated fish head sticking out under a round white breast had started it perhaps.

Donnie touched his hand and relevance surged electrically up his arm. The dinghy rocked. Donnie looked startled, even offended at the unseamanly movement: Alan recalled Selena's unsatisfactory toerail. 'Sorry!' he said, laughing. When is a fulmar not a fulmar? Donnie too had a gentle tilt of the head, characteristic when he wanted to communicate something which mattered to him.

'I just meant had you seen these?' he said, pointing to a shadowy vertical crevice just above them, nearer than the fulmars.

Alan's eyes adjusted from the golden westering sunlight and the white birds. He saw first the pale nest-heaps of bleached tangle, and then the dark incumbents against the dark rock, long necks watchfully raised, bills up in frozen postures of apprehension. The nearest shag was not twenty feet away. They could see the membrane flicking up and down on its turquoise eye, and the yellow skin pouch under the mandible filling and sagging with anxious breath.

'Poor things!' said Donnie, softly.

As quietly as possible, they weighed anchor and left, catching a lucky breath of fainting wind.

'They're nervous, that kind,' said Donnie, when they were out of the lee. 'Maybe it's because people shoot them.'

'Do people shoot them? Why?'

'To eat.'

'Eat *shags*?'

'Yes. They're all right – well, I mean as – as good as anything else like that— '

Alan smiled at his confusion.

'You take the helm. The wind's dying. See what you can catch.'

It increased again as they tacked out of Kilmory Bay. There was more south in it than before.

'Good,' said Alan, remembering the spinnaker. 'We don't want it dead astern. Point as high as you can till we clear Vatasgeir: don't forget the tide. Then bear away and I'll see if I can get this thing up.'

Donnie kept his course and adjusted the kicking-strap at arm's length without prompting and did the right things with the spinnaker guy.

'You're incredible!' Alan said, and other remarks like it, in a combinative euphoria of infatuated sentimentality and manly admiration. And though much affected by these expressions, so that his eyes shone and his cheeks burned, Donnie continued to do exactly what he should, responsive to the tidal eddies and the light shifts of the gently freshening breeze. Soon the hull lifted and sang, and soon after that Donnie was singing too, in an undertone, but recognisably Mairi's song of the evening on the hill.

Alan leant his head back to listen. 'What's that you're singing?'

He stopped at once. 'It's called *Calum Sgaire*.'

'How does it go?'

'Och – I can't sing.'

'Yes, you can. Eleanor says you can.'

'I could when I was a wee lad.'

'You can now you're a big lad too. Go on.'

'No, ask someone else.' But he laughed, and pushed Alan's shoulder with a new and intimate disrespect. After a minute he began to sing, and in no cracked adolescent monotone. His voice was a flexible Celtic tenor, well-breathed and confidently phrased; and the melody he sang of the most bittersweet Celtic beauty. After a few verses a wave jarred the highest note and

rolled the boat, and he laughed and said, 'That's enough – I should
be watching for that.'

'So should I.' But he felt curiously drunk. The breeze and the light
swells and the humming rigging were no longer in his power. Their
pattern was webbed into the evening of white wings and bird calls,
of islands floating in a gold and opal sea, of inter-reflected sea and
sky. Rousing from the enchantment, he fiddled unnecessarily with
the spinnaker guy.

'It's drawing well,' he remarked. 'What's your song about, then?'

'Och, I dunno, it's a Lewis song. About a sailor is coming
home I think. It is the places he passes on the way.'

'It doesn't sound like turn left at the lighthouse.'

Donnie looked bashful. 'It's a love song I suppose,' he admitted.

Boys of sixteen do not utter the word love without embarrassment.
Alan eyed him sideways with tender amusement. It was enough that
he had chosen to sing it.

Donnie gave a sudden gasp and startle.

'What— ' Alan began – '*No!*'

He ducked as the boom crashed across, braking it with a hand,
but too late. The mast shuddered fearsomely, the shrouds howled,
the boom dipped. He flung himself outboard, with his heel behind
the tiller. The boom swung back obediently and he slid into the
helmsman's place.

'The spinnaker's snagged round the forestay. Get it down and
keep the jib out,' he said, between his teeth. He was shaking violently
and couldn't think why. It wasn't grief for the new spinnaker: it was
probably intact anyway, as it wasn't trailing.

He winced at the sight of Donnie on the rounded foredeck.
The evening calm seemed placid no longer. Dark rocks loomed
to either side. Tidal eddies sucked at the hull and disappeared
with sinister speed.

Alan had never been more than enjoyably frightened at sea before,
and now he felt sick: on a tranquil spring evening in his own boat. He
was absolutely furious.

'Why on *earth* did you do that?' he asked with gritty emphasis,
as Donnie settled amidships.

'There was a rock.' His voice was schoolboy sullen.

'Where?'

161

'Straight ahead. Off where that big seal was.'

Alan hadn't noticed the seal. 'There are no rocks that aren't showing by this state of the tide. Not on the chart, anyway.'

'There is, then.'

Silence.

'You should never— '

'I know!'

'Keep that boom out!'

He stretched his right arm to do so, and since his left was already doing duty for a whisker-pole, began to sniff, being without a hand to wipe his eyes.

Alan was appalled. 'Oh, God, I'm sorry. It was my fault – you couldn't be expected to know.'

Donnie's shoulders heaved.

Alan reached out his free hand and withdrew it, anguished. A fast dinghy is an unsuitable venue for emotional scenes, but discretion almost failed him.

'Please don't cry!' was all he could say.

Donnie gulped. 'There *was* a rock, Alan.'

'All right.'

'There was!'

'Yes. O.K. – you could have given a shout, though. If I'd been knocked out – I know you can handle the boat, you could get home yourself, probably, but – I mean if we'd capsized in those eddies, you wouldn't – you can't swim, can you?'

'No. You don't believe me.'

Since he didn't and tactful evasions were obviously unavailing, he said nothing. Donnie sighed: more of a whine than a sigh.

A strange thought occurred to Alan.

'Donnie! Is it – like you found those nests?'

'What d'you mean?'

'I don't know – I mean you just knew the rock was there? You didn't actually see it?'

'I couldn't see it. The sails was in the way.' He sounded justifiably peevish about it.

'Well!'

He turned his head as Alan laughed.

162

'I am awfully sorry, really. I'd forgotten you Borerayans can see through things. It could be very useful. Come on, you take the helm again.'

'I don't want to.'

'Yes, or you'll lose your nerve.' He caught his outstretched arm and pulled it back to the tiller, settling the hand under his own. Donnie's was cold and blood-drained. His own palm was warm: there might have been Rodolfo-like sentiments expressed if the boom hadn't been swaying. He slid forward and steadied it.

He was disconcerted, not only by the risk of drowning his crew, but by the novel experience of its mattering so much. It was not pleasant to find a normal responsibility causing such incapacitating nervousness. If he didn't get used to it he might really drown him.

'I'll have to teach you to swim, anyway,' he said.

'All right.'

And how he was going to handle a naked Donnie in the water when the boy's merest touch made him dizzy was another problem.

Neither spoke again till they had got the boat ashore and were dumping the loose gear in the shed.

'Coming out again tomorrow?' The casual question belied a growing anxiety: perhaps he had been put off.

Donnie looked downcast. 'No, I got to go to peat. Probably most of this week.'

'That's a pity.'

He added hesitantly, 'Murdo's away. I'll not be in school either.'

There was silence while they both considered this with dismay.

Alan had a bright idea. 'I'll give you a hand with peat tomorrow – in fact every evening – oh hell! There's Eleanor tomorrow, but I can get away by six or half past.' He continued as a sop to decency, 'If I help, they might let you off for a sail by Friday.'

'Och, you wouldn't want to bother with that, Alan.' But his eyes were hopeful.

'Yes! Where will you be working?'

'Ours is above Roddy's croft. His is below the road and then we go on to Lal's.'

'Right.'

'That's great!' He hopped up and down with delight and pivoted on Selena's stocks. 'See you tomorrow then.'

*   *   *

It was the muddiest week of Alan's life and one of the happiest. Each afternoon he joined five or six neighbours on one or other of the crofts, working backwards along the slippery sulphur-smelling banks of peat, slicing slab after black slab with rhythmic thrusts of the iron *teasgair*. There was little talking at work, but earthy banter when people came and went, and convivial pauses for food and drink. That the empty containers were jettisoned in the bog was a matter of regret to Alan; his liberally educated conscience suffered from keeping quiet on that point; but everyone was so good-natured, so intent on giving him the best iron, the least-sloping bank, the first can of beer, that the reservation faded from his index of neighbourly virtues.

They worked in pairs, one cutting on top of the bank, and the other braced in the oozy ground below to catch the weighty slabs as they fell from the iron and throw them beyond the cutter onto the heather. Whoever Alan started work with, somehow, in minutes, it was Donnie who was standing below him: one shy smile of greeting, and then silence and a bent back for the rest of the session. His looked the harder task. The sodden heavy peats had to be cast above head-height, well out beyond the bank, and without overlapping. On the first occasion, noticing the cruel wrench of the farthest-out slabs on his slight body, Alan jumped down beside him.

'Change places. My arms are longer.'

But he shook his head in wordless deprecation.

Why not?'

'I'll change if the grownups go before we finish,' he muttered.

Alan took the hint. Two hints: one, that the lower-status task was throwing – women and youngsters squelched in the bog, while men and strangers kept their dignity above; two, delightfully, that he was no longer classed as a grownup. He no longer felt like one; in fact, he never really had.

The grownups went. Each evening Alan and Donnie worked on after them into the luminous dusk, keeping the same steady rhythm of cutting and throwing, but released by solitude into talk and laughter, silly private jokes and limitless curiosity about each other's past and present, likes and dislikes. Their dissimilarity of age and background was no barrier, rather a gateway. The most mundane circumstance of

164

the other's life filled each of them with a simple wonder, which mercifully there was no one there to laugh at. Donnie, shy and excited by turns, talked about his brothers and sisters (so many in such a small house: Dad had meant to do it up, but never would now, he was ill and the family had gone mostly), about his first day at school, about the right way to strain a fence and how to deliver a breech-first calf, and what a good dog Ben would be for the hill. Alan countered with his father's desertion, a pain he was glad to share for the first time; with definitions (compared and contrasted) of opera and orchestra, with descriptions of foreign places, of climbing and skiing, and of course, most of all, sailing. By Saturday evening the biographical infill was almost complete, only a figleaf of reticence remaining to veil the present. Donnie was too innocent to know what they were hiding; but he grew wistful as he cut the last sections, listening to Alan's account of a double knockdown in the Irish Sea.

'Och, Alan, you've done everything,' he said, softly. 'Been everywhere too. Why did you want to come to a place like this?'

Alan, crouching to take the lowest cut, smiled up at him. 'I've never been happier.'

'That's funny. It's not much of a place.'

The last block of peat flopped across Alan's wrists. They washed the teasgair and their hands in a stream, and lingered, stretched out in the sweet-smelling young heather.

'You really like it here, then?' asked Donnie, wonderingly.

'Yes – not for good: but now.'

Now was snipe drumming in the pellucid sky, lambs bleating on the croft below; an iridescent blue beetle striving through the moss; benevolent Venus hanging above the shoulder of the hill, and the joyful scent of growing things.

Alan had had a week's practice at keeping his hands to himself and his tongue under control, but he had not learned not to look or smile. Donnie's clear eyes looked back at him, candid and happy; there was nothing in his experience or expectations to cloud that frankness. They lay at a little more than arm's length in the heather, gazing in delight and silence while Venus sank behind the hill and the moon rose over Rona. There was no one there to be scandalised by their gravity: the grownups were at home preparing for the Sabbath.

Donnie started at last and leapt to his feet.

'I better get back. I forgot it's Saturday.'

But when they reached his door he hesitated. 'I'll walk down with you, Alan.'

'No.' Alan put the teasgair into his hands. 'Go on in, or you'll be in trouble. Come and see me tomorrow, if they'll let you out.'

'I'll come.'

Alan walked on, healthily tired, and happy enough to burst. Mairi's song – Donnie's song – moved in his mind in cadences of longing and fulfilment, not an opposition but a harmony. He remembered – it seemed a long time ago – the Mozart larghetto which had so offended Eleanor, and how Donnie's eyes had haunted it. Not much wonder she had been offended. The thought of Eleanor was uneasy. It didn't linger long with him: there were plenty more thoughts to think about Donnie. He thought as many as he could in a mile and a half, till the still-rosy twilight with its edge of lunar silver took its beauty from that human face, and the whole world turned to pastoral, and pastoral to the secret of the universe. Alan had read very widely, but though his heart was easily touched, he had not had occasion to apply any of it till now. He applied all of it, with rapture. The rapture was no less real because he had done his homework; only the practicalities had not been gone into. A grownup could have told him that; to deaf ears. He bounded along the flowery path with his thoughts running from Donnie to Dante, to Florizel and Perdita and 'Carmina Burana'. *Mout a dur cuer qui en may n'aime.* He forgave his father and mother and even Harold, and there was not a grain of practicality in his head.

As he breasted the last rise above the stream he heard women's voices, chatter and laughter. Roddy's girls must be out late, in spite of the coming Sabbath. It pleased him to think of these dark-haired slender beauties playing in the long spring dusk. *Ludunt super gramina virgines decore.* Looking round for them, he was startled by a sudden explosion of wings. A group of hoodies erupted from the bank of the stream. One perched on the old ruins with a roguish laugh, its neck stretching in comic silhouette against the glowing sky.

'Hallo, you're up late,' Alan said, and cawed back at it. It hobbled a few crone's paces and flapped away up the darkening glen. He turned home, smiling, in good humour with the birds and the world.

Down by the stream, he almost trod on the thing that had kept the crows awake. It was what he had often heard about but never seen. They had pecked a lamb's eyes and tongue out. With an involuntary gasp of horror, Alan backed from it. In the fading light he could not see if its frail ribs moved. He touched, with flinching hand. It was warm, but still. The innocent white curls were rape-red, the weak muzzle ravaged and dumb. He straightened up, and looked round for the ewe, but there was no other sheep in sight. He remembered then that he had noticed a miserable hunched lamb all alone that morning as he set out; and the previous afternoon he had hurried past one, it must have been the same one, and maybe the afternoon before too. With growing distress, he looked again at the limp body. It had two black legs and two white. He had seen it in its birth-blood, by the fence, ten days before: on that day. It was dead now, and he could have saved it, if he had had room in his thoughts for anything but Donnie.

His mind glanced at the paradox, love and its corollary, and shied away. He was afraid. He fetched a spade and buried the thing, and washed the spade and put it back in the shed. The house door stood open, blackness beyond it. He did not want to go in. He did not want to stay out.

Chapter 18

Week followed week of long northern sunlight, flat seas and light easterly winds, a magical interlude in the harsh island year. Lambs grew fat and woolly and played king-of-the-castle on rocky outcrops. A corncrake skulked in the rough growth of nettles and yellow flags among the old ruins: it rasped day and night in hypnotic self-satisfaction, escalating to frenzy when the evening calm rendered a neighbouring bird on Roddy's croft audible. Above Skalanish Island the air sparkled with the vibrant wings and voices of many terns, and the first common seal pups appeared, reproachful-eyed in the incoming tide. The otter with her two growing cubs, whose tracks Donnie had noticed on their first excursion from the den, played and fished every day off the point where the blackbacks dropped their urchins. As the kingcups faded, orchids sprang up as thick as bluebells in an English wood, and later heady meadowsweet filled the lush hollows. There the corncrakes had retired into silent domesticity, and the nights were quiet again.

Donnie was at Skalanish whenever he could escape from the tasks laid on him by his family, and often before they could catch him to state their requirements. To procure leniency, Alan made himself as useful as possible to the Morrisons. The ailing father was glad enough of another strong set of limbs about the place. Increasingly enfeebled, increasingly withdrawn, he took less and less part in the croft business, but the fine weather brought him out to potter aimlessly up and down the fences, stopping now and again to test a post for rigidity, for the sake of seeming to do something; or standing hands in pockets to watch the young men at work. Alan knew that he had been a strong vigorous man in his prime, that in his courting days he had rowed the swirling passage to Rona, still inhabited then by one family, to visit Mairi Anna, three times a week, summer and winter: he had heard that from Lal. There was nothing to show it now, in the grey, lined face and sagging shoulders. Alan felt sorry for him, but disliked the inhibiting surveillance, the impassivity which seemed like a silent mockery of youth and love. But gradually, Angus's daily greeting changed, from 'Good day to you, Mr Cameron,' to 'Ay, ay, Alan': and one morning, after a more than usually long and irritating scrutiny (they were clearing rock for the foundation of a new byre), to 'Well, Alan, you're putting muscle on that lad of mine.'

Surprised, Alan looked him in the eye, and for the first time saw a flicker of what had been, and bewilderment and loss. He stammered – something: there was nothing of comfort to say. He swung the sledgehammer down, pityingly aware of his own strength and youth. Angus went in. Donnie, heaving on a crowbar, straightened up, wiping sweat from his brows with the back of his wrist.

'Is that true, Alan?'

'What?' For once, Alan's attention was not on him.

'What my father said. Am I really getting bigger?'

His eyes were hopeful. Alan laughed then, feeling more like crying from very tenderness.

'Yes.'

His neck and shoulders had knit, and his chest deepened.

White rock-dust accentuated the new sculptured hardness of his upper arms. But the light fan of ribs was still childish, lifting with a sudden drag on the navel when Alan said what he wanted to hear. He was growing taller, too. Alan stood close for a second, the boy's hair brushing his chin.

'You were only up to my shoulder last September,' he said, picking up the hammer again. He could not look any longer.

Mairi Anna also gradually unbent towards Alan. At the time when he had come to plead for Donnie and sailing, he had found her formidable, a big, straight-backed, straight-mouthed woman, black-browed and hawk-nosed, with hawk-pale eyes. It was difficult to see in her the winning beauty of her youngest children: but sometimes, when Donnie was tired and yet stubbornly attentive to something he would not give up – at the end of that backbreaking day with the crowbar, or drenched and tense on the trapeze on a too-windy, too-late evening sail – he had the look of his mother. That enabled Alan to see in her face her history: hard work, little means, no complaint. If there was no softness either, it was not to be wondered at. She was generous; almost every day he went home with eggs or crowdie or fresh baking. As for old Johane, the grandmother, almost deaf, almost blind, full of wrinkles and chuckles – if she were by she would catch her daughter-in-law's arm: 'Oh well, well, give him more Mairi Anna, give him more! He's a big lad,' and turning then to him, patting his hand, 'Och, it's time you got a wife, *ma tha*!' If he gave her his arm up to the road, she was all the way bubbling with laughter and old woman's teasing, and he would not get out of her house without she made good the imagined deficiency of Mairi Anna's hospitality. Her companions were her cat and her cow. She sang to them on her stool in the field at milking time, in a thin cracked voice, pausing with a chuckle and a shake of the head. 'Oh well, well! Where is the song now, eh? Mairi will sing it. Donnie will sing it.' Sometimes they did. Alan grew to know it well enough to sing it too:

> *Il a bholagain il bho m'aghan,*
> *Il a bholagain il bho m'aghan,*
> *Il a bholagain il bho m'aghan,*
> *Mo chrodh laoigh air gach taobh an abhainn.*

The cow wouldn't give her milk without a song. She preferred

169

a woman's voice, though she would stand for Donnie. But when they tried to give Alan a milking lesson, she turned her head with an earsplitting moo and snaked her tongue round a mouthful of his hair.

It was good to be with them all. Only old Effie muttered against him, malign in her chair by the fire, which had to be lit for her even on the hottest days. In another setting she might have crossed herself at his entry, or spat against the evil eye. She was the oldest remnant of grim Rona. Her grandfather Donald Cam had been one of the young men driven with their families from fertile Fladday, towing their few cattle behind the boats, when the landlord had taken their land for sheep. None of the Morrison family would have been unmannerly enough to tell that to Alan, who was so obviously in voice and looks one of the oppressors' race: but Eleanor told him, with some satisfaction.

And there was Murdo. Murdo ignored him, with silent resentment. How deep it went was difficult to tell.

'He's like that with everyone, Alan,' Donnie said, apologetically. 'He never open his mouth to me last week.'

Whatever Murdo's feelings about Alan's intimacy with the family and Eleanor, he availed himself of the gains in his own time by joining up with the *Maid of Rona*. Do'l Alex thanked Alan. 'You sent me a crew, lad. No room for the two of youse in Gnipadale!' He slapped his back, with a bellow of laughter. 'You better not be giving that girl up! But you should come out with me yourself some day – some evening Murdo's with the lady, eh?'

He made the suggestion several times, but Alan, remembering the lobsters, always managed to find some excuse. There was potato-hoeing and haymaking. There were incessant fanks: gatherings, dippings, shearing and marking. Donnie protected him from anything nasty, though; he never saw castration or ear-punching or the AI man's assault on the grandmother's friendly brown cow.

When they were free, they sailed and swam, basked like seals on offshore islands, and wandered in the wild expanses of moor and sand to the west, usually with Ben lolloping beside them. They were so much together and so anxious to please one another that sometimes in the first weeks there was nothing left to talk about; and then each grew timid, fearing the other's interest waning, till a shy meeting of glances made things right again. As summer wore on, these uneasy hiccups subsided, so that they could be happily mute for hours, without awareness either of silence or of time passing. Then both might speak at once, commenting on the same fantastically shaped cloud or the same bird overhead, and there would be shared wonder and laughter at the coincidence; afterwards deeper silence, and both adrift in it. But often Donnie would not be quiet at all, not for a minute, any more than the young gulls jostling on the rocks, not even if Alan told him to shut up and threatened to push him head down in a peat hag. He was full of questions. He knew every inch of his native area, every white vein in the grey rock, every grassy hollow in the heather, the otter slides and eel pools and which nests the cuckoo visited, yet he craved definitions and particularities of what he could point to but not name. Alan got books out and read him the details of spotted redshank, creeping salix, calcareous algae, snakelocks anemone. He forgot most of it himself immediately: but he could apply to Donnie next day, who nearly always remembered, whose starved mind devoured information like that of a child of five; who wanted to know, when Alan and Ben had slumped in a chair after a long day in the open, how to set a saw, or tie a Turk's head, or take a flute to bits.

He was fascinated by Alan's music.

'You're the most gratifying audience.' Alan had been warming up the instrument on the cave music from *The Magic Flute* before applying himself to the unpleasant piece of Poulenc Eleanor had decreed for the next week.

'That's like – ' Donnie wriggled in the thyme and daisies, excitement in his eyes. 'It's like – ' He broke off, looking down and frowning, then laughed and said, 'Play it again,' turning on his back with his arms behind his head.

Alan played it again. 'What's it like?' he asked, afterwards, but the only answer he got, and that unwilling, was 'Like things you hear sometimes.'

To which he replied that the next thing he would hear, he would certainly hope never to have to hear again. Alan detested Poulenc, and was certain beyond reasonable doubt that that was Eleanor's chief motive for the choice. They grated on each other increasingly. She was puzzled by his sudden interest in crofting affairs, but not

171

pleased by it. She suspected condescension and sentimentality; when he accepted these misaccusations with ill-concealed relief, she was even more puzzled and even less pleased. Alan knew she resented his easy infiltration into the Morrison household, and pitied her accordingly. He was aware that he was, in a way, poaching on her preserve. She, who so much desired to be part of the community in which she saw all social virtue, had found it less easy. Murdo was not a pleasant route. She did not – could not, surely – love him, and yet, perversely, she had chosen this veritable via dolorosa as an entry to that world. Still, residual feminist independence, if no tenderer feeling, kept her determinedly attached to Alan, as to the wearing of trousers and the drinking of spirits. Such immodest insistences were anathema to Murdo's mother, and, presumably, to Murdo; though what went on behind that narrow shut face with its opaque slate-grey eyes was anyone's guess.

As for Alan, he would have been glad enough to be relinquished, at least for most purposes. Eleanor had her uses: he was succeeding in treating Donnie with Socratic purity, but that left something to catch up on. He was ashamed of degrading her to a sexual machine, but not so ashamed that a combination of healthy lust and growing personal animosity could not produce justification; because after all that was also how she used him, while maintaining a more decorous role with Murdo.

She intended to be away for most of the summer holidays, but in the event they quarrelled before she left. He was disrespectful about Poulenc. She tossed her head and called him a tiresome brat. He was abjectly conciliatory then in case she would send him home without what he had come for; but she was already looking at her watch and declaring a babysitting engagement. He felt relieved in a way, because if he managed to hitch a lift back there would be time to call in for Donnie and go for a sail. He glanced with momentary equanimity at her tense, decisively-waisted back as she pushed music away, and began to whistle as he gathered his own things together. That was calculated to annoy her: first, because she disapproved of whistling (a sloppy habit) and second, because she regarded that same melody which was like nothing Donnie could name as a self-betraying but not isolated triviality on the composer's part.

'You're very gay today,' she said, sourly.

Alan's pulse raced with alarm. 'Mind your language, Eleanor,' he said, pulling her round by the hips, and kissing her hard: as he did so noticing in her eyes that even such a crude double meaning was too double for someone of such obstinate literality, and then forgetting everything except the need to get her trousers down as quickly as possible. She seemed as ready as he was: but at a most critical moment she pushed him off violently, and sat up with knees folded. Alan stared at her, speechless with shock at this indignity.

'I don't like sweaty heaving performances,' she said, icily, though her face was still flushed. 'You're altogether too randy these days.'

He was furious, because it was true. 'You ill-natured bitch!' He grabbed her arms, with what intention he could not afterwards decide, perhaps merely to avert the coming slap in the face. It did not. She hit him hard several times and stalked out of the room.

Her recollected exit saved Alan from total humiliation: as, unlike him, she had shed all her clothes, her shapely nakedness would have rescued her dignity, except that her perspiring backside had picked up a rash of blue fluff from the rug. She had been sweating and heaving too. By the time he reached home, on foot, skulking from prospective lift-givers, he was beginning to find it funny. He couldn't quite face Donnie, though. He presumed the affair with Eleanor was over, and felt on the whole relieved; but he wished he hadn't handled her roughly, and that he had been kinder in general. He had exploited her really, just as she always claimed about men. Perhaps not kinder, kindness would have infuriated her; more honest.

But even Alan could see that this time honesty had not been an option. He sighed. The vague sensation of guiltiness had not disappeared entirely with Eleanor.

There was a note on the kitchen table: *Dear Alan, Your Mum was ringing Roddys she wants you fone tomorow I finished that varnshing hope you had a nise time   Yours, Donnie.*

Yours, Donnie. He smiled and forgot about Eleanor for the next six weeks.

Donnie was his, body and soul. As far as the body went, the boy's imagination extended only to daydreams of rescuing his idol from burning buildings or throwing himself in the way of an assassin's bullet. He had seen such things on television. He remembered, searched for, and pored over by night a storybook about David and Jonathan which Alex Angus had had as a Sunday school prize. It was very affecting, but not instructive on other than heroic matters. Not that Donnie was looking for instruction. He knew about sex: it was what happened between rams and ewes, bulls and cows (if they were lucky enough to escape the AI man), and Johane and her boyfriend in the byre. The outcome was birth, in a mess of blood and shit. Its attraction was minimal and its relevance nil.

It did not seem strange to him to worship Alan. He came from a society abundant in elder brothers and young uncles, whose brawny chests and capacity for drams were the boast of their young adherents, and whose rough good nature made men out of little boys. There had been a lonely gap in Donnie's life, a grief and a humiliation, in that his brothers had not stood so to him. At thirteen, when Uncle Ewan died and the workshop days were over, he had followed Murdo forlornly for a time, meek to foul words and blows. But being unwelcomed, his affection soon turned to hatred. To hate his own brother had been a deep secret shame to him, a gnawing worm in his spirit, till the contrast of Alan's gentleness had lent it justification: at which stage it had ceased to matter.

Nor was it strange that such loyalty should be unexpressed by word or gesture. That was a penalty of growing up. Children were kissed and petted, but he was of an age when men scowled in embarrassment if he so much as stroked the cat. He had never seen his father kiss his mother. People shook hands and patted shoulders at funerals, and the more swashbuckling sort of elder brother would punch a boy in the ribs occasionally: but while David and Jonathan might embrace (a word which Donnie took to mean merely 'hug'; the implied kiss was beyond the bounds of probability) such behaviour was plainly outlandish, like circumcision and dancing before the Ark of the Lord, and would certainly not do in Boreray.

So he was content enough, most of the time, to lean against Alan's shoulder to look at the chart, which he couldn't read, or to catch his hand, which being goat-footed he didn't need, in scrambling up slippery rocks: to get close to him when possible, and when not to admire him constantly, in and out of his presence. The long hours of church, family mealtimes, family prayers, any other spell of five

174

minutes upwards when they were apart, he spent in contemplation of Alan. Yet when Mairi nudged him during tea and demanded to know what he was dreaming about, or when his mother scolded him for forgetting half her shopping at the grocery van, he could not have said what had distracted him from passing the jam or asking for Auntie Effie's indigestion tablets. He had a vision, no words: an image in his mind so steadfast that any competitor for his attention was a perplexing intruder. Mairi's sisterly screech in his ear hardly dimmed the gilding sunlight on Alan's untidy curls; her elbow in his ribs caused only a shimmer on that bright reflection, like a breath of wind on a calm pool. He scarcely heard his mother's remonstrances for chasing the lights and shadows on Alan's muscles as he worked at the sawhorse, steady powerful strokes falling easily through his broad shoulders and long arms, a log dropping away, then he would raise his head to speak maybe, pushing his hair out of his eyes. They were sea-blue, startling in his tanned face, and his hair was lighter at the ends in summer than his skin. He was strong, but he was not like other strong men, he never swaggered or shouted like Ewan or Do'l Alex, he wasn't slow or clumsy like Angus Shaw. Every movement was light and easy, as if all life was a game and the only thing that mattered was to enjoy it, not to win. He was never rough to anything, he would jump the veins of seed mussels in the rocks not to crush them and catch a fly or bee off the window in the hollow of his hand to put it out of doors.

Remembering this or that incident, that smile, that tone of voice, Donnie would be drawn by their sequence into definition, description; and lost again in inexpressible delight, the eye of his mind dwelling on every line and tint and movement with wordless love. But because he had no words for it, he did not call it love, or call it anything, or know that there was any other way to see or feel. Alan: he lived and breathed Alan, thinking only that he wanted to be like him. 'I wish I was strong like you,' he said sometimes, with eyes of unremitting ardour; or 'I wish I could swim like you,' or run as fast, or helm as expertly. He never said, 'I wish I looked like you,' though he thought he did wish it; it did not seem a right thing to wish. There were reasons to want to be a head taller and broader and stronger in proportion, but there was not a reason in his world for wanting fair hair rather than dark, or blue eyes rather than grey.

175

And that was not the wish exactly, only he could not discover more clearly what the identification was that he longed for. Wishing it, or wishing something, there at last he came to a doubt, a shadow in the brilliance Alan cast for him: so that sometimes, lying in the grass beside him, scanning his long, tanned body and tangled salt-bleached hair, he was suddenly abashed. If that direct blue gaze turned on him then, he looked away, troubled.

Alan meant to avoid such occasions, but he was not over-conscientious about it. Donnie's adoration was too beguiling. He had never been so unconditionally loved, except by the spaniel he had had for his eighth birthday, whose shortlived affection had made things tolerable in the early days of Harold, till it was ended by the back wheel of a coal-lorry. To bask in such devotion was no common experience, and inevitably it lulled doubts and self-criticism. There seemed to be no graver responsibility attached to it than to accept it gratefully, and give himself up to the present moment.

That would not have been so easy if the present had not been delimited. At the beginning of September, Donnie would go to his brother in Glasgow, not because he had ever wanted to, but because his elders, Alan foremost among them, had decided it was in his interest. If Alan's persuasions had been left till later, so he told himself, they would never have happened. More likely, if things had not been already so arranged, the meeting on the hill on that spring evening would never have happened: or if so, its radiance would never have spread, illumining the here and now, the passionate, piercing present. He was not required to project a future which included Donnie, and had not even thought of trying; but a summer pastoral, fourteen weeks lifted out of time, heightened by the poignancy of anticipated parting – to that he abandoned himself utterly. He accepted the chance of a further term's teaching, wriggled out of Torquil's offer of a trip to the States, telephoned a reproachful Celia to tell her he wouldn't be on the mainland till October, ignored mayday calls from a couple of short-handed racing skippers: and every sleight to stay on Boreray was an intoxicating delight, a further surrender to the novel and absorbing hobby of being in love.

There seemed no reason to be wary. Donnie was as happy as he was, happy with every day as it came, without forebodings about the future or the shadow of past wretchedness. He was growing and blossoming, and in every way open to him he made it clear that it was Alan he thanked for all of it. Alan, proud of that happiness as of something he had brought to birth, was fatally ready to assume that his worth was as he saw it reflected in the other's eyes. He had forgotten how unequally they were matched, that Donnie's youth and simplicity were easily-taken pawns, that when the game was over there would be no restitution. The time limit set for it made it seem safe to play, but the end hazard was incalculable loss.

Chapter 19

'Over you go, boys.'

Roddy cut the engine and Donnie and Sandy slid over the bows, thigh-deep in the surf, to keep her nose from digging into the soft sand. Eager dogs leapt over their shoulders. The girls teetered forward, shrieking and catching at each other as the boat jarred in the surges. Murdo and Lal pushed past them, waded ashore, and strode off up the hill, whistling their dogs.

'Get out there or we'll throw you in – eh Alan?' Roddy gave Mairi a good-natured prod with the boathook. She screamed, loving it, seizing Alan's arm.

'All right, who's first? Come on, Mairi!'

He swung her out and carried her ashore, enjoying her pink cheeks and smiling eyes. Then Morag Ann, more decorous, with a protest or two and a determination, not acted on, to wade: next Dina, a solid little dumpling, jumping into his arms with a whoop of sweetie-tainted breath. Kirsty had hung back, but before he had landed Dina, she had slipped over Donnie's side of the boat, and with a screech and a well-timed slither, and a clinging of arms round his neck, had forced him to heave her ashore. He dropped her unceremoniously, and braced his shoulder again to the prow, scowling. Alan smiled to himself: it was the first time he had noticed sly-eyed Kirsty's preference.

'Oh help, the bags!' Morag Ann waved her arms at her father.

'You're a useless lot, you!' He handed out an assortment of plastic carriers, clanking with beer cans or cloyingly perfumed with girlish necessaries.

'Ach, you would think you were here for a week, with all that rubbish you're carrying!' He threw the last bag to Alan, who narrowly rescued a flying copy of *True Romances*. Sandy scrambled back into the boat and Donnie pushed her off. Roddy would moor at the jetty which lay further round to the north, in a sheltered inlet below the cliffs.

'*Seventeen . . . Jackie . . . True Love . . .*' Alan examined the contents of the carrier, jerking them above Mairi's snatching hands, till Ben leapt at him with a joyful bark, spattering pouting lips and half-closed eyes across the sand. The girls swooped on them, scolding, and turned their backs in a self-conscious hip-tilted huddle. Alan followed Donnie, who was already halfway up the steep hillside above the bay. He waited at the top, perched on a boulder. Alan sat down beside him, grinning when he saw the changed state of affairs on the beach below. The four dark-haired figures were racing along the tideline, pushing and splashing each other. Mairi's skirt was tucked into her pants, Kirsty sported a brief scarlet bikini, and Dina was stark naked. He looked at Donnie to share the joke, but he was squinting under his hand at the higher summit to their right, which plunged off almost sheer into the sea, forming the sombre cliffs which so dominated the seaward view from the south of Boreray.

'You got the glasses, Alan? There's the eagles' eyrie over there, one of the birds has just gone down to it – no, you're looking the wrong way. It's on the land side of the summit.' Crouching behind Alan's shoulder, he pulled the binoculars to the right angle. The nest lay beneath a low crag, with a steep scree under it. The bird, though partly hidden by a rock in front, was apparently tearing at something with its powerful beak.

'What's she eating?'

'Half a lamb. Just as well Murdo not got the gun today.'

'Christ, does he shoot these too?'

'You bet, anything that moves. That lamb's probably been dead a week, anyway.'

Alan passed him the glasses, scanning the island while he studied the eyrie. It was the first time he had been on Rona. There was nowhere to bring the dinghy in except two small shell-sand coves, the one they had started from that day, on the north-west corner, and another in the south, and both were prone to heavy surf and a fierce undertow. They had sailed beneath the awesome northern cliffs several times, always into the wind, with one eye for the tight ranks of auks, excitable as commuters in a rail strike, and the other on the vicious cat's-paws rushing on them from the rock faces. Rona looked grim from the sea, and scarcely less grim from the land. The northern cliffs rounded up into a steep brow of shattered rock and boulder screes, which swept off in a descending spine south-eastwards. The inland side of the ridge dropped in steep terraces and overhangs towards a sort of triangular basin running from an apex below the hill where they sat to the southern shore. It should have been a sheltered fertile pasture, but it was not: already in mid-August, it was faded to acidic russet, speckled with cotton grass and patched with black where the peat was too liquid to support any life at all. At the farthest end, a few small pools and a larger one caught the blue sky; beyond that was the straight line of a boulder beach, and the sea. To the west the land was higher again, more gently sloping, but bald and grey, broken and weathered rock too leached and ancient to nourish anything but lichens. Yet these decayed and desolate slopes were beaded with white strings of moving sheep, where already Lal and Murdo were driving their first flock towards the pens by the jetty.

'What on earth do these poor animals find to eat out here?' The thought brought a sombre memory of winter; he spoke more to himself than to Donnie.

'Very little. But look at Out End now. It's so green – the most of them will be there, if they got through the wall. That's why we got it – the longest walk and the most beasts, so that Murdo can curse me for taking my time.'

There was an unusual bitterness in his voice, which Alan did not care to pursue.

'I thought that was a separate island. Why is it so green?' He looked curiously at the steep emerald whale-back humping from the south-west tip.

'They are saying it is the black rock. It's not like the rock here or on the other islands. There are cliffs on the sea side – they drop right in, just as black as anything.'

179

'Basalt?'

'Yourself will know that.'

He set off with the steady hillman's stride which Alan, in spite of his longer legs, never outpaced. They traversed a shallow saddle, meeting an old drystone wall, which seemed to dip towards the house, fank and jetty. Its grey thread was visible as far as Out End, dividing the dead hillside from the scarcely less deadly valley. It was of impressive size, five or six feet high and three thick. On the far side a dead ram lay half sunk in a stagnant pool, a glimmer of livid skin showing through soggy fleece, jaws worn to bone and pointing skywards between the spiralling horns which lent such nobility to the live beasts.

Donnie glanced at it briefly. 'Lal's,' he said. 'It was an old one. See the teeth.'

Alan did not much want to study the teeth, beseeching Heaven in a grimace of fixed pain.

'Who built the wall, Donnie?'

'Mostly old Effie's grandfather.'

'Your great-great-grandfather, then.'

'Ay. There's another on the far side there, but more broken. No fences in them days: no grants either. Nothing but stone.'

And from these laconic remarks in the dreary wilderness, Alan began to understand what life had been like for Donald Cam, late of green Fladday, who might have lain down to die like the ram outside the wall, but had endured.

Distant whistles and shouts on the ridge opposite made Donnie pause, eyes narrowed against the sun, searching for Roddy's movements. Head up and alert like that, the line of his jaw made his ancestry disconcertingly credible. A dog raced into view below the crags, driving a little knot of sheep up to the skyline. Donnie sprang ahead again, calling back Ben, who had started downhill to join the fun. His voice was as fierce and guttural as the voices opposite: no hint in it of the many times he had sprawled in the grass kissing the dog's nose, with the pink tongue reciprocating. Alan began to feel oppressed by the unyielding starkness of the terrain, and the colour his companion seemed to take from it. Ben, though, was undaunted: he leapt at the boy's bare back, leaving two muddy pawmarks.

'You wee devil!' said Donnie, in his normal tone.

Alan felt encouraged to fish for enlightenment.

'Not much wonder Auntie Effie can't stand me,' he said, as they reached the summit. 'My mother's garden would grow more crops than this whole island, and all she's got in it is roses.'

Donnie's head tilted against the blue sea.

'Och, I would rather roses than a lot of cabbages, Alan,' he said, with a smile of summer, he who could hardly have seen a rose in his life, except maybe the doctor's sweet-scented rugosa hedge in Port Long. There was not much of Rona in him, after all.

Things were better for a bit after that. Donnie kept by his side, telling what he knew about the old days, naming the unfamiliar skerries and islands appearing beyond Fladday, occasionally leaning dangerously over the uncertain edge of the cliffs to point to where the peregrines nested or where he had seen a fight between a raven and a buzzard. The ground sloped downhill towards Out End. Heather appeared and grew more luxuriant, and with it wheatears, very tame, chacking boldly from their favoured perches. Ben chased them, barking, ignoring all recalls.

'Tess doesn't think much of him.' Alan laughed at the older dog's flattened ears and basilisk eye.

'He's all right,' said Donnie, defensively.

'He's useless! I've never seen such an idiotic sheepdog. Look at him now!'

Ben had broken off his chase to roll with flailing legs on some unidentifiable piece of carrion.

'He's not useless. He's got a good outrun.' There was an odd edge in his voice.

Alan glanced at him in surprise, and said hastily, 'Sorry. I don't know anything about it.'

Donnie looked away. He pointed to the deep sandy cove coming into view below them. 'That's the seals' beach.' He had told Alan Rona meant seal island. 'See the green bits going up to the pools behind. That's where they slide up and down. It's all just mud then. They're wallowing in these pools. I've been here and seen them a few times, but the weather's often too bad to get across. It's some sight. I wish you— ' He broke off. His face, which had been eager with recollection, went suddenly blank, like a child's caught out in some naughtiness, before the lie forms.

Alan's heart pinched in dismay. The unspeakable fell between them. In October the grey seals would hump on the mudslides to pup; in October the two of them would be in separate worlds.

Donnie bounded across the nitrogenous swathes of scurvy grass and bladder campion, splashed knee-deep through the wallows, and ran out along the narrow isthmus from which the green back of Out End rose, dotted with watching and wary sheep. He turned there, directing the dogs with harsh cries and gestures; and was off again, leaping up the steep slope. Alan followed, trying not to think.

The next hour or so was all at a run, and by the time they crossed the isthmus again, with the wave of white and meal-coloured backs flowing ahead of them, they were sweat-drenched and winded, with no thought except where to find fresh water. Donnie led the way to a small rivulet trickling down to the seal wallows through the sphagnum. It smelt of sulphur, but it was cold and sweet tasting. After that it was another hot hour's work to drive the flock down through the gap in the old wall and pen them in the fank.

'God, that was tiring.' Alan dragged the hurdle into place. He was, in fact, tired, but he had said it because, pitying the panting unwatered flock, he had turned to mention it to Donnie, and noticed the exhausted pallor beneath his tan. There was nothing pity could do for the beasts, and nothing Donnie could change: so he occupied himself for a few minutes in covertly untying and retying the ropes which held the gate closed, till the boy's shoulders had straightened again and his head lifted.

The desperate identifying bleats of lambs momentarily separated from ewes faded as they walked up the track. The final separation would come the next day. They passed Mairi Anna's old home, the only house in the ruined clachan which was still roofed, a grey two-up, two-down cottage, with salt-bleached windowframes and rusting rones. It faced north, and backed against a precipitous slope, always in shadow.

'I'll show you the house after we get something to eat,' said Donnie.

On the other side of the wall there was sudden sunlight and turf sweetened to greenness by the sand-blow from the beach where they had landed. The girls had spread out a picnic, and the other men were there already, lounging and smoking, red-shouldered in the burning sun.

'You been taking your time, boys,' remarked Roddy, jovially. 'These girls got nobody but Sandy to admire them.'

Sandy was indeed admiring them, with silent wistful adolescent lust. He looked aside sheepishly. The girls tossed their heads and sniffed. They sat in a demure group apart from the men. They had made up their faces and styled each other's hair: even Dina had acquired blue eyelids and an extraordinary topknot drooping over one ear. It had a wilted bunch of daisies stuck in it. Murdo glowered across at the latecomers, though it was hard to tell whether his ill humour was occasioned by suspicion of laziness, by exclusion from Roddy's list of eligible youth, or by outrage at his ravenous brother's snatching a sandwich without saying grace. Donnie dropped it, muttered the customary formula, and bit fiercely.

The talk was all of sheep, and of expected prices at the forthcoming lamb sales. Lal and Murdo continued their conversation in Gaelic. Roddy, embarrassed, took them to task for their discourtesy. 'Alan will be thinking you are making your fortunes and not telling him.'

Alan, equally embarrassed by the constraint he placed on them, said quickly, 'Don't mind me, Roddy. I can't talk any sense about sheep anyway.' He finished eating, and stretched out on his stomach, biting at sour clover leaves. Sideways, with affectionate amusement, he watched Sandy watching the girls. They were worth looking at, pretty and knowingly coy as Dresden shepherdesses, cool and creamy-limbed in pastel cottons. Kirsty's scarlet bikini glinted when she moved under her white blouse and skirt. Mairi and Morag Ann put heads together and whispered and giggled; Kirsty cried out an indignant negative, clapped her hand to her red mouth and looked eloquently at Donnie.

Donnie, who had been sitting, as was proper, beside Sandy, came over to Alan and dropped silently beside him. The others rose to go back to work.

'Bloody dog,' Murdo aimed a kick at Ben, who was thieving biscuits.

'Ben!' Donnie called, without looking up, knowing who the bloody dog was. He raised his head to watch Murdo out of sight, his jaw clenching.

With the men gone, the girls, like so many pigeons, suddenly fluttered to life; pelting each other with crusts and ringpulls as they

183

packed up the remains of the meal, squealing protests at Ben, who joined in by hurling his muddy body at their icecream-tinted finery. Mairi prodded her brother with sandalled nailpolished toes. 'Oh well, aren't you the lazy ones! It's time you got going.'

Alan sat up, groaning. 'We've brought all our beasts down. I'm shattered anyway.'

Mairi gave his head a shy push and tripped off. 'I can't make them move!'

Donnie stretched out his hand for an apple before Morag Ann put them away, and flopped down again on his back. Kirsty, taking advantage of her cousinship, seized her chance. 'Up you get, lazybones!' She stood over him, pulling at his wrists. He resisted, with a convincingly gruff string of Gaelic oaths, but as he tried to bite the apple again, Mairi was on him too, pinning his arms while Kirsty bent to tickle him, reducing him to helpless giggles. Alan lay back, laughing at the animated childish faces and flying crow's-wing hair. Ben yapped, Dina whirled round and round and hurled herself with a yell across Donnie's ankles. Kirsty was warming up. With gleaming eyes and lips and a flash of red bikini, she squatted on his pelvis, bouncing up and down. Donnie writhed.

'Stop it!' His voice was sharp enough to make Alan sit up again.

'She's got you now, boy!' shouted Mairi, gleefully.

Kirsty wriggled, her fingers playing on his bucking belly, on his belt, under his belt.

'Stop it, you're hurting!'

'Kirsty, you brat!' Mairi gasped with merriment.

Kirsty's prying hand swept round. There was a tableknife lying in the grass. She held it to the boy's throat and drew a buttery trail down his chest, then with a sudden swoop she had it at his genitals. 'I'll castrate you, boy!' she shrieked, twisting it.

Morag Ann descended on her just as Alan grabbed her arm.

'Kirsty!' She caught her sister by the back of her blouse. The buttons flew open and so did the red bikini, revealing upstanding nipples. She leapt to her feet with a scream, pulling her clothing together, and Donnie, wrenching free from Mairi and Dina, landed in mid-writhe across Alan's thighs, hot, panting and tousled; and slumped gratefully against his chest in unmistakeable surrender. Alan's arms were round him and his face down, for an instant only.

He struggled upright, pushing the boy off, none too gently. Donnie jumped up and raced towards the fank.

Alan frowned down at the bitten apple in the grass. He stooped to pick it up, not sure what had gone wrong, but remorsefully sure that he, at least, was old enough to know better, and should have intervened. Kirsty and Morag Ann were in shrill altercation. Dina had lost interest and was turning cartwheels. Mairi looked at him sidelong, shamefaced, biting her lip with the same mannerism as her brother. He smiled at her, because after all they were only kids, and set off to find Donnie.

Vaulting the gate, he almost kicked him in the head. He was crouched in the shadow of the wall. He straightened up slowly. His face was flushed and bewildered.

'Watch out for Kirsty, then,' said Alan, trying to tease him out of his misery, 'she's obviously got a fancy for you.'

His stomach heaved in and out with stressful breaths. 'Well, I haven't for her,' he said thickly.

His eyes showed plainly that he had noticed Alan backing treacherously away from him; and Alan, taking fright, increased the distance, setting off down the track. Donnie didn't follow. He hesitated and went back: it would soon be over, surely he could be kind for another three weeks – less. Thinking that, he began to tremble, and would rather have been anywhere than there, but managed to say, 'Come on. Come and show me the house.'

'There's nothing there.'

'I'd like to see it.' He leant against the wall beside him, tossing the now-sticky apple from hand to hand for something to do. It was a Port Long ex-Common Market apple, a red one: they came in two colours, neither tasting as if they had grown on trees. The open flesh has not browned, as a young apple should in August. He took a bite and chucked it to Donnie. 'That's yours.'

He looked up smiling then, the tension easing, and at the house he was himself again. He turned at the door, pointing to the stream, in that dry season only a lazy wisp of spray on the precipice behind, which gurgled in small brown pools to the west of the house, down to the shore.

'Mairi and me were always playing there. My sister Effie used to bring us – she was cooking for them at lambing time. It was great – no school.'

'You never did like school, did you?'

'Neither would you if you couldn't read or write.'

He pushed the door open. Inside it was dark and dank, smelling of rats and mildew. Donnie snuffed the stale air.

'What a place! I don't know why I'm showing you this.' It seemed to bother him: it was not a mere deprecatory politeness.

'I asked to have a look,' Alan pointed out.

The room on the left was ceiling-high with sacks of wool waiting collection. On the other side was the kitchen, with a rickety table and half a dozen wooden chairs with twenty-three legs. The twenty-fourth lay on the floor, well chewed.

'Ben?' asked Alan.

'Of course!' He laughed, but almost at once his face was anxious. 'It's horrible this place, isn't it?'

Alan was listening. 'No,' he said at length, 'hear that waterfall.' It was only a faint manifold rustling like a light evening breeze makes in the crown of a tall tree. In other weathers it would tinkle, or swish or roar.

Donnie's eyes shone. He said nothing at all, till, on the narrow low-lintelled stair, 'Mind your head.' His hand brushed it, briefly.

On the landing, a rag-sealed skylight admitted a single sunbeam, its daily arc on the floor traced in dead bluebottles. Their footsteps started a faint buzz, and a few expiring corkscrew turns in the dust. The upper rooms each contained four black iron bedsteads, with rust-spotted striped mattresses and pillows communally stained by many heads. It reminded Alan strongly of dismaying early schooldays. He stifled the thought, in case Donnie, in the uncertain mood of that day, would be hurt by it: and stood still, at the sudden realisation that he had long ceased to reckon thoughts as private property.

Donnie was kneeling on one of the beds in the right-hand room, looking out of the window.

'I always grab this one if I get the chance,' he said, turning as Alan came up to him.

Alan smiled. 'Sea and waterfall.'

'Yes.'

186

Outside, they leant against the doorposts, looking from the shadow of the hill behind across blinding water to Boreray, warmly sunlit. The saddle between its two summits shimmered. The distant mainland blotted and reformed in a mirage of heat.

'Rain, that means,' said Donnie. 'We need it, too.' Then, 'I love this place.'

'I'm beginning to see why. Sorry I didn't think much of it this morning.'

Donnie scanned his face for the honesty of this, and finding it, said, with eyes of eloquent sadness, 'I wish we would have come here before.'

'So do I.'

There was not so much truth in that, but Donnie was willing to settle even for a little.

'Alan – they'll be making several trips over tomorrow – we could stay here tonight if you like.'

'No.'

It was out too quickly. He heard the boy's breath indrawn in a barely audible sound of disappointment. It was the wrong thing to have said, the only possible thing. He knew Donnie was importuning him, as plainly as Kirsty had Donnie; unlike her, he did not know what he was asking for. Alan glanced at his bent head with a sickening twinge of pity and loss: the May evening on the hill, Donnie's bowed head, the same gentle profile, the same delicate, maddening, uncaressed hollows of neck and throat. There was nothing that could truthfully be spoken. He found something that was not entirely a lie, and used it, desperately.

'I can't stand the thought of separating these lambs in the morning. I'm going to give it a miss.'

Donnie looked at him thoughtfully, but seemed to swallow it. 'I knew you wouldn't like that. You won't be coming tomorrow then.'

'No.' He softened it with, 'Not unless it leaves you short-handed, anyway.'

'No, we'll be fine.'

The crisis seemed to have been averted gracefully. It was even Donnie who said in quite a matter-of-fact voice, 'Here's Lal back with the last lot. We'd better go down and help.' But walking to the fank, discussing the next day's weather, Alan was filled with a deso-

187

late sense of receding and betrayal. He dragged the hurdles to and fro for Lal in a black spasm of anger. What else could he have done, what choice could he ever have made that would have been the right one? The stream of white backs, splashed red or blue or magenta in the insolence of ownership, poured into the pen, unresisting. Only one or two beasts tried to bolt, jumping on each others' haunches, but the dogs soon had them inside and they subsided, panting but submissive. He secured the ropes for the second time that day. Donnie lifted the last escaped lamb over the wall, placing it gently by a ewe who was somehow the right mother. Alan looked away in helpless anguish, and wished, with the obsessive passion of a Death Row prisoner, that it was all over.

In the boat Donnie kept a stranglehold on Ben, who wanted to play with Lal's dog Dileas, crouched between his master and Murdo. Morag Ann and Kirsty were not on speaking terms. Dina was devouring a stick of malodorous pink rock which beat against all the other odours of sea and engine fuel, men and dogs and cigarette smoke, and the coal-tarry alginate nip of hot August haze. The sea was glassy calm, dully reflecting growing banks of cloud.

'Looks like rain,' said Lal.

'Well yes, and we could do with it,' said Roddy.

'We could do with it right enough.'

Chapter 20

A grey breathless day brought no rain, only midges, an early dusk, and the first really dark night since April. The downpour began after midnight. Alan woke with a start, imagining voices, and heard instead the long-unaccustomed squall and rattle on the roof.

The clock said ten past two. He watched it with dread while another minute fell away, and two, and three, slow ineffectual flakes of time scarcely depleting the night's weight of hours, which pressed on him with compassionless inquisition: what now, till dawn? What after that? What, after? He had got through the experimental day without Donnie, the first for twelve weeks. He had sawn driftwood, fitted the cockpit coamings, practised a sonata or two, sorted out books for the new school term; even scrubbed the kitchen floor, all with the unreasoning diligence of a child under threat of a spanking; the time had passed, and he had managed not to think ahead at all, except to the following afternoon, when he would see Donnie, and it would be just like any other day. Now as he lay awake in the darkness, each inexorable minute found the hidden wound and scraped it raw: the days to come were few, and after that, nothing. Yet he had known the end from the very beginning. In that equilibrium it had been light and shadow on every moment, the form in which the precious thing was cast, the perfected pattern inviolate to time. Now it had torn loose, dragging all down with it in a black horror springing out of darkness and sleep. He faced it as it clawed, but tried to escape, his mind scuttling for the rhythms of wind and rain, the ticking of the clock, the trivia of the coming day, the coming days and weeks and years. And there it was waiting for him, with studious talons.

He buried his face in his forearms. It was so dark there was no sight to be shut out; nevertheless the attitude was self-protective, an instinctive reversion to the past. In the first few dreadful weeks at prep school he had lain like that, biting the back of his hand to keep himself quiet. There had been a saving bedtime fantasy, that he was dreaming a bad dream, and would wake up in his own room, with sunlight streaming through the galleon-patterned curtains, Rocky at the back of his knees, and his mother in her foamy white negligée calling, 'Wake up, darling'; and no Harold. His particularisations of the scene had been more minute the more he was wretched: the night after his most relentless tormentor had locked him in the lavatory for two hours, he had visualised all twenty of the pearly buttons on his mother's nightdress, how the second one was loose and drooped, and the fifth was a replacement with a more yellowy colour, and the ninth had a bit of thread sticking up behind it. Now lying awake in equivalent desolation he turned his back on the eviscerating future, calling up protection in an image of Donnie, smiling from his eyes in the spring twilight, an image complete in every muscle and strand of hair, which he regarded without desire and without affection: it was not a representation of the living boy, but a magic formula. That realisation came to him, eventually, with a recall of the childish circumstances which had first created the method. He loathed himself then for using Donnie, and for seeking to evade the pain, but the claws flashed again, and he scurried for shelter. He fell asleep abruptly, with his teeth still clenched on his hand.

When he came back from work in the afternoon, Donnie was in the kitchen, cleaning paintbrushes. 'What got into you, Alan? You scrubbed the floor,' he remarked cheerfully.

It was just like any other day.

It was too windy for sailing, and intermittently raining: good boat-repairing weather.

'Nice to see that burn full again,' said Donnie, as they went out to the workshop.

There was more day-to-day gossip than usual to catch up on, and plenty to do on Selena; she had been neglected during the fine spell. Donnie whistled off and on, and teased about the standard of Alan's varnishing, as about the lack of anything to eat in the house.

'I just never remember to go to the shop,' he said apologetically, half-laughing with relief that everything was just as usual. There was cheese and some not very fresh bread, so they ate that, and went back to Selena.

The previous night had left a cold lump of fear in Alan, but it was melting in the warmth of the everyday. Things could not be so bad: it must have been mostly the business with Kirsty that had made Donnie so moody on Rona, and he had seemed on edge about Murdo too. If he could survive, if he could be happy, then it really wasn't the same mess. He himself could stand his own loss, if it was only his own. The bargain all along had been that the summer idyll had to be paid for in parting, that he had to let Donnie go without laying any claim to him. The abyss really only started to open if Donnie wanted to be claimed.

For the next few days there was no sign that he did. There were two good sailing evenings, and a dipping on Saturday. After it there were visiting aunts and cousins in the Morrison kitchen, quizzing him about his incipient departure. He wouldn't be drawn; but he seemed incurious and indifferent, rather than miserable. When a fat sentimental auntie hugged him and cried, 'Oh, you'll be homesick, laddie. Mairi Anna, I'm sure he'll be homesick,' he shrugged and looked embarrassed, as well he might.

190

Alan went home then, feeling fairly miserable himself, but relieved. Of course Donnie would be homesick: none of the many young men and women who left Boreray and childhood for the city could be otherwise, at first. But he had skill and loved the practice of it, and there was every chance that he would do very well in his trade. It would not take long for him to lose all relish for the position of Murdo's downtrodden younger brother. If he remembered the summer that had just passed wistfully, it would not be in terms of the companion he had lost, but of the things they had done together. The memory of his home island would have a radiance it might never have possessed, but he would not know why, and need never know, leaving now. It was time. It couldn't be long, even for dreamy Donnie, before some chance-heard remark suggested possibilities he had never thought of. There was no place for exotic experiment in his social background: the realisation that he was attracted to another male would force on him an immediate choice, traumatic and final, a choice he was too unformed to make.

Alan had been over it all so many times that it came glibly enough. Common sense and common decency showed it was crazy, even criminal, to pursue Donnie's life further. Perhaps they would meet, casually, after a time, when it was safe. The certainty that it would be safe, that Donnie a few years hence would not be the boy he had loved, cost him an awful pang of grief; but it offered comfort, too: once the dead are dead, they can be mourned, and life can go on again. He told himself for the hundredth time that week that he wanted it to be over now, while there were no bad memories for Donnie; not adding, while there was no burden of guilt for himself. He had all but suppressed the disquieting voice which whispered that he was breaking faith, that the decision was not now his to make. But he might have been more wary of his sudden adherence to common sense: it was a quality in which he had always been markedly deficient.

On Sunday afternoon they raced each other up Gormul in the mist, and got back with half an hour to spare before Donnie had to be home for church. He collapsed on the floor, laughing and gasping, and doubled over with a groan, clutching his side, but still laughing.

'You've overdone it.'

'Yes – I wasn't going to let you beat me.'

'But I did anyway.'

'Of course, you always do. I keep trying.' He stretched out full length. Alan tossed him the cushion from Uncle Ewan's chair.

'Thanks.' He settled it under his cheek; then sat up, pushing it away.

'Has that cushion bitten you?' Alan looked at him curiously. He was glowering at the innocuous faded floral object with twitching nostrils.

'Eleanor was here last night.'

'This morning. Yes, she was sitting in that chair.' He had been surprised by her visit: she didn't usually come on Sundays. For that matter, he had been surprised to discover in the previous week that she had apparently decided to forgive him their quarrel.

'You seeing each other again, then?'

He had never told Donnie the details of that occasion, but he had presumably heard something.

'Yes – sorry if that's treading on Murdo's toes,' he added, rather awkwardly, because they usually kept clear of the subject out of respect for family loyalties.

'I don't care about Murdo.'

He scowled at the floor, his lashes very dark against his cheekbones. Alan wondered what Murdo had been up to. The next question took him completely by surprise.

'Do you sleep with her?'

With a nasty jolt, Alan divined jealousy. There had never been any sign of it before. But he could only say yes.

'Why?'

'That's obvious, isn't it?'

'Just that?'

'Yes – well, yes, I suppose, just that. Scratching an itch, really.'

Donnie continued to scowl at the ground, with an expression so lowering that Alan added, unwisely, 'Look, I don't want this to prejudice her chances with Murdo. You won't—'

'Of course I bloody won't.'

Donnie's eyes were suddenly on him, pale with anger.

'Sorry.'

There was a strained silence. Donnie still watched him, a strange

192

intent look from which the anger had quickly faded. Eventually he said, 'Be careful.'

'What do you mean?' Alan wondered if Murdo was threatening a punch-up, but this time had sufficient wit not to mention him.

'She's not good for you.' Donnie's eyes were unwavering.

'I'm not good for her either. I don't actually much like the way we treat each other.' Donnie's scrutiny was unbearable. He turned away, before it forced out of him everything he must not say, beginning with how little Eleanor meant to him. He wandered to the open door, leaning against the jamb. The mist was down almost to the burn. A fat black slug was inching over the doorstep. 'It won't be for much longer, anyhow,' he muttered, 'I shan't be hanging around.'

'You don't hang around for anyone, do you?'

Alan managed this time not to ask what he meant: and anyway it was painfully obvious, although his voice was quiet and his face still. He sat crosslegged, as he often did, watching his own fingertips brushing the floor. He had learned to be jealous, and learned not to show it, and what else? Alan picked up the slug, which was hopefully questing at the threshold, and replaced it in the water-beaded grass. His heart felt like lead.

Donnie came to the door. His face was very white. 'When are you going, Alan?'

It was a subject they had avoided.

'October.' After a glance at Donnie's beseeching, puzzled eyes he watched the slug.

'Selena won't be finished.' He spoke almost in a whisper.

'No. I've asked Roddy if I can leave her here just now. I'll have to come back for her some time.'

'When?'

'I don't know.'

There was a moment's shared hopeless grief. Alan looked away. He didn't want Donnie to see the desire to escape taking over.

Donnie said, 'Time to go, then,' and stepped outside onto the grass.

Alan, shocked by his own treachery, said, 'I wish they'd let you skip church for once.'

It was the only Sunday he hadn't wished it. Donnie wasn't fooled, and he knew it.

'See you tomorrow,' he said, civilly.

193

Alan could not even wait to watch the mist close round him. He walked off in the opposite direction, and kept going till he reached the end of the island, as far away from Donnie as possible. His mind was frozen: he didn't think at all; but by the end of that evening, he had already left Donnie, and he moved through the remaining days with the predetermined compulsion of a ghost.

Donnie pleaded a headache, and skipped church. He lay on his bed perfectly still for a long time. When the downstairs clock chimed seven, he roused, and took the diary out from under the lining paper of a drawer, where it had lain unheeded since May. He read the last entry several times, and withdrew into stillness again. The church bus stopped in the passing place. He put the notebook away in the drawer.

Next day he wrote: *Mon Aug 21 it is not long now I was not thinking about it befor but now I am thinking about it al the time.*

When he had written it, it didn't seem worth the effort. There was nothing to say.

There was no one to talk to either. He didn't know why it had become impossible to speak to Alan. They met every day and things went on as usual, with the usual number of words between them. But it was like being in a dream where you think you are running, and find you haven't moved. He came home each night cowed and bewildered. His mother was fussing about his clothes for going to Glasgow; his father, with more to say to him than he had ever had before, was full of his own father's young days on the Clyde steamers, and of distant cousins he must go to visit. They had never had anything but silent docility from him, and were too preoccupied to notice the change in the quality of the silence. Their words and movements had become for him a meaningless blur. After a while he would leave them arguing about his best interests, and take the diary off to one of his customary hiding places. Sometimes he would write something, as often not. What he did write was usually the least miserable incident of the day, as if by vouching for its reality he could disown the rest.

Tue 22 Aug I went down to Alans he was at work I was going to fit the new cleets but I was just hanging around waching the rabits the are nice ther is a blak one they were eting al his lettices in the sumer but he didnt mind.

That evening Alan was with Eleanor and Donnie hadn't seen him at all, though he waited as late as he dared.

Wed aug 23rd I was looking at a book Alan has about Tahiti he has somone wants him to help with cruses round ther it will be very intresting nex yere

The kitchen table and half the floor were littered with maps and charts, and Alan, when he appeared after a series of very long-distance telephone calls, immediately started to type the letters which would commit him to treason.

Friday Aug 25 I been woried abowt Ben he is no good at the sheep in cas Murdo will shoot him I asked Alan he sai he wil take it if they are geting rid of it. I was offen taking Ben ther I am glad it will be alrigt.

Alan was unenthusiastic. 'I shan't be here long. Isn't there anyone else who could take him?'
Donnie looked at him disbelievingly.
'Well, of course I'll take him. I'd find a home for him, I expect. Tell them to be sure and let me know if they're sick of him, will you?'
Donnie did not seem much encouraged. Alan sighed.
'What's wrong? Do they want rid of him right away?'
'No. They haven't said.'
'Well, find out.'
They left it at that. Donnie said nothing to Alan about the possibility of a weighted sack rather than a bullet.

Sat Aug 26 At sheep al day drenching hogs but I got away later we went out to the big sands haven't been ther for a whil ther are more shels when its windy.

Alan had lost interest in sheep and had missed out on hog drenching. When Donnie escaped to Skalanish, it was to find that Porky's brother Alex and two of his classmates had homed in on Selena; whether by Alan's invitation was not obvious, but the mere circumstances was desolation. He climbed the sidhean and lay in the

195

grass listening. There was a high laugh once or twice but mostly it was wailing. He drifted into a half-sleep where his parents seemed to be arguing over him and Kirsty tormenting him somehow, and drifted awake again to find Alan standing beside him.

'Aren't the others with you?'

Donnie stared, blank and exhausted.

'Alex and co. I thought you were all up here.'

He shook his head, shivering slightly. The grass was damp and the shadows had spread. Alan said nothing for a bit, then, 'It's going to be a lovely sunset. Coming over to Tràigh Mhór?'

Monday 28 aug We were going out in the boat after Alan got back, he was geting changed when he came throuh I supose I wasnt looking to hapy he said cheer up I said I cant stand going away he was teling me then al the things they al sai, how theres no chanse here and so on and I was not saing any thing then he said I sound just like a bloody techer dont I. I said yes I coudnt look at him, he said God Ill miss you Donnie he was rufling my hair then I wonder is that true if he will miss me we had great time this sumer in the boat and evrything we were saling after that it was breezy we dint talk much again.

He did not add that what talk there had been had consisted mainly of such unpleasantries as 'not another bloody shackle pin' and 'for Christ's sake don't luff her.' When they got back to the house Eleanor had just arrived. She had her violin case, but also she was wearing extremely tight lemon-yellow trousers.

'Your mother wants you home, Donnie,' she told him at once.

He took a long time over getting there, by way of the summit of Càrn Bàn and his grandmother's house. She was napping in her chair by the fire, with her old freckled hands peacefully folded upon the cat and the *Christian Herald* on her lap. He crouched on the hearthrug for a few minutes, seeing her smiling toothless jaws mumbling together in sleep, her green and purple paisley apron over a pink nylon overall and shapeless grey skirt, all a little grubby with years of wear, and her veined ankles in thick wrinkled stockings, ending in pompommed slippers slit to allow her bunions space. She had a faded old-woman smell, like dead grass warming

196

in February sunshine. She moved and muttered in her sleep, and he rose silently and slipped away.

Tue Aug 29 We coud have gone in the boat it was a nice evning but I didnt feel like it much so we didnt.

'I feel sick,' he said, when Alan suggested a sail.

There was nothing Donnie much felt like for the rest of the week, except sick. When he was at home he did as he was told: 'Give me that shirt to wash, Donnie.' 'Donnie, be sure now that you take your bible with you.' 'Go you and say goodbye to Lal and Katie.' When he was with Alan, he curled up on the rug in animal withdrawal, completely inert, as if stillness offered some protection. Sometimes he fell asleep for a while; it was difficult to tell from his shallow breathing whether he was asleep or awake.

Alan watched the downward spiral of misery with paralysed guilt. As Donnie's wretchedness became more apparent, his own focussed on a desperate desire to escape from him and from everything connected with him. The suffering was his fault, and that burden was so crushing that it overpowered all habitual feeling. He told himself over and over again that things must go on as before, till Donnie was safe and he was free. 'Safe' and 'free' achieved incantatory power. Clinging to the importance of seeming normal as an absolute requirement, he embarked on a dedicated programme of seeming normality: but as he operated in a state of numb derangement, the effects were as grotesque as a drunk's attempt to walk a straight line. He was conscientious, but it was difficult to work out even what constituted kindness; impossible to recall the luminous empathy of love. He tolerated the white-faced silent boy with distant pity, while his imagination ran febrile races in a post-Borerayan never-never-land.

Friday Sept 1 I said goodby to Alan now. He walked with me to the fense he was saing goodbye and good luck shaking hands like I was someone he only met yestrday I coudnt beleve he would go just like that I didnt let go his hand then he said thanks for this sumer Donnie his voice was so diferent I coudnt take that I just started to cry he said oh dont, he sounded realy sad but mabe he was angry I count see he pulled his hand away

197

and ran of down the hill. I dont know what he was mening he did not even say see you agen maybe he is not coming back at al this is the end of it then it feels like the end of evrything I dont know what it is is making evrything so bad I wish I coud die.

He cried until there were no tears left, and on the dawn voyage next day vomited till that was impossible too, but dying proved beyond his capabilities. Nevertheless, his sister-in-law was shocked when she saw how wretched he looked, and treated him at first with maternal solicitude. But he was puzzlingly unresponsive, which piqued her. He wouldn't eat and wouldn't talk, and took no interest in the children, or in anything. After a time she found him extremely tiresome.

'He's just sulky,' she told her husband, following a few weeks of this.

'He wasn't like that when he was wee,' said Alex Angus. 'I'll talk to him.'

He did, and it made no difference. The boy persisted in fading away before their eyes, in dumb insolent rejection of family feeling. Not that he was rebellious: he did what he was asked to do at work or in the house, sometimes more than he was asked.

'He dug the whole garden today,' Rhoda told Alex Angus one evening in October. 'But he gives me the shivers. There's something not right about that boy.'

There was very little right about him. Only a germ of stubborn pride kept him from total breakdown. Endurance was in his blood, from the grim wastes of Rona.

Alan too wished he could die. He wept for hours in utter desolation, and most desperately when Donnie's face and voice escaped recollection, a second and terrifying loss. At last the grey thought dawned that to lose these shadows was nothing: he had lost the reality. He quietened then in beaten fear. Dreadful images split the darkness, Roddy's sheep strangling in the wire, Murdo's disembowelled wedders, the lamb with crowpecked eyes, Rocky in two halves, one squashed and one kicking, a little arctic fox curled up in caged misery in a London pet shop. The fox was worst: he could not remember the occasion of seeing it, it was scarcely a memory at all. It lay as

198

Donnie had, in mute animal pain. He had caused that suffering and watched it indifferently. He had slaughtered the innocent. He had claimed to live by compassion as a guiding principle, shrinking from causing hurt and taking life, and all along he had been tearing another creature to pieces. He remembered Donnie with the injured gull he had been too squeamish to kill, and foundered in self-hatred, hating himself for what he had done and more for the spurious decency of belated, fatuous remorse; hating himself for having dared to think he loved, when he had only exploited. Donnie had suffered in the end as Richard and Sally and all the others had. He had merely been playing with him, then, playing at innocence, playing at shepherds, using and devouring. He lacerated himself with these accusations, till unmistakeable, heartrending love flared up and showed them all to be lies.

In the next days he punished himself savagely, pursuing every element of his culpability with remorseless zeal, searching for the mainspring, the heinous deceit, the black decision. But he could not find what he was looking for, although he would have been glad to accept any fault as his own. He could not pin down the first step, the fatal choice he must have made for rapine and slaughter. There was nothing to arraign but a series of insignificant accidents, of unforceful retreats and small yieldings, slight parcels of blame which did not add up to the felt totality of guilt. There had not been a choice; in the first moment in the dingy classroom, he had looked into the eyes of someone who already loved him. Rejection, if he could have carried it out, would have been injury too, casting him still as destroyer and the other as victim. Withdrawal had never been possible, there was harm in all quarters. Not that he felt excused: to be the inevitable catalyst of misery, to bear inherent mischief in his mere presence made the guilt more terrible. Nothing in his previous experience had prepared him for this doubtful tear in the fabric of a humane and orderable universe. A chasm full of lurking Furies had opened in his harmonious world.

As one who on a lonesome road doth walk in fear and dread: he wandered the hills and shores they had explored together in Oresteian despair, accursed, and glad of it, because it was the only meaning to be found in loss. Re-analysis of the cosmos stopped him thinking about Donnie. But not always; an otter's print in the mud or the call of a plover was enough to set him sobbing with raw heartbreak, only wanting him back.

The rest of the inhabitants of Boreray lived in the same cosmos as before. In the first few minutes of each working morning this seemed to him utterly baffling. He adjusted during the day, was genial with the boys, practised whatever Eleanor demanded, gave his neighbours a hand now and again, even called on the Morrisons. They told him news of Donnie occasionally.

'He's doing well,' said Angus. 'Ay, he got a good chance there. We are very grateful to you that you put in a good word for him.'

'Yes, they're very pleased with him,' said Mairi Anna, adding, 'he's a bit homesick, right enough.'

And Alan accepted it hopefully, blinking a bit in amazement that he had let his imagination run riot: Donnie would be all right, of course he wouldn't pine away over something that had never happened. But when he was alone again, he knew better.

A week before the October school holiday, Murdo shot Ben.

'I'd have taken him,' said Alan, white-faced.

'Och, yes, I knew that,' said Angus. 'But I would not be bothering you with it. Och, not at all!'

Alan, sick and deadened, was not surprised to learn that he had betrayed Donnie again. He smiled politely at Murdo when they passed at the gate.

Two days after that, Torquil shot himself.

'I shall shoot myself when I feel I've had enough of myself,' he had said frequently, raising a whisky and soda. Alan reflected that if he had accepted the invitation of that summer, his father might not have shot himself so soon. He said as much to Celia, when he broke his journey to New York to see her, at her request.

'Oh, how dreadful! How perfectly dreadful!' she sobbed.

'But he always said he'd do it, Mummy. It was sooner or later, that's all.'

'But suicide! It's so pathetic – it's just too awful.' She wept with her face on Harold's shoulder.

Alan said nothing. It seemed to him it was a very good idea, and eminently sensible to prefer to be dead. He felt vaguely resentful that Celia's apparently genuine aversion to it made it difficult for him to do it himself.

PART THREE

Dawn points, and another day
Prepares for heat and silence. Out at sea the dawn wind
Wrinkles and slides. I am here
Or there, or elsewhere. In my beginning.

— 'East Coker', T.S. Eliot

Chapter 21

Jessie and Neilie had a new great-grandchild. Eleanor hung over the pram, cooing and crooning, tickling his tummy. He kicked with feeble pumping movements, his face dull red and wreathed back from angry toothless gums. Eleanor's supple fingers played voluptuously on his steamy-warm crown.

'Oh, that lovely wee soft patch! He's gorgeous, Catriona, just gorgeous. Can I lift him?'

'Yes, he'll no go back to sleep now. It's nearly time for his bottle.' The first-time mother looked importantly at the picture-clock on the wall, a thatched cottage in a garden of pink and red roses.

Eleanor tutted. 'Aren't you feeding him yourself? Come on, wee mannie, up you come – how can you bear not to?'

Catriona made a face. 'They were telling us we should at the hospital right enough. But och, I don't know, I don't fancy it really.'

'Shame on you!' Eleanor smiled a slow smile, rocking the child back and forward on her shoulder, lulling herself more than her charge, who was uttering sharp coughs of outrage at every movement.

'Och, he'll do very well on the bottle.' Jessie was behind her, chuckling and waving an old crooked hand at the infant's tight-screwed eyes. 'The bottle is very good. I would be putting a bit of sugar in it. His legs are as thin, Catriona! He is not getting enough, surely.'

'Not *sugar!*' Eleanor's arms enfolded the angry starveling. 'They mustn't give you sugar. Milk's all you need, isn't it, my pet?'

'They were saying no sugar at the hospital,' Catriona agreed.

'Och well, a wee bit of steeped oatmeal, then. That's what I was giving your dad. When he was a week old he was taking that strained. Ay!' She clasped her hands round her son's brawny forearm. 'He was a big strong baby. Och yes, oatmeal will be better than sugar, I would be giving him oatmeal.'

'No, you'll make him fat and give him bad teeth,' protested Eleanor.

Catriona smiled indulgently.

'It was doing me no harm, eh, Mam?' Do'l Alex guffawed, with his great paw on her frail clasped hands. 'Gave me bad teeth right enough. Not many left now!' He pointed cheerfully to the ever-increasing gap in his top jaw.

'I was putting a wee drop whisky with it sometimes,' his mother added proudly. 'Whisky is very good for the teething and to make them sleep.'

'So it is now, isn't that right, Murdo?' Do'l Alex, looming in the doorway, slapped his companion on the back and hoisted his grandson aloft between his vast hairy fists.

'Mind him!' snapped Eleanor.

'Oh, careful Dad!'

'Och, Do'l Alex, you are making him cry!'

The small creature screeched with rage and fear, working blue nylon extremities in passionate hatred.

'You are too rough, too rough!' remonstrated Jessie, stretching her arms up ineffectually towards the child.

Do'l Alex brought the small red mask of fury down to his own broad red smiling countenance. 'He's a boy. He'll take a bit of roughness. A boy at last, thank God for that! Too many women in my life.' A gusty roar of laughter tensed the infant into a silent paroxysm. His grandfather, beaming with pride, planted a lipsmacking kiss on the contorted face, a kiss so generous it covered eyes, nose and mouth at once.

'We'll have him a sailor yet, eh?' piped up old Neilie. He had cataract, and could no longer see anything but shadows, but he sat leaning forward in his chair, listening eagerly.

'Ay we will that!' Do'l Alex dumped his descendant among the frilly white quilts, and stumped across to sit by his father, with a 'How's yourself today?' that made his feeble old head shake.

The three women converged on the pram, with searching hands and soothing voices. Catriona, in the gravity of maternal privilege,

203

raised the child to her face. 'There there! There there! Och, your grandad is just terrible!'

Eleanor's envious palms patted his back and bottom. 'He needs changing. Let me do it.'

Catriona relinquished her son, who squalled anew in the stranger's arms, so that she reached out for him again. 'Oh, I'd better take him. He won't go with anyone else, not even his father.'

Eleanor frowned, holding tight. 'No, please let me! Come on, my precious. Come on, darling!'

Catriona, sympathising, smiled and rummaged in her basket of necessaries, while Eleanor swung the baby to and fro, singing to him softly. He fell silent, squinting and twisting his mouth. Perhaps it was her clear voice, or the sunlight from the open door making a copper halo of her hair; at any rate, rapport was established.

'He's fairly taken to you,' said Catriona graciously.

'Och, yes, yes indeed. You have a way with him, my dear. It is wonderful indeed.' Jessie's faded eyes dwelt kindly on the girl's absorbed face and slim upright figure. She turned to Murdo, silent on a chair by the door. 'She will be a good wife to you, Murdo. You are the lucky man, eh?'

Murdo grunted, 'Uh-huh.'

That strangled disyllable of public affirmation came unwillingly. He would have kept it to himself; he would keep to himself everything to do with her, buried, safe. He resented the old woman's probing, her open smile and trespass on his private being, resented even that Eleanor should be in that place where he was too, so that his least word or look might give away something from the depths, the fleck of gold in her right eye, the sharp static crack of her underslip coming off, the obliterating darkness between her thighs. Her name in his mouth, his intercepted look, the flash of the ring on her finger made these things common, flagrant; robbed him and displayed him naked.

He would have gone outside, but he could not take his eyes off her. She hung over the child, petting, murmuring, taking it into her darkness, giving herself away from him. He had to watch. He had to see what she did, what she was depriving him of, how she split him open, squirming, with the lingering tips of her white fingers and the two sharp teeth gleaming in her smile. She picked the thing up.

'All finished, pet! Who's got a nice dry bottom now?'

She twirled and danced with it in her arms, her lips moist and parted, kissing its head.

Ah, you bastard, damn you, damn you.

Do'l Alex thrust a big dram into his hand. 'Slàinte, Murdo!'

'Slàinte.' He drained the glass, the first of the day. The fire of the liquor brightened his anger. She was laughing with that pudding-faced cunt Catriona, with the brat held between them. Fuck her, he thought, and because he had, often, and the whisky was flushing his veins, he smiled behind his hand, and said, 'Another dram would be good, man.'

That turned her head. 'No, it's time we went. Catriona's going now.'

'Petticoat government. You'll get that for the rest of your life, boy!' Do'l Alex screwed the cap back on the bottle ostentatiously. 'Now, would he have permission to come to the pub with me – just for a pint?'

Eleanor looked up briefly from the pram. 'If I come too.'

'Oho! And it won't be a pint for you, but a dram. Is that right, girl?'

'That's right.'

Do'l Alex strode out in great good humour. He liked her, because she was different, because he liked everyone. He winked at Murdo. 'Come on, we'll get there first. Just to order the drinks, Eleanor.'

Murdo followed him, brushing by the pram in the doorway. His fists clenched. It was making everyone laugh that he had a girlfriend who went in the pub. It would stop when they were married. It would have to stop. How? How to change her at all, because she might take herself away, had done it before. Rage fidgeted impotently in his clenched hands.

She sat down beside him while Do'l Alex was fetching the drinks.

'I've got something to talk to you about. We'd better get back to my place as soon as possible.'

The rage was still on him. 'I'm in no hurry.'

'Well, I am. Just one drink, then we go.'

They had two, though he was afraid of her and of what she could take from him. Her nostrils whitened, but she was polite to Do'l Alex. He said his farewells, and left. She stood up, waiting.

Murdo stared into his last inch of beer. She tapped her foot a bit, then sat down again.

'Right!' She clasped her hands on the table. 'Since you don't seem to want to move, I'll say what I've got to say here.' She took a deep breath. 'It's your mother.' She added sharply, 'You might look at me. I can't talk to the side of your head.'

He turned unwillingly. She appeared less angry than he expected. Taking courage, he said sullenly, 'What about my mother? Are you complaining?'

'Yes, and with good reason. I know I'm not what she wants for a daughter-in-law, but if I'm to go and live under the same roof, we'll have to do better than this.'

She was tense, pushing her hair back with fast-moving fingers, crossing and uncrossing her legs. He hoped she would not start shouting. He glanced furtively around to see who was in earshot. It was early and the bar was nearly empty, only a couple of tourists and Shonny cadging a drink from them. That was bad. Shonny was on the dole and drinking hard these days, unlikely to keep himself to himself.

'Keep your voice down,' he mumbled.

'Is that all you can say?' Her voice rose.

He took fright. 'No, no. You tell on. What's bothering you?'

She swallowed, looking at her hands. 'Everything,' she said, after a pause.

'What do you mean? You said it was my mother just now. What's she been saying to you?'

'You know what she's like. It's all the time – I ought to go to church, I go to church and I have to wear a hat, I mustn't wear trousers, I mustn't have bare legs, I shouldn't come in here with you – just one trivial thing after another. I'm so damned sick of it!'

'Better not let her hear you using bad language either.' Murdo smirked. He felt as hostile to his mother as to his fiancée; their mutual antagonism amused him, even though he was afraid of what might come next.

Eleanor thumped the table. 'Hasn't she heard you? You're certainly foulmouthed enough to shock me.'

'Och, it's different in a man – she says.'

'Yes, she says! D'you know what she said today?'

'What is it now?'

'I drove down there specially to give Mairi a lift up – not that it's the first time: not that I mind. I'd given some hiker a ride, and there was mother glowering at the door. "You shouldn't be driving around with men, Eleanor. It doesn't look good when you are marrying Murdo." Well, really, I just about slapped her face.'

A new horror gripped Murdo, scrambling over his lurking jealousy of the unnamed hiker. 'What did you say to her?'

'What did *I* say to *her*? What d'you think? The truth! I told her she was a vile suspicious old hag. I said I wasn't marrying her and it was none of her business.'

'You said that? Oh God, you didn't say that, Eleanor!'

'I certainly did! And there's a lot more I'll say if she doesn't mend her ways. You'll have to say something to her yourself.'

Murdo looked glazed.

'I said you'll have to say something to her. I'm not going to take any more of her cheek.'

'You shouldn't have said that to her, Eleanor. She'll never . . . she . . . oh, fuckin' hell!'

'What *do* you mean?' Her eyes were blazing, her voice icy. 'She'll never let you marry me, is that it?'

'Ay.'

She laughed sharply. Shonny, leaning on the bar, turned to look.

'Be quiet,' muttered Murdo.

'Be quiet! Is that all you can say? You worm.'

'Ach, forget it. I'll say something to the old woman. Just be quiet now. We'll go over to your place for a bit.'

'No we won't. Not now or later. I want this sorted out. I don't believe you intend to speak to your mother about this at all. Do you?'

'Och yes. Yes, I will. But she is my mother – I got to be careful what I say –'

'And what will you do if she says you're not to marry me?'

He had no idea what he would do. He would do as his mother said. He would not do without Eleanor. He put his hand round her elbow, the fingers between her arm and her breast. 'Come on, let's go.'

'Go where?' She pulled away and stood up, facing him. 'I've had enough. I'm not going to wait for the boot from your mother.'

She slapped the table, turned on her heel and walked away. It

207

was only after the creak and crash of the swing doors had subsided that her late fiancé realised that he was looking at her ring, lying in a small pool of beer on the table. He stared at it for several minutes. Her fingers were very slim and white and the circle small. There was a streak of beer from it to the outer side of the table where her hand had swept across it. After a bit he picked it up and put it in his pocket.

Shonny appeared opposite and set drams down. He was yellow with drink, but not completely drunk.

'Having a bit of trouble, eh?'

'Bloody hell,' said Murdo at last, with hell indeed opening for him.

'Forget it! She'll be back tomorrow.'

'Not her.'

'Any of them. They're all the same. Say something nice – take her a box of chocolates—'

'Shut up.'

Shonny wagged a finger. 'Now now! That's what you get with them mainland girls. Liberated. Eleanor's a liberated woman. But she'll be back – maybe.'

She'll be back. He repeated it to himself several times. He didn't believe it, but the words had enough force to keep him sitting there, to hear Shonny say them again.

'She'll be back, don't you worry man.' He placed a solemn hand on the other's shoulder. 'I'll give you a bit of advice.'

'I don't want your advice.'

'My advice is good advice – a friend's advice, Murdo.' He drained first the pint and then the dram, and licked his lips. 'Listen now! Once you fucked one you fucked them all. They're all the same.'

Murdo rose, staggering more with rage than drink.

'She'll be back!' Shonny waved a hand. Murdo slumped down again. The swing doors creaked and crashed and he looked up.

'Hullo, it's your nice wee sister.'

Mairi came towards them, pulling her cardigan round her, looking away, abashed, from the eyes of the barman.

'Off duty, Mairi? Have a quick one.'

'Och no, I'm no staying. I was just looking for Calum. Is he about, Shonny?'

'Haven't seen him all day.' It piqued him that his middle brother had got there first with Mairi; he thought he had got pretty far, and resented it. He put his arm round her. 'I'll do instead.'

'Och, get off!' She pushed him, giggling. 'I'm no staying here with you. If you see Calum tell him I'm looking for him.'

'Will do. Now sit there by your brother and have a drink. A snowball?'

'Ay, that'll do.' She sat down beside Murdo. 'Where's Eleanor?' she asked, but he didn't answer. She shrugged. There was silence till Shonny returned. He squeezed into the seat beside her, and tried the arm again. This time she didn't resist; she was glad enough of the warmth on her shoulders.

'What's the news, then?'

'Oh, not much.' She looked down, sniffing slightly, and peered sideways at Murdo. 'I nearly forgot. I got Dad's pills here – you better take them home with you. I'm on late tonight, I'll be staying over.'

Her brother took the package without a word. Shonny's arm settled more intimately further down. She edged away, uncomfortably silent, then said, with a sudden giggle, 'I got one bit of news!'

'What's that?'

'Alan's coming back. Remember Alan Cameron? He was ringing Roddy this morning.'

'Oh ay. I remember him. That's interesting, I wonder does anyone else know about that yet.'

Murdo got up and made for the door, almost at a run. Mairi stared after him. 'Here, what's the matter with him?'

'Nothing. Just a wee lovers' tiff.'

'Oh, no!' Mairi eased away into her brother's vacated place. 'Oh well! With Alan coming back and all!' She put her hand to her mouth, laughing, but shaking her head too. 'You should hear what Eleanor said to my mum. That would be what done it. That would be it.'

'What did she say?'

His arm pursued her along the back of the seat. She slipped off the other end.

'I'm on in five minutes. 'Bye.'

Kirsty, decent in black and white for the dining room, was peeping round the door, waving to her. Mairi, going towards her, huddled into her cardigan, and began to sniff. By the time she reached the door, she was dabbing her eyes with a tissue.

Kirsty was agog. 'Are you, Mairi?' she whispered, clutching her arm.

'Yes!' with a sob she tore herself free and blundered into the ladies.

'Oh good God, girl!' Kirsty clapped her hand to her mouth and ran after her.

In the bar of the ferry, Porky was filling in the details of recent local history. Alan had met him on the pier – taller, broader, hairier, and divertingly tattooed, but much the same about the snout, on his way home between spells of roughnecking.

'Your redheaded girlfriend's got engaged,' he volunteered, rolling a cigarette.

'To Murdo Morrison, presumably?'

'Ay. Surly bugger. Pity you took so long coming back, eh?' He winked and lit up.

Alan grinned, backing away from the smoke. 'Unlike you, Porky, I can manage without it. That's what old age does for you.' He felt, in fact, distinctly listless. He had put it down to the non-stop drive from London, but wondered if it went deeper, when he surveyed Porky burgeoning before him in his riggers' boots, with bulging denim crotch and checks straining across his barrel chest.

Porky treated him to the familiar cross-eyed leer. 'You're no looking that bad. You been somewhere in the sun anyway.'

'Yes. Two seasons in the South Seas. Tahiti – most beautiful women in the world, you'd like it.'

Porky made appreciative noises. 'They willing?'

'Very. You can't stop 'em.'

'Oh boy! How d'you get there?'

Porky's repertoire of bodily expressiveness was as beastly as ever. Alan laughed out loud, relieved he no longer had any responsibility for keeping order over the obscene writhing of eyebrows, hands and ears. 'Swim,' he said.

He ordered another drink for Porky, not for himself, and made his escape out to the deck. Gannets were knifing into the sea. He blinked at them, fuddled by the fresh air after the whisky and the long journey. One after the other they dropped with split-second accuracy. Beyond them the Port Long light was coming up on the bow.

He slumped down on the nearest seat. It was the same scene: three years almost to the day; to the hour, because the ferry timetable hadn't changed. He had thought a lot about what it would be like coming back, and dreaded it and longed for it. He waited in trepidation for the expected rush of memories, but they did not come. It was just a trip to Boreray on an average late summer's day. He could remember every detail of that first voyage, Selena chafing the big BMW, the two ministers in the cafeteria, the flat basin of Port Long pockmarked with rain after the turbulent passage. He remembered it, but it had nothing to do with him. He was very tired and rather drunk. He hoped the bed at Skalanish wouldn't be too damp.

The hope was so shockingly inapposite that he got up and wandered round the deck. He hadn't left the South Seas to worry about damp beds. He couldn't remember ever even noticing if a bed was damp in his life. It must be true what he had said to Porky. Getting old; growing up – he had always thought when he was a boy that when you grew up you didn't feel things any more, not real things worth feeling about, only money and health and what to eat – and damp beds. Perhaps it really did happen, then. His knee hurt. It had had a nasty encounter with a python-like hawser six months previously, but it had not occurred to him till that moment that it would always ache now, or that it would matter if it did. He sat down again, scowling, disliking himself greatly. He thought he would have been better getting properly drunk in Porky's reprobate company. Then it struck him that Porky himself might appear at any time, and instigate a conversation. He shut his eyes defensively and curled as far into the corner as possible.

It was a puzzle why he was there at all. When he had left, he had not intended to go back, Selena notwithstanding. The memories had been too bad; they were not good now, only enfeebled by two years' determined turning away. What they might be back on Boreray he did not know, and couldn't imagine why he had set himself to find out. He had told Roddy he was coming to complete the work on the boat and take her away, about four months' work, finished by New Year, probably. It sounded convincing enough, but in fact he had no relish for it: Selena had ceased to live for him before ever he had left the island. Yet there was a sort of loyalty about it, because he had brought her there as a forlorn wreck. There was a promise to be fulfilled. It had been that feeling of things left undone that had brought him home.

Home. He had not realised until then that by home he had meant Boreray – had he? It didn't seem like going home. Boarding the plane in Brisbane he had had an elated feeling about it. 'Going home': he had thought of working beside carpenters with slow Devon voices, of the richly fragrant Etoile de Hollande outside his mother's drawing room window, of long iridescent evenings on the sea lochs of Argyll. Selena had been merely a sneaking guilt, and Boreray carefully buried. Perhaps it was just the usual restlessness that had sent him back. Certainly he had extricated himself with relief from the too-smart boats and too-rich clientele. He was sick of using his skill to make a living, sick of being charming to spoiled daughters and their bootleather mothers, sick of taking their fathers' money, sick of endless vapid questions, of champagne parties on board and unspeakable barbecues on land. He had made the decision to retreat while vomiting up a lobster that might as well have been roast long pig: he had been so drunk he wouldn't have noticed the difference anyway. So perhaps he hadn't been thinking of unfulfilled obligations at all, but of mere escape, as usual.

But why Boreray? He opened his eyes, frowning in the sudden light. The gannets were still diving, blindingly white against blue water and the low green promontory of the lighthouse. It was beautiful, but he had seen it before. It held no answers, any more than the blood-warm perfume of the roses in his mother's garden.

She had been in poor spirits. A hysterectomy in the spring had left her pale, gaunt and aged: and depressed. 'I don't feel like a woman any more,' she had said; and if her life as it had been had constituted being a woman, she was right. There were no men any longer, the men who had been the mirror in which she assured herself that she was as she wanted to be. Harold was unimaginative but conscientious, brought her flowers every second day and looked permanently guilty. 'He's sleeping with his secretary, darling,' Celia told Alan. 'You can't blame him.' She didn't blame him, but she had cried.

Alan kept her company for a fortnight, as long as was tolerable. She wanted to know what he was going to do, but seemed resigned when he told her. She hadn't much fight left in her; it had gone with the shine in her hair and the firmness of her body. He had promised to go back for Christmas: 'Before, if you don't feel better soon.'

Driving north through the night, he had been alive with the intention of fulfilling the things undone. The exits and intersections, the border, the deserted Highland roads sang going home. A roebuck leapt the beam of his headlights at Crianlarich, and dawn broke in Glencoe, golden on the head of the Great Shepherd and grey in the river valley where dun horses moved indistinctly through the brown rushes. He had been feverish with anticipation; but of what? On the pierhead it had evaporated, although the sea was dancing blue and white, and the ferrymen had the speech and features of the islands. He could not imagine what his expectation had been: not Selena, a matter only of spars and chandlery and so many tins of paint and varnish; not Boreray, beautiful as it was. Not Donnie, certainly: that was irrecoverable. On the journey he had taken care not even to think his name. He thought it now, and since it proved bearable, which it should not have been, thought further, cautiously, as one explores a bad tooth. He allowed an image to surface, and that didn't hurt either, till its very powerlessness summoned a dull ache of loss. He knew he could no longer recall the living features. All that remained were the frozen attitudes of a few photographs, Donnie with Ben on Traìgh Mhór, at the helm of the dinghy on a nearly glassy day, with Mairi milking Johane's cow. He had been afraid to look at these pictures for a long time after the event, but when he had, it was to find them so dead to reality that they provoked only a faint echo of grief. He carried them with him constantly, but hardly ever glanced at them. They had imposed a desolate distance more final than the natural wasting of memory, and he regarded them with the same distaste as the string of beads round his neck. But he didn't get rid of either. He found his fingers sliding now in the habitual manner under the necklace, and thought of the two boys struggling on the classroom floor. It was irrelevant; there was nothing he expected to find left outstanding from that life he had lived.

The ship was drawing alongside. The *Maid of Rona* bobbed in the surge from her rear-thrusters. A trio of young herring gulls perched on the neat stack of creels on the deck. Port Long was totally familiar, with a familiarity neither exciting nor repellent. He didn't wait to see the warps thrown.

Porky was lurking on the car-deck. 'Any chance of a lift?'

213

'Sure. I'd have offered, but I thought you'd be hitting the town tonight.'

Porky's eyes crossed with warming comicality. 'I'm scared of the *cailleach*. She'd skin me if I didn't go home – oh well! Where did you get this then?'

Alan, key in the lock, looked round vaguely to see what he might have got where.

'The car, man! This fantastic machine – oh boy! you come up in the world, all right!' He moved round the sleek Porsche, patting it lasciviously and chortling.

Alan laughed. 'It's a nasty petrol-guzzling aberration. Port Long to Skalanish in five minutes, holing the exhaust on the triple bump at Ardbuie – unless they've done some roadworks?'

'No chance! This is great! What a car, eh?' He pulled out his half-bottle to celebrate.

Alan declined, but felt slightly cheered. He was ashamed of the car, but at least it would entertain his neighbours. Ashore, he put his foot down obligingly, since it didn't really bother him whether the exhaust survived the road or not.

'Six and a half minutes! Good God!' Porky was ecstatic as they hurtled down the Ardbuie turn-off, scattering his mother's hens.

'Come along some morning before you hit the bottle and you can have a go.'

'Will do!'

Four or five of Porky's siblings spilled out of the house, open-mouthed and round-eyed. They were all two inches taller than last time. Alan had forgotten he would know everyone. He realised then that collecting the key from Roddy would mean a social call, and wished he hadn't telephoned in advance.

In the event, by the time he had been with them half an hour, he was reluctant to leave, to go on to the empty house with its uncertain memories. Chrissie had a meal waiting, and Roddy poured enormous drams. Their welcome was wholehearted and disarming. They pressed him to stay the night, but he resisted, though with an effort.

He walked down the familiar path in the dusk, hesitating on the last bend, wondering how it would be. The house was just there, itself, as it had always been, with its back sturdily to the rising ground

214

and its long and short chimneys, the long one smoking; Chrissie had lit the stove and cleaned and aired, and also, he noticed as he went in, set a mousetrap. He bent to disengage it, glad it had no victim, and straightening up bumped his head as usual on the lintel of the kitchen door. He stood in the quiet, looking around at the familiar objects in their ordinary places, and it was not appalling, or not yet. But as at any moment it might become so, he went hastily backwards and forwards unpacking the car, filling the house with things that had not been there before. He went to check on Selena, but briefly, only for the form of it. Returning, he noticed a pale orb glimmering on the darkening windowsill. It was Donnie's sea urchin. A hail of prickles fell from it as he picked it up, although it must have sat there in the wind and rain for two years. He turned it gently in his hands, and waited with obedient dread for the agonising rush of memory. Instead, he felt merely rather wistful; and when he went into the house again, opening doors aimlessly, it seemed incredible that he had lain on that bed weeping for a whole night, and for nights after that. It was difficult even to imagine what it felt like to shed tears.

Chapter 22

It was drizzling next morning, with midges. Since he had left the window open overnight, Alan woke up scratching, wondering with sleepy ill-temper why on earth he had wanted to come back. But the unanswerability of the question raised spectres worse than midges; he put it away with a bleak determination to do what he had purportedly come for as quickly as possible, and leave. Of course there were social decencies that would have to be observed: it would be offensive not to call on neighbours who had treated him so kindly in the past. During a midge-discouraging cold bath, he decided it would be as well to get the visiting over quickly, so that he could hide with an easy conscience, and be forgotten about.

Nevertheless, he would probably have found enough reasons to prevent him seeking anyone out, at least for that day, if Porky hadn't appeared to remind him of his promise of the previous evening.

'Stone cold sober!' he said proudly, with a corroborative puff of peppermint and stale smoke.

He had three younger boys in tow, whose round expectant faces made excuses difficult.

'All right,' agreed Alan, reluctantly, 'but no smoking. You can put the thing in the ditch if you want, but I'm not having it stinking of tobacco. And no bubblegum either,' he continued, remembering the habits of the under-fourteens. A mile or so towards Port Long he had cause to add fiercely, 'No murder!' as Porky swooped with maniacal glee on a panic-stricken rabbit.

'Och, they're vermin, them.'

'Nice little bunnies, right?'

'Right.'

They screamed round every bend on Boreray three times, without bloodshed, stopping twice to change the consignment of brothers and cousins. When they eventually drew up at Porky's door in a spray of mud and gravel, it was before a reception committee of all the Ardbuie males whose age and dignity had precluded begging a ride. There was general handshaking, with approving looks and comments. Porky's sister photographed him and the vehicle in various heroic poses, and there was scuffling among the younger children to have their pictures taken as well. Very little pressing was required to persuade their fathers to make trial runs, and shortly the policeman appeared to find out what was happening and had to have a go too. After that there were drams and cups of tea, and the occasion turned into an agreeably wasted Borerayan day; or rather, as far as the humdrum routine of money-pinched and unemployed Ardbuie went, not wasted but enlivened. Alan thought of it that way as he drew up at Skalanish, and almost liked the Porsche for the first time since the day after he had bought it, as an easy way of getting rid of cash in hand when Torquil's will was settled.

The relief of having painlessly re-established friendly relations with Ardbuie encouraged him to promise himself Gnipadale the following day. In the afternoon he walked along the shore in that direction, but was intercepted by Roddy and Chrissie. They found the house quiet, they said, with only Dina at home. Morag Ann was at catering college in Edinburgh, and Kirsty was working at the hotel in Port Long. Alan did not resist their hospitality.

Next day he started from the other end of the township, at Lal's. He found Sandy at home, doing nothing, as monosyllabic as ever, but unmistakeably eager for a turn at the wheel of the Porsche.

'I haven't passed my test,' he mumbled, looking stricken.

'Never mind.' Alan hadn't the heart to disappoint him; that was by far the greatest number of words Sandy had ever spoken to him in one breath. In the event, he suffered very little damage, only a smashed rear light and a hard look from the policeman.

He found that old Johane had moved in with Lal and Katie after a bad stroke.

'She will not know you, but you will go through to see her, will you?'

Lal's question clearly did not brook a negative reply. Alan was dismayed: he remembered her kindness and good humour, and had no stomach for seeing her now, bedridden, witless and degraded. But Katie had already gone to tidy her up for her visitor.

The room was cramped and foetid, and the old pale face shockingly blank. So as not to look at it, he focussed on the collar of the new pink bedjacket, embroidered in coarse shades of orange and mauve, with harsh white lace.

'It is Alan Cameron here to see you, Nanan,' Katie said, repeating it in Gaelic. 'She does not have any English now,' she explained apologetically, 'but just speak to her a wee bit. It passes the time for her.'

She smoothed the ugly collar gently, as if she divined Alan's thoughts – as indeed, being an islander, she probably did – and slipped away. Ashamed, he clasped the empty hands lying loose on the turned-down sheet, and looked into her face. It changed, one-sidedly, warming into a smile and then a chuckle, with a lightening of the eye as the failing brain searched after intelligibility. Her hands tightened weakly, the one more than the other.

'How are you tonight? It is good to see you,' she said, with the same gentle courteous manner she had always used.

'I am very well. And how are you yourself?' His Gaelic just about stretched to that, but he stammered, disconcerted by the familiar dignity of her greeting, issuing from that blue-lipped life-in-death visage.

'Och, I am well indeed!'

Her voice was tranquil. He dared to search further in her face, and saw that the half which moved and was alive was kind and serene: the eye not vacant, but expressive of what she uttered, that she did believe she was well indeed. He could summon up no more in her language, but said in English, 'It's good to see you again. I don't think you remember me, but I used to go to Angus's house a lot. You were always very kind to me – kind to everyone. I'm sorry I don't have Gaelic to talk to you properly.'

She pulled at his hand, and he leant towards her, while she looked and smiled and nodded, bright as a little child in that side of her face which was not frozen. 'Oh well well, it is a bonny lad here to see me tonight, Katie,' she said, patting his hand in the old way.

He glanced round for Katie and help, but she had not in fact reappeared. He was at a loss what to say. The feeble voice lapsed into a mutter and then a whisper, and in her eye the fragile web of understanding began to dissipate. It was injury to let it go. To hold it, he spoke what was in his mind. 'I remember you with your brown cow, and Donnie and Mairi singing. We were very happy.'

It was safe to say it because she had no English now, but his voice shook and he broke off. She smiled and talked. He didn't understand much of it, but he caught the names of the two youngest grandchildren; then '*Piseag, piseag – seo bainne.*' The cat's milk, in the blue chipped saucer on the grass, the first squirt from the udder her portion.

Katie came in then, and up to the bed, rearranging the pillows and bedspread, talking all the time cheerfully in Gaelic. Then she said quietly in English, 'She's away again now.'

The face was blank once more. Alan stood up, still holding the limp hands, till he saw Katie wanted to cover them. She smoothed the sheet and pulled the curtains across the window, and stood waiting to usher him out.

He glanced at the inert figure, propped image-like against the pillows. 'Is she – she seems so cheerful. Is she always happy when she comes round like that?'

Katie regarded the shapeless hump with tender pride. 'Och, she is wonderful really. She is never complaining.'

What was wonderful was Katie. He had hardly felt he knew her: she was indistinguishable from so many other respectable island housewives, with features forever composed and nothing to say but

218

agreeable commonplaces. She must be nearly sixty, and would expect now to nurse her mother-in-law till she was old herself. Yet her face spoke more than resignation. She turned to the bed as they went out and said, 'Goodnight, Nanan.' Then to Alan, with her hands clasped in the decent attitude, 'Well, well, it is the will of the Lord.'

Not feeling at ease with the Lord's will, he said what he knew she would want to hear, though it seemed to him a gross insult to put it in such terms: 'I can see she's very well looked after.'

'Och, there's no much we can do.' But she was pleased, he could tell from her voice.

They went into the sitting room, and Lal, smoking silently by the fireside, shook his head and repeated, 'Well, well, a big change, eh? But it is the will of the Lord.'

This time Alan agreed halfheartedly that it was; and his primary impatience with Jehovah flickered slightly before the complexity of the issues facing the divine mind. Katie was smiling and bringing in tea.

Driving home he noticed Johane's house dark above the road in the twilight. It had never been other than a corrugated iron shack, but while she lived there, it had lived too, with the faded brown door open in the daytime and warm yellow light in the window in the evening, peat smoke in the chimney and a cat on the doorstep. It was dead and shrunken now under the lowering night-black crags, a formless mess of rusty iron and smeary glass.

As he walked down his own path, that house too came into view dark and humble, and unkempt in outline. He stopped outside and looked at it hard, seeing the frayed edges of the rusting roof, the cracked window, the peeling paint, the loose handle of the door; but it would not empty itself of meaning, as Johane's house had done. He gave his doorknob the usual cautious jiggle, pushing it in and then quickly up before turning it. The movement was friendly, habitual as a neighbour's face or a well-worn garment: the house lived in it. It was not physical decay or physical darkness that killed, but the fading of daily life, of the continuity of custom.

There was a phrase hovering in his mind which he couldn't pin down for the moment; the ceremony of innocence. He stood in the blackness of the narrow lobby, while his head filled with sunlight and the smell of grass. It was only after he had picked up the photographs from the bedside table that he remembered to switch on the light.

The two children with the brown cow appeared, a faint and tenuous symbol standing for a memory so razor sharp, so white hot that it left no sensation. He turned the light off absent-mindedly, and on again, and put the photographs away, which was the intended move, without looking at the rest of them.

He slumped into Uncle Ewan's chair with his arms behind his head and wondered why, being so cauterised, he was reluctant to visit Angus and Mairi Anna, unwilling to walk down the path past the cow's milking stance or along the shore below the ragged patches of green corn; afraid, as he now realised, to hear news of Donnie. Yet what could he hear that would hurt? It would only be that he was training successfully or wasn't, that he liked the city or didn't, that he came home sometimes or didn't. All of that would be common knowledge in the township anyway, and none of it could make any difference now. Except perhaps if he were expected home: there was a residual terror of meeting again. He told himself, as he had before, that it was simply enough dealt with; he could either be away coincidentally, or grit his teeth and put up with it. The latter would be better, if he could force himself to it. After it had happened, that would be that, the ghost would be laid, because whatever else remained the same, it was absolutely impossible that Donnie would feel for him as he once had, with the unqualified devotion of sixteen. He was bound to be changed in that respect at least, and probably in almost every other as well. Nevertheless, his imagination began to explore the not unlikely case that he would be friendly and open, and eager to talk about interim events. He clamped down on it ferociously: if friendly, also final. There could be no attempt to put the clock back, no trespass on whatever life he now lived. He thought that over grimly with all that it implied: what it would be like meeting again and never saying, 'Do you remember . . .', alluding only to the two years in which they had been strangers. He shrank from such a meeting; and yet, if it could happen like that, without reference to the past, it would be so much easier to accept finality, knowing that he was happy, or anyway well adjusted: or at least (Alan grew more desperate) set in some course that made it impossible even to contemplate the never-possible alternative. Surely he would be changed, like all the other boys who went away and did well and came back to strut around for a week, swearing and drinking hard, with black moustaches and hairy throats, and an obsessional interest in football or barmaids. Like Porky – not that Porky had ever been much different, but Alan stifled that thought quickly, continuing the unlikely scenario. If he had a girlfriend, as he probably had by now: a steady girlfriend, perhaps pregnant. He grasped at this solution eagerly, till a sobering twinge of conscience reminded him that, if true, a shotgun marriage at eighteen would hardly be in Donnie's interests. He shook himself and paced round the room, angry at his own absurdity in running ahead of events; it was not even likely that they would both be on the island at the same time, since he intended to leave before Christmas. But the thought would not rest that if they could meet, if there could be a meeting with no meeting-point, with no common ground, then the past would be dissolved; it would really, finally be over, the injury he had caused and the guilt which had injured him at last wiped out.

He decided he would visit Angus and Mairi Anna the next day, but he put it off, and then Sunday intervened. By the middle of the week, though, it was worse not going than going; and once he was actually in their shabby living room, oddly more familiar than his mother's drawing room, he found the occasion surprisingly painless, if depressing. Mairi Anna had aged, her dark hair turned iron-grey and her face thin and anxious. She had three separate selections of pills for Angus during the evening, small white ones and big round brown ones. He seemed frail and self-absorbed, talking alternately of his youth and of what the doctor said, when he spoke at all; but he had never been conversational, and it was Mairi Anna who related news of the family. Old Effie had recently died.

'Only five weeks,' she said, pulling at her black cardigan, 'and that was a great pity with Angus's mother, though I should not be saying it. We did not have the room we have since Effie died when she was taken ill, and so she went with Lal and Katie. But Angus would rather she had been with us here.'

'Ach well, that was not to be,' said Angus quietly.

Looking from one to the other, Alan saw it grieved them that the old mother was not with the eldest son, and was amazed and humbled that they would have welcomed another such burden, after a lifetime of Auntie Effie's maledictions.

'Och, we won't talk all night of bad news,' said Mairi Anna, glancing at her husband.

'How's the rest of the family?'

He learnt that Ewan had got his mate's ticket, that Alex Angus and Rhoda were expecting another child 'any day', that Effie was a ward sister now, and Chrissann working in a dress shop in Inverness.

'And Johane is thinking of coming home. She can't get work out there, and the wee one is getting that foulmouthed. It is very rough there in Livingstone. She would be better here with us.'

'Ay, she would,' agreed Angus. 'Better if she never went away.'

'Och well, she was only young!' Her mother sighed, and paused. 'And Murdo? I hear he's engaged.'

There was a longer and very sticky pause.

'Well, we'll see,' grunted Angus, at length.

In embarrassment, Alan remembered that all had not been well between Mairi Anna and Eleanor. Poor old Eleanor, he thought. But he was glad enough of an excuse to change the subject.

'What about Donnie?'

'Oh, he's doing very well over there.'

They would have left it at that. Being the insignificant seventh child, he was not much in their minds. Alan questioned further, with sweating palms. Yes, he had work, though how long it would last was doubtful, the firm was in some trouble or other, and they didn't train apprentices like in the old days. Yes, he had got used to the city. No, he didn't come home much.

'The young folk never come home much. Too much life in the towns,' said Angus.

That didn't sound like the boy he had known. He filed it as evidence for change, and told himself he was relieved; but he found the rest of the evening's conversation difficult.

Having got the visits over, he applied himself to Selena, and hid. He was far from easy in his own company, and every day seemed to last a long time. Such casual meetings as he had with other people – with Roddy as he went about his sheep, or with the Ardbuie children cycling along the road – filled him with grateful warmth, enough to cheer up a whole morning; but he avoided deliberate encounters.

Yet he had never previously been so aware of the richness of sociality around him, of the ties of kinship and neighbourliness. He

222

had more time, being alone, to ponder what those ties meant to the people who lived by them. He wondered why he had never seen the community so clearly before, though he should have done, in the summer when he had helped Angus's family and enjoyed so many kindnesses in return. He had accepted the practical implications of mutual assistance and tolerance, of course, without which the events of the crofting year simply could not take place. He supposed he had assumed it was somehow mechanical, because so apparently efficient, an intricate machine fuelled by reciprocal obligation. But things looked different to him now. He had been shown such unexpected welcome and affection: Roddy wringing his hand till it hurt, Chrissie working all day to make the cottage homely, undemonstrative Mairi Anna's dignified reproach, 'It is good to see you again. We were thinking you had forgotten us.' There was no practical reason why anyone in that long-term community should treat him so kindly, when he would be gone for good in a few months' time, no reason why they should be glad to see him, as they obviously were, or why they should expect him to be glad to see them, as they obviously did. He remembered, feeling humbled, how Eleanor had once cut him down to size by assuring him that the welcome he was offered had nothing to do with his own merits: 'You don't think it's because they *like* you, do you?' He recalled how her acid tone had stung at the time. He had taken her to mean that the relationship involved, the duty of friendliness to strangers, was a cold and rigid formality. He saw now that it was not like that at all, but on the contrary so warmly felt that it would have been extended to him whatever his own worth or lack of it. It was not duty as he had ever comprehended it. It was not duty that heartened Katie or grieved Angus in their dealings with old Johane, or that brought the failed and faded old men of Ardbuie out to admire Porky in his hour of youthful glory. The network that held families and townships together was not of obligation but of love, unindividuated and spontaneous, the ceremony of innocence. For the first time he really understood what Eleanor had meant, that a place was the people who live in it, and why she was driven to give up her freedom in order to belong to it. He thought of her often, as he shaped spars and cut down endless coats of varnish. He hoped she would find what she was looking for, and thought perhaps he ought to go and see her, to wish her well, but he didn't do so, and

223

knew he had no real intention of it. He preferred to be alone: it was all he felt fit for.

He had brought various devices for staving off emptiness, a radio and a record player and plenty of books. He had had none of these in the old days, and had never missed them. He was aware of the contrast, but at first glad to drown it out by listening to music all evening, or rereading favourite books he hadn't seen for years, or doing both at once and gaining nothing from either. But after a few days, he found his reliance on these things so depressing that he wanted to do without them, and could not, because the silence in the house after nightfall was so final. He quickly took to working all evening as well as all day; and gradually perceived through the soft monotonous swish of sandpaper why it was better to be out there with the boat than inside listening to the St Matthew Passion. With the music, and even with the books, it was as with the community: he could admire these but he was apart from them. He could not have them, and they could not have him. He was on the outside; and better to stay there than live a lie.

There was enough work in Selena to fill the hours. Most of what was left was the internal fitting-out and rigging. He stuck to his intention, as there seemed no point in changing it, of preparing her for short ocean passages in high latitudes, up to a week, perhaps. He had meant to take her round home waters first, then to the Orkneys and Shetland, and on to Iceland. But he had not envisaged starting in January. She should certainly be ready, probably stiffening in the water by late November, if the weather was reasonable. He considered trailing her to the mainland and starting out in the spring, but such a delay conflicted with an impelling desire to get things over with. When he thought about it, that seemed silly. Getting something over with meant starting something new, and there was nothing he wanted to do. But any direction was better than none. He clung, on the whole, to the idea of sailing her as soon as possible, substituting Ireland and waters south for the Orkneys and the north. A singlehanded winter voyage seemed appropriate, and in a way he began to look forward to it.

But when he glanced at his watch to see how things were progressing, he could never believe that it was only three o'clock, or only the tenth of September. To break up the days, he walked along the coast or in the hills as he had in the first autumn. He was conscientious in tabulating what he saw in accordance with previous impressions: the late sprigs of heather trembling by a sheltered stream, cormorants coursing the same flightpath on a windy day, the glistening wrack of shells after a strong north-westerly. There were the usual rainbows; they implied rain, and he had taken a dislike to being rained on. He acquired a new measurement of time, in that when his bad knee began to hurt noticeably he knew that he had done an hour's rough walking, and when it hurt so much he couldn't think of anything else, two hours. Then he caught himself turning back one afternoon at the base of the great dunes behind Tràigh Mhór because an hour was up, without even climbing them to look out to sea. He became so furious that he walked till after dark, all the way to Garve along the beach and back through the saddle of Gormul and Càrn Bàn. By the time he reached home, he had bitten a chunk out of the inside of his lip with pain: but at least after that his walks had a more challenging purpose than filling in time, and in fact his leg did strengthen, unpleasantly but quickly.

Returning from one of these forays on a grey damp evening, he glimpsed a figure on the path making for his door, and hastily doubled back, unseen, to avoid whoever it was. But as the chill drizzle gave him some compunction about his unwanted visitor, who would get wet to no purpose, he hesitated and turned again, swearing to himself.

It was Eleanor. He slithered down the last steep bank calling her, suddenly as delighted as he had been grudging a moment before, and would have seized her in his arms if he hadn't remembered that it would probably earn him a slap in the face and send her away. He drew up short beside her.

'Eleanor! How lovely to see you.'

She stood there straight-backed in the misty amorphous evening, neat and defined from her water-pearled russet curls to her glossy black boots. Her arms were by her sides but she was smiling, thrusting her chin up in the remembered way to counteract the discrepancy in height. That made him laugh.

'Same old Eleanor! I promise I won't look down on you.'

'Same old Alan – aren't you going to ask me in out of the rain?'

In the narrow doorway, her warm perfume was in his nostrils, erasing the damp pungencies of heather and peaty water. She stood in the middle of the kitchen, shedding gloves and coat and scarf. She glanced around with a slight snort.

'This place doesn't look any better.'

'Doesn't it?'

'Neither do you.' She turned a penetrating gaze on him. 'Are you ill?'

'What? No, of course not.' Her intent, flecked appraisal did nothing for his self-esteem. 'I think I forgot to shave probably.' His knee was hurting abominably.

'Yes,' she agreed, mercifully losing interest as she noticed the record player. 'Quite a nice one,' she allowed, crossing to inspect it.

He followed her, drawn by her familiar backview, the tapering waist and round hips. Suddenly he remembered, and retreated.

'I hear you're engaged – congratulations.'

She didn't turn. 'Who told you that?'

'I think it was Porky.'

She faced him, with hands held up and fingers spread.

'Well, I'm not. See? It's been off for some time. Where have you been buried since you got back?'

'Sorry – I haven't been out much. I haven't seen anyone for days.'

'Well, Ben Gunn! What about that smart car, then? I even thought you might drive up to see me in it.'

'I meant to!' He felt as if he really had: couldn't imagine why he hadn't. The featureless solitude of ten minutes before seemed suddenly insupportable.

She tossed her head, with another snort, and marched over to the stove for the kettle.

'Sorry, I just didn't get round to it.' He followed her again as she filled it at the sink and took it back to the stove, and hovered behind her as she inspected the mugs with apparent disapproval.

'Have you got a sheepdog in your ancestry?' she snapped over her shoulder.

He sat down meekly. It had become very important to keep her in a good humour. He struggled against a dangerous impulse to ask her about Murdo. Though the news of her engagement had left him unmoved at the time, he was suddenly burningly curious to know what had happened; and about what might happen next, and whether she might stay. He kept quiet, on the assumption that if he said anything at all it would be the wrong thing.

'Lost your tongue?' she asked, briskly, banging a mug down in front of him.

Since it contained coffee rather than tea, he deduced that she was feeling friendly. She didn't seem put out by his silence. She talked enough for both of them, expounding two years' happenings, or non-happenings, in Port Long and Fladday, and examining him on his conduct in the meantime. Couldn't he have managed to send a postcard or so from such exotic places? Had he taken lots of photographs? Really not *any*? And had he kept his music up?

Before he could reply to that one, she gave him her most withering schoolmarm look and said, 'Of course not!'

'Well – no.'

'You'd better start practising again, hadn't you?'

'Yes! I will, but—' he stifled the admission that he had no idea where his instruments were, or even if he had brought them with him.

She eyed him sternly. 'You can start tonight. I'll come in on my way from Fladday tomorrow.'

'Yes – good God, you'll be absolutely horrified!'

'I dare say.' She stood up and reached for her coat and scarf.

'Do you have to go already?'

She shrugged into her coat, evading his hands on her shoulders. 'Yes, I want to get home before dark.'

He spent the rest of the day catching up on the musical backslidings of two years, and went to bed with a headache, a sore throat and an anticipation both fearful and happy of what she would say when she discovered the extent of his negligence.

Next morning he felt extraordinarily limp and shaky. After half an hour of leaning against Selena telling himself he must start work, while coloured lights flashed in front of his eyes, he concluded that Eleanor had been right about his being ill, and went back to bed. When she was due to arrive he got up and dressed, reeling, lay down again, and drifted into a groggy doze. Her cross voice from the kitchen woke him with a start. He leapt up, got halfway through the door, and fainted at her feet. As the blackness trickled away, he became aware of her arms round him, and her voice at a great distance saying 'Oh, Alan darling!' This was so gratifyingly affectionate that he made no attempt to recover, other than nestling against her. But Eleanor was not that easily fooled.

'Stop playing dead, you idiot! You scared me. I knew you were ill yesterday.' She prodded him into a sitting position.

'I'm never ill,' he said hazily, 'absolutely never.'

'Don't be so silly! You're mortal, you know. You'd better lie down.'

She disappeared into the bedroom, and he heard vigorous pillow-thumping noises. It was incredibly difficult to get on his feet and stay there. He leant on the high bed-end while Eleanor buzzed round him.

'I suppose I might have picked up something abroad,' he said, doubtfully.

'No need to romanticise! There's 'flu about in Port Long. I expect you've got that, like everyone else. You're sweating like a pig.'

'Do pigs really sweat? I've never worked out if that's true.'

She turned back the bedclothes and pointed severely. 'Get undressed.'

For the next night and day he was conscious of very little, except that Eleanor seemed to be there whenever he woke up, sponging him with cold water or otherwise pushing him around, and telling him he was talking nonsense.

'I'm not talking at all,' he said, aggrieved, when he had gathered his wits sufficiently to reply.

'You've been raving for the past twenty-four hours,' she replied shortly.

She went out to fill an empty tumbler, while he considered this. When she came back he asked, 'Eleanor, have you been here all the time? Did you stay last night?'

She didn't answer. 'If you're not a whole lot better by tomorrow I'm going to get the doctor,' she said, with menace.

The threat was effective. Though he was still very feeble the next day, the fever and headache had subsided. Eleanor came in the middle of the morning and said, 'You look awful.'

'No, I'm fine.'

'Dreadful. Half dead.'

'I was just wondering where you were.'

Even to his own ears his voice sounded querulous, and he expected

228

a reprimand, but she merely said, 'You big baby! I went home for a change of underwear.'

She stayed for the rest of that day and returned for most of the two following, treating him with uncharacteristic forbearance. His own patience was more quickly exhausted: he wasn't used to lying in bed doing nothing, was incapable of anything more arduous, and soon became plaintive. When she saw he was getting better, she began to snap again, castigated him for feeling sorry for himself, told him he could do his own beastly washing now, pushed him away when he dared to put his arm round her: and then, when he came back from having a bath, was lying naked on his bed.

'I thought you looked more lively tonight,' she explained, matter-of-fact.

Chapter 23

She was different: definitely softer. Over the next few weeks they spent increasingly long periods together without music, sex or argument, though most of the time they still engaged in at least one of these. Occasionally she remained with him for a whole night, or even better, though rarer, a whole day. She began to bring her knitting as well as her violin, and passed evenings listening amicably to his records. She tidied up after him without jibes, fed him sometimes, and expected him to fix her kitchen shelves and broken hairdrier in return. She was no longer angry if she came home from work or babysitting and found him in front of her television. She took to kissing him hello and goodbye, and even goodnight.

Alan, sprawled on her sofa with a book, considered the change in her rather sleepily. She was knitting a pink thing for some baby; she seemed to know every infant in both islands. She sat with her slim legs crossed and fingers moving deftly between the clicking needles. He watched her quietly, yawning now and again, unentertained but not unhappy. He was curious about this new undemanding coexistence, in the very poses of conventional domesticity. As they were at that moment, they could have been married for years: she could be knitting for the fourth arrival. He wondered idly how she would look pregnant, if she would assume that drugged, smug sort of expression that a lot of women seemed to wear, and turned hastily back to his book in case she would look up and ask why he was grinning. But his concentration was poor; Hegel came off second best in a tussle with the fantasy of being married to Eleanor. It was enticing for a moment, and then alarming. A fourth child was an appalling prospect, a previous trio quite horrific. She would be bound to have dozens, she was mad about babies. And she hated boats. Anyway, while it was pleasant to spend an evening thus when it was only (he counted) the sixth in his life, the sixtieth or six hundredth might be a different matter. Besides, he reminded himself, she had never suggested marrying him; she presumably would if she wanted to.

He yawned again and buried his face in his arms and *Phaenomenologie*, slightly wistful, in spite of her uncongenial bent towards motherhood. Away from her, he was too haunted by loneliness not to wonder, sometimes.

'I was speaking to Murdo today,' she offered, suddenly.

'Mm?' He raised his head. She never mentioned Murdo to him. He hadn't even been sure that she had stopped meeting him.

Her fingers moved as before in the pink wool. She was counting under her breath, frowning.

He sat up. 'What's that supposed to mean?'

'Just what I said. I met him on the pier.'

'Accident or design?'

'I don't go in for accidents. He's been trying to get me to meet him for ages – since I broke it off, really. I decided it was unfair not to, so I did.'

He considered this uneasily. She didn't elaborate, or look as if she intended to.

'The pier's a bit public, isn't it?' he remarked at length. Surely even Eleanor wouldn't choose such a venue for a grand reconciliation.

'I don't feel like anything too private at the moment.'

At the moment. What did that indicate? He remembered she was rumoured to have broken off her engagement in the hotel bar: that was hardly private either. With growing anxiety he watched the pink thread drawn by her slender fingers into the lacy web.

'Well?'

230

He saw at once that his unformed question irritated her by its timidity. She twitched the ball of wool with a warning movement, like an angry cat's tail.

'I mean, why are you telling me?'

'I thought you might like to know.'

'Thanks.'

'But you'd rather not.'

There was a silence. He was aware that he was looking sulky.

'Yes or no? Don't know.'

'Of course I don't know! I don't know what you said to him, or what you feel about him. You've never told me.'

'You've never asked.'

'Ask you that? I wouldn't see you for dust if I did.'

She actually smiled. He wandered restlessly round the room, and dropped on the floor by her chair. 'It doesn't mean I don't care,' he said, disconsolately, fidgeting with the ball of wool.

'Leave that alone!' She kicked his hand away from it. 'Don't be silly, Alan,' she went on briskly. 'Of course you don't care – not that much, anyway. You're not that sort of person.'

'What sort of person?'

'Jealous.'

'How do you know I'm not?' He was beginning to feel he might be.

'Oh, *really!*' The needles clicked louder and faster. 'How do I know the moon's not made of green cheese? Now, Murdo's quite incredibly jealous – even today, when he was totally abject. He'd cut your throat if he got the chance.'

'Charming! Did he tell you so?'

'Yes, he did.'

Unwilled images stirred in his memory, the limp-winged gull, Ben. He felt suddenly sick.

'Can't you stop knitting for a minute?'

'Is it putting you in mind of the guillotine? You've gone a bit green.' Her tone was sarcastic, but she put the needles down by her side.

'I don't know what you see in him. He's crazy.'

'He's not automatically crazy just because he doesn't like you. I told you, he's jealous.'

Alan got up, agitated, though he knew looking down at her was dangerous. 'If he's jealous, it's not just of me, it's of everything that

231

breathes. He's completely warped – for God's sake don't get mixed up with him again.'

'Are you giving me advice?' Her tone and look were freezing, in the old mode.

'Yes!' Then, striving to keep bitterness out of his voice, 'No. I've no right to give you advice. I'm simply telling you what I think. There's a horrible negative something about Murdo. I don't know what's wrong with the man, but I find him absolutely repellent, and I always did, before I knew he had anything to do with you. He's – he really is a killer, Eleanor. He enjoys it. Birds, sheep—'

'Oh, there you go again!' She jumped up, furious. 'It's just your usual hobbyhorse, isn't it? Murdo is an efficient crofter and does what he has to do. Unlike you, he hasn't had much choice about what that is. You can't grow brown rice on Boreray, you know.'

'I do know. And you can't eat seagulls either.'

'You can if you're hungry enough – starving. I dare say Murdo's ancestors did. Limpets – that's what they lived on on Rona, limpets and tangle stalks—'

'– And scurvy grass – all right, I know that, but I also happen to know that Murdo lives on mutton and whisky—'

'Oh, you are so childish!' She screamed her words with lips drawn back, shockingly angry and anguished.

He sat down in an immediate bid for de-escalation. 'Yes, I am. I'm sorry.'

Her breath hissed through pinched nostrils. 'Is that all you have to say?'

'Yes.'

'You're not even looking at me!'

Her pupils were pinpoints. There was a streak of saliva at the corner of her mouth. It demeaned her and he hoped she wouldn't notice it.

'You're sulking, aren't you? You – oh!' She brought her clenched fists down murderously on nothing. 'What *is* the use of arguing with you?'

He rose warily, withdrawing from the palpable field of her anger. She smelt acrid; her rage distorted the form and colour of her face and collapsed the room around her. Formerly, he had suffered her temper with incredulity, even amusement. Now it dismayed him: it was a rent in her nature, a mad black pit.

When he was safely behind the sofa, he said, 'I don't even know what we're arguing about. I'm sorry I upset you. I certainly shan't interfere, whatever you do.'

This did not mollify her. She picked up her knitting and hurled it at his head. He caught it, or some of it. A needle fell to the floor and the ball of wool twisted round his wrist and bounced onto the sofa, unravelling the loose stitches under its weight. He watched in stupid consternation as the pink web in his hands rapidly diminished.

Eleanor began to laugh, with flushing cheeks and hands pressed to her mouth. 'What an idiot you are!'

'There doesn't seem to be much of it left. Sorry.' He held the reassembled bundle out to her gingerly, over the back of the sofa.

She snatched it from him, scowling. 'Sorry again! You'd apologise for breathing, wouldn't you? You're always crawling!'

She flung herself into her chair and set to work on the tangle. She was edgy, but no longer furious. The room recomposed itself around her. Alan watched her with his hands in his pockets, uncertain. A minute before he had been intent on escape: now he remembered that the world outside her door was uninviting.

She glowered and clicked and counted. He waited for a pause and said, with inevitably irritating politeness, wondering what he should say instead, 'Would you like me to go, Eleanor?'

'No! Sit down and read your book,' she ordered crossly.

He picked it up and put it down again.

'It's boring and largely irrelevant.'

She stuck the needles deliberately into the ball of wool and got to her feet. 'Let's go to bed, then. Is that what you want?' She tossed her hair back, eyeing him with a mixture of scorn and perhaps amusement, perhaps even affection: whatever it was, not enough of it showed.

'Not if you're going to kick me out at midnight.'

She smiled, as neat and controlled as she had been abandoned a few minutes before. 'Well, you do have some pride after all!'

The rent in her had closed; hadn't she even noticed it was there? She smiled, with eerie somnambulistic nonchalance.

'No, I don't think so.' He felt and sounded bleak.

233

Her smile faded, revealing a shadow of perplexity. She turned away quickly. 'Oh, go home, Alan. I'm in too bad a temper.'

He followed and put his arms round her. She turned back to him. Her eyes were quite sane and serious. He held her without kissing her, because he wanted to look at her like that, but she pushed him away, though unrancorously.

He protested then, pulling her closer, but she was firm, 'Go on. No, go *on*, I mean it! I'll come and see you tomorrow.'

He had reached the far end of the village before he remembered about the car. He would rather have walked, to try to set some order on the miserable jumble of events, but he couldn't leave it at her door overnight. She had never tried to keep their affair secret, but she didn't like the intimacies of time and place to be open to comment or ridicule. Especially ridicule: he remembered how she had scolded him one day when he had kissed her outside the school gates, with grinning onlookers. Yet half an hour after that, she had marched into the doctor's surgery to collect her contraceptive pills, demanded loudly and clearly in front of all the decent old ladies in black waiting to have their blood pressure taken. Having followed her in unsuspectingly, he had been snorted at for his embarrassment. The memory of that previous ludicrous incongruity softened the present one slightly: one moment knitting like an Edwardian grandmama, the next snarling like a wildcat. Still there was something in her contradiction that wouldn't be dissolved by laughing at it. The naked face of her anger was too recent, pale lips strained back over pointed teeth, rage-widened tawny-flecked eyes, the circle of mascaraed lashes blanching her skin in their stark blackness. That concealment of natural gingerness was the only make-up she wore; she wore it even in bed, a badge of mistrust between them.

He reached the car, wondering what it was she didn't trust. The car was another thing. She had let him know, with some malice, that everyone on the island believed he possessed untold wealth, because of the Porsche. When he thought about it, this was hardly surprising, but the implied envy disturbed him. He was thoroughly sick of the car anyway, and she liked it; he had offered to exchange it for her more modest vehicle, and when she realised he meant it, she had been very angry. She didn't trust gifts.

It's me she doesn't trust, he thought as he drove off; and as the doleful reflex to the thought, the shadow of warmth of contact, dwindled along the road in solitude and darkness, he concluded grimly that her instinct was right. She had become his protection against emptiness. She kept it at bay, even filled it, when she was present, with her wholehearted vigour in the everyday, her definite opinions and confident movements. Yet she remained a means to him, not an end. The lack she obliterated was not lack of her: when he was not with her it returned, the grey insoluble riddle, the whispering recrimination. If he thought, as he often did, 'I wish Eleanor would come,' it was not for herself, but for her power to stave off the darkness, as an infant screams for mother to dispel the nightmare. He was using her: again. He would as long as he could. The loneliness she could suppress was too tormenting and he too unheroic for the other choice.

He swerved for a sheep in a skid of gravel and realised he was driving much too fast. Running away, he thought. She would go back to Murdo. She had done so in her mind already. As usual, the question arose, why? As usual, he could not answer it. He supposed he was being unfair, and tried repainting. He was quite good-looking, in a mean impassive sort of way, perhaps very attractive to her. Not unintelligent, trapped on the croft by circumstances: everyone agreed that, not just Eleanor.

He ran out of charity. The contemplation of Murdo was revolting. He was bitter, cruel, violent, inseparable from bullet and knife. For anyone who didn't mind that, he might be a bosom companion.

Eleanor? He thought her over uneasily. There was an affinity. He had never found her cruel: not actually cruel, maybe verbally so. But her temper, that disproportionate rage. Her anger was frightening, because she lost herself in it. The Eleanor of brisk common sense and impatient witticisms was not to be found behind that mask of fury. Eleanor, who knew no surrender to other passions, who never babbled nonsense in bed, never forgot to turn a page of music in the delight of the previous phrase, never relaxed in laughter and scarcely in sleep: in a rage she was transported, drunk, self-abandoned.

He had forgotten a torch. He walked down the path at Skalanish slowly, stepping in all the puddles which she so objected to, aware of jostling movement in the pitch darkness. Sheep would be sheltering in the hollows. She was afraid of that dark path; that discovery had made him feel protective towards her. But it must be the black

235

ecstasy in herself that made bogeys for her, and he couldn't protect her from that. He had very little to offer her, really; she might well do better with Murdo.

In this expansive sentiment he caught himself with the reminder that he had never offered her anything at all, except a car which he didn't want, and that he had drawn from her a great deal of comfort. He owed her some return, but what he couldn't imagine. Wading knee-deep through the flooding stream, he thought wrily that he could at least, in all that time, have put down a couple of planks to save her smart boots, and filled in the hole in front of the door: it was ankle-high. Inside, he leant against the still-warm stove, shivering and dripping. A pair of her gloves lay on the table, shiny brown leather in the slender mould of her hands, a stamp of her presence. Her presence: seeing them there, he knew he would miss her when she went, for herself. She was more than a mirror in a budgie's cage after all.

Murdo and Shonny had a half-bottle in the car after closing time. Murdo saw the Porsche pass as Shonny was taking his pull. He said nothing. His mouth was dry with hatred. Shonny had better not notice, better keep quiet.

'She's sent him home early tonight,' remarked Shonny, passing the bottle.

He drained it in one gulp. Shonny snatched it back and held it up to the light of the last streetlamp. 'Ah, you shit!' He wound the window down and hurled it grenade-like at the lamp post. It burst in glittering fragments. They had four cans left in the plastic carrier. He took out one each. '*Slàinte.*'

There was no reply. He eased himself round in the passenger seat to focus, with some trouble, on his companion. 'You taken it bad, man. I tell you, you got your chance now, go down and see her, eh?'

Murdo drank silently. The other prodded his elbow. 'Eh? Go on, go and see her now. Get her alone.'

'Fuck off.'

'What's wrong, man? You seen the bastard go past. You got your chance. She's on her own.'

He broached another can, goggling and taking hazy umbrage at the unresponsive silence. 'All on her own. Give her what you got, man,

236

show her you can do it – if you can do it.' He prodded again with clenched knuckles. 'You scared of her? That won't do. Not scared of a woman.' The prod became a rhythmic punch. 'Go down there and get her knickers off! If she got them on yet after the other fellow—'

Murdo lunged. Shonny had kept a precautionary grip on the door handle throughout his exhortation, and escaped neatly. He waved a sardonic farewell as his victim drove insanely out of the village.

Murdo needed more drink. He kept off it in the day, but he needed it at night. After the first dram, that was it, he needed more, or her. There was a half-bottle in the byre, in the hay. I'll get it there, he thought, I'll get it there, and it changed in the miles home to I'll get the bastard, I'll get the bastard, singing it aloud. He parked and got out, quiet with the door and gate, moving silently on the path, mouthing now silently, get, get, get.

In the byre he switched the light on with a jerk, leaning against the door. 'I'll – get – you!' he said emphatically. It was his byre. He could do what he liked. His hand found the bottle neck in the hay. He unscrewed and drank.

'I'll get you.' He swayed and slumped against the pile of hay. The tortoiseshell cat mewed as her nest subsided under his weight. He noticed her, a disintegrating patchwork of white, black and tan. He addressed her solemnly.

'She's my girl.'

The cat mewed and purred.

'My girl. She's my girl. Why'd she do it, eh?'

The cat purred, licking the first of her litter in the hay. The rest heaved inside, under the tan fur of her flank.

'English bastard!' He brought his fist down on the cat's belly. She screeched and shifted, nudging her kitten along beside her. He frowned. His hand pursued the russet patch of fur. It reminded him of something. She edged away and tissed at him, but his hand followed.

'Shut up, you.'

She purred again, eyes narrowing in hypnotic felicity, licking and licking.

'Shut – up!'

She licked and purred, twisting her head back as her belly contracted and shuddered. He felt it under his hand three times, the colour and the movement.

'Fuck you!' His fingers gouged under her ribs. She screamed in agony and terror. He kept hold. He held her down on the concrete floor and pulped her, screaming, with the heel of his shoe.

'I'll get you!' he said to each scream.

When it was a red and bluish pink mass with no fur showing he stood back, and sat down heavily. 'Bloody mess,' he said. 'Christ, what a mess.' He picked up the blind kitten and pulled its head off, dropping the pieces by the rest. Some others were squirming weakly inside the shiny membranes. He took another long gulp from the bottle, examined the level, screwed it up and put it back in its hiding place.

'Bloody mess. Have to clean it up.'

It was Mairi's pet cat. He would have to be careful. He scraped the stuff up with a spade, cursing Mairi, into the old fertiliser sack he would have used to drown the kittens. He got a bucket of water and sluiced, but the crimson stain was ground in. He trampled loose hay on it. 'Have to do,' he remarked, looking round with satisfaction before switching the light off. He carried the sack to the shore, slowly and quietly in the darkness. He put some stones in it and tied it, and held it up, heavy and swinging in front of his face, though he could not see it. 'I got you,' he said triumphantly. He let it swing for a minute before he hurled it out to sea.

'I got you!' he muttered again, hearing the splash.

Alan left Eleanor's gloves on the table, glad to see them there. He was reflecting that it seemed pretty silly to have breakfast beside them when she arrived. He hadn't heard her over the din of the flooding burn.

'What are you grinning at?'

'Your gloves.' He held them out to her.

'What's so funny about them?'

'There's something about gloves in *The Changeling*.' Not that he could remember what it was. 'Nuts and bolts in the muesli again,' he added, inspecting a piece of scrap metal with a view to identification.

'I thought it was supposed to be good for you?'

'So it is. Proves it's organic, bits of old tractor in the compost heap.'

'You didn't get that stuff in the village, did you? What about the local economy?'

'It's worse off by about ten pounds. I bought a whole sack at a terribly earnest worker's co-operative in Fort William. You can't object to that, now, can you?'

She seemed in two minds, but relented, rather to his surprise, when he hugged her and begged her not to be cross.

'I'm not cross. It's a lovely day: are you coming to Fladday with me?'

She had given all the inhabitants of Fladday who wanted it as much clarsach tuition as they could assimilate. Her new project was a music-making playgroup for the under-fives.

'You can stay if you like,' she shouted over the shrill voices. She had immediately hoisted a fat infant on each arm, and two more in the press round her knees were blubbering to get up there.

'I don't think so.' Alan backed away from a small girl with a very snotty nose who was embracing his calf. 'I'll go for a walk.'

The wind was blowing strongly from the west, sifting sand halfway across the low green island from that side. He kept to the rocky east coast. Soon he wished he had not: Rona was too much in view, a long unforgiving battlement above the surf, with the whaleback of Out End cut off sheer and black, veiled by slow plumes of climbing spray. The pale yellow indent of Port nan Roinn showed near the isthmus. The seals would be there, it was late in October. Memory was powerful: Rona was not much visible from Skalanish, so that the hot August day returned unsoftened by the gradual and familiar. He was glad to get back to Eleanor.

She spent the weekend with him, leaving late on Sunday. She seemed unusually good-humoured; she didn't mention Murdo, or behave like the sort of woman who is fatally drawn to dark handsome psychopaths. She sent him out to the workshop to repair two xylophones while she cooked dinner, and afterwards complained about the dubious cleanliness of the saucepans and the lack of scouring pads. He felt encouraged. She took an evening class on Monday; she told him to come to her place on Tuesday.

On Tuesday, Roddy had been fishing in the bay, a late run of mackerel. He had a boxful for Do'l Alex, to be salted for next season's bait. Would Alan deliver them, since he was going that way? Alan regretted it when he saw the beautiful iridescent fish stiff in the crate, and more when he realised the errand might involve bumping into Murdo. He reached the pier hoping the *Maid* might be deserted or gone so that he could take them to the house instead, but she was tied up by the slipway, with both men on board. Do'l Alex bellowed greetings. Murdo leapt ashore and passed him with face averted, but not enough to conceal a split cheek and swollen nose. Alan looked away, embarrassed, with a twinge of pity. He had presumably been in some drunken brawl. Hearsay was that he had hit the bottle badly since Eleanor broke with him.

'Leave it there!' Do'l Alex pointed at the barrel marked *MOR* in the line on the pier. 'I been springcleaning. I don't want no fishguts here, boy!'

He stumped cheerfully up the slipway, jerking his head in the direction taken by Murdo. 'Bad blood there, eh?' His discreet whisper reverberated pharyngeally in the quiet afternoon air. 'Ach well! All's fair in love, they say!' He delivered a congratulatory slap on the back.

Alan was unconvinced, as well as winded. He hadn't thought of Murdo as an injured party before, and the new aspect bothered him. 'Is he – has he taken it very badly?'

'Terrible! Just terrible!' roared Do'l Alex. He thrust a powerful index finger into Alan's ribs. 'No need for you to be down in the mouth. You did all right there, didn't you now?'

'Well –' Alan scuffed an oily patch in the concrete doubtfully. 'I'm glad the break-up was before I got back, anyway.'

Do'l Alex laughed loud and long. 'Oh, by God, you're cool, Alan! About half an hour before. He didn't get much warning, poor Murdo.'

This sank in slowly.

'What? D'you mean that?'

'Ay!' Do'l Alex was plainly surprised at his amazement. When he had worked it out he chortled mightily. 'Oh well, lad! Smart girl Eleanor, eh? Oho, smart girl!'

'Good grief.'

Do'l Alex went back to the *Maid*, chuckling and shaking his head. Alan forgot the car again.

Chapter 24

Murdo had orders to pick up his mother from Jessie's at five o'clock. He rapped on the door and stood with his back to it, keeping his face out of sight as long as possible, but the old woman came outside to draw him in, and at once exclaimed, 'Och, what has been happening to you? Oh well well!'

'Tripped on the pier this morning.' He had left home very early, so they wouldn't know it was last night; but his mother, as he unwillingly entered the sitting room, looked at him hard.

Jessie didn't believe him either, but she had endless indulgence for the follies of young men. 'Indeed, indeed! You should not have been leaving it like that all day. Wait you and I will get a plaster.'

'It's nothing.' He looked anywhere but at his mother. He had not dared take a dram before facing her; if he had he would have felt bolder now. She stood glaring at him with Jessie's old-fashioned wooden wool-winder frozen threateningly aloft.

'Your father will—' She bit off the rest of the remark. 'You need to watch yourself,' she said instead, quietly but very grim.

'I'll wait at the car. You'll no be long,' he muttered, still not meeting her eye.

She recognised her son's appeal. 'One more hank,' she said, pulling again on the bobbin of the spinning wheel.

'Och Murdo! You will not be going without seeing Neilie, he is just having a wee lie down. You'll stay for a cup of tea now – for a dram –'

He went out silently, shutting the door on Jessie's protests.

Mairi Anna wound the wool with deliberate hands, but her face was set. Jessie's gentle plaints and exclamations continued. 'Oh well, he should be staying a minute! It is a nasty cut that, he should be putting a plaster on it.'

'He should not have got it in the first place.'

The asperity of her tone silenced Jessie for a moment. She pulled her apron through her hands unhappily, and bent to poke up the fire.

Mairi Anna pulled the last hank from the winder and held it up to let it twist round on itself. She put the wheel back in its corner behind Neilie's chair. 'That will keep you knitting for a while now,' she said, 'and mind I will be expecting some socks for the menfolk.'

'Och yes indeed, I will be starting right away at that.' Jessie peered into her face, pitying the strained attempt at a smile, and patted her arm. 'You are worrying too much, Mairi Anna. Murdo is a good lad – a good worker, very steady at his work, Do'l Alex is always telling me that.'

'He's too heavy on the drink.'

'Och, the young ones are all at that. Do'l Alex was just terrible. He is still taking a big dram but there is no harm in it. Many is the night I was sitting up waiting for him here, and his father was so soft with him too! But he is a good son to us and he got a good wife.' She chuckled and shook her head at her recollections. 'Wait you, my dear, Murdo will be settling down once he is married.'

'No sign of that!' Mairi Anna's eyes hardened.

'Yes, yes! They will be getting married. It is just a wee quarrel they are having. She had the ring, she will not be for leaving him now.'

Mairi Anna's face was stony. Jessie sighed. 'But she should not be treating the poor lad like that, indeed. She should not be seeing the English boy when she is going to marry Murdo, that is right enough.'

'She is not going to marry Murdo, that's certain. She gave back the ring.'

'Oh, quiet now!' She waved away the unlucky words with old fluttering hands. 'Oh yes, she will be marrying him. She would not be doing that to him!'

Mairi Anna's tight face twitched; she did not often speak of her anxieties, but they were welling inside her. 'I wouldn't have him marry that girl. He's better keeping away from her.'

'Och no, my dear!' Jessie looked up at her earnestly. 'You must not be saying that. Murdo is missing her terrible, that is why he is at drinking like that.'

'Why is he picking on that one? A mainland girl like her – she is not a Christian girl –'

'Och, now! She is in church every week I am hearing. We are all sinners, yes every one of us! Eleanor is not a bad girl. She's bonny right enough, that is bringing the boys round her. She is a teacher too, that is a good job, she is a clever lassie.' She prattled on, patting Mairi Anna's hands, trying with innocent cunning for the right words

242

to soften her face and ease her heart. 'And Murdo was always a clever lad. Mind when he was wee we were all saying he would make a minister, he was that good at school!'

His mother remembered well. The stunted ambition pulled her straight mouth down at the corner momentarily. She recovered herself at once. 'Och, that was just a notion,' she said briskly. 'Good enough if he would stop his drinking and not be running after that – that girl. It is his father he should be thinking of just now.'

Jessie sighed. 'Oh well, the Lord knows you have your troubles, Mairi Anna.'

'Ay, the Lord knows.' Reminded, she composed her features for the Lord to see, buttoned her coat and picked up her shopping bag.

Jessie followed her to the door. 'Don't now be too strict on the lad. He is working hard there on the croft and when he is married he will be very steady, he will not be drinking and that carry-on. And Eleanor will be a help to you in the house there, dear, yes she will that!'

Mairi Anna maintained her self-control; it had been thoroughly tested by Auntie Effie. 'He is young enough yet to be thinking of marrying. Now look after yourself, Jessie, and I will be seeing you next week if I'm spared.'

'Byebye, now! I will be sending the socks down with Murdo.'

Jessie waited at the door waving as they drove off. Mairi Anna remembered to smile at her. After that her mouth set, and neither she nor Murdo spoke on the way home.

'What have you done with the car?' Eleanor shouted from the porch. She was in a bad temper.

'I forgot it. It's on the pier.'

'Oh, really, how absurd!' She bounced through the dim living room and into the kitchen. 'You might have put on the kettle. *And* the lights.' She snapped the switches emphatically.

He opened his mouth to apologise and decided he had better not. She whirled round to tell him disapprovingly that she supposed he'd want coffee instead of tea.

'Yes, please – what happened to you?' She had a bruise on her upper lip.

She glared at him. 'Murdo,' she said, reaching for mugs.

243

'Eleanor! You mean he thumped you?'

'No!' She crashed the cupboard doors impatiently. 'I thumped him.'

Alan, about to catch her in his arms, stopped in his tracks, recalling Murdo's face, and burst out laughing. 'Good God, so you did! I've seen him.'

'*You've* seen him? Why?'

'In passing. Don't thump me too.' He sat down as a precaution.

'Oh, shut up!' She banged the milk bottle forcefully on the table in front of him. He jumped and she began to laugh. 'I'll tell you about it later. Give me an hour, I want to wash my hair.'

Perhaps she timed herself by the clock. At five forty-five she removed Hegel from Alan's hands and settled herself opposite him with folded arms. Her eyes glinted and her newly washed hair had a Valkyrie's burnish of fire and bronze. Alan pulled himself respectfully out of his customary slouch.

'Are we sitting comfortably? Right!' And she began.

She did not, in fact, describe the occasion of punching Murdo's nose; but she had plenty to say about Murdo's failings, from his incipient alcoholism to the infrequency with which he changed his socks. Within that arena, she slashed back and forth. He was foulmouthed, he had sworn at her. He didn't like her going into the bar with him. He had got rid of her ring and wouldn't say where. His father had called her a slut. His mother was impossible, immune to all friendly overtures. He wore the most awful suit to church. He needed a haircut. He kept company with Shonny who was a bad influence. After intercourse he went to sleep without thanking her. He wouldn't practise the pipes. He wouldn't tell her how much money he earned with Do'l Alex. He was negotiating for four new rams and they couldn't possibly need more than two. He wore a horrible string vest just to annoy her. He ate with his elbows on the table.

She started with sarcastic scorn, progressed through angry detachment, and finished with a torrent of hysterical abuse: he was a coward, a liar, a hypocrite, mean, unshaven, stubborn, morose, sly, evil-smelling, narrow-minded, unappreciative. At the end she burst into tears.

Alan, having sat through this bewildering catalogue of irrelevant crimes, approached her cautiously. He had never seen her cry before, and doubted whether she would accept comfort, but he couldn't help offering it. She seemed quite prepared, in fact, to cry on his shoulder; she wept for some time, loudly and angrily, till his neck was hot and wet. She stopped quite suddenly, and blew her nose hard.

'Thanks,' she said. 'I feel much better now. Get us a drink, I'm going to wash my face.'

Alan poured two large gins in the kitchen, looked at them for a while, and topped them up a bit more. He would have downed one at once if it hadn't been for what she had said about Murdo's drinking habits. Poor sod, he thought.

She took a long time restoring her face. He couldn't find what she had done with Hegel. There was a copy of *Pins and Needles* under her chair, and he had a look at that, but it didn't make much sense. Her outburst obtruded, though he would much rather not have remembered in what precise and pungent details she detested Murdo; but since they wouldn't go away, he considered them, and was baffled. They were an extraordinary mixture of gross incompatibilities and petty annoyances. It was difficult to detect, in the abusive superficiality of her tone, that she could ever have wanted to marry him, or even that she had liked or trusted him: or even that she cared what he felt about her, beyond according her proper respect. Obviously he hadn't done that. Perhaps that was the trouble, perhaps it was all hurt pride on her part. He had an unwilling vision of Murdo, up at dawn to haul lobster pots all day, back home to a few hours of drudgery for father, then shaken out of exhausted post-coital sleep by a furious Eleanor. He remembered Ben then, and told himself it served him right, but the punishment seemed inapplicable to the crime. There was a strange pathos about it somewhere that he could not pinpoint. A man so eaten into by bitterness and envy, to have almost acquired the dignity of a mate, and to be spurned by her for faults that were hardly faults at all, mere accidents, circumstances: part of the very social system that Eleanor admired and aspired to. There wasn't a man on Boreray who didn't defer to his mother and smell of sheep or fish. Yet there was hardly another who would shoot anything that moved, as Donnie had said, or who glowered on the world with such constant resentment, unlightened by affection for family or neighbours. It was as if she had never bothered to notice his real, deforming vices; didn't care, certainly didn't think of helping him out of them. He had always rather assumed she must have some self-sacrificing feminine notion of saving Murdo from himself. It didn't look much like it.

Alan was shaken. He eyed the drinks and wished she would hurry up. Things might be clearer when she did. She might have something else to say.

She had quite a lot else to say, in a more orderly fashion, and it did make things clearer, or at least it seemed to after the third large gin.

'I've had my say against Murdo,' she remarked, after another, more qualified tirade. 'I'm not blaming him. It just couldn't work. I can't change him and I can't change me.'

'Have you tried?'

He wouldn't have asked that if he hadn't been lying on the floor with his head against her knee, and half drunk. Even so she was indignant.

'What on earth do you mean? Are you suggesting I go back to him?'

'No! No, of course not. I just thought, well, maybe you were looking for the wrong things.'

'Wrong things? What are the right things?'

'Oh, I don't know. I'm scarcely competent to judge am I? I can't stand Murdo, never could.'

'You weren't expected to marry him.' Her knee tensed with annoyance.

'Another drink,' Alan suggested hastily.

She looked at the clock. 'Some food would be more to the point. You're staggering already.'

'Another drink first.'

Her glass was empty too. She didn't protest further. He refilled both and settled beside her again.

'What I can't understand is, why you thought of marrying him at all. It doesn't sound as if – I mean, did you actually love him?'

There was an awkward silence. 'I suppose I must have done. I don't know.'

'You can't have done. You'd know.'

'Would I? How are you such an expert in the matter?' She tugged his hair, but didn't wait for an answer. 'I'm not sentimental like you. It takes more than that to make a marriage work. It's all these minor

246

irritations that wreck a relationship.'

'But they wouldn't have irritated you if you loved him.'

She snorted, rapping his head with her knuckles. 'That's a classic recipe for disaster. Most people wake up a month after the happy day and discover they're very irritated indeed. It happened to your parents, presumably.'

'I don't know. I wasn't around.'

'It happens plenty, anyway. Well, I'm glad it didn't happen to me. I'm just not the marrying sort.'

She said it, he thought, with a commendable lack of self-pity. He was suddenly terribly sorry for her. He hugged her waist in a muzzy excess of intoxicated sympathy. 'But you want lots of babies, don't you?'

'Yes.'

'So you'll have to get married some day, you poor thing.'

'I'm not a poor thing! You have an outdatedly patriarchal view of the world. I shall have as many babies as I want.'

'But you ought to get married. Murdo's just the wrong person. You don't love him.' He wanted to tell her what love was, how nothing else was anything, but the fumes of gin dissipated the grand design. He buried his face against her midriff.

'*I'm* the wrong person. Marriage is the wrong idea. I'm going to live my own life.'

'No, that's terrible. Living your own life is awful – desperate.'

'Stop biting me. And don't drink any more.'

'Sorry.' He relapsed against her knee in silence, unable to express the utter emptiness of a life without love, or how he had wanted to live his own life before he knew, or how helplessly sorry he felt for her, and Donnie's grey eyes swam before him.

'It's finding the right person,' he managed at last, indistinctly.

She sniffed. 'You're very silly when you're drunk.'

A magnanimous thought occurred to him, springing freshly out of a quarter-bottle of spirits; he had forgotten he had ever previously given it consideration. 'Eleanor, would you marry me?'

'Is it likely, soppy?' She laughed, worrying his hair with her fingers. 'You'll be asking if I love you next.'

'I wouldn't dare,' he said, suddenly much more sober.

Since he didn't dare, he didn't find out.

Chapter 25

She was splenetic the following morning. When he enquired solicitously how she was feeling, she snapped that she didn't know what was supposed to be the matter with her. She went off to work, and he shut himself in with much-neglected Selena for the day. But Eleanor was there immediately after school, actually running down the path to meet him.

It was the same the next day and all week. He was gratified, but disconcerted. Always before he had been the one who leant on her, for one reason or another. Her sudden dependence on him was entirely new, if limited. What she wanted was to talk; she needed a listener, even an adviser. That astonished him: she had always been so totally self-sufficient. The one thing she didn't tell him was what had made her punch Murdo's nose, but whatever it had been, it had evidently caused a crisis in self-confidence. From that point, she coursed backwards and forwards in her life, struggling, it seemed, to bring it under control. Every day a new monologue brought another layer of skin off her. He learned about early days in a slummy council flat, where mother wouldn't let the children out in the morning till she had scrubbed off the graffiti in the common entrance, because she thought she was too good for the place: how father had done endless overtime at the carpet factory to get them up in the world, and they had moved to a vast anonymous Barratt-house estate, where mother wouldn't speak to the neighbours because she soon didn't think they were good enough either. They had moved three times and she still didn't speak to anyone, had nervous breakdowns. Eleanor hated her mother. She didn't seem to like her father much either, he'd gone over to being a rep because the image was more genteel, had taken to speaking in a phony accent and wearing flashy cufflinks. They gave themselves ridiculous airs and thought Murdo was beneath her: 'Maybe that was a reason I stuck to him,' she said, as if it had just occurred to her. And she had never got on with her sister. She had married a very stuffy man who worked in a bank. They had a huge mortgage and a really dreadful plastic house, and wouldn't have children because they couldn't afford it. 'Imagine that!' she said, fiercely.

'At least there was no nonsense like that with Murdo. He thinks it's sinful taking the pill.'

Alan was amazed to discover that her allegiance to the island way of life had not grown out of a close-knit family background. It gave her a new fragility, that her most passionately held ideal was not a happy gift of upbringing, but a defence against its deficiencies. She had trained as a teacher and come to Boreray in pursuit of a dream, though she didn't state it that way.

'They didn't like my left-wing friends at university. They didn't like real people at all – that's why I came here, to be amongst real, solid people. I could have got a place in a respectable orchestra – they'd have loved that. They were always wanting to see me dressed up in a party dress on a concert platform when I was a child.'

'Parents do like that sort of thing.'

'Oh, Alan, they were awful!'

'Parents are all awful. One day you'll be an awful parent yourself.' He added, 'I've always been highly embarrassed by mine. I suppose one gets over it eventually.'

But she shook her head crossly. She had not lived down being thirteen, and not allowed make-up for the school concert.

What he had taken for complexity, the tension between liberated, socialist Eleanor and Eleanor the traditionalist, was disturbingly revealed as unyokeable opposition. She would not, could not, reconcile her contrarieties. She was naively wounded that Murdo's mother considered her morals dubious: 'Just because I've had other boyfriends she thinks I sleep around.' There had been another man on Fladday and one in Inverness in the two years of Alan's absence, he learned: 'But they were perfectly serious, adult relationships.' By that he supposed she meant impermanent, unloving and mutually enjoyable, but put like that it sounded unkind, so he said instead, 'I can't see any harm in that, but it's very foreign to people round here, isn't it? It must have seemed awfully humiliating to Murdo, and to his family.'

'But I'd join in the system, in everything that mattered.'

She could not see that, in the system which as an outsider she had appraised so sensitively, everything mattered. Her theory about it was perfect, but she had a different and conflicting theory about that part of her which shouldn't matter to the system, about the very individuality which by her other theory she claimed should be sacrificed to the community. Or perhaps it was not conflicting, but only dismally confused.

'If I'd married him, I'd have fitted in. I'd have been respectful to his beastly mother and knitted his socks and all the rest of it. But I couldn't until I was part of it, could I? I'd have been nothing then – a non-person.'

She held on. She didn't want to be a non-person. She clung to being Eleanor, even when Eleanor fell apart in her hands.

'You need to get away,' Alan said with feeling.

'I don't want to.'

But she admitted she didn't know why she didn't want to. She couldn't reveal to herself why she had been attracted to Murdo, though she wheeled round and round the uncertainty, approaching it from every angle of her life. She would not let it go, could not just pack up and leave it. It was a scar on her inmost self, and she had to know what had hurt her and how it had got there.

Alan was quickly enough bored with her relentless circling. He couldn't understand why, if the attraction was there no longer, she would not forget it. But he was touched by her new need of him, which went some way to repaying what she had been doing for him. Even though he might be surreptitiously reading a book upside down or quietly considering a revision in sail specifications while her voice went on and on, he felt more tender towards her than he had ever done: she was so unexpectedly adrift, and it came so hard to her to trust anyone. He was unsure why she had decided to trust him now, and was prepared for her to turn round at any moment, snarling at him to mind his own business.

'Do you really want my advice?' he asked, more than once.

Yes, she wanted it; she wanted to know why she had come unstuck, what she should do next, why she couldn't stop brooding about Murdo, though she hated him.

He ventured the only explanation he could think of that did her any credit. 'He's crazy about you, isn't he? I suppose you're sorry for him.'

She shrugged. 'Not any more. It's his own fault, after all. There are other things he'd rather have.'

That rankled with her, obviously. Being Eleanor's guru was an uncomfortable charge: he tried again, more doubtfully. 'Perhaps you do love him in a way? Or did,' he added hastily, as her eyes narrowed with anger.

'No, I loathe him. I don't believe I could ever have loved him, but now I hate him. I hate him, I really do!' And she wept, in sheer bitter fury.

'Oh Christ! Sorry.' He wriggled his way round Selena's transom and perched on the bench beside her. She had followed him into the workshop: she had followed him everywhere for the last few days. He remembered her mother's nervous breakdowns and hoped he wasn't going to precipitate one in her, through ill-advised remarks. When she had calmed down, he asked, 'Why do you hate him, exactly?' in his best approximation to the analyst's manner.

After a pause she said, 'I'm afraid of him – no, not of him. Of how miserable he is. You know the phrase, miserable as sin? Well, that's Murdo.'

So she was not totally oblivious.

She went on, with rising voice, 'I hate remembering about it. I hate the way I'm not free. Why am I not?' She pressed her face against his arm. 'Oh, Alan, I envy you your peace!'

'Peace?' he repeated it rather absently. It was an amazing thought. 'I don't have much of that, Eleanor.'

'Oh yes you do, you are –' she hugged him, uncharacteristically. 'You don't hate anyone or anything, do you?'

He agreed only warily. 'No.' After a bit he added, 'I don't think not hating is worth much. It's not loving that's the problem. Using people, thinking the world owes you a living – exploiting things generally –' he paused, glancing at her half-hidden face. 'Well, the next stage in that argument is a lot of greenie claptrap I'm sure you don't want to hear again.' They had fallen out over that part of the subject before.

'It's not my scene.' She shook her head. 'But I see how it makes sense for you, at a personal level. You've never struggled and fought and never hated –'

She sounded resentful. He expected a harangue on social and sexual privilege to follow, but she broke off and looked at him intently.

251

'What is it about you, Alan? What do you know that I don't?'

'Nothing!' He was most alarmed. She seemed to be waiting for enlightenment. 'I might ask the same about you. What do you know that I don't?'

She stared at the floor, swinging her crossed ankles. 'I don't know love and you don't know hate. It's far from the same.'

'Well, things change. One of these days someone might do me a bad turn and I'll hate his guts, one of these days you might fall in love. But you'd better try somewhere other than Boreray. You must have explored most of the possibilities here by now, haven't you?'

He wanted to make her laugh, or even take offence. He wanted to get back to fitting the rudder: intense discussion on life and love with Eleanor was surprisingly frightening. He was quite relieved that she was going to spend the weekend with a friend on Fladday. It was a Thursday-to-Sunday one, because of the autumn communion season.

She would not be diverted. 'Have you ever been in love, then?'

She said 'in love' as if it belonged in inverted commas.

'Yes.'

'You don't talk about it. Didn't it work out?'

'No.'

'Who is she?'

She had trusted him. He had to trust her. He took a deep breath first; his heart contracted.

'Not she.'

She looked puzzled. 'Who?'

'Donnie.'

'*Who?*'

'Murdo's brother.'

'What, that boy?'

She sounded so scandalised that he laughed: not only a boy, but *that* boy, that particular reluctant pupil and family liability.

'Yes, that boy.'

'You mean, the summer I was away? All that sailing and so on?' She stared, with a stirring of hostility in her eye. 'Well, you certainly kept it nicely concealed!'

'There was nothing that had to be concealed.' He felt drained by her incomprehension. 'What do you take me for, Eleanor? With

252

a kid of sixteen?'

She watched him curiously, considering this. 'What happened then? Apart from nothing.'

He turned from her, anguished that she didn't understand. 'What you would call nothing, that's all.'

She caught his hand. 'No, tell me, Alan. I want to know what – what it meant to you.'

'I loved him.'

She searched his face quite gravely, without scorn or malice. That way it was easier to meet her eyes.

'You still do.'

'Yes.'

'But you let him go.'

'There wasn't any alternative. But I hurt him dreadfully, that's the awful thing. It's – unforgiveable.' He paused, at a loss to describe the implacable guilt he carried around with him.

Her face was alert, as if they were practising a difficult sonata where she expected him to make a mistake soon. 'How could you hurt him if it was all so innocent?'

He suffered a moment's incredulous pain. It faded quickly: how could she understand? She probably thought he was being disrespectful about sex, and she was bound to take that as a personal insult. He couldn't tell her that Donnie was the only innocent human being he had ever known, which was what he most wanted to convey to her; she didn't believe in innocence, could not speak of it without a sneer. He said at last, 'I think I was the first person who had ever taken an interest in him. He was – he became very fond of me. It was a frightful wrench for him leaving after that – entirely my fault. I – mishandled it. I was such a coward.'

'I expect he got over it.'

'I expect so.'

She scanned his face carefully. Her pointed canines pressed on her lower lip. 'You're surprisingly discreet. I certainly never realised you're gay.'

'An inept term, Eleanor. I'm bloody miserable.' He felt light-headed with anger. 'Can't you stop thinking in categories? There isn't a set of rules for everything, you know. Homosexual, heterosexual, bisexual – all they mean is join the club and kick the outsiders. You

253

can't label the world like that. You miss the point.' He was desperate she should understand; it was something she needed to know. He had passed his threshold of coherence, but he took her wrists and pulled her round to face him. 'Listen. I usually fancy women more than men and boats more than either. But I just happen to love Donnie.'

'Who just happens not to be a woman or a boat.' She smiled, unexpectedly.

'Do you understand at all? Do you, Eleanor?'

'Don't pull my hands off – yes, I do. I see you mean it, anyway.'

'But you don't see what it means – I wish you could, if only you knew –'

'Now don't start raving. Oh, really!' She was laughing, holding his head between her hands. 'That time you were ill – you were muttering about him all day. I thought it was some exotic South Pacific girl's name. That was silly, wasn't it?'

He agreed, bemused, that it was.

She glanced at her watch. 'I must go, or I'll miss the ferry.' She was brighter and brisker than she had been for days. Her friend on Fladday had recent twins; they were the occasion of the pink garment and its double. He walked up to her car with her, holding her hand.

'I'm glad I've told you,' he said, hugging her. 'I've never told anyone else.'

She kissed him and got into the driving seat.

'See you on Monday,' he said, closing the door for her.

'No – evening class. I'll come down on Wednesday.'

'Wednesday! That's nearly a week.'

She smiled, looking over her shoulder for the fence as she reversed. 'You won't miss me that much, Alan.'

He missed her considerably, and looked forward to her coming back. Yet he was remarkably content, resting in the new trust between them, the promise of a fresh start. He worked at Selena with some of the old enthusiasm, liking her again; she was far behind schedule and he intended to make it up to her. He whistled to himself, sorting out deadeyes and swivels on the floor. The tune was 'Calum Sgaire', and it came back gently, with the golden light of a spring evening. He knelt on the concrete wondering how it had become possible to remember with so much love and so little pain.

She set course for Orkney, with new masts and white sails;
beautiful weather was it with us for the sea.

He had got the translation in the end, in bits and pieces, about
how the returning sailor climbed the hill and saw the girl going
round the cattle.

Happy am I today, here is the one I love.

Eleanor arrived cheerful and talkative. Murdo seemed to be out
of her head at last. The twins had been lovely, real little pets; just
seeing them had done her a world of good, she said. It was obviously
true: she was her former vivacious, perky, practical self. Alan listened
patiently, though not attentively, to her raptures on their tiny button
noses, their miraculous little fingers, their identical pink ears, feeling
quite benevolent towards them for the good they had done her. She
scolded him with vigour for having spilled black paint on the table,
and broke off to ask if she had told him yet about the twins' first
excursion in the double baby buggy. He said hastily that she had,
although in fact he couldn't remember; but she had a dozen other
tales of the wonderful doings of the twins anyway.

She eventually stopped talking about them in bed. She was more
affectionate than usual, and he fell asleep with his arms round her.
He half-woke later, hearing her moving about in the darkness. After
a bit he switched on the light to see what was happening. She was
dressed, just zipping up her boots. He blinked at her, puzzled and
sleepy. 'I thought you were staying.'

'No, I'm going.'

'Can't you stay? Please.'

She shook her head, and went through to the kitchen for her coat.

'Wait and I'll walk up with you, then.'

'No.' She stood in the doorway, belting her trenchcoat. She
pulled on her gloves, and looked at him unsmiling.

'Alan, I'm going to marry Murdo.'

He stared at her. She stared back unflinching.

'Oh, Eleanor!'

'I'm sorry if you don't like it, but I am. On the fourteenth
of January. I've got my own life to live.'

She turned quickly. Her feet tapped across the kitchen and
the door slammed. The doorknob rolled over the floor and
rocked slowly to rest.

Chapter 26

A week later Dina ran into the workshop at dusk. 'Oh well, it's dark!' she giggled, sidling up to him round the boat. 'This place is real creepy. I don't know how you stay here.'

'Hello, Dina.' He found he was pleased to see her. She was solid and cheerful. He had been in hiding, and his world was peopled by uncertain wraiths.

'There's a man been phoning you, he wants you to ring him back. My mum's got the number.'

'Oh, thanks. I suppose it's the sailmakers.'

'Might be. He said as soon as possible, Mum said to tell you. You could come now – come on, I'm scared going along there myself!'

She hopped up and down, grinning at him through her chewing gum. She was the tomboy among the sisters. Twelve had put breasts on her and shoes with silly heels, but she was still boisterous and frank-eyed. He went with her gladly enough, warmed by her shrill chatter and skipping gait. There was something about her that reminded him of Donnie; she was merry and animal-quick, though not pretty by Boreray standards. Thanks to her, he reached Roddy's house capable of friendly greetings, and excuses for not having called for some time.

Chrissie handed him the scrap of paper with the number.

'It's just my mother.'

'It was a man that spoke. I couldn't catch the name.' She left him in the hall with the telephone, shutting the living-room door discreetly.

He did not recognise the voice at the other end at first. 'Harold, is that you? It's Alan. The line's shocking.'

The strange noises resolved into drunken mumblings, punctuated by groans.

'What the hell's the matter?'

This time he caught, 'Your mother's ill.'

'Is she ill again? She seemed better last time I rang.'

'Much worse. You have to see her. You have to come.'

'What's happened?'

'Very ill. Very – very – ill.'

The slow drunken emphasis infuriated him. 'What's wrong with her, you fool? Tell me!' He shouted 'Tell me!' again through the incoherent reply.

'Cancer. She has cancer, Alan. She's dying. You must see her. She only has a few weeks left – just – a few weeks –' The voice disintegrated in sobs and whispers.

'I'll come tomorrow. It'll be late.'

He put the receiver down slowly and slumped into the chair by the telephone. After a minute or so Chrissie came out cautiously.

'I hope it is not bad news.'

He started, confused by her presence.

'My mother has cancer. She's dying.'

'Oh no! Oh well, I am sorry.' She patted his arm, with soft sounds of commiseration. Roddy appeared, shutting the door behind him on a rise and fall of maniacal television laughter. His broad weatherbeaten face showed concern. Chrissie said something to him in Gaelic.

'Oh well, that's a terrible thing, ay!' He repeated 'a terrible thing' in a lower voice, adding, with transparently false cheerfulness, 'Och, it may no be so bad, eh? It's wonderful what they can do in them hospitals these days. Maybe you'll get down there and find she's right as rain, eh lad?'

Chrissie shushed him sharply, but Alan had scarcely heard him. He stood up, looking at them apologetically because he couldn't understand what they were saying.

'I should have known,' he said, as a sort of explanation, making for the door.

'You'll stay here tonight, Alan. You will be better not by yourself,' Chrissie remonstrated.

'No.' He looked from one sympathetic face to the other, wondering that they should be so troubled on his behalf. 'Thanks. I'll have to get packed up to go. I'll put the key in your post-box when I pass.'

He had plenty of time on the long journey to reflect on why he should have known, if he had bothered to think about it.

'But why didn't you tell me?' he asked her in the morning. 'I'd have stayed. I wouldn't have left you.'

She smiled at him wanly. She was the colour of ashes, hair, face, hands, even the whites of her eyes. 'I couldn't keep you here, darling. You'd have been so bored. I do know you better than that.'

Cowed by the totality of his failure, he offered no denial. He leant on the deep windowledge, watching the early mist thinning between the sparse blotchy sycamore foliage. In the orchard a few red apples and a scatter of yellow leaves floated evanescently on the shadows. The paddock was grey with dew, like rough neglected fur. She had written some weeks before to say that she had sold the bay hunters.

She watched him, but with dull flickering eyes in gaunt sockets. They had talked for half an hour or so, and she was exhausted already.

'I'll leave you to rest,' he said, bending to kiss her.

'No, stay till Dr Simpson comes. I need you to cheer me up, it's not very nice to think about things.'

Her voice was matter-of-fact; she could have been telling him his shoelace was undone. Her manner of speech had always been dependent on the mood of the moment, indifferent to the real extent of joy or horror. He sat on the edge of the bed, unable as yet to start the process of cheering her up. He had to find out the worst about himself first.

'Have you known all the time? Since that Christmas when you said you had 'flu?'

'I did have 'flu, my sweet. Everyone did, even Yasmin.' She stretched her hand inelastically to stroke the aged decrepit creature lying on the quilt at her side; Yasmin mewed a silent toothless mew. The hand was an old woman's. She wore her rings, loose and twisting on the in-curling fingers: Torquil's sapphire, her mother's and Harold's diamonds, the abstract opal cluster that he had always supposed came from Enrico.

'But you did know then?'

'Yes.'

'I should have known. I should have seen it.'

'I didn't want you to know, lovie. It was too awful.' She took his hand. Her fingers scrabbled nervously, dry as grasshoppers. 'I couldn't bear you to know, it would have made it all come true. I didn't have to think about it if you didn't know.'

'But you told everyone else.'

'Only all the oldies, darling. I wanted to see you young and happy. It's horrid being old.'

'You said it was time I grew up.'

258

'Oh yes, I wanted you to marry Sally, didn't I? How funny. I thought I'd tidy everything up nicely before – you've always been rather a worry, sweetie.'

'I'm sorry!' He put his arms round her, but she paddled at them weakly, pushing him away.

'Have I hurt you? Where does it hurt?'

'No, I'm not in pain. These pills are absolutely marvellous. But you mustn't get upset, I can't bear that. You mustn't talk about it or even think about it – promise?'

She was urgent, glittering-eyed. He promised, hastily. She sank back on the pillows, licking dry lips.

'Just be nice and cheerful, and tell me what you've been doing.'

He tried to think of something, anything, that would be nice and cheerful.

'No girlfriends?' she asked hopefully.

'Oh Mummy, that's all you ever think about!'

They both laughed. Her gums and teeth were ashen too.

'There was one till recently, but she's going to marry someone else.' There seemed to be nothing else she would rather hear about, though it was not a subject he relished.

'Oh, how dreadful! Would you have married her?'

'I don't know.'

'Oh, darling, you almost sound as if you might have! Couldn't you make up your mind in time? You are hopeless! I'm frightfully sorry.'

He hadn't felt that his face betrayed much, but she was animated; it was exactly her subject.

'No need to be sorry, after all it's more or less what I did to – to Sally, and others.'

'Oh, I do wish I'd met her! I might have managed to arrange things for you.'

That made him smile. 'No, it doesn't matter. We weren't well suited anyway.'

She shifted, causing Yasmin to pull a plaintive face, and pushed back her hair with a shadow of the old vitality. 'Oh, you are rotten, sweetie! If you hadn't kept things so quiet I could have asked all about her, it would have been such fun! It seems in bad taste to ask now. You never mentioned her in your letters – not that you write many.'

'I'm sorry, I'm a useless correspondent. I'll—' He was going to say, I'll try harder in future. Four to six weeks of it.

She saw the change in his face and ignored it determinedly. 'Tell me what the girls are like on that island of yours. Are they buxom country wenches?'

'Ravishing. Very graceful, dark with light eyes mostly – rather romantically proud and pensive – they're all out of Wordsworth's solitary Highland lass by Burne-Jones, if you can imagine.'

Her hazed eyes positively lit. 'How divine! Is that what this girl you might have married looked like? Oh, you are exasperating, Alan!'

'Eleanor? No, she's a redhead from Dundee. I'll show you a photograph later.' That was a betrayal, and not to was a betrayal; he hoped Eleanor wouldn't mind if she knew the circumstances.

The doctor's arrival released him, after introductions. He hesitated in the hall, recollecting the recently installed housekeeper in the kitchen. There were nurses too, they came and went from the room next to his own. Harold had presumably gone to the office. He looked in the study to make sure, and in the dining room; he would rather have seen even Harold than another unfamiliar face or no face at all. As he recrossed the hall he heard the sound of scrubbing behind the internal vestibule doors, and remembered Mrs Jenkins.

''Allo love,' she said, still scrubbing, as she had said at every meeting for the past eighteen years. He almost expected her to add, 'My, you've grown!'

'My, you look worn out!' was her more topical version. 'How's your mum today?'

He shrugged indecisively. 'I don't know how she's been. She looks dreadful to me.'

'Oh, dreadful. Wonderful spirit, mind. She don't let it get 'er down. She says to me last time you was comin' like, "Don't tell Alan," she says, "I don't want no funeral talk." Well, I says, "'E'll take one look at you, Mrs Fordyce," I says, "an' 'e won't need no tellin'." She lost all 'er looks, like. Well, she says, "Don't you tell 'im nothin'. I'm goin' to enjoy 'im while I can." Mind your feet, love. You're in me way.' She stopped scrubbing momentarily. 'Poor soul, she can't keep it 'id no longer. She 'ad to tell in the end.'

'I should have known.'

She reapplied herself to her scrubbing. 'Don't think about it when you're young, love, do you? Me water needs changin'. Did you bring all this mud in?' She heaved herself up on thin but varicosed legs.

'I'll get it for you.'

'Don't go in the kitchen, love. She's fierce, that one. Got a thing about 'ygiene – Swiss, she is.'

He refilled the bucket in the cloakroom.

He fed the cats and replenished the bluetits' containers under the formidable eye of the large Swiss housekeeper. She addressed him as 'Meester Fordyce'.

'Alan,' he said, hopefully.

After that she called him 'Meester Alan'.

'I do not like to have the animals in the kitchen, Meester Alan. We do not have the mice, so, we do not need the cats.'

Shan curled round his neck, yowling at her defiantly.

'I'd do as she says, if I were you,' Alan muttered to him as they went out to the garden.

In the garden Ted was pruning roses.

'Morning, Ted.'

'Morning.' He wiped the recurrent drop from his thin blue nose with a brown thumb, and jerked his head towards the paddock. 'Hosses is gone. Grass is gettin' terrible long.' His tone indicated grievance. 'Mr Fordyce says leave it. Looks a mess I say.' He had kept the lawns fanatically for ten years and fed the bays his windfall apples; he was doubly injured.

'If it dries I could scythe it. Have you a scythe, Ted?'

Ted gave him a bleak look and set to on the roses again. 'Wouldn't touch one. Lop yer feet off with them things.'

The sweet-scented hay of Boreray, crimson clover, vetch and yarrow, counterpointed by the iodine tang of the sea: Alan regarded the forlorn paddock hazily. Shan leapt from his shoulder, tiptoed through the distasteful dew, and sat down to groom on the drier ground under the great cedar. Alan looked from Ted to Shan; both squinted at him malignly.

Ted wiped his nose again, a prelude to speech.

'How's She today?'

'Not too good.'

'Big change these three years.'

'Yes.'

'She hardly come in the garden last summer. Winter before that, first one she never planted a new rose. "I shan't see them," she says, "plant petunias." Nothing but damned annuals last year – let the place down. D'you notice that when you was here in the summer?'

'No. I didn't notice.'

No scythe was forthcoming. In the weeks that followed there was nothing to do. The housekeeper kept house with inexorable efficiency; the nurses dictated Celia's meals and rests, and shut the window when he opened it for the cats. For much of the day, and increasingly, she was in a more or less drugged sleep. He would reach her door to find it closed, with the nurse standing guard like a blue and white Saint Michael: 'Mrs Fordyce is resting, Mr Cameron.' The nicer plump one said, 'She's having a little nap, dear,' but it came to the same thing. When she woke, she demanded him at once, and kept him there till she was overborne by pain and the nurse with tablets or, later, a syringe.

He kept to the house, to be there when she wanted him. He spent most of the time in the music room. It had been Celia's fancy: she had established it as a surprise for him one school holiday, though typically, the pretty instruments she collected were not those on which he was most proficient. There was a good grand piano; a soft-voiced, much-inlaid lady's guitar, which rested unplayed from year to year on the arm of the chaise longue, against a fringed and flowered black Spanish shawl; a set of mysterious twangy Middle Eastern instruments, made of gourds and goat hide; and a derelict spinet, a leftover from Torquil. The case of the last had been reveneered and repolished, but most of the keys either wouldn't go down or didn't come up. She had had the room done in *trompe l'oeil* a few years previously, by a frightfully expensive man whose name she couldn't recall, though she could have found his signature behind the spinet if she had remembered to look. The walls, seen on entering, were continuous with the view of the garden seen through the French windows. The door was in the trunk of the great cedar, Etoile de Hollande blossomed behind the chaise longue, the knot garden offered a pleasing perspective from the piano stool. Dryads disported themselves in the orchard; one, with Celia's face as it had then been, held out an apple to the bay mare over the paddock gate. The décor was eccentric, given the weighty mock-Tudor proportions of the room, but it was charming. In the first week or so, Celia was well enough to come down for a short while in the afternoon, and that was where she chose to be. 'My winter garden,' she called it. She had him play to her: 'Nothing too demanding, darling.' He played 'Nocturnes', and 'Moments Musicaux'; she leant on the chaise longue as gracefully as pain would allow, with the Spanish shawl round her shoulders, her face above it in a cruel unconscious decay that Goya might have enjoyed.

When she was resting, he stayed there playing or reading desultorily, taking the spinet to bits, or simply hiding from Trudi, with Shan round his neck. Trudi, who was far from the girlish lightness implied by her name, disliked him thoroughly. He addressed her in adequate and respectful German, and she snubbed him by replying in English; and after he had asked her not to buy veal again (though even Harold wouldn't eat the stuff) she treated him as if he were as insanitary as the cats and bluetits. 'My, she'll 'ave you for that!' exclaimed Mrs Jenkins in a hoarse whisper, catching sight of the pieces of spinet laid out on the floor in the dust of two hundred years; and she was right.

After perhaps ten days, Celia said brightly, when he went up to fetch her, 'I really don't feel like coming downstairs today, darling. Sorry to be such a bore.'

He took the guitar up to amuse her, then fixed a string of peanuts for the tits on the wisteria outside her window. Yasmin watched, slit-eyed. The wisteria was her scaling ladder, and she had once been a mighty hunter, but she knew she was past it. 'Poor old toothless crone,' said Celia, laughing at the cat's expression. She never came downstairs again.

She held him to his promise. She would not talk about death or her fear and pain. The vicar or his curate brought her communion, and afterwards she invariably said she felt better, but she shied absolutely from what she felt better about. She would move on restlessly to discussing the vicar's younger daughter, such a plain girl, but frightfully worthy, doing something in a clinic in Mozambique; or wondering what Trudi had cooked them for supper and whether Harold was cheating about his artificial sweetener in the coffee; or enquiring which of the winter shrubs were flowering – he brought in some yellow jasmine, which Shan liked to nibble, and told her the viburnum was glorious, though in fact it had failed that year. When visitors called, she discussed them avidly later in minute and increasingly repetitive detail. Sally came one afternoon with her mother, and the visit provided food for several days. What had he thought of her hair, her outfit, her infant daughter; hadn't she put on weight, and did he know her mother thought she was unfaithful to George?

She craved small talk, the smaller the better. He did his best to give it, though wretchedly aware of the incongruity; and she was resolute in not noticing any hesitancies. He became her lapdog, to be shut out or detained unprotesting, performing the tricks she asked for. Acting a continuous lie was dully painful, but there was nothing else she wanted and no other way to help her, except by such denial of her coming extinction. Since the future could not be touched on, the present was only available for comment in attenuated form. When the invitation to Eleanor's wedding arrived, it was the best thing that had happened for days, she almost clawed it in her excitement, full of questions about the groom's personality and, more important, looks; but when she saw the date, fourteenth of January, she handed it back and talked about something else.

As time went on, even the present, with its implication of a future, became too fearful for her. She had him pull out the old photograph albums. Her weak fingers flickered over and over the pages, picture after picture of the consciously adoring madonna holding her passive pretty child, pensive among daisies, smiling in a rose arbour, sensuously naked on a French beach. There was a pastel drawing over her bed in the same mode, and an oil painting in the dining room. He was used to these, and used to not looking at them, but the photographs were repulsive. If they had been totally feigned they would have been merely insipid; it was the pathos of truth struggling under the make-believe that made them unbearable. But he was not required to comment, merely to be there while she talked till she was exhausted, gloating over his childish likeness to herself, his beauty, his sweet nature, his thousand precocious talents: he was her son, not Torquil's; Torquil had never really understood either of them, had been inattentive, moody, penny-pinching, but she had protected him and borne with it, because it was so important for a child to be secure and happy. She moved from maternal reminiscences to more general matters: how Torquil had been crazily jealous, how she had

264

always needed friends, how one man had broken off two engagements because of her and another had sent her anonymous presents of model gowns from Paris, how this one had praised her seat on a horse and that one her dress sense. She grew more garrulous the further from the truth. Frantically, it seemed, she was searching for the grounds of her self-esteem, scraping her life together, assuring herself there would be something left to become a ghost; and a ghost it was, obsessive, plaintive, gibbering. It was a ghost that smeared eyeshadow with shaking fingers on pain-darkened eyelids; a ghost that gushed over Sally's baby and when it cried complained of a headache. Of her real, lovable, substantial self, her generosity, her quick interest in others, her wit and gaiety, she apparently reckoned nothing worth saving. Alan watched, and humoured her in agonised pity: it was too late to do anything except mould himself to her requirements. After a day of empty chatter with Celia and an evening swilling unwanted vintage port with Harold, he was dazed by the sheer hopelessness of what he was about, the prostitution of energy and will. It had never occurred to him that not only pleasure but even integrity might have to be set aside for another's sake, but there was nothing else, now, that would suffice. Celia should not have been running away from dying, Harold should not have been drinking himself into a hypertensive stupor; nevertheless, for the people Celia and Harold were, in extremis, there were no other anodyne possibilities. There was no help he could give except to acquiesce.

By the middle of December her mind was only intermittently lucid. She resented Harold's presence in her room, or ignored it. 'I want my son,' she would say tearfully; later, 'Go away!' Later still, 'Where's Alan? I want Alan,' when he was standing beside her holding her hand; and Harold, heavy-faced, heavy-breathed, his small feet under his weighty bulk creaking the floorboards as he withdrew, would go downstairs to drink. When she fell asleep, Alan would join him.

In the week before Christmas she no longer called for him; she was straying in the ghostly past she had painfully scrabbled together. Mostly she lay still, propped up and breathing stertorously, whispering sometimes in a voice of indistinct blandishment, or breaking into a repeated laugh, her hostess laugh, under her breath, like a parrot practising. Occasionally when she spoke it was to the child Alan, but so confused that if he had not once been that child he would not have caught the significances. When he replied she did not react. If her mind cleared at all, it was to such appalling pain that no face or voice on earth could comfort her.

The vicar came every day, anointed her, fed her communion by intinction. He had begun, on the way out, to address Alan as 'my boy', and look clerical; betraying thereby an unease with death no less than that of laymen, which made Alan sorry for his embarrassment. The organist broke an arm two days before Christmas: the incident provided a few minutes' blessedly unawkward conversation.

'My wife will have to stand in. It will be rather much for her, with all the family at home, but we shall cope.'

'I'll do it, if you like. I could manage hymns and a few chorale preludes, anyway.'

The vicar looked relieved, if somewhat guilty, at the success of his hint. 'It's laying too great a burden on you at this troubled time, my boy.'

'I'll be glad to.'

He was desperate to get away from the house. A smell of death had settled on it, a lying miasma of disinfectant and air freshener, which wreathed its way even into the music room. The dryad with the apple had become a pathetic obscenity.

So on Christmas Eve he sat at the organ, with the scent of rich women and candle smoke in his nostrils as in other years. Purcell's Chaconne in G then *Nun Komm der Heiden Heiland*; both too introspective for the bland faces and careful coiffures. The little boys and girls of the choir scampered on slight pretexts to and fro, bobbing to the altar as they crossed it, tense with excitement, and back into hiding in the vestry.

Oh come, oh come Emmanuel. The children sang with bright Christmas eyes and a giggle and a nudge, *Disperse the gloomy clouds of night, And death's dark shadows put to flight*. It was not like that at all. Dark shadows have the dignity of fallen angels, or at the least the glamour of villainy, of Borgias or pirates. They can be put to flight by light and life and courage. But dying. A rotting effluvium of bedsores, surgical spirit and cologne; lies and fear, a fading whimper, a ghost dissolving in the midwinter evening. The dead lay in the devouring wind of Boreray: a dessicated auk in the dried wrack at spring-tide mark, a sockful of drowned kittens washed up in a cleft of the rock, an aged ewe half sunk in the peaty mire. Trudi had a dead thing on the kitchen table, a pale pink scalded unfeathered thing which had lived no life at all. Every home would have one of those tonight. The dead lay under the old damp headstones outside, inemotive nothings disintegrating in the earth. Their agony in death was nothing, their life was nothing, they could no longer even be pitied, there was nothing to be put to flight.

Midnight, communion. After the communion hymn, *Allein Gott in der Hoh' sei Ehr*: the left hand's bubbling energy, changing and changeless as a cascading spring. If that was all it was, a going back into the earth to grow again as grass; but it was not that, with the pain and the obliterating drugs.

The final hymn, then *In Dulci Jubilo*. He escaped by the vestry door, unnoticed by the shrill-voiced children.

Harold was puce and sweating. He had been drinking, but that was not all.

'Thank God you're back.' He lurched into the hall to say it. 'She's been in the most awful pain. I couldn't get hold of anyone – I tried for an hour, I couldn't get anyone.'

'Christ! Hasn't the nurse got anything?'

'The doctor came in the end. He gave her an injection. It's impossible – it's becoming impossible. I couldn't find anyone—'

'I'm sorry, I should have been here.'

He was peevish at once. 'You couldn't have done anything. If I couldn't, you couldn't.'

'No, of course not. Have another drink.'

'No soda, if you don't mind.'

They sat down slowly opposite each other, with mutually averted eyes. The silence changed to a heavy pause, as Harold shifted in his seat and rubbed the rim of his tumbler, working up to speaking.

'She must go to a nursing home. She must have proper treatment. Things are impossible.'

'No.' Alan stared at the ashes of the fire, avoiding Harold's eye, which would rouse his anger. 'Leave her at home, she hasn't long now.'

'No, I insist.' He rose, placing his glass with slow emphasis on the mantelpiece. 'She must have the best attention. She must have proper treatment.'

'No one can do anything for her now, Harold. Let her be.'

'I insist! I absolutely insist.'

Alan leapt to his feet, with the blood draining from his face. 'No! She's my mother—'

'She's my wife! My – wife –' His voice foundered in ponderous, drunken sobs.

Alan ran for the stairs. He got as far as the bottom step and sat down suddenly, with his head against the newel post. The thought formed that she was no longer his mother and no longer Harold's wife; she was no longer anything. He waited till Harold was quiet, then went back into the drawing room and poured them both another drink.

'All right, Harold, you decide about a nursing home. If it will make things better.'

So Celia died, on the day before New Year's Eve, on a high bed in a brightly lit pink cubicle full of stainless steel, not in her pretty sky-blue bedroom with the creeper and the string of peanuts at the window, and the cats on the quilt.

It was almost dawn when they got home.

'I'll make all the arrangements tomorrow, Harold, don't worry,' Alan reassured him for the tenth time. His own voice sounded like a stranger's, promising it. He poured a whisky for him with two sleeping pills crushed in it, made sure it went down his throat, got him upstairs and into his pyjamas. Harold sat on the edge of his bed, with his podgy feet together and his fat cotton-clothed knees apart, staring through the open door of his room at the closed door of Celia's, with slow tears trickling down his nose. Alan shut the door, and found himself, with distant surprise, still on the same side of it as Harold.

Harold wiped his eyes and blew his nose. 'You'll stay, Alan. You'll stay for a bit, won't you? After it's over.'

In that ugly gross body too there was a guileless child. There was no growing up after all.

'Yes, I'll stay till you get sorted out, anyway. Why don't you get into bed now, and I'll put the light off.'

He switched the lights out downstairs as well and opened the curtains. An uncertain pallor crept over his hands and the furniture. He went out to the garden. The dawn was grey beyond the orchard, the misty night yellowish with streetlamps above the cedar. The motorway sounded two miles away, dull and insidious as the sodium glare: the city dawn of loneliness and estrangement, haunted by unsteady self-images and directionless ghosts, the broken remnants of its thousands. The sheep and the razorbill might dissolve on Boreray and be free to the elements, but she was trapped, her way out occluded by drugs and lights. She couldn't stay and she couldn't go. She wouldn't acknowledge water and dust. She was afraid.

Something white was under the cedar. It was Yasmin, crouched, mewing toothlessly. Her fur was damp and bedraggled. Yasmin, the bird-tormentor, the skittish night prowler, who got her name because she loved blood and was frightened of the moon; she was no longer smooth and white. Her mistress had gone and the window was closed against her, the back door too, and the cat-flap latched by Trudi to deter burglars and rapists. He lifted her and held her close to his face. 'Yasmin.' She rubbed her ill-smelling old mouth against his in a purring frenzy of love and relief, kneading his neck with chilled pads. 'I will take her home – shall I?'

PART FOUR

Where Mercy, Love and Pity dwell
There God is dwelling too.

'The Divine Image', William Blake

. . . gille nan caorachan, gaolach thu.

Chapter 27

The journey north took longer than he expected. He hadn't reckoned with the slower east-coast route, or with the slower vehicle. He had exchanged the Porsche for an Escort van, which was unexhilarating on the motorway. It had seemed necessary, though, as a gesture towards inconspicuous non-consumption, after the routine luxuries of home counties life; a ludicrously empty gesture at that, he felt. He had been disturbed to discover what an excessive sum the transaction left him with, in spite of the undoubted dishonesty of the used-car salesman, but after a few minutes in a traffic jam calculating his future, he had recognised that he would need the money. A further few minutes revealed the dangers in such a recognition: he might end up needing life insurance and a mortgage and the *Financial Times* share index. Oxfam had a poster on a hoarding opposite, and in between fiddling with the radio to see if it worked (surprisingly, it did) he wrote a cheque to them and another to Trudi, with considerable relief. Trudi's went into her menacing black leather handbag with a very handsomely worded reference when she wasn't looking. He hadn't dared offer it openly: she would certainly have refused it out of spite, if she could have done so to his face, knowing it was conscience money.

He had got rid of her at the very end of her agreed two-month trial period, at the last possible moment, after finding the cats shut out overnight a second time; if Shan hadn't yowled unstoically under his window, poor old Yasmin would have died in the snow. Harold had been nervous about the proceedings. 'Do as you like,' he said, 'but I shan't have anything to do with it. Only if you get another one, let's not have such a man-hater.'

But it was on grounds of cat-hating that he dismissed Trudi. For ten minutes he had quaked before her while she told him in

272

both German and English what she thought of him, of cats and of Harold. Then suddenly her face swelled and reddened, and to his consternation she wept.

'It is not my cooking. It is not my housekeeping. You want someone young and pretty – that is all. Men!'

That had been dreadful. His protestations that he was unmoved by youth and prettiness, and that anyway he was going away, only increased her fury. It was veal for dinner and she hid the bread so that he couldn't feed the birds. But she went next day, the same day as the Porsche. The replacement from the agency was, in fact, both younger and prettier, and had the air of one who liked men as well as cats. Alan felt confident Harold would find her an improvement.

The whole train of events was vaguely discreditable; he pondered his part in it from time to time during the journey north. Self-respect was becoming increasingly hard to find, but he was becoming used to not having any. At least he was left without any money to worry about; he would have to finish Selena quickly, because he wouldn't be able to pay the rent much longer, and that clarified things considerably.

Scuffling for toll change at the Forth Bridge, he resigned himself to being late. He examined the possibility of not turning up at all, but it was really only of academic interest, though certainly he had not originally intended to go to Eleanor's wedding. The contra-indications were strong: he would meet Eleanor, and worse, Donnie. The indications were strong too: if he didn't, he would offend the Morrisons, and he would not meet Donnie.

He stopped to change into suitable clothes at a service area. By the time he was on the road again, he had worked out, if he hadn't known it all along, that the Morrisons would not be offended if he kept away, because his mother's death was a decent excuse; in fact, attending a wedding so soon was more likely to be considered indecent. But that was what he was going to do: therefore his only aim was to meet Donnie. He was incredulous that this was so. They would be two out of two hundred people in a noisy crowded room. There could be no point of contact, they might not even recognise each other. He reminded himself grimly that he no longer fitted the part of a schoolboy's hero in either looks or spirit, after two months of lounging in a sickroom by day and hard drinking by night; and that

273

anyway, Donnie was no longer a schoolboy. He would, of course, be completely different. He repeated that to himself over and over, and kept the radio turned well up to batter down any musings around the subject. All the same he was soon shaking noticeably, and felt so sick that he had to stop twice between Queensferry and Dundee. Every disregarded junction for Crianlarich and other points west provoked a new and more wretched shudder: Dundee itself looked about as inviting as one of Kokoschka's worse visions of Prague.

Eleanor had sketched directions to the church on the back of the invitation, and he found a parking place half a block away. He had come only to lay a ghost, he reminded himself, as he locked the van with trembling fingers; but looking up at the gaunt Scottish neo-Gothic steeple against the steel-grey January sky, he knew with miserable certainty that he preferred a ghost to nothing. There was no one else visible and he could have turned back, but he realised he would not. He could always attend the service and miss the reception if things were too bad: that let-out made it possible to open the door quietly and slip into the pews at the end of the first hymn. Sandy, hovering dozily near the door, made an indecisive move towards him. Alan returned his nod of greeting and thereafter looked forwards, petrified. He was incapable of taking much in, except that any one of the youthful dark heads on the Boreray side might be Donnie's, that he was not necessarily near Sandy a few yards behind, in the deep shadows under the gallery. Distractedly, he pursued the ins and outs of Eleanor's headdress, dainty sprays of satin blossom ringleted round her burnished curls under a rather papal white skullcap. The back of Murdo's neck looked hot and anxious, just like any other bridegroom's; perhaps he would even smile later. Ewan's powerful shoulders, hunched bashfully in a churchgoing posture, strained his unaccustomed pale grey jacket. The matron of honour was taller than her sister and yellowish blonde, and Mairi – poor Mairi the bridesmaid, he noticed with sudden pity, was all too obviously a maid no longer.

When it was over, he bolted without looking right or left. He retrieved the van and drove off in what instinct told him was a westerly direction. He had no instinct, though, for the one-way system: he went round it three times, was hooted and sworn at, and when he had narrowly missed squashing a pushchair and contents on a zebra crossing, decided he was unfit to continue. He jumped the next set of traffic lights, shot up a cul-de-sac and reversed down it, and somehow found himself in the environs of a multistorey carpark. He collected his wits sufficiently to discern a vacant space, drew into it, and slumped trembling in the merciful half-darkness.

He switched the radio on and off several times. He read the van's service record from end to end. His trembling passed into shivering, as it was a freezing east-coast day and he was de-acclimatised by indoor living. He stretched into the back for a pullover, and stared at it with chattering teeth, but it seemed a defeatingly complex manoeuvre to take his jacket off and put the other garment on, and he lost interest in it. He thought about Murdo's detested string vest and wondered if he'd be wearing it for his wedding night. He wondered if Eleanor's sister's hair was really that colour. He turned the radio on again, and off. Eventually he realised with a mixture of relief and despair that he was not going to leave without seeing Donnie.

He walked for half an hour or so, again in a westerly direction, before it impinged upon him that Donnie was not inevitably to be found in that quarter of open horizon and setting sun. After accosting a series of passers-by, he at last found himself in the right hotel, surrounded by friendly Borerayans who shook hands warmly and offered condolences. After the condolences, Do'l Alex and Roddy severally suggested a visit to the gents for a wee private dram: the bar was still closed, and they had arrived furnished with half-bottles to while away the interval of the wedding party's photographic session. Alan could have done with a dram, but not in the gents; his refusals of the time-honoured Borerayan custom were tolerated gently because of his recent bereavement.

It took about ten minutes of hesitant glancing around to be sure that Donnie was not yet present. He warmed up and stopped shaking, and became capable of answering people coherently and of remembering most of their names. Every household on the island seemed to be represented, with only Katie left in Gnipadale to mind old Johane and all the crofts. The official festivities would not begin until the bride and groom arrived, after which drink would start flowing and continue to do so for a good eight or nine hours, but Boreray was already working up to it. A dignified procession of broad-chested, great-fisted island men filed in and out of the gents, without unruliness, but redder and more Gaelic-speaking when they came out than when they went in. A less obvious traffic in twos and threes circulated through the ladies, Alan soon realised, speculating curiously on the contents of the large handbags. The feel of a Highland wedding was coming back to him; he had had an erstwhile nanny who married a gamekeeper from Ardnamurchan. Eleanor's side of the affair, recognisable from their city pallor and inferior physique, seemed to be regarding the other contingent rather askance already.

He went out with Porky for a wee stroll, which turned out predictably to mean a dram beside the dustbins. This time he didn't refuse. His churning stomach felt considerably calmer immediately.

'Thought you'd given the stuff up then.'

'No – afraid not. I just don't fancy it in the loo. I had a nasty experience in a school lavatory once, gave me negative feelings about such places.'

'Tell me about it, come on!'

'Nothing to leer about, fatface! I got locked in, that's all.'

'Oh well, I thought worse than that happened in them posh schools –'

He cuffed, Porky ducked, a dustbin fell over, and a determined-looking female in black appeared at a kitchen window. Porky ogled and waved and Alan scarpered. It had made him laugh, which was just as well, since the bride and groom were installed and greeting their guests, a moment he had not been looking forward to. Fortified by Porky's drams and absurdities, he kissed Eleanor peacefully enough and clasped Murdo's hand with a sort of bewildered affection, because the man actually did smile.

Borerayan glee was mounting. Do'l Alex's cheerful voice was raised in incomprehensible oaths, countered by shrill remonstrances from his five daughters. Alan took a drink from a passing waitress, grinning at her expression of outrage as Do'l Alex's astounding gutturals assaulted her ears.

'You have your hands full of wild highlanders tonight.'

She tutted, 'Uncivilised barbarians, I'd call them,' she said, in an accent very like Eleanor's.

He laughed. Another voice spoke behind him.

'Alan.'

He turned, saw no one he knew; then a moment's blinding recognition, then a stranger again.

'Donnie.'

They shook hands. He was pale and his hair was shorter or somehow different. His eyes were guarded, or perhaps grown up, or perhaps they had never been as he had imagined them. He had a girl on his arm.

'This is Carol,' he said. 'Carol, this is Alan I was telling you about.'

'What was he telling you?' Alan shook hands with her too. She had long nails.

'I told her you were the one with the untidy hair. Carol's a hairdresser, never forgets it either.'

She had obviously tidied his up. He looked down at her with a certain pride.

'Shut up, Donnie.' Her voice was middling-strong Glasgow, and his had more than a touch of the accent too. She was a small, neat, nondescriptly pretty girl. Alan's heart quailed. If it was not hatred he felt for her it was the nearest he had ever been to it.

'Donnie!' came a shout across the room.

'That's Ewan wanting me – come on.' He turned, pulling her along with him; but looked back, saying in his old quiet civil tone, 'See you later, Alan,' with the beginning of a smile; or rather, he had been smiling all the time, with the hard gloss of the city, and it had gone, revealing briefly his former sweet gravity.

Alan started after him, stopped, and forced himself to walk off in the other direction, where he was soon engaged in some sort of conversation. He had no idea what it was about, but no one expected anything better of him, because of his mother's death and Eleanor's marriage.

There were further drinks and dinner, toasts and speeches and wedding cake, more drinking, ever-increasing noise, the tinkle of breaking glass followed by a gust of pejorative Gaelic, a band tuning up, dancing. All the time Alan was eerily aware of Donnie's position in the room, though when he actually caught sight of him, the young man with the quick level stare was not anyone he knew.

The dancing was wild and Scottish. Jackets, ties and shoes flew to the wall, and warlike whoops resounded above the over-amplified instruments. Even Eleanor's relatives began to look cheerful by the second eightsome. Alan caught Mairi for it.

'I can't!' she said, pink and bashful, but she did, at least three-quarters of it. Then she clung to his arm, gasping and laughing. 'I'll have to stop, Alan! I'm six months gone.'

They fell back to the wall, she clinging to his arm with both hands, and sobbing for breath.

'Are you all right?'

'Yes, in a minute.'

He noticed the ringless hand on his arm. She was pale and quiet when she stopped panting.

'Who was it, Mairi?' he asked.

'Calum MacDonald – Crabbit's brother.'

'Oh God, that family – has he – I mean—'

'He left me, you bet. Said it was none of his. It is, though.'

'I'm sorry. I've made you cry now.'

She gulped, trying not to. 'Mum and Dad were taking it badly, because of Johane being the same way before. They were that ashamed!'

'Have they got over it?'

'Almost.' She managed a tremulous smile, looking up at him with childlike eyes. 'Eleanor's been great. She's so good to me. She – she says she's looking forward to the baby.'

'I'm sure she is. She loves babies.'

She gave him another quivering smile: so like Donnie, as he had been. 'They weren't going to let me be a bridesmaid with this big belly on me, but she said yes. She made all our dresses too.'

'They're lovely. That blue suits you, Mairi. The style's clever, too. You don't notice the bump.'

It was probably the longest speech he had ever made in praise of a woman's dress. It had the desired effect.

'Och, get away! You see it a mile off!' But her smile brightened and her eyes shone. She laughed and pointed at Kirsty skidding across the floor on her bottom from a boisterous partner's swing, as the dance ended in gratulatory shrieks and tangled heaps of bodies.

Eleanor approaching leading Murdo. Mairi pulled a face. 'Here's big brother. I'm off.'

It was Murdo who was leading Eleanor. Her chin was determined

278

and her eyes fiery, but she was definitely being led. While Alan was musing over this extraordinary circumstance, they stopped in front of him. He smiled nervously and remarked that everything was going very well. Murdo's face was dark rather than red, and he was breathing hard. Alan concluded that he had come to deliver an insulting speech or a threat, or perhaps a few punches. Instead he said, 'It's good to see you here tonight.'

Alan was astonished, but collected himself quickly. 'It's good to see you both looking so happy.'

'Happy' was not a just term, but he delivered it without hesitation: he had glimpsed the chill thing contorting behind Murdo's words, and respected his attempt. He had his own recent acquaintance with jealousy for comparison.

Murdo pulled Eleanor forward. 'No ill-feeling, eh? You'll have a dance with her.'

She was smiling, but he could feel her fury, although with him she had never hidden it behind a smile.

'I'd like to. What do you say, Eleanor?'

'Certainly.'

There was an outburst of execration from the exhausted reelers as Strip the Willow was announced. Alan, at least, was glad it was nothing more intimate.

'I'm sorry about your mother. We didn't really expect to see you,' she said, as they took their places.

From her eyes he could see that she had left at least one unpleasant remark unvoiced, but he was saved the necessity of fielding it by the outbreak of the music. She had her Valkyrie look. He held and twirled her gingerly: her voltage was definitely high. Conversation was fortunately impossible. She did shout at him half-way through. 'You dance quite well. I didn't even realise you could.'

'Highland balls in privileged youth,' he shouted back, hoping that irritation to her socialist principles might distract her attention from whatever the more intense grievance was which set her hair on end and made his arm tingle. But he forgot about her abruptly. He became aware that Donnie was standing by the door, without Carol. Perhaps Eleanor was aware of it too; when the music stopped she turned her back on him at once. He didn't notice; he remembered his discarded jacket only because he tripped over it, caught it up and made for the door.

Donnie did not look at him till he was at his side, and then it was the new hard flat stare. 'Come on,' he said, turning immediately.

It was better not to be looked at. Alan followed his dark head through the crowd in the lobby. 'Where?'

'The bar, of course.' The insolent city-touched intonation died in his next words. 'Carol's in there.' He jerked his head towards the room they had left; his fleeting glance betrayed that it was not in order to get even drunker that he wanted to keep out of her way.

Alan halted, as the estranging press of bodies closed in outside the bar. 'The last thing we need is more drink. Isn't there anywhere else?'

Donnie swung round, brushing against him in the packed corridor. He was tense and hostile, Murdo's brother. 'Only the gents.'

His eyes were shockingly unrevealing. Alan looked away, shrinking from the several unpleasantries he might intend, but followed him back through the lobby.

'I'm going to throw up,' said Donnie indistinctly, and hurled himself into the confused din of flushing urinals, retching and joyful Gaelic song.

Alan sank back against the wall. He wanted to think things out, but the only thought his head would accommodate was that the girl might come out looking for Donnie. That made him sweat with panic. He pushed his clenched hands hard down in his pockets to stop himself quaking. Donnie returned, very white.

'Coming for a walk?' Alan asked quickly, with what seemed like brilliant presence of mind.

He nodded. 'I can't take much drink,' he said, rather sheepishly. In the admission he sounded more like his old self.

Outside the cold pressed on them like a weight after the smoky warmth within. Donnie glanced up at the frosty haloes round the streetlamps. 'You driving north tonight? Hope you don't run into snow.'

'It doesn't matter really if I get stranded. Which way?'

They stood at a corner. The streets were deserted, the pavements glistening with untrodden hoar frost.

'Doesn't matter either.' He looked up sideways (he still had to look up) with an echo of familiar shyness.

They took the broader road, a straight modern shopping street extending in a menacing unpeopled perspective of glass and concrete. The rhythm of the band still boomed faintly behind them. An unseen distant motorcycle snarled and faded, followed by another, and a third. They were both awkwardly silent, then they both spoke at once, and laughed.

'Go on.'

'No, you.'

'I was going to ask about Selena, but I should have said first about your mother. I was sorry to hear.'

After that they remembered what the friendly and appropriate things to say were, and conversation was easier. The boatbuilding details kept them occupied for some time. They walked fast in the cold, and talked with animation, in the relief of finding a mutually congenial subject. Donnie's new sharp edges began to soften, or at least to be revealed as for defence rather than attack. They turned off down a narrower and meaner street, with shuttered and padlocked pubs on either side, and occasional knots of youngsters sniggering in doorways. Donnie eyed them warily. He had acquired urban suspicions, Alan realised with a pang; but perhaps necessarily, since he was not built on the lines of his elder brothers.

'When do you think you'll finish?' he was asking.

'Probably early March. I should get her in the water then, anyway, if the weather's reasonable. Depends how much she leaks when I can sail her realistically.' He spoke with enthusiasm: Donnie's interest had made it seem genuinely attractive.

'Then you'll go.'

'Yes.'

He was silent. Alan glanced at him. His jaw was set and his mouth sullen.

A drunk tottered towards them out of a doorway, a straying-haired down-and-out with a blue nose and red eyes. He shambled between them, stretching a wavering hand to each shoulder. Alan stepped aside.

'Fuck off you stinking bastard!' Donnie was hoarse with fury, fists up and eyes narrowed. The old man lurched away, complaining inarticulately. Alan looked from one to the other, dismayed.

'Plenty of that sort in Glasgow.' Donnie stared at him defiantly, daring him, it seemed, to voice his silent disapproval; but he bowed his head as Alan looked away, and when he turned to him again, his face was his own, gentle and beseeching, almost as if he were ready to cry.

Alan felt pretty much like crying too. 'How's Glasgow?' he asked, before things got any worse. 'We've been talking about me. How are you getting on?'

He shrugged and seemed to be thinking out his answer, but when he spoke it was to say, 'You got a limp, Alan. What happened?'

'Oh, old age – decrepitude.' The weeks of inactivity had weakened the tendons again. 'It's nothing much, I had an accident on a yacht.' He remembered, suddenly, the boy with a splinter in his foot, limping and jumping by turns through the kingcups and peat-pools.

'Was that in the South Seas? What was it like?'

They talked about that, about Rangiora and Moorea, Suvarov and Pago Pago, till Alan broke it off. 'What about you? How's the work?'

He was evasive: the work was all right, the tradesmen were all right, the other trainees were all right, the firm was all right.

'But what sort of work do you do?'

'Shopfitting mostly.'

'Is it interesting?'

'No, bloody boring.' He laughed. 'Half of them can't tell a screw from a nail in that place. It's all machines – if you can plug them into a socket that's all you need to know. Machines and chipboard. I haven't cut a dovetail since Selena's halfbeams.'

'God, is it really that bad? Couldn't you change to some other firm?'

'They're all the same – any would have me, at least. I'm lucky to have a job, it'll do. Might not be one much longer. They turned off six before Christmas, they're all on the dole.'

'They wouldn't get rid of you. You're too talented.'

Donnie cast him a quizzical glance. 'Last in first out. That's the rule.'

Alan was shamed into silence. It was a harsh rule made for people who didn't have wealthy parents dying off at convenient intervals. The reality of that way of life appeared starkly; he remembered the long-ago day in the technical classroom, Donnie quivering with chagrin over a blank sheet of paper. He was quivering now, though

282

whether with cold or anxiety was difficult to tell. His face was tense but gave away little. The childish oval had gone: a habit of clenching his jaw left a hollow beneath his cheekbone. Alan ached with sadness. He had hoped he would be unchanged, although he had told himself it was impossible. It was impossible; his new world plundered the innocent. His fault there must be that his defences were not thorough enough: every softening of that shadow in his cheek was a failure in survival. The only good to wish for him was that the change should be completed.

Donnie halted suddenly. He had been far away. His eyes had that strange inward look Alan knew but had never interpreted. It reminded him that the old world had not been kind either.

'Where are we?' Pragmatic alertness reclaimed his features.

'I've no idea.'

They stood in a wide unwindowed area of warehouses and locked yards. A thin air barbed with oil and salt sifted the uneasy detritus of the town, dirt-obscured scraps of paper, colourless dust of traffic-worn thoroughfares. A discarded lager can rolled to and fro on a grating, briefly displaying a big-breasted pin-up on the back: Janis, red-lipped among broken glass and disintegrating cardboard, making a small empty sound as the wind pushed her here and there.

'Near the docks I think. Freezing, isn't it? What's the time?'

Alan glanced at his watch. 'Just after midnight.'

'Better get back or you'll be missing the ferry.'

'How do we get back from here? I haven't been noticing where we've been going.'

'We'll find it.' He set off purposefully.

'I've no idea where I left my car either,' said Alan, suddenly.

'Multistorey?'

'Yes.'

'I'll show you. It's nearly back where we started. We pass it.'

Alan was doubtful, remembering distantly that he had walked for a long time and asked directions from a lot of people. 'Is there only one in the city centre?'

'I don't know.'

'I walked for miles. I think it was probably another one.'

Donnie laughed. 'You're hopeless! I bet you went round in a circle. That's the one – well, look there first, anyway.'

Alan wondered, as usual, how on earth he knew: uncharted rocks and mislaid vehicles. They smiled at each other shyly. The unspoken recall of the past made things easier. Alan took the chance; there was something he had to know.

'What about the girlfriend?'

'What about her?'

His tone was warning, but Alan gritted his teeth and pursued it. 'Serious?'

'So so.'

There was a charged silence. Then he said, 'No, it's not. But she's pretty, at least.'

'Yes, she is.' In his relief, Alan sounded quite enthusiastic.

'I don't sleep with her. Wouldn't get the chance the way Alex Angus and her mum are. I don't want to anyway.'

To this unsolicited and unclear revelation Alan could think of no reply. After it Donnie distanced himself. He had plenty to say, but his voice had taken the Glaswegian edge again; his gestures were sharper, his face wary. He seemed intent on turning aside Alan's initiatives. Further questions about his way of life in Glasgow got short answers or none. Alan kept trying, searching for some reassurance that he wasn't totally unsatisfied with it. He wanted to ask, simply, 'Are you happy?' The need to know that had bedevilled him since the day they parted. Now it seemed obvious that the answer could never have been yes: and equally evident that to question in what proportion he was and was not would be trespass. The moment for such intimacy had gone; Alan cursed himself bitterly for using it to find out about Carol. The defences were up again now.

'There's the carpark. Hotel's up that street. You going now?'

'No, I'll walk back with you.' Alan fell into desperate silence, and at last, as they turned the corner with the beat of the dance band already throbbing around them, into desperate speech. 'Donnie, isn't there anything you like about the work? The city?'

'I'm lucky to have a job.'

'But do you like it?'

'No.' He walked on up the steps without change of pace. A few uncertain flakes of snow had begun to fall, touching his hair and dissipating in the drift of confetti before the glass doors.

'You don't go home much.'

'No.'

'But you would rather never have left?'

He gave no answer as they plunged into the heat and noise of the vestibule. Siblings and cousins were already swallowing him up. He greeted this one and that. Mairi advanced giggling, unsteadily arm-in-arm with Kirsty.

'They've just left, you missed it. Did the car pass you? What a laugh! They're dragging everything but the kitchen sink behind them.'

'Your girlfriend's looking for you, boy,' warned Kirsty, with wantoning eyes.

'She's wild, too.' Mairi smacked his cheek playfully.

They swayed away, laughing and pushing each other. Donnie shouldered into the crowd and din. Carol was standing at the door of the dance hall in company with other bored and aggrieved women.

Alan made a last attempt. 'Was it the wrong thing, Donnie?'

He stopped. They were pushed close in the crush, so that he had to look up. His face was guardedly blank. 'Yes.' He averted his gaze. At Alan's slight wince of indrawn breath he looked up again. 'Yes, totally wrong. But it wasn't your fault.' Suddenly his eyes cleared to naked sadness. He lunged away through the crowd towards Carol, who received him with a frown and a raucous reproof.

'What ya playin' at? You makin' a fool of me?'

He silenced her with the basic conciliatory move common to all the erring males who were reclaiming their partners after clandestine visits to the bar, an open-mouthed kiss and a hand on her buttocks. She slid a thin arm round his waist, talking angrily at odds with her gesture as soon as his mouth lifted, and they disappeared among the milling bodies.

Chapter 28

On Boreray it was a mild winter; 'mild' implying mere absence of frost. It was a life-sapping, twilit season of incessant rain and gales, scouring exposed pastures down to sterile black slime. Storm-driven spring tides gnawed chunks out of the land and spewed rocks and flotsam far up the crofts. Between storms, the land and its creatures oozed and dripped dismally. Alan fed the birds and sheep around his door, but without any of the satisfaction of successful benevolence. For the four or five draggle-fleeced animals pushing hopefully against his hands every day, he knew there were twenty more dead out on the hill, and that the starlings and crows did well enough off their corpses. All the same, they were vociferous in their expectations when he went out to the workshop in the mornings.

He worked assiduously on the boat, although things were so far advanced that it was often a case of refining details that would have done well enough without it. It was time for setting the mast and rigging, but since the continuous rain made outside work unrealistic, she remained in the shed, acquiring extra layers of paint and varnish till she shone as glassily as a child's new toy. To occupy the rest of the time decently, he patched up Roddy's leaky old boat with painstaking scarfs that would have lasted half a century if they hadn't been on to planks that were at best half rotten rather than very rotten. 'It'll do a year or so yet,' was Roddy's hope; he was proud of the immaculate renovations Chrissie had masterminded for the house, but boats were not Chrissie's department, and left to himself he was happy-go-lucky. Sandy provided Alan with a further outlet for futile good works: he gave him driving lessons, though he was privately of the opinion that if you tested Sandy's head with an awl it would be no more hopeful than Roddy's boat. He didn't forget Harold; he telephoned him with a regularity that would have astonished Celia, and gathered that the new housekeeper was very satisfactory. He even telephoned the housekeeper on the appropriate day in February to ask her to surprise Harold with a birthday cake. '*Financial Times* pink icing,' he couldn't resist. She laughed a slow warm chuckle which made him remember how long it was since he had had a girl in bed with him.

He could have found one easily enough with minimal exertion of charm, but he took care to keep clear of such involvement: he had decided on a harmless life. He was aware that his conduct was hardly to be dignified by the term 'decision', since it was not a matter of integrity or even choice. It was more like the impulse that prompts drowning sailors to sing hymns or penned sows to chew the bars of their cages: a self-drugging mechanism to anaesthetise against the

286

unbearable. He realised in the exercise of it that he was Celia's son.

If he kept his mind safely inactive most of the time, he found intervals when he could think quite normally: or by the standards of the normal, quite crazily. He had seen Donnie and he knew the Furies were still after him; he wanted to meet them face to face. There were no steps of reasoning, no further arguments to be gone through, only two incompatible certainties: he had acted with decent motives, and he had caused destruction. He wanted to know why. The continuous train of the causes and effects of daily choices was merely the working out of the equation, how, not why, no more a reason than the length of Donnie's eyelashes or the tilt of his pelvis were reasons for falling in love. These were discoveries after the event, retrospective explanations.

He set himself to search for connections. He looked from Donnie outwards at the rest of his life. Torquil, Celia, dead. Eleanor, incomprehensibly abandoning herself to a fate as bad as. Further back, Sally, unfaithful to George: she had looked at him wanly in Celia's sickroom. Frances: he had dropped in on his way south to tell her to take the dinghy if she could be bothered to collect it, and his brief presence had been no kindness, in spite of her new bearded and jolly boyfriend. Richard, Daphne. Destruction and loss spread out from him like ripples from a stone in deep water. He caused the ripples, though he had not willed the plummet. He wasn't a reason.

He went all his usual ways in the hills and along the shore. The harmony he had seen and shared was broken. He perceived that he was the cause of this breach and that it was actual, not subjective. His unresponsiveness might make him blind, but it was not all: it was not a reason.

He spent hours crouched among the rocks staring at the swirling water, the changing and changeless waves and eddies, and saw that tides and landforms were not reasons. He studied the lights of the township at night and thought of community, and knew that mutual benefit was not the reason. He watched a rabbit in the sun on a rare bright day, washing its ears with all the joy in the world, and it was obvious that absorption of vitamin D was not the reason. He saw mated ravens somersaulting in the sky above the rabbit and knew that survival of corvine genes was no good reason; afterwards he reread *The Selfish Gene* and concluded that DNA was no sort of reason for anything. All reasons were retrospective explanations and the connections implied were spurious.

He played music and listened to his stock of records with attention, grim attention, in case he might miss the answer. He pondered most often the magic music that Donnie had looked at with his inward look: a shepherd's improvisation, a nursery tune, throwaway, sweetly merry, a still small voice. It was the music of a ceremony of innocence. It was beginning to be a reason. Was that all? The unity of the lovers perceived it; it was there already in the ancient oak tree. If it did not exist unity would be two. Why should 'I will be always at your side' be a convincing rejoinder to 'Here are the gates of terror', if it were not for that voice, that reason?

He saw there were connections, but they were out of reach.

By the end of February, Selena was chocked up outside. It still rained, but less vehemently. With the boat out of the way, it was possible to shape the new mast in comfort. The boom had caused some trouble, as he had worked on it stooping in the narrow space alongside the hull. Nevertheless, it was finished and varnished to astonishing perfection. It looked pleasing, but it would have been better to be certain about the weight. It was long in proportion to the hull and it could perhaps have stood more of a hollow to lighten it. He was anxious to try the boat's performance so that any such defects could be remedied before he abandoned the workshop; he had told Roddy he would be gone by mid April. They might find summer visitors to rent to after that: he used some of Selena's blue paint to smarten up the front door in case, and even mended the doorknob. These unfamiliarities made his departure seem more imminent. He began to study the *West Coast Pilot* in bed, and sent for charts of Icelandic waters, not as many as he would have liked. He had intended to sell the van to pay for such last-minute paraphernalia, but put it off because it seemed unkind to Sandy, though unlikely to lessen his anyway negligible chance of passing a driving test.

One uninvitingly grey morning when the *Pilot* had offered an alternative to getting up immediately, he was roused from contemplation of Islands and Dangers in the Sound of Barra by a knock at the door. As his shout of 'Come in' was unanswered by

288

the time he had pulled on jeans and a sweater, he expected to see a stranger, but it was Roddy.

'Roddy! You should just have walked in.'

Roddy took his bonnet off and clutched it before him in both hands. 'I came to tell you, Alan, Angus has passed away.'

'Oh – I'm very sorry.' The news was unexpected, but hardly shocking. He had been sent the previous week to Edinburgh for treatment, the second visit since Murdo's wedding. 'Come in.' Alan stood back awkwardly, not sure what else to say.

'No, no, I will not come in just now.' But he remained on the doorstep, unhappily twisting his bonnet.

Alan searched for appropriate comment. 'Was it yesterday?'

'Ay.' He shook his head at the hat in his hands. 'Ay, yesterday. Oh well, we never know the day or the hour, eh?' The cliché ended in a wrenched sob.

'Poor Angus,' said Alan, after a pause. He had always found Angus taciturn and self-pitying: it made him seem different when his craggy-faced cousin wept for him.

'Ay,' Roddy recovered himself, circulating his bonnet slowly. 'The remains will be coming this morning.'

'Oh – yes.' He worked out what the remains were. 'When's the funeral?'

'The day after tomorrow by the time all the family can get home.' He replaced his bonnet. 'Well, I'll be leaving you now. I will go to the plane with Murdo.'

'Thank you for coming to tell me.' He just remembered to say it.

He went in and fetched the usual rations for the waiting birds, wondering why on earth Murdo was going to the plane. The remains, of course: the body would be sent home by air. There would be a service in the house each evening the corpse lay there, as the custom was. Being a near neighbour, he would have to attend those and the funeral, and probably ought to call on Mairi Anna herself too. The prospect was unpleasant; he had had too much of that sort of thing too recently. His stomach tied in knots so that breakfast became unattractive. He made some coffee and took it out to the workshop, but concentration was difficult. At last, reluctantly, he admitted to himself that the knots were not tied by incipient funeral rites, but by the knowledge that Donnie would be home. He had no wish

289

to see him. He frowned into his coffee; more accurately, he had no wish to be obsessed by the expectation of seeing him, which was not the same thing.

For that reason as well as others, he was anxious to get the visit to the Morrisons over as quickly as possible. He wasn't sure of the form; perhaps it wouldn't even be necessary to go in. And should one approach by the back door as usual, or did death demand greater formality? He could have done with a briefing from Eleanor, he thought, with a wry grin. He stopped on the way to ask Chrissie's advice.

'Och, you will not go to the front door – only the minister will go to the front.' She began to sniff, wiping her eyes. He escaped hastily, though with sincere thanks: it would have been a grave breach of etiquette for a sinner to use the minister's door.

His momentary jauntiness disappeared as he stepped into the Morrisons' kitchen. They were grouped round the table, in a pathetic double-take of times past. Murdo and Eleanor sat in the seats that had been Angus's and Mairi Anna's, Johane's little boy on the stool where Mairi used to sit, Johane in the place that had been Donnie's: and Mairi Anna herself, suddenly a shrunken old woman in black, hunched in the chair that had been Auntie Effie's. There were whispered greetings. He took Mairi Anna's outstretched hands. She keened softly, clasping and patting his fingers with a basic human affection that astonished him. It was difficult to speak: he did not know the formulae of local mourning that would answer her need. The others sat silent with bowed heads, with the big black family bible dour and closed on the table in their midst. The door from the living room opened, and Mairi came in, pallid and heavy. Donnie was behind her. Alan's heart jolted: he hadn't expected him to be home that day. Their eyes met briefly, then the lashes were down, smudging pale cheeks.

He repeated to Mairi Anna some of the things he had heard people say to Harold. The sense was poor, but the intention was right, and reached her. She nodded, muttering broken affirmatives in Gaelic and English, ending, 'It is the will of God.'

'Mummy, I'm bored!' The child's high voice pierced the rickety fabric of adult comfort ruthlessly. Johane shushed him and took him out on tiptoe. Mairi Anna looked round, with dazed eyes.

'The will of God,' she repeated with determination, almost defiance. It was a tone Alan had heard her use to reprimand Donnie and Mairi for laughing at Mr MacNeil.

She turned to him again, her face now dignified and composed. 'Would you like to see him, Alan?'

It was a moment before he realised what was intended, but he managed to clamp down on a horrified negative. 'Yes.'

'Take him through, Donnie.'

The coffin lay open on the bed in what had been Auntie Effie's room. The dead man's face was covered. Donnie put his hand on the sheet. 'You don't have to look. It pleases her you said yes.' But in spite of the warning, filial piety apparently required that he fold it back; his own eyes were averted. An uneasy exhalation of embalmer's aromatics rose from the coffin, which Alan had not forgotten: looking could not be worse. Angus's face was blanched and fined by death and the undertaker's art. It held no memories of his life or personality; only for the first time Alan saw a resemblance between the hollow-cheeked dead father and his unhappy hollow-cheeked son.

'Oh, Donnie.' He spoke in a whisper of pity. The boy replaced the sheet. He could not or would not speak, or turn to face him, but slid past him and back into the kitchen.

Mairi Anna burst out in a paroxysm of sobbing when they entered. She rocked to and fro, her arms clasped round her body. '*Aoghnais, Aoghnais – o mo ghradh, mo ghradh!*' Alan looked at her, amazed. In Angus's lifetime they had seemed merely to tolerate each other, without smile or converse: so too the rest of his family. Now poor sweet Mairi howled with her head on her arms, her swollen belly heaving in a too-tight black skirt with the zip down. Her hand above her dark head was twisted in Donnie's; she was crying, surely, not for her father, who had scarcely acknowledged his youngest children's existence, but for the man who had abandoned her, who should have been holding her hand now. Donnie stood frozen at her side, his head bent, tears streaming down his still face. Eleanor, white and upright, stared ahead with pinching nostrils. Murdo's sallow cheeks were ashen, the bitter downcurve of his mouth drawing deep lines of strain. Alan looked from one to the other, appalled and humbled by their grief, helpless to remedy it. He made quietly for the door. Alex Angus came in as he went out, and shook hands tightly, though they hardly knew each other.

'You are very welcome to stay. They will be here for the service in a couple of hours.'

'No, I'll come back for it.'

Alex Angus shook hands again. Grief seemed to demand human contact, the palpable presence of others. Alan walked home slowly, thinking about it. As far as he could remember, he hadn't shed a tear for either of his parents.

That evening and the next he arrived for the house-services as late as possible, stood near the door, and left as soon as they were over. Those who relished such affairs stayed on for tea and sandwiches and subdued gossip. Such entertainment seemed unthinkable after the long sad cadences of Gaelic prayers and the heartrending yearning of Gaelic psalms. Alan found it scarcely bearable, and couldn't stay even knowing he might have a chance to speak to Donnie if he did; though if Donnie had shown any sign of wanting to be spoken to, he might have felt differently.

The funeral would be at midday. It would evidently be succeeded by a sober but plentiful feast for all the members of the family. In the two preceding days, the better part of the contents of Chrissie's freezer seemed to be spread out in her kitchen, thawing, cooking, and cooling in preparation.

'Katie is doing the rest of it,' she explained. 'Poor wee Mairi is not fit, and Eleanor will not know what to do yet.'

'The rest of it?' Alan's eyes wandered over the two whole salmon and the dismembered sheep and chickens on her kitchen table. 'However many are you feeding?'

'About thirty maybe. They will be hungry after standing about in the cold.'

The actual ceremony was as solemn as could be wished, and certainly cold. Every room of the house was crowded with women, but only the most respected and most infirm old men and Angus's sons and brothers were indoors with them. The rest of the men, at least a hundred of them, stood outside, ranged up the croft, dark-clad, quiet and dignified in the slow misty rain. A dog whimpered in the shed, a small sound audible in the waiting silence. An old ewe stalked up to the fence to stare for a few minutes, then turned with a toss of her horns and a hoarse disapproving bleat: Alan stifled a hysterical impulse to laugh. Nothing was actually in the least funny.

The mourners stood in confident simplicity, assured of the need of their presence. For an hour the soft wavering voices of the minister and missionary came faintly through the open door, interspersed with psalms, each line given out thin and high by the old precentor, and sung back by the whole congregation: or rather, wailed and roared, with little melody and less harmony, but throbbing with utter lamentation.

After the last prayer there was stillness and silence more tense than before: a sheep's jaws busy in the poor pasture, a brittle sound of small tough roots tearing out of damp soil; then women keening in the house, and footsteps as Angus's sons carried the coffin out, Alex Angus and Ewan red-eyed, Murdo impassive, Donnie deadly white. Behind them the women stood in the doorway, the four sisters in a sobbing knot, but Mairi Anna stern-faced and proud now: and it was Eleanor, with high head and straight back, who held her tightly by the arm, supporting her. Alan stared at her in amazement, and felt like cheering. He was distracted by Do'l Alex nudging him and pointing discreetly at half-mast: the coffin had passed to the dead man's brothers and brother-in-law, while the first bearers stood to either side with bowed heads, and the other men were forming a slow procession behind, as the coffin shifted gradually down the line, from near kin to more distant relatives and neighbours, followed by those who were neither. Do'l Alex steered Alan into the appropriate position, as the long line of dark figures wound up the hill and along the road, silent except for the slow tramp of feet. Those who had already taken their turn fell in again at the end. They would carry him, Alan saw, only a few hundred yards, to the all-purpose island bus, the same which conveyed the children to school, the faithful to church, and tourists to Ardbuie three times a week in summer. That circumstance should have been comic, but was not; no head of state could have been conducted to the grave with more dignity than was shown to Angus Morrison, who must have shared even that undistinguished name with thousands of other obscure crofters, as they carried him across his little patch of unyielding land, from his shabby house to that familiar bus, the coffin passing from shoulder to shoulder of all those he had been tied to by blood and obligation, necessity and love. Had dour Angus loved, was he loved? He had stood as father to his younger brothers and provider to his mother

293

when he was a mere boy; he had rowed the dangerous strait to Rona to court his wife. Everyone who carried him now knew that, knew the best of his past as well as his defeats and failures. A few had helped to carry his father fifty years before.

Once the coffin was stowed, solemnity slipped a little. There was a low mutter of conversation and a rolling of cigarettes.

'Oh well, poor Angus, eh?' remarked Do'l Alex in a chastened half-bellow.

The burial ground was on the machair beyond Garve, the only area with sufficient depth of soil for the purpose. In his wanderings, Alan had often come upon the old coffin trail marked by resting cairns which led from the back of Càrn Bàn nearly to Port Long, more or less parallel to the modern road. In the past the long procession of bearers would have walked the whole way. His throat tightened thinking about it, on the slow drive to the graveyard. He was very stirred: the driving mirror showed a slightly wild-eyed reflection. He was relieved no one had seemed to need a lift, he wanted to be alone. It was all so different from the disguised squalor of prosperous city funerals. He thought of Celia's burial, with that hideous blanket of poison-green artificial grass over the turned winter earth in a travesty of spring, and the shovels hidden discreetly behind an aggressive Victorian headstone; and of Torquil's cremation, the obsequious flunkeys with bought faces, the coffin sliding silently behind the curtain, and the nauseating, deceitful, perfumed miasma, worse than any stench of bodily decay. He had switched off as thoroughly as possible on both occasions, and practised forgetfulness since, but the ceremonies of Angus's death had brought it back, and made it tolerable to face. There was some meaning in this mourning of a whole community, an affirmation of the event in the train of events, in the succession of ancestors and descendants, birth and death: an acknowledgement of the once-and-for-all cessation of a particular life and a dissolving of it into the other lives that had been and would be. A good send-off: Angus was certainly getting that. They were helping him on his way, mourning him as the best that he had been, all that he might have been, setting him free as the young man of courage who had held his household together half a century before. His friends had not gathered to remember the ailing, ineffective, self-pitying shadow of his later years, his grieving family did not take into account that he had shown them little affection or interest. Almost with indignation, Alan recalled his casual dismissals of Donnie: 'daft', 'no use at anything', 'too soft'. He couldn't remember ever having heard him speak either to or about Mairi. And Murdo: he had heaped drudgery on him, with curt commands and no thanks. Only the ones who got away, Alex Angus, Ewan and Effie, ever brought a word of praise to his lips. And yet they loved him; it was enough for them that he was their father.

He thought about Torquil. He had always resisted being called 'Daddy'; Torquil he had been. No one had wept for him. Then he remembered that Celia had; while he had assured her with monstrous indifference that his death didn't matter, she had cried out of old affection. She had died and he hadn't wept for her either. Her women friends had dabbed their eyes at her funeral and he had avoided them in embarrassment. He had felt pity, for suffering and the wasting of her personality in the charade of her last weeks; and guilt for not having loved her, for not grieving. He had said, and meant, that he was glad her suffering was over. That was all.

He braked suddenly as the train of vehicles swung slowly round into the main street of Port Long. The village was totally deserted, the shop doors closed out of respect for Angus. Respect: with a flinching of dismay he remembered sitting up all night after Torquil's funeral, because he was in a hurry to sort out his papers, scarcely noticing the handwriting of the dead man, the whisky-glass rings, the bundle of letters from Celia before their marriage. There had been holiday photographs like those in Celia's albums, and an envelope marked 'Alan's' with a lock of fair infant hair. He had incinerated everything quickly after the manner of the corpse, rather than see what he didn't want to see; had stuck to the story that the man who refused to be called Daddy had lived the life he chose and ended it when he chose. What had he expected his son to be, on those long-ago summer holidays? There was a memory of a later visit, introducing Richard, flaunting the relationship; and all Torquil would say, as unpaternally detached as ever, was that while that sort of thing was great fun at Oxford, in the wide world it simply made you a laughing stock. That had wounded. The resentment and humiliation of it made his ears burn now. He snorted with laughter at himself for still minding, and suddenly found he was crying, at last, for his mother and father; not for his failures or their suffering, but for loss, because he had once loved them, when he was a little boy in Celia's scented bedroom under the ornate plaster ceiling rose.

The cortège drew up decorously by the burial ground. It was simply a patch of machair behind the dunes, stoutly fenced with concrete posts and wrylock to keep sheep out. Some had got in nevertheless; they tripped out peevishly through the gate when it was opened to admit the coffin. Alan smiled at the sight of them, but lurked evasively in the rear, still sniffling slightly.

It had begun to rain in earnest, a flying fine drift misting in from the sea. There were more slow-cadenced prayers. The spades lay openly against the mound of fresh sandy soil, white-speckled with ancient cockleshells. When the coffin was lowered, the four sons first and then by turns the others took up the spades and filled the grave. There was a last prayer, then murmurings of condolence and the beginnings of muttered conversation, and handshaking. Donnie's hand was icy cold and gritty with earth, his damp hair streaked across his forehead. His fingers clenched tightly in Alan's for an instant; he didn't look up. Someone else came towards him with outstretched hand, a cousin with more right and sentiments proper to the occasion.

Alan walked away thinking that it really was the last time. Had been the last time: it was fixed already in the unassailable past. At home he went straight to the workshop, calmed by a finality which brought with it a sort of frozen clarity, making it almost a relief. He worked late, ending with a first coat of varnish on the mast. The weather was poor for that job, but he wanted the boat in the water by the following week. He went into the house tired, but not tired enough to sleep. He tried the radio, but it was an Ash Wednesday homily of platitudinous vacuity; he turned instead to the intellectual athletics of a Bach partita. He finished playing with the sense that he had solved some problem successfully, and yawned and stretched, waiting for it to surface.

It was not, as he expected, the optimum weight of the boom. He knew at last why the Furies pursued him: it was for the breaking of a vow. Even the unspoken vow of an unconsummated, unconfessed, unallowable love was binding, and could be broken. Love absolutely required trust, and he had not given it. He was surprised, even disbelieving, to realise this: he knew it was so, but he could not at first perceive how he had failed. There must have been, somewhere, a guardedness, a reservation. He searched after its nature, but it eluded him: it was so long forgotten in origin, so deeply buried. He took himself back to the first meeting, the ecstatic instant of drowning in another; and to the weeks following, the Saturdays with Selena, Donnie's transparent adoration. He had resisted, but surely with good reason, not only for his own sake. And in that summer of insouciant delight in each other, he had never said 'I love you,' but it could never have been said without harm: that was still as plain as it had been at the time. He had meant it, the desolate years since left no doubt of that. So what had been held back that could have been given, what promised that had not been fulfilled? Donnie's face was before him, killingly sweet, as he had been on that spring evening with the strayed lamb in his arms. How had he regarded him then, following him down the hill, lost and found, and how in the summer after? Beautiful, innocent, trusting: the words rushed in with their attendant images, shimmering in the glamour and anguish of the glimpsed unattainable.

He waited. There was something more. He looked into terrible depths. Poor, stupid, illiterate: a boy who would grow up to be at best a conscientious dull artisan, at worst a drunken, weak-willed black sheep; someone who would bore him to death in a week, or a month, or a year.

A desperate stillness fell on him. He had thought like that about Donnie – had he? And he knew he had. He had refused to give himself up, had insured himself against commitment to what might prove a fantasy; despicably, even against becoming what Torquil had forecast, a laughing stock. He had lacked the courage to believe in love, even when it was clear that nothing else had any meaning at all.

So now he knew. In practical terms it made no difference. Donnie was undoubtedly better off left to his own devices, there had never been any other realistic solution. But in the only terms that mattered, he knew himself a betrayer. He was relieved to have found it out. Harold had said that when Celia learned the truth about her disease, she was glad, really glad, though she would not afterwards look at the implications; so he faced the new knowledge and put it behind him. There was nothing else to be done with it.

Chapter 29

Alex Angus led family prayers and read from First Corinthians, 'And if Christ be not risen, then is our preaching vain, and your faith also vain,' and his mother went to bed comforted, she said. The girls went through to the kitchen to tidy up for the night, gossiping in low voices; a little shriek of laughter was stifled as Murdo returned from the byre.

Donnie sat in the corner behind what had been his father's chair, reading the bible. Alex Angus, coming into the room scarved and overcoated, noted this with surprise and some resentment.

'Come on, it's time you got your things together. We'd better get down to Roddy's now.'

'I'm not coming.' Donnie didn't look up.

'You might as well. We have an early start tomorrow.' His tone was slightly huffy: he was already a communicant, and would be an elder in a few years' time, and there was something that did not please him about the sight of his graceless youngest brother reading the Good Book on this appropriate evening.

Donnie closed the big black bible and raised his black head. 'I'm not going back with you tomorrow.'

'How not? You'd better, you have work the next day.'

'I'm not going back at all. I'm chucking it.' He slung the bible irreverently under his father's chair.

'What?' Alex Angus fumed and reddened. In his early thirties, he was already respectably hypertensive; speech deserted him as his blood pressure rose.

Ewan strode in, with his coat and holdall over his arm. 'What's going on, eh?'

'Ask him! He's crazy!'

'What are you up to, boy?'

'I just told him. I'm not going back to Glasgow again.'

Ewan snorted and took out his cigarettes. 'You're a bloody fool then. Nothing doing here. You'll change your mind in a week.'

'I will not.' He stood up warily. Eleanor had just come out of the kitchen, with Murdo behind her.

'What's this?' she asked, glaring at him.

'I'm staying,' he said, glaring back. But he was frightened of her.

His shoulder blades pushed against the wall.

Chrissann tittered. Murdo cursed softly. Alex Angus shifted from foot to foot, angry and offended.

'You'll have to come back with me. You'll never get a job in this place, anyway. Think of your mother – she's not going to want you at home idle.'

'No, indeed!' That was Effie, clicking her tongue.

'What d'you want to stay here for? You need your head examined!' Chrissan's own head sported a barrage of yellowish green spikes.

'You're bloody daft.' Ewan lit up.

'After all we've done for you!' Alex Angus, overheating, loosened his scarf.

Donnie stared back at them with the hard flat look he had learned in beleaguered urban situations.

'You can't possibly stay here,' Eleanor put in, crisply. 'There's nowhere for you to sleep, not even tonight. You'd better get along to Roddy's with Alex Angus.'

'Och, come on now Eleanor!' Ewan drew on his cigarette, scowling a bit, though not in support of Donnie. 'My mother brought up eight of us in this house.'

'Eight children, maybe. We're not children now. There's Johane and wee Angus, Mairi, your mother, and Murdo and I. That's four bedrooms, living room and kitchen. That's all we've got.'

Donnie looked at her opaquely. She was pregnant, but nobody seemed to know. It made her worse.

'I'll ask my mother in the morning. If she doesn't want me in the house I'll go up to Nanan's old place.'

'Hey, no!' Johane was immediately plaintive. 'I might be going there. I'm waiting till spring to see about it, that's all. I'm going to get the grant for it.'

Donnie scanned the half circle of hostile faces, then fixed his eyes on a point between Ewan's shoulder and Effie's head. He clenched his jaw and said nothing.

Alex Angus knew the look. Flustered, he broke out, 'It's hopeless. You can't do anything with that boy. He's obstinate, ungrateful – I've done my best for him, the Lord knows I have. We gave him a good Christian home, Rhoda and me – got him a job, stopped him from going wrong in the city – what thanks do we get? Hardly a

299

civil word out of him. Well, you'll have nothing but trouble from him here. He's a waster.'

'He can't stay,' Eleanor pointed out.

'Oh, he'll stay – he'll stay if he's determined. Stubborn as a mule. Well, I know I shouldn't say it, he's my own brother, but I'll be glad to be rid of him, and that's the truth!'

'Rhoda will be glad too,' said Donnie quietly. He had handed over half of every pay packet and made her kitchen units and fitted wardrobes which were the envy of all her friends, but she detested him.

Alex Angus looked away, redder than ever. 'No use talking to the boy, no use at all. He's up to you now, Murdo. Well, I wish you luck.' Luck was a risqué concept for a would-be elder; he added quickly, 'And may the good Lord help you!'

Murdo's lip curled: he had scant expectation of help from the Lord. 'I don't want him here, lazy little bugger.'

'Och, he's not wise!' Chrissann was anxious to fill in past details for her admired new sister-in-law. 'They were all teasing him in school, saying he was daft. He used to get mad.'

'Well, yes indeed!' Effie was indignant. 'He's a terrible boy, always wanting his own way. He's always been just the same – remember, Johane, when he ran away on us that communion time, he was just a wee lad then. Near broke Mam's heart!'

Johane's objection was of a more practical nature. 'I'm not moving out yet, anyway. Once I get back in Auntie Effie's room, that's me in this house till the weather's better. I'm no going in there for a night or so yet, though!' She shuddered.

'I'll ask my mother,' said Donnie again. No one paid any attention.

'I'm off. Are you ready, Ewan?' Alex Angus jerked his bag off the floor irritably and went to the back door.

'Ay. Pick us up at seven, Murdo. So long, girls. Hope it's a good big one, Mairi.' He gave her a slap and a wink.

In the kitchen Alex Angus too recalled his fraternal duties. 'The Lord bless you, now. Remember there's a welcome for all of you in Glasgow, any time. Mairi, God willing, we'll be hearing news of you soon. Rhoda will be sending you some things with her cousin next week.'

In the suddenly empty living room Eleanor and Donnie glared at each other with the strange comprehending intimacy of utter hatred.

'You'll have to go.'

'I'm staying.'

'You can't stay.'

'I'm not going.'

They stared with eyes locked in silent conflict. The blood had drained from Donnie's head so that he swayed dizzily. He pressed against the wall and faced her out. 'You or me, Eleanor.' The faint voice was his own. It surprised him. He lowered his head, shaking himself slightly, bewildered.

She stamped her foot sharply so that he jumped. 'Oh! You're a spoilt little brat! You'll go whining to your mother now, as if she hasn't enough to put up with. Well, if you stay here, you'll work for it, I can tell you!'

Murdo had re-entered. 'You bloody well will. You can start by driving them to the plane tomorrow. I'm for a long lie.'

He went upstairs. By the slam of the bathroom door, Eleanor had locked herself in there.

He had defeated her, he had no idea how. Not for good, he knew. He sank down on the sofa, arranging himself in an insolent city sprawl, while the girls bustled and tutted to and from the kitchen and bathroom, and one by one disappeared upstairs to Mairi's room. When they had all gone, he put a few more peats on the fire, and sat on the floor in front of it, cross-legged.

Mairi came in again, in dressing gown and slippers, almost sticking in the doorway because of the quilt and pillow she was carrying next to her big belly. 'Oh well, I'll be glad to get rid of this,' she said, giggling and patting the bump. She dumped her burden on the sofa. 'The wee one's gone into my bed. There's too much of me to get in beside him, I'm coming down. You staying here?'

Donnie got up. 'I'll go,' he said. He had had enough.

'Where? In there?' She indicated the door of the room where the corpse had lain.

He shook his head; not because of the coffin that had stood there, but for Auntie Effie's presence.

'We can get some covers out of there anyway. You'll have to let me have the sofa, though. Floor's too hard in my condition.' She switched the light on cautiously in the bedroom before entering, and snatched pillows and blankets off the bed at arm's length, hurling

301

them out in a heap on the living-room floor. She shut the door quick-ly. 'Come on, lazy, give me a hand! You'll have to do better than that if you're staying here. Eleanor won't stand no nonsense, boy.' She threw a pillow at him to cheer him up, kneeling heavily to arrange the rest of the bedding on the rug. He dropped on the floor beside her. She looked at him sideways and tucked her arm in his; for a moment they crouched together in the silence of inexpressible trouble.

She levered herself up leaning on his shoulder, switched off the light, and lay down ponderously on the sofa, squealing with laughter as the aged springs creaked. 'Oh God! Can't get comfortable at all at all, with this thing in the way. You're lucky it can't happen to you, boy. Don't you go getting any poor girl into trouble.'

'I wasn't thinking of it.'

'Lie down then, can't you.' But he still knelt with shoulders drooped, staring into the fire. She propped herself up on an elbow.

'I'm real glad you've come back, Donnie.'

'Are you?' He looked round with doubting eyes.

'Ay. Here, I might call the baby after you, if it's a boy.' She added, a little regretfully, 'I was going to call it Justin. I think that's a really nice name.'

He lay down with his head on his arms. 'Call it Justin. There's no luck calling it after me.'

'Well, we'll see. Might be a girl anyway. I'd like a wee girl. 'Night, Donnie.'

''Night, Mairi.'

When her breathing was deep and even, he stretched a hand carefully under his father's chair. His fingertips encountered the marker ribbon, and he pulled the bible quietly towards him. Turning to the firelight, he opened it. He found the place quickly. It was by now familiar, but he had to make sure. Leviticus 18, verse 22: 'Thou shalt not lie with mankind as with womankind. It is abomination.' And verse 29: 'For whosoever shall commit any of these abominations, even the souls that commit them shall be cut off from among the people.' He leafed through to the other half of his sentence: Matthew 6, verse 28: 'But I say unto you, that whosoever looketh on a woman to lust after her, hath committed adultery with her already in his heart.' If so with adultery, then how much more with worse abominations. Looking into his heart, he had no doubt at all that his soul was cut off.

He closed the bible and pushed it back under the chair, and lay gazing into the fire, caverns of glowing orange and dull pits of sombre red, a colourless flicker of flame, ashes curling and falling from the peats like tortured bodies. That would be Hell. He was damned and he would burn in it. He stared at it defiantly. God could take his saving Grace elsewhere, he didn't want it, he would never want it, even when the next few weeks were over and Alan had gone for good. He was proud to be damned. He had given his soul with his heart.

He watched the falling ashes, feeling the hot breath of Hell on his cheek, smiling.

Chapter 30

Alan stepped the still-tacky mast experimentally the following morning, and left it up all day for consideration. It was of course too late to change his mind if restoring it to its original position was a mistake, but he eyed it from all angles as he came and went, imagining the practicalities, or more likely impracticalities, of managing the old-fashioned rig singlehanded in uncertain northern weather. At least she would look lovely, with her billowing wide-footed gunter lug. It was a rig which always made him think of a preening swan rousing its feathers on the water; though uncanvased, with her shiny blue topsides and red bottomsides, her stalwart clinker hull and jaunty bowsprit, Selena was not much of a swan, more like a busy, sturdy little duck.

He divided the day between resealing parts of the deck, which was leaking at the gunwale even in rain, and preparatory work on the standing rigging. There was going to be a frustrating hiatus, just waiting for varnish to harden, before any of it could be attached. He scrutinised the sky hopefully, wondering if there was any chance at all of varnishing the mast in situ and continuing with the rigging at the same time; but the wind was increasing, and the clouds south-westwards were pewtery dark. By mid afternoon he concluded rain was imminent and got the mast down on deck. It was unpleasantly sticky and grimy and should obviously have had a day's rest.

As he contemplated it thoughtfully, he became gradually aware that he was himself being contemplated. It was not an unknown sensation: he had had it often when he had lived at Skalanish before, a feeling of being watched, or perhaps not so much watched as discussed. Whether there was anything audible associated with it, he had never been able to decide. He looked around curiously, as always. There were a few sheep grazing above the stream, one staring back at him: a flock of starlings around the ruins, stabbing the grass with a constant wheezy chittering. No doubt there were usually starlings and sheep around, nothing more uncanny than that.

A familiar voice behind him brought him down off the deck in more of a fall than a leap. 'I thought you'd gone!'

'No.' He half-smiled, his eyes flickering at once to the boat. 'She's looking good. Nearly finished now.' He walked round her, stroking and patting. 'Selena.' He ran his fingers over the flourishes surrounding the name.

Alan's silent confusion was focussed by a sudden squall of rain. 'The mast! I'll never get the bloody thing varnished at this rate.' Donnie took one end as he swung it down. 'It's sticky, mind your clothes.' He was city clean, in an improbably pale grey pullover and white bomber jacket. 'Come on in,' said Alan hastily, as he slid the mast under cover. 'You can look at the boat when the rain stops.' He had a fear that he might dematerialise as suddenly as he had appeared.

In the kitchen, Donnie ranged about restlessly, silent.

'Sit down.' Every chair seemed to be heaped with books, charts and sheet music. Alan glanced round, incapacitated by the overwhelming, forbidden question of how long he would be staying. Distractedly, he tipped a few piles on to the floor among the sails and bits of rigging, and at last thought of something neutral to say. 'Like some coffee?'

'Have a dram instead.' He pulled out a half-bottle and placed it on the table. Alan eyed it anxiously; he had caught the smell of whisky on his breath already. Not much wonder, he told himself, the day after the funeral. All the same he said, 'No, too early in the day for me.' Immediately he wished he had not snubbed the initiative; it was difficult enough to think of anything to talk about.

Donnie flung his jacket over the back of Uncle Ewan's chair and stretched himself out in it in a pose of studied brazenness, not totally convincing. 'It's my birthday.'

'Oh yes?' Alan smiled uneasily, opening the bedroom door to bundle the sails out of the way.

'It is.' His voice was small and hurt. It had Alan at his side in an instant.

'Really?' He stepped back a pace, remembering to be careful. 'Not much point saying Happy Birthday in the circumstances, I suppose. But I will have a drink, then.'

He found a couple of glasses, small ones: the island custom being to fill whatever receptacle was offered to the brim, which Donnie accordingly did.

'Smallest glasses in the house these, aren't they?' he said, smiling.

Alan grinned. 'Yes. *Slàinte.*'

'*Slàinte.*'

'When do you go back, then?'

'I'm no going back.'

'What?'

Donnie drained his glass. 'That's what they all say. No one seems very pleased.'

'Oh, for God's sake, I . . . but what's happened? What about your job?'

'I'm jacking it in.' He refilled his glass and waved the bottle in Alan's direction enquiringly.

'No, I'm fine, thanks – but what are you going to do instead?'

'I've got work here.'

'Already? How on earth did you manage that?'

'I fixed it up this morning.' There was some pride in his tone. 'I start tomorrow on the coal. There's a boat in late tonight.'

'Christ, that's much too heavy for you!' As soon as it was out, he saw the boy's eyes widen with humiliation. He added quickly, 'Sorry, I'm not implying you're a weakling, you've grown a lot – that sounds condescending, doesn't it? Oh hell.' He fidgeted with his empty glass.

Donnie looked up with a Glaswegian-hardman stare and down with a trembling lip. Alan made another attempt. 'It's a grim slog that job, for anyone.'

'Yes, no one else would take it.'

'I'm not surprised.'

'I'll survive.'

There was an awkward silence. Alan tried not to look him over; but he had noticed as soon as he removed his jacket that though he was broader in the shoulders and taller, he was painfully thin. He had always been slight, but previously there had been a certain animal sturdiness about him, a healthy rustic roundness of limb. Now there was a tense deep hollow above his collar bone, visible under the open neck of his shirt, and even seated he showed an incurve at his hips. 'The coal' was the heaviest work on Boreray, though it included other things as well as coal-heaving. It meant acting dogsbody to the island's only haulage contractor, nicknamed 'Bleeder' for obvious reasons, loading and delivering whatever heavy goods arrived at the pier, coal being the most usual load in the low-on-peats season between February and May. There was a high turnover in the job: it was one nobody ever took on except under threat of having unemployment benefit stopped, and the doctor did a brisk trade in medical certificates for men who had decided to opt out of it, before or after fair trial. Even Alan knew all about it; it was a notorious local joke.

Donnie reached for the bottle. Alan's eyes followed his thin wrist. 'Have another one.'

'No thanks.'

He looked at the bottle with regret, but put it down. Alan screwed the cap on it firmly. 'Rain's off, come and see Selena. You'd better take this.'

Donnie pushed it away forcefully. 'No, you'd better keep it. I can do without it.' As they went out he said, 'I don't drink much. It's just so bloody miserable over there.' He looked up pleadingly in the doorway.

Alan managed to confine his sympathy to a vague grunt, with hands in pockets. When he could trust to sounding brisk enough, he said, 'I expect your mother's glad to see you back, anyway.'

There was a tangibly negative silence. Alan cursed himself inwardly for tactlessness, wondering what on earth was behind it all. Donnie cheered up as he inspected the boat, admiring the cabin, which he hadn't seen completed, but critical of the leaky deck. 'Should have had a second go at canvasing that bit. Why don't you still?'

'I'm not taking off that toerail, after the fancy job you did on it.'

His mouth twitched disparagingly. 'You'll regret it. That bunk's like a bath.' Jumping to the ground, he looked up with laughter running into his eyes. 'Paintwork's better than I expected.'

Alan laughed too. 'It was raining. There wasn't anything else left to do. You may have noticed the mast is more my usual standard of finish.'

'I had.'

They smiled at each other, relaxing caution, then tensing more than before. Donnie's uneasy glance slid in the direction of home. 'I'd better go. I'm in the bad books already.'

'Wait a second.' Alan had a sudden bright idea: at least it seemed brighter than a casual goodbye. In the workshop he rummaged for a carrier bag under the bench, and with his back turned scooped his moulding planes into it. He pushed the bag into the boy's hands. 'Birthday present.'

Donnie saw what he was holding. 'I can't take these!'

'Why not? You always liked them. If you can't use them, sell them sometime you're hard up, people buy these old things for ornaments.'

'I'd never do that. Alan, I can't –'

'Oh, shut up! You can make pretty doors for people's kitchens and so on – Donnie, have you thought, you could probably get quite a bit of joinery work locally? Better than heaving coal, anyway.'

'I was wondering about that. Maybe I will later on.' His face brightened a little, but hesitantly, as if he were ashamed to be found out in some laughable daydream. Whatever two years in the town had given him, it was not self-confidence.

'You easily could,' Alan persisted. 'Look, why not try to get hold of this workshop? I'm sure you could fix it up through Roddy.'

A warning look shuttered Donnie's eyes. The implication was clear: he had had his future organised for him before, and he was wary. Alan dropped the subject then, and concentrated on disarming his reluctance to take the planes. He accomplished this only by resort to abject pleading and, in desperation, a hard shove: a breach of his no-contact rule which left him ludicrously hot and shaking, with any remnant of hope that he had grown wiser in the past two years forcibly routed. Donnie's bird-boned elbow harried his evening, in a disarray of spilt varnish and lost screws.

In the next few days he spent much of the time overhauling his tools, grinding and filing everything that could conceivably be sharpened, and laying things away in oiled wrappings with the ritualistic absorption of an Egyptian embalmer. He had some doubts about it: Donnie's pride was evidently too raw these days to accept much in the way of gifts, but if everything was simply left there and he could use it if he wanted, he might. The scheme kept him excited and happy, even to the extent of cleaning paintbrushes, until he remembered the separation it implied, and reminded himself that this was borrowed time, and not much of it.

There was less of it even than he might have hoped. Donnie appeared only every second or third day, never staying long, sometimes only hovering at the workshop door for a few words before turning for home. He seemed restless and uncommunicative. Alan did his best to face that he came at all only out of a sense of past loyalty; that he was probably bored, and certainly exhausted after a day slogging for Bleeder. Questioned about the work, he would only say, 'It's all right.' He made one complaint, as a true peat-loving Borerayan: 'I don't like stinking of coal all the time.'

'You don't.' He smelt of remedial soap and shampoo.

'Well, it's in my nose. In the bath too. God, you should hear Eleanor! I spend longer scrubbing that bath than I do myself and she's still on at me. You didn't miss much there, Alan. What a woman! "Donnie, carry that washing for Mairi." "Donnie, go and feed the hens." "Donnie, we need more peat in." She's no much better with Murdo either.'

Alan laughed. He could imagine it well enough. 'What does he think of it?'

'Oh, puts up with it. Not allowed to think.'

'Well, you could use the bath here any time. It's filthy to start with so you wouldn't have to bother cleaning it.'

'I might then. I get sick of her.'

After that he turned up more often, for an hour or so after work. Alan was surprised and gratified. He did not guess what was implied in being sick of Eleanor. It was a sickness of fear, a physical nausea which made it increasingly hard to speak or breathe in her presence. It had been worse since she had been overruled on the question of where he slept. Mairi had offered to share her room, after the other girls left, and Eleanor's protest had been borne down by his mother, whose whole family had slept in one room till the new house was built when she was twelve. Eleanor's definition of impropriety brought a steely glint to her eye, though she was unrelenting in her bitterness against Donnie for being there at all; he had humiliated her well-doing eldest son, and that was unforgiveable. But though unwanted at home, his absences were grudged. It was too soon after a bereavement for the family to go out socially; they must at least pretend to be at home with the bible. The elders called frequently to see if they were. Donnie tried various excuses, but his escapes were difficult. A deadly instinct warned him that Eleanor should not know where he was; mentioning that he would be late home in the evening only as he went out the door in the morning at least postponed cross-examination, and sometimes obviated it, if he timed himself to return while the elder was calling, or during someone's favourite television programme.

Seeing him at that time of day, Alan was appalled by his state of exhaustion. After the black was scrubbed off, he was pale and listless, scarcely capable of speaking. It emerged that though he usually got a lift part of the way in the morning, he often walked home at night.

'Can't Murdo let you have the car?'

'Not him.'

'Take my van then. Take it tonight, I hardly ever use it.'

'No thanks.'

'Why not?'

He scowled.

'Why *not?*'

Alan supposed the unforthcoming answer was to do with independence. Donnie had become understandably suspicious of any renewed attempts to manage his life. He turned silent when the question of approaching Roddy for use of the workshop was brought up again, and positively sullen at the suggestion of permanently borrowing all the tools in it.

'They'll just rust to bits then. I certainly don't have any further use for them.' Alan was equally sulky. They glowered at each other, mutually offended, and looked away, mutually wretched: Alan because the old trusting affection had faded, Donnie because he was being bribed to go away; Alan because whatever he offered was rejected, Donnie because the one thing he wanted wasn't being offered.

Alan kept trying, because time was short and precious. 'Anyway, you might at least take this box of old chisels and things. They're all duplicates, but they're usable.'

Donnie picked one up. 'Old chisels, bloody hell! I remember when you got them. You were carving AC on the handles first day we came over to work on the boat.'

'Was I?' Alan began to laugh. 'Well, carve DM on them instead. Stop scowling at me.'

'Och Alan, you would give away your head!'

'Who'd want it?'

He did stop scowling, with a momentary look almost of the old affection and simplicity; but he wouldn't take the chisels. Alan gave up, when he saw he had pushed him to the verge of tears, but he was himself very downcast by the boy's refusal: other than the boat, his favourite tools were the only belongings for which he felt a sentimental attachment. He knew that was a bad reason for forcing them on Donnie, a mere possessiveness at second hand, but he remained wistful about it.

At first hand there was not much to be enjoyed either: he had grown wary of anything that recalled his former joyful boyish subordination. Treated with gentleness, he resented it as a sign of patronising; if criticised, he was defiant, then sulky. Yet he was no thicker-skinned than he had ever been, though his reactions were different. All their encounters had rough edges; Alan dreaded them, told himself that was a good sign, and pined miserably when he didn't come.

Selena fell behind schedule again. Ten days of violent southerly weather made it impossible to launch her. He laid a mooring for her in Skalanish Bay, on the Gnipadale side of the shallow glen where the house stood. It was sheltered from all the quarters, but not sufficiently so to make manoeuvring an untried boat there in a gale inviting: or leaving her on an untried mooring. It was well enough weighted, with scrap iron and concrete poured into old wheel hubs, but the only chain available was a rather short one from Uncle Ewan's loft. A second anchor would probably have been a safer way

310

to moor, but lack of money had become an irritating problem; the cost even of her single anchor and its chain indicated semi-starvation for the next few weeks. Searching along the shore yielded rewards, not only the scrap metal and orange marker-float for the mooring, but a small fibreglass dinghy, by the look of it not much more than a child's beach toy. It was badly cracked and without rowlocks, hardly as seaworthy as a fishbox, but with a bit of patching and a further raid on Uncle Ewan's legacy of rowlocks and oars, it was just about possible as a tender. Alan began to feel somewhat guilty about his depredations on the contents of the loft, but reasoned that he could always leave a cheque with Roddy, once he had succeeded in selling the van, if he ever did. Sandy's driving test was at the end of the month. It was most unlikely he would pass it, even though Port Long didn't sport so much as a set of traffic lights, but even less likely if he changed vehicles. Failing Alan's, his choice would be confined to Murdo's, without a handbrake, or Roddy's, without a silencer.

Sandy was in his way grateful, and gave a hand with the preparations for Selena's launching. Laying the mooring with Sandy from the wobbly tender was nerve-wracking work. He was about as confident on the water as a hen, and seemed to produce inextricable knots and tangles in everything he touched. Alan tried to be amused by the contrast with Donnie, and succeeded only in making himself depressed thinking of it.

Donnie agreed warily that if Selena went into the water on Saturday he might come along to help. His lack of enthusiasm was not cheering; though it should have been, in a way, Alan decided, as he attacked the rusted-up trailer with spanners and easing oil. The more indifferent the boy became, the less difficult it should be to leave him. He failed to convince himself, and finished the job dismally aware that leaving him would be unmitigated hell in any case.

Launching the boat from the trailer would be simple at high tide. The only problem was that a persistently onshore wind made leaving under sail from the narrow rock-bound cove seem unattractive in an unknown craft. He asked Roddy for a loan of his outboard engine as back-up.

Roddy looked at him disbelievingly. 'You not got any engine in that thing?'

'No. I shan't need one out at sea.' It struck him that this sounded absurdly like the Flying Dutchman. 'I mean, once I get used to her.'

Roddy stared and scratched his head. 'Well,' he said at last, 'it's a risk.'

Donnie elaborated on Saturday. 'Roddy says you're completely off your head. He says you'll never last a day without an engine.'

Alan grinned wryly. He had intended to carry an outboard, but it was either that or a compass, as finances stood.

'Can't afford it, I suppose,' commented Donnie.

'I might get one some time,' Alan replied shortly, wondering how Donnie knew what he could afford.

Roddy and Sandy turned up to help, Roddy out of concern for Alan's lunacy and Sandy because he had nothing better to do. In fact the procedure was anti-climactic in its simplicity.

'Not the same job it was getting her down that track, eh?' Roddy remarked as the bow slid into position on the trailer.

'No.' Alan made the last few stiff turns on the ratchet, utterly miserable at the recollection of that evening: the neighbourly kindness, the unexplored cottage in the vibrant twilight, the battered old boat and all his expectations for her. It seemed a world away; the world before Donnie. There had been a dark-haired boy sickling corn below the road, an image on that first evening insignificant, now heavy with memory.

He looked round for him to take a line from the rocks to the stern once the boat was half afloat, to stop her swinging and bumping when her nose came off the trailer, but he was already in the water, holding her bodily so that the keel wouldn't grind in the shingle. The sight of him standing patiently waist-deep in the icy water was an obscure addition to Alan's wretchedness; though perhaps at that moment between recollection of a more hopeful past and dread of the future as Selena finally slid into the sea, the sight of him however engaged would have been painful.

They picked up the mooring without incident. Roddy and Sandy did a tour of inspection and were returned to land one by one. Alan rowed back to collect Donnie. He was head down in the bilge. 'There's a bit of water coming in by the fourth frame already, and the forward pump isn't working,' was his verdict.

'I dare say there will be worse than that,' said Alan gloomily, fidgeting with the starboard runner.

Donnie replaced the bottom boards, watching him covertly. After a bit he said, 'You're not sailing her today then?'

'Wasn't thinking of it. The forecast's another southerly gale tonight. I don't want the main in shreds. It doesn't seem worth putting it on till I can leave it there.'

Donnie looked noncommital; in fact he looked very like Sandy. Alan sighed. 'I'll take you back now.' He bent to draw the dinghy alongside, but turning, surprised a look of deep disappointment. He let the dinghy go, catching the painter just in time.

'Would you like to try her out today?'

He shrugged. 'Not unless you—'

'I said would you like to?'

The roughness of tone made him scowl, squaring his shoulders; but when he met Alan's eye he said shakily, 'Yes.'

'Why the hell couldn't you say so? You told me you had to get home.' Alan hurled the sailbags at him. He caught them, laughing.

'I do. I'm supposed to bring Jessie down to see Mum. Och, Murdo can do it.'

'He'll be delighted. Are you sure this is wise?'

'No!' He was animated and smiling. 'How do you rig this anyway?'

Alan explained the tackle for the standing lug as he fed the luff on, and went forward to shackle the headsail, leaving Donnie to lace the main to the boom.

'Not much room, is there?' he said, hanging over the counter to haul out the clew. The small cockpit was billowing with sailcloth.

'I might rethink that. If I left the foot loose it could be pulled up to the mast to keep it out of the way at this sort of stage.'

'If there's no one else to trip over you'll manage all right, anyway.'

Alan was silent. He didn't welcome the prospect of having no one to trip over. Sliding back into the cockpit he collided with Donnie scrambling forward for a line to lash the swaying boom. His proximity was warmth and life, but to touch, he was cold, wet and shivering.

'You're soaking, boy. I forgot.' Alan pulled off his sailing smock and the heavy sweater underneath, and handed him the latter. 'Put that on, anyway.' He protested. 'Go on!'

He smiled, struggling into the warm garment. 'All right, I do what you tell me in a boat.'

It was true. He was as excellent a crew as he had always been: none of the recent argument, sulks or scowls. There wasn't much chance to consider the change. The wind was increasing and the boat slightly overcanvased. She was less responsive to the helm than Alan felt was comfortable, but closer-winded then he had expected. Donnie was bright-eyed with excitement. 'She's fantastic! That main's setting just lovely. I bet she looks great from the shore.' Alan remembered, *With white sails and new mast – I saw her going like a roe deer* – but she needed concentration. Even though they stuck to familiar channels, the consciousness of her solid lead keel and the poor visibility her short, wide mainsail afforded to leeward required alert helming.

'At least you can see under that small jib,' remarked Donnie cheerfully, charging past a foaming shoal with six feet to spare. Alan gritted his teeth. It was almost as bad as Sandy's driving lessons. But Donnie knew what he was doing. It was difficult to believe he hadn't been in a boat for more than two years; difficult to believe anything had changed at all.

Back on shore he was different again.

'What happened to the Fireball?' he asked suddenly as they carried the tender up the beach.

'I got rid of it soon after you left.'

'No crew, eh?'

'I didn't look for anyone.'

'You wouldn't find anyone with the nerve for it here. What did you do with it?'

'I dumped it on a girl I know in Argyll.'

'Another one. Before or after Eleanor? Or in between?'

'Not a girlfriend, properly speaking. Just someone who was nice to me.'

Donnie looked opaque, as if he did not intend to be nice. His posture had reverted to the urban slouch, his intonation, the poise of his head, even the shape of his face had altered. Alan regarded the little werewolf with resigned dismay. Still he could not help asking, 'Can you come out again next week?'

'No – I've got work, haven't I?'

'Saturday?'

'I suppose so, unless you've gone by then.'

'By next week? Hell, no! There are loads of adjustments to

314

make – the compass hasn't come yet, even. There's Sandy's driving test, I mean, he needs my van – anyway, the weather's rotten.' He floundered in the cool gaze of the one real reason. 'I'll probably make it by the second week in April,' he ended desperately.

'I might get another sail yet then,' said Donnie, as if he didn't care, turning off towards home.

It was growing dark as he came down to the shore opposite Holm rock. Murdo was crouched below the path with the rifle. Donnie sensed him there and froze silently, ready for a detour. But he knew it was the otter he was after, so he went on, whistling and kicking stones to scare it away.

Murdo wheeled round as he came up. 'You shit!' He knew what the noise had been for. Donnie would have walked on, but Murdo barred his way, pointing the gun unpleasantly at his stomach. Donnie looked down at it thoughtfully. It wasn't broken and Murdo breathed rage. His scalp tingled.

'Get off,' he said, quietly, stepping aside.

'Where've you been?'

'At Alan's.'

'What doing?'

'Putting the boat in the water.'

He walked on. His spine crawled, the gun barrel touched his ribs. 'Stop fooling with that thing,' he said, without turning; but it was an effort not to. His hands were shaking as he pulled off his boots at the back door.

Eleanor looked up from washing the dishes as he went in. 'You're late again.'

'Yes. I'll go straight up for Jessie.' He knew she hadn't been fetched because the television was on in the next room.

Her eyes fixed on him with venomous intensity. He realised suddenly that he was still wearing Alan's sweater. His arm pressed defensively to his chest, only for a second, but she knew why, and he saw it. They looked at each other with total hatred, while the routine bickering continued.

'Your mother's complaining about you being out so much. People will be talking about it, your father's not been dead three weeks yet.'

'If she doesn't like it she can tell me herself.'

315

'Don't give me cheek!'

Murdo came in. Donnie perceived with a chill that Murdo hated both of them, and hated Alan more than either. He couldn't work it out. He knew how much Murdo had wanted her, that he spoke to her civilly and did as she told him. Eleanor put her hand to her waist as she straightened at the sink, and Murdo's eyes were on the gesture. There was something in his look bewildered as well as hating, like a penned bull. In an icy flash Donnie thought he knew. He went through to the living room. He didn't want to think about it. He shivered, huddling into Alan's sweater; it smelt of him, of his warmth and strength.

Mairi was lying on the sofa, drowsing in the firelight and television chatter. 'You been at Alan's?'

'Yes.'

She shifted a cushion at her back, moving restlessly. 'I never see him now. He doesn't visit us like he used to.'

'Not much wonder, with herself there,' he muttered.

Mairi dropped her voice. 'Does he still fancy her?'

'How should I know?'

'Thought he might have told you.'

'No.'

Donnie stood still, looking into what Alan hadn't told him. A rainbow came and went. It had hovered in the dusk on the way home, separate bands of clear colour. The first colour was red. They were bound to each other from the first moment. Alan knew it but he wouldn't have it, he had gone away, he was other colours too, depths and distances away, across seas, among people and places fabulously out of reach, in a past and future he wouldn't share, and he was with Eleanor, linked with her still. He was not hers, she was purple darkness. Everywhere was danger except that first colour.

'I don't understand.'

'Mm?' Mairi looked round from the screen in surprise. She had forgotten about him.

Eleanor called through sharply, 'Donnie, hurry up and go for Jessie.' She slammed the door shut between the kitchen and the living room.

'The truth. Tell me the truth.' Murdo hunched forward, looking at his clenched hands, not at her. 'Tell me the truth.' His voice rose with each hoarse utterance.

'Be quiet. That boy's probably listening.' She did not understand that Donnie's awareness did not come from listening to the audible. She waited till the front door banged to. 'I've told you the truth. You should be pleased.'

'It could be his. Is it his?'

'Most unlikely.' She sniffed disdainfully, as if she were arguing with his estimate of the cow's rations or tomorrow's weather.

'You know. You must know.'

'As far as I know it's yours. You're the one who doubts it. You're being ridiculous.' She clattered cutlery angrily, slamming drawers and cupboards shut. He followed her round the kitchen, with hands out, but not daring to touch her.

'Tell me, damn you!' he choked, as she made to open the living room door.

'Don't you speak to me like that!'

He was cowed. She turned, with folded arms and snapping eyes. 'Now, I have told you. I'm going to tell everyone else tomorrow. You just keep your nasty suspicions to yourself, right?'

He avoided her eyes, but his face darkened. 'Nasty suspicions – what d'you mean? I've a right, haven't I? You were sleeping with that bastard, wasn't that nasty?'

She glared at him warningly. 'Not just with Alan, if that's who you mean. You knew my views on that subject before you married me, so you needn't whine now. We're married and that's over. You can forget it – or not, as you like. But I won't have your insane jealousy.'

'Anyone'd be jealous.' He came close to her, breathing hard, dizzy with what she had done, with how many other men. 'Anyone'd be jealous, Eleanor.'

She removed herself. 'You have no need. And as for the baby, you'd better be good to it, because if you're not I'll leave you.'

'No, Eleanor – no!'

'Yes!' She laughed, showing her pointed teeth, ready to bite. 'And you can put your silly thoughts out of your head right now, because it won't be born with black hair. You might as well stop tormenting yourself – and me.'

317

A red-haired baby. A fair-haired baby. He wouldn't know. Her hair was redder than ever, standing up in a halo round her head. He touched it, ran his hands over it and down her body. She shrugged him away.

'Not here.'

'Come on upstairs, then.'

'Not just now.'

He swore, but in Gaelic. She narrowed her eyes at him.

'Anyone but me. You didn't say that to him, did you?'

'Yes, frequently.'

'Ah, you bitch – you're a whore –' It excited him. He pulled her back against him.

'How *dare* you call me that!' She slapped him resoundingly. 'With your family history. Well! You're not short on bastards in this place. Or other vices.'

'What d'you mean?' he said, thickly.

'I told you about the boy.'

'The filthy little sod. I'll murder him.' He kept following her, trying to catch her round the hips, but she was cunning. She turned smiling, running her fingers up his arms. 'You needn't do that. He did you a good turn.'

'What's that?' He tried to kiss her.

'If I hadn't found out about your little brother, I mightn't have decided to marry you.'

He clutched her violently. She swung her pelvis away from his, laughing in his face. 'You can regard Donnie as a pawn in your game. Him or me. Perhaps we should call the baby after him.' Her eyes and teeth gleamed, her hair was on fire. 'Just teasing.' She closed with him, pinching with her thighs, and broke away, maddeningly. 'Outside,' she murmured.

He followed her to the byre. He drove into her viciously. She cried out. She loved it.

'The truth, tell me the truth.'

She laughed and cried out where the tortoiseshell cat had lain.

'I'll kill it.'

'Go on, go on.'

He killed the thing inside her that was not his and lost himself in the darkness.

'Yes, yes, it's yours,' she whispered, swaddling him afterwards in her arms and legs.

Chapter 31

Zwei Herzen die von Liebe brennen
Kann Menschenohnmacht niemals trennen;
verloren ist der Feinde Müh,
die Götter selbsten schützen·sie.

The last record of the set was wearing badly. The voices were indistinguishable in the sibilants and the unison octaves following were furry at the edges. Alan felt suddenly foolish about it, realising that he must have played it a dozen times – dozens of times – in isolation from the rest of the opera: he began to imagine what Eleanor would have had to say about such philistine self-indulgence. In her absence, the thought of it still produced a grimace of embarrassment. False pride: a cold breath of solitariness blew it away. There was no conceivable audience for a public image. He could wallow in whatever spurious emotion he chose. So he wallowed, though it felt more like a cold sea-dive than a warm bath. Trembling, he so far forsook decency as to switch Papageno off after three bars: that was demoralising and invigorating, like losing one's virginity, except he couldn't actually remember that, when he thought about it.

In the ensuing silence he looked at his watch, having meant to avoid it, and was then solely demoralised. It was Wednesday. Donnie would have finished work early, since it was Bleeder's day for delivering goods to the Fladday ferry, and he would have dropped him off at Ardbuie. The previous two weeks he had appeared, tired and grimy, before five o'clock. It was already almost six. Alan reached for the *West Coast Pilot* and began to study the Approaches to St Kilda with impatience and dislike.

There was a light footstep at the open door. He came in with the borrowed sweater under his arm. He put it down on a chair and was sidling out again almost before he had voiced the customary island civility, that it was a lovely day.

'Where are you off to?'

'Looking for our cow. She's wandered.' Outside the door he seemed easier. 'Have you seen her?'

'No, I don't think so – no, I haven't. I might not have noticed her.'

'She might have gone over to Traìgh Mhór, the bull is out there. I'll go that way.'

'Mind if I come with you?' He braced himself for a grudging reply, but Donnie smiled sweetly.

'Boots,' Alan reminded himself, rather absently, after a moment's contemplation. He had left them somewhere when he came in from the boat.

Donnie leant on the doorpost, whistling half under his breath. With one boot on, Alan jolted upright, listening. It was only a minor uncanniness. He had been used to such coincidences between them at one time: the gloomy realisation that they were unusual now arrested the donning of the other boot. At length he pulled it on and followed Donnie across the stream.

'Donnie, do you remember what you said about that music?' He wished immediately that he had not asked the question. He would not possibly remember; that he had even retained the melody was surprising enough. And if he did remember, he would pretend that he didn't.

'Oh ay,' said Donnie, smiling, but not at Alan.

'What did you mean?' His heart raced. It seemed extraordinarily important to know.

He hesitated, with a quick mistrustful glance, but said, 'I meant it is like the music of the sidhean.'

'The what?'

'The sidhean. The fairy hill.'

'What's that?'

'We're on it now.' He laughed, as Alan started and looked around. He halted, leaning against one of the big rock slabs above the ruined cottages.

'I didn't know I had a fairy hill for a neighbour. You kept very quiet about it.'

'Enough other people were telling me I was daft. I didn't want

320

you to start.' He glanced at Alan suspiciously, as if expecting an immediate accusation to that effect.

'What's the story then? Come on.'

'Nothing much. Just one of them old stories.' He checked again for signs of ridicule, and seeing none, went on with growing animation. 'They were saying that was why they left the clachan. They were saying they were afraid of the fairies. Didn't put old Ewan off, though. He came here when he married – the only one who would. She wouldn't stay, like that, after he died. She went to Ian in Glasgow.'

Alan looked at the ruins below them with a slight frisson, and back at Donnie, who was watching him intently, wide-eyed. 'And is it true?'

'Ach, who knows?'

'You will, if anyone does.'

Donnie hid behind his lashes. 'I dunno. You live here. You ever heard anything?'

'Yes, when I think of it. Not recently so much, but the first year I was here. Music, and people talking, but that could easily be the wind, I suppose, or the water. It always stops when I listen – I don't know, you've put the idea into my head. Sometimes the door was open – once—' he stopped, remembering the night when he had run down the hill in the rain, convinced Donnie was there. It came to him then that all these strange things had had something to do with Donnie, who kept looking at him now and away again, hiding bird-shy under his heavy dark hair and downswept lashes.

'What do you think about it, Donnie? do you think *I'm* daft?'

He shrugged, curling his lip with a resurgence of urbanised insolence.

'You do.'

'No.' His eyes were on him then with all the old gentleness. 'I don't know what to think about it, Alan. I've heard strange things here, but maybe it's in them that hear it, not in the place – yes, and see it. I don't know. The old people were always believing in that sort of thing, but nowadays you'll not get anyone to admit it. But you might have noticed, there's no one will come near this place after dark.'

'Except you.'

'Ay, and you. And old Ewan, he wasn't scared.'

Alan remembered. 'Eleanor was always afraid here. She hated this

321

place – the house, the path. I didn't know why – I don't know why. Are the stories scary? Are the fairies good or bad?'

Donnie looked at nothing with unnerving intentness for a minute. 'There isn't good or bad with them. They're called the good people, but you might get bad – but it might be there already, it might be in us, or somewhere, I don't know. It might be a lot of daft talk. Hearing things.' He was backtracking, with a suspicious covert glance, his voice losing its soft native intonation.

'Don't!'

He assumed the expression for asking 'Don't what?' but gave up on it. When he spoke again it was in his natural tone. 'It wasn't that I thought you would be saying I was daft that I didn't tell you. It's – it is not knowing what it is meaning for us. *If* it is meaning. See, before you came, Alan, I was always at this place. I wasn't telling anyone that, though, for what they would say about me. Well, Uncle Ewan was gone, it should have been lonely here, but it wasn't, I was feeling all the time I was with someone, that I could just turn and speak to someone.' He frowned, running his hand over the dry crotal on the rock beside him, grey convoluted lumps darkened as if charred on the underside where they buckled up from the stone.

Alan, still pondering what he had said, followed the movement of his fingers, teasing under the edge of the crotal, out lightly over the ice-green fur of sea ivory, tracing round the yellow whorls of xanthoria. There was an anxiety in watching him which dissipated and turned to delight. The puzzle of why that should be led him away from his words and into them. It was a fine-boned hand, but he had seen it often enough before and could never touch it; it was, besides, far from clean, and he bit his nails.

It rested a moment outspread on the top of the rock and fell back to his side. 'It was what was going to happen, but it was there already.'

The delight was in knowing what was going to happen, that he would not pull chunks of lichen from the rock, or scratch or crumble it from its legitimate living place; any other idly moving hand might do that, but not Donnie's. The delight was that because small pellets of lichen had not coursed carelessly through the air, the already known was true, he was not other than himself.

'Do you see what I mean?' His glance was sidelong, but now without distrust.

'Yes.' He saw, in a light so bright it was blinding. He could not tell what he saw; only that it seemed most natural and obvious that whatever would be, was there already. *There* already, in that small green place between the hills and the sea; or elsewhere.

Donnie's eyes brimmed with secret laughter. 'Where were you that time, really? Halfway across the world, I suppose.'

With you. He stifled the words before they were out, in a double dowse of resurgent prudence and self-ridicule. Careful: writing silly postcards to Sally from Punta del Este maybe. And Donnie lying in the grass at Skalanish with unfocussed eyes, not lonely.

His withdrawal communicated itself, a chill like a passing cloud-shadow. Donnie looked round uneasily, and shook himself as a dog might, waking up. 'Och, there were other things too, not so good either, some of them. It's a funny place, or it's me that's funny. It's better not to talk about these things maybe. It might – talking about it might make it happen – no, that's not it! It is there already. I can't say what I'm wanting to say.'

They both fell silent. Alan said at last, 'It's a lot of not-its. You can't get any nearer. I've been trying.'

Reasons, voices. Neti, neti. He looked down the grassy slope at the world suddener and more of it than you think, the ruined clachan fallen into shadow, the square little house with smoke in the chimney, Selena rocking gently in the bay with the late sunlight tipping her mast, Fladday still warmly lit behind, gulls flying sun-high as golden angels and shadow-low as grey wraiths. But two of these same phantom birds alighted on the bank of the stream, nodding and beckoning each other, and they were solid with life, bright-eyed and flat-footed.

Donnie was watching them too, with forgetful love, the shadow gone from his features; and Alan, looking into his now unguarded face, saw also the gulls, hopeful vibrating springtime bird-souls, and was aware of a secret wren busy among the boulders under their flat pink feet, a small eagerness with beetles on the brain, and of the first clump of uncurling primrose leaves, with a tassel of pale buds and one early flower half-open, the scent of one flower filling the whole evening, and roots spinning new white threads from the residual warmth

323

of day. The boy's eyes turned on him. What he sees, he thought, is what I am. The birds were still there and the flower. I am what he makes me. His eyes were too clear to be borne.

'I better push off,' he said, anxiously, as Alan looked away, and the world lurched uncomfortably back to normal opacity.

'What about the cow?'

'Oh, she's above Roddy's. I'll pick her up on the road.'

'But I thought you said . . .'

'I did. I was making it up.' He was walking fast ahead, on towards the road. Alan followed, bemused. When he caught up, Donnie had a question about the boat, and more after it. They found the cow half-way along Roddy's fence. She snuffed at them with a damp tranquil nose, and turned for home. Donnie stopped determinedly, in an attitude which indicated it was time Alan went back. He looked worried, almost frightened: Alan remembered about Eleanor, and smiled, but felt too much in awe of him at that moment to tease him about it.

'See you on Saturday,' Donnie said, giving the cow a push and Alan a smile of bone-dissolving beauty.

Alan went home in a state of hazy contrition, not sure what had happened, but knowing something had. It had somehow become possible to leave him, or at least to resign any lingering hope of possession. There could be no claim on that self-forgetting innocence which saw into heart and mind, root and stone. It was enough that it existed, an undeserved bounty to have seen it. He stood at the open door long after it grew dark, listening gratefully to the call of peewits and the soft voices of running and lapping water. Eventually he grew hungry, but hunger seemed unworthy; in any case, there was no food in the house except some forgotten potatoes sprouting under the sink. Acknowledging this less elevated reason for abstinence, he turned in light-hearted.

Holy innocence was poor protection against common misery. Donnie was helplessly miserable. Alan treated him with gentle patience and intended to leave him. That intention was as tangible as a closed door, barring every path. The world had become a maze in a nightmare. Eleanor and Murdo lurked in the dead ends. She had taken to getting up early in the mornings to give him instructions for the evening before he left for work: prayer meeting, collecting seaweed for the potatoes, planting same, repairing creels for Do'l Alex, fetching a strayed wedder from the missionary's garden, meeting Sandy's brother from the ferry. He didn't protest; he knew she was capable of worse, if pushed. He was afraid when he saw her expanding midriff. She had begun to stick it out proudly since she had told the family, and to knit spider's-web things in pale, dead colours. He was afraid of Murdo too, though he could not have said why. It was not because of the way his brother had taken to calling him filthy little this and dirty little that, presumably with reference to the abominations he had not had a chance to commit. She must have told him, however she knew. He put up with that, it might stop Murdo thinking about the other thing; he was more afraid when he saw him looking at Eleanor's belly. He was afraid going to Alan, drawing the scent there, and afraid away from him, off guard. At nights he lay awake and listened to his fear. By Friday of that wretched week he whimpered at it too.

'Donnie!' Mairi's voice was sleepy. He froze. 'What's wrong?'

'Nothing.'

She switched on the bedside lamp.

'I hurt my back,' he said, to stop her enquiring further.

'Och, you're a pest, you are. You've got me wakened up now, I'll have to go down for a pee.'

While she was gone he turned on his face, hoping she would think he was asleep, but when she returned, she came over and prodded him. 'What you done to it?'

'I don't know.'

'It's hurting you bad, anyway.' She turned the covers back and poked around till he winced. 'There? It's bruised right enough. You do that on the coal?'

'Ay, a bag slipped. It's all right, it's no bad.'

'You were crying.'

'I was not!'

'I heard you, boy. You should be ashamed of yourself at your age!' She tousled his hair roughly and slid her hands under his neck. 'You're an awful misery these days. What's wrong with you?'

'Nothing.'

'I don't believe it. Tell!' She throttled him a bit.

'Och, go away Mairi!'

'You wakened me up, see! I'm going to torture you till you tell.'
She twisted his wrist up to his shoulder blade. 'What happened to
that girlfriend, for a start?'

'Nothing. Leave me alone.'

'She ditch you?'

'No.'

'You ditched her.'

'No.'

'Come on! Must've been one or the other.'

'I just didn't go back, that's all.'

'She might be waiting to hear from you, then.'

'Not her. She'll have found someone else.'

'Time you did too, cheer you up a bit.' She prodded him in the
ribs. 'Get your face out of that pillow! Kirsty's still keen on you.'

He flattened himself visibly and said nothing.

'Well?'

'Well what?'

'Don't you fancy her?'

'No.'

'Why no?' She pulled his hair. 'What's wrong with you? She's good
fun – good-looking, too.'

'I'm not interested.' He spoke between his teeth and into the pillow.

Mairi gave his hair a final exasperated tweak. 'What are you
interested in, I'd like to know?' She put her hands on his shoulders,
because they were shaking. 'What is it you want?'

She had got little of what she wanted herself; she leant back beside
him, sorry, with her head against his.

'I want to go with Alan.' His voice was strangled.

'In that boat of his? Why don't you then?'

There was no answer. She wrestled him to make him turn over,
but when he did and she saw his face, she said, 'You're daft,
boy,' and let him be.

'Nothing keeping you,' she added, after a minute. 'Why don't you
go, get away from Murdo? Have you asked Alan about it?'

It was a foreign thought. The barriers were absolute, fatal, certain
as damnation. It had not occurred to him to question why he was
betrayed, or whether anything could be done about it. It was such a
strange idea that he rolled over, blinking at Mairi. 'No,' he said.

'Well then, why don't you?'

'What's the use? I know the answer.'

'You ask!' She twitched the covers over his head and padded heavily back to bed.

He sat up suddenly, with a bitten-off yelp at the pain in his back. 'Mairi! Don't say anything about it. Don't tell anyone, right?'

He was always like that, about not telling anyone, always afraid of everyone. 'I won't say anything,' she assured him, patiently.

Murdo met Shonny up on the road after closing time and they had a good dram between them. He was quiet coming in. She pretended she was asleep, but he didn't believe it. There'd be hell from her in the morning, and from the old woman too. Worth it: he needed the drink, stop thinking about things for a bit.

He heard Mairi go downstairs and up, and the murmur of voices in the next room. They might be talking about it, laughing at him. She might have told Mairi, they were thick together. Mairi had suspected about the cat, she'd be glad. The boy too, snivelling little sod, his boyfriend might have told him. If that was true what she said. If it was true, the other couldn't be, not to father a child, not that sort. But he'd had her often enough, she said so, everyone knew it. Do it with both, do it with anything, it could be.

Carefully, inching his hand under the bedclothes, he felt her belly. It didn't feel much, not more than four months. Five more to go. He clenched his fists till the nails bit, straining eyes and ears against the darkness. Mairi was giggling. At me, he thought, forming the words silently. Laughing at me. What's he telling her, what does he know? Squirming soft little bastard, always whining about something, might as well have been a girl, kissing the dog's stinking nose and stroking the sheep when the knife goes in, probably does it with the animals as well as men, the filthy little bugger. I'll get it out of him what he knows, get it out of him somehow, give him something to whine about.

He tensed his biceps, looking forward to it. There were things to pay, had been a long time, Mother's pet, she'd have kicked him back to Glasgow if he wasn't. Always like that, Mum and the girls and that whimpering brat, only a baby, not strong enough, not big enough, don't make him cry. Always crying in corners about nothing, but you could hammer him and you wouldn't get a squeak out of him, kick the guts out of him, he'd not open his mouth. There's some way. He knows all right, I'll get it out of him.

He craved more drink. It was in the byre. Out of bed, inch by inch, trousers on, the stairs, inch by inch, silent, dark. He could do it without a creak. The old woman was snoring, he could hear her but she wouldn't hear him, never did. The dark was safe, he knew his way. He touched the guns passing, shotgun, two rifles. The English bastard, I could go there now, put a bullet through him. The thought was a surge of delight. In the byre he enjoyed it as he drank. In the stomach, hurts more. Can't be done, though, questions, police. Never get off with it, a mainlander, friends and influence. Fucking bastard. Shotgun in the eye, blast his balls off. No good, pity. He nursed the bottle. 'They'd all split on me,' he murmured aloud, sorrowful. 'No one back me up.' He hunched silent, listening. 'Don't make a sound. Not a sound, right?' The boy would tell, he'd know. He knows. How does he know, what does he know? He'd tell. Get him first. Kill him. 'Can't kill your brother,' he reminded himself sternly, wagging a finger. 'Not your nice wee brother.' Mairi and Donnie in the pram together, pushed it over and got a hiding. Cut his head open, smash his head in. She was watching, I'd have killed him, good thing too, look at him now. Everyone talking, talking about me, bastard baby, brother like that. Thought we'd got rid of him one time, that time we killed the sheep, first one I did, did it good too. Got the little brat screaming, all that fuss over him when they found him. She always made a fuss of him, picking him up, cuddling him, the girls were at it too. Eleanor too. 'Eleanor wasn't there,' he told himself peevishly. 'Not that time she bloody well wasn't.' Eleanor's got some sense, can't stand the little bugger. She's my girl. Maybe it's mine, she won't tell. You can't get strangers, mainland, they'd sort you out, you can't get women either. 'You never get women, boy. Too clever for you.' She'll smell the drink, what the hell, finish it.

He gulped and prowled back noiselessly through the fiery conspiring darkness, feeling it with his hands, the knife in the block, the dark outside, the closed door, the rifles, the shotgun, the dark on the stairs. He stroked the dark stair-rail and a streak of fire ran under his fingers and up behind his eyes, he put the door of the bedroom on fire with his hands, he fell on the bed and pulled her towards him. She told him to stop but he didn't. Hell to pay in the morning. Too bad. She dug her nails into his arms and threw him off.

'Och, you're hard on me, Eleanor,' he said mournfully. 'Too hard. You're too hard. No one back me up.' His eyes filled with tears and he fell asleep.

Chapter 32

'Planting Uncle Kenny's potatoes again, Roddy?' Alan, with time to fill, stopped to chat on his way back from the Saturday morning telephone call to Harold.

'Oh ay! Same damn nonsense as usual. Och well, it keeps the old man happy.' He turned a spadeful of dubious black mud laced with buttercup roots upside down on top of a tuber.

Alan noticed a second spade. 'I'll help for a bit. I'm taking Donnie out in the boat later, but I'll give a hand till he comes along.'

Roddy grinned. 'Oh well, might be long enough till he does, he'll have work to do first. Murdo had a bad night last night, I hear.'

'What happened?'

'Hit the bottle – hard. Got the works from the women in his life this morning. Kirsty was along for the milk, said you couldn't hear yourself for the shouting was going on.'

'God help Murdo, then. Eleanor won't spare him.'

'Oh, she's a terror!' Roddy forked seaweed with emphasis. 'A terror right enough. He has to do what she says, eh?'

'I think so, Roddy.'

'Well, you know this, I'd never have thought it would be like that with Murdo. He's always been that hard – too hard, really. Another one like Uncle Kenny, just, I'd have said. Oh well, maybe if poor old Bella had shouted at him louder, she would have been alive today.'

'He used to beat her up, did he?' Alan, good-humoured in the bright morning, found the idea faintly entertaining. He had often seen the tremulous nonagenarian, bent double on two sticks, inspecting the potato patch; a hook-nosed tottery Punch to Bella's Judy.

'Oh ay, he did that, something terrible too. Many's the night when

329

he had a drink on him she was running from the house with the children, and walking up and down the road there.' Roddy paused for a moment, shaking his head, and dug his spade in again forcefully. 'I mind one morning – it was winter too, terrible weather – I was just a wee lad then, I went out with my father to the cow – the byre was in the end of the workshop then. Well, there they all were, lying up against the beast to get warm. Oh, the face that woman had on her, I'm telling you I'll never forget it. I never seen a woman bruised so bad. The wee ones was crying, saying they were thinking she'd been dead. I believe he fractured her skull that time, great clots of blood was in her hair. Well, poor soul, she could hardly stand, it was a shame on him to do that.'

Alan's amusement had quickly evaporated. 'What happened?'

'Och, nothing. My father gave them milk, sent me into the house to sneak some oatcake. He'd some whisky in his tool chest, he put that in the milk and sent her off. Nothing we could do. We told Mam the cow kicked the pail over. Ach, maybe she knew.'

Alan was puzzled. 'Why didn't you tell her?'

Roddy adjusted his potato sprouted side up. 'Oh, very difficult. Kenny's her brother, she'd no side with Bella. If Kenny had found she'd been to us, he'd have killed her, putting shame on him to his sister like that. My father wouldn't say. He would never make trouble for anyone.'

Alan pondered this, over the next three potatoes. 'What happened to the children?' he asked at last.

'That's his daughter Marion he's living with. The boys are all away, the eldest was killed at the end of the war, just eighteen he was, it was sad. The youngest girl, Kennag, she's that daftie, you'll have seen her. She's living with her other sister in Port Long.'

'Is that that cripple woman, the dumb one?'

'Ay.' He turned another few spadefuls. 'Well, I tell you this, Alan, that woman's a cripple now and near enough an idiot, but when she was a wee lassie she was a bonny wee thing, bright and lively too. He did that: Kenny did it. Got her one day when Bella was out, and near enough killed her, would have done if the oldest boy hadn't got her away from him. It was a crowbar he took to her they say. Well, some people were saying a pick handle.'

The precise details of what he had used seemed irrelevant. 'How

330

awful. Wasn't he had up for it?'

Roddy shook his head.

'Not even after that? But people must have known, surely.'

'Oh well yes, they were hearing the screams every night, near enough. It was stopping them sleeping down there. But what could anybody do? They were neighbours. His brothers were telling him right enough, and my mother too, that it didn't look good. The missionary then was preaching against him, but the very next day Kenny was at his door, said any more of that and he'd throw him off the cliff. Oh well! Fancy saying that to the missionary, eh?'

Alan dug with subdued violence, wishing Uncle Kenny's neck under the blade. 'Worse what he did to his wife and kids, wasn't it?'

'Well yes, I suppose. Still and all, there is not many would talk like that to a missionary.' Roddy leant on his spade. 'Well, well, old Kenny! you would think he was harmless to see him now. Oh, but he was coorse!'

Alan straightened up, pushing back his hair in agitation. 'But how could people know what was going on and stick it? Not try to help?'

Roddy scratched his head. 'Well, if there had been a stranger in the village, now, it might have been different. He might have been stopped. Someone like yourself, Alan, would have taken the police in for what that man was doing – yes, for the half of it. It's a pity in a way there was no one in a position to do it. Poor Bella might have been alive today. He murdered her, really, and that's the truth. Bit by bit. Oh, it was a shame!'

Alan opened his mouth to protest, and shut it. He had learnt wisdom from Eleanor on such points. There stood Roddy, broad and kind, sweating over the surly ground to please his murderous uncle, who would be better under it. And when his wicked century was up, he would be buried in it with the same ceremony as Angus or any other, carried by men who had heard the shrieks of his wife and children. And his beasts: Alan could imagine that bit, dogs in sacks, cats in fires. The sunny day seemed less inviting than before, the breeze chill and fitful. There was no sign of Donnie.

'I think I'd better go now,' he said, at the end of the next row.

Donnie was waiting for him, lying on the grassy bank above the stream.

'Sorry I'm late, I've been with Roddy. I thought I'd meet you on your way over.' Alan dropped beside him, noticing then that he was very white, his eyes lemur-ringed with strain. 'You look ghastly! What's wrong?'

'I hurt my back a bit. I'm no good in a boat today.'

'What have you done to it?'

Donnie moved cautiously, indicating his right side. 'Torn muscles I think. It's stiffened up, I can't use this arm properly.'

'Was that at work?'

'Och, I'm all right, it's nothing much.' His voice was high with tension. There were other things: lack of sleep, Eleanor's crazy rage, the kick Murdo gave Tess because he was watching. He bit his lip on them.

Alan remembered what Roddy had told him, and pieced some of it together. 'Come on in,' he said. 'The wind's cold. You'll stiffen worse than ever lying here.'

'No, I'd rather stay here. I'll just hang around while you're out in the boat, keep out of everyone's way.'

'I'm not going out if you can't.'

Donnie frowned, and sat up painfully. 'You don't want to waste the weather. I'm just here hiding, getting away from them at home.'

'I wish you'd come in to hide, then. You can lie down if you like, I'll leave you in peace. I'm not going out in the boat, though.'

'You're not staying here because of me.'

'Yes I am. You look ill, I'm not leaving you.'

Donnie turned a sudden menacing look on him, eyes paling to startling ice-grey between his black lashes. 'You'll be leaving me soon enough. You might as well go.'

Alan jumped up, confused by his bitterness. 'For Christ's sake, I can't be bothered going out in the bloody boat on my own. I'll have plenty of that – years of it.' His recent reconciliation to leaving had fled at the mention of it.

'Aren't you pleased with her?' His tone was accusatory; he sounded as if he took the remark as a personal insult. Perhaps he did: he had always loved Selena.

'Yes, I suppose so.' Alan paced up the bank, out of the line of his scowl.

'You always wanted to do this.'

'Yes.'

332

'Lucky to get what you want, then.'

'Yes.'

'Did you want Eleanor?'

'No – not much. Why on earth ask that?' He stopped pacing, baffled by that morning's reversion to pointless squabbling.

'None of my business, you mean.'

'I'll tell you anything you like.' He sat down again, close enough to be aware of his taut misery.

'Doesn't matter.' The clenching of his jaw made a muscle flinch above his eyebrow. He scrabbled tiny pebbles out of the soil, flinging them with a fierce click against a boulder in the stream. Every toss made his nostrils twitch with pain.

'What the hell's wrong with you? Why are you so angry?'

He shook his head slightly, perhaps denying anger. Alan saw desperate, cornered exhaustion. Knowing that whatever he said would touch raw nerves, he kept quiet for a while, but the imagination of Donnie in that state lugging coal and cement for Bleeder proved too much to bear in silence. 'You'll have to give that job up, Donnie. It's far too hard for you.'

'It's all there is. I'm not going on the dole as long as there's anything to do.' He threw pebbles insistently.

'Why not? Everyone else does it.'

'Well, and I'm not everyone else.'

'But there isn't any work here.'

'I got work now.'

'It's half killing you.'

'It can whole kill me, for all I care.'

'It will, too. You're too bloody proud.'

He rose, turning a sulky back. 'What about yourself, then?'

'Me?'

'You're not on the dole.'

'No, I'm not looking for a job.'

'There wouldn't be one anyway. You'd be safe enough – like everyone else.' He swung round, with unsteady resentment in his face. 'You got no money, have you?'

'I don't need any. I'll have thousands when my mother's affairs are sorted out – a really disgusting amount.' It revolted him to think about it, with Donnie standing before him half crushed by the

333

pressures of the bottom of the social heap.

'I'm not talking about then, I mean now. When did you last have a square meal, Alan?'

This was so extraordinarily different from the way anyone had ever attacked him before that he simply stared, first astonished, then angry and embarrassed, then repentant when he realised that he had certainly asked Donnie questions equally humiliating. 'That's just absent-mindedness –'

'More like bloody-mindedness.'

'Oh, all right, it's choice. I don't want money, I've always had too much of it.'

'Who's proud, then? You're prouder than I am.'

'Look, it's entirely different for me. I'm on my own, I haven't got anyone to compromise for. You're with your family. I just drift around, it doesn't matter what I do.' He was conscious of poor reasoning, unwilling to meet his eyes.

Donnie fixed him with an icy stare. 'Different. You mean . . .' He took a deep, uneven breath. 'You mean, you make allowances for me. I got to have different standards, you mean, because I'm just a crofter's son – a peasant, a halfwit—'

'Oh, Donnie, for God's sake! What are we fighting about?'

'You wouldn't put it like that, I know. You're too kind. That's what's in your mind, though. That's what you always thought.'

Alan's denial was lost in the memory which showed in his face: that was what he had thought.

'You did. You do still.'

In the silence, Donnie's eyes changed, darkening, quivering with sadness. He said, without reproach, 'I'm beneath you.'

'What do you mean?' Alan was lost. The familiar prison had opened. He did not know yet how to leave it. It had grown to be a refuge, dismal, but safe.

Donnie looked at him as if from a swiftly increasing distance. 'That's all.' He turned quietly to walk back along the path. His movement was so unemphatic that Alan stood dazed for a few seconds, watching him go, before the import of it reached him.

He sprang after him, seizing his wrist. Donnie pulled away violently. 'What d'you want?'

'I don't think that. How could I?' He grabbed for the other hand.

334

Donnie retreated, wild-eyed.

'Donnie, it's not like that!'

'It was! Is it now?' He shouted it.

'No!' Alan yelled back at him.

In the jangling silence which followed they stared at each other across a crevasse of habitual anguished prohibition. Donnie jumped first. He was suddenly there, in his right place, hard-armed, hard-skulled, laughing and crying between rough boy's kisses.

Chapter 33

Donnie's hair was peat-brown where the light caught it, soot-black in shadow. Alan stroked it almost hesitantly, inhibited by a residual grumble of guilt. After such long and well-reasoned restraint, it seemed outrageous that a few minutes from the heart-stopping purity of Donnie's 'I love you', they should have been tumbling into bed with undignified urgency. It had been that first and talk afterwards, all the explanations and avowals, memories and outpourings, hopes and plans for the suddenly brilliant future. It should, surely, have been the other way round.

'What's wrong?' Donnie's eyes were anxious.

'Nothing!'

'Yes – something about . . . I'm sorry, I'm not much good in bed, I haven't had any practice.'

Alan held him close, shaken by such humility, murmuring, 'You're perfect. I love you as you are,' with other things in the same blessedly unoriginal vein, and many kisses. After a bit he said, 'You don't think that's all I've been wanting you for, do you? To drag you into bed?'

'You didn't drag me!' He seemed to find that very funny. 'You were still saying didn't I think we ought to wait when I got your trousers off.'

'Was I?'

It seemed very funny to Alan too. Everything was either hilarious or heart-rending. Laughing softly, Donnie ran a finger under Richard's necklace. Alan caught his hand, feeling the tiny smooth beads sliding over work-roughened skin; it was a miracle to be allowed to link fingers.

'You see, Donnie, Crabbit was right about me.'

'Och, Alan!' He thrust his head against his neck, tangling his hair with both hands. 'He was not right at all. What he meant is not what you are at all.' He unburied his face. His eyes were almost fierce, blazing with love, obliterating, unbearable as the sun. Alan pulled the dark head against his shoulder again.

'I can't look at you,' he whispered. 'I can't not look at you either,' he added, almost immediately, caressing the young face between his palms. For a long time they lay still, blue and grey eyes lost in each other, while thoughts became common property and limbs melted without definition. When at last Donnie shifted position, it was Alan who said 'Ouch!' feeling the pain in his back.

'I should go home,' said Donnie, when they had unconfused themselves sufficiently to speak; but he made no move to do so. 'Nothing but trouble there anyway,' he added, so light-hearted that Alan felt no need to encourage him to go.

Later they wandered along the shore, not very far, because every other step ended in a long embrace; went back ravenously hungry, and ate what they could find, which was, as usual, not much.

'You'll starve me to death,' Donnie complained, searching in the pantry.

'You can take over that side of affairs. I'm completely incompetent.'

'Not much room for food in Selena anyway.'

'Not much room for anything. I hope you realise you'll have to sleep on the chart table?'

'I'm going to sleep with you tonight anyway. I'm going to sleep with my arms round you and wake up like that too.' He wound his arms round Alan's neck in an anticipatory stranglehold.

'Hadn't you better go home?' Alan surfaced with difficulty from this beguiling prospect. 'And what on earth are we going to tell them?'

'Nothing.' But a shadow crossed his face. Alan remembered about Eleanor and Donnie saw her come into his eyes. 'Did you tell her about me?'

'Yes, I did. God, you look sick about it. I'm sorry, my darling!

336

She'd told me so much about herself, and I thought we'd never see each other again, I thought . . . I don't know what I thought. I should never have said anything.'

'It's all right.'

'It's not. You look so anxious – surely she . . .' He had been going to say, 'Surely she won't make trouble for you,' but he had a disconcerting feeling that she might.

'She hates my guts. Never mind, we'll soon be out of her reach.'

He knew about Eleanor's hatred, how her lips drew back and the air crackled round her; but though he recollected its symptoms, holding Donnie in his arms he was incredulous of its reality. 'Why should she hate you? You've never injured her. She's snappy with everyone, it's just how she is.' Donnie looked unconvinced. 'She couldn't hate you!' His mind teemed inexpressibly with the manifold impossibility of hating him.

Donnie's eyes registered amazement, then amusement. 'Alan, you're soft,' he said, after a moment's scrutiny.

'Eleanor said that too.' He was perplexed by the coincidence.

'She was right there anyway. Thank God you are, *Ailein a ghaoil!*'

He nestled his face against Alan's throat. The flick of his lashes and the soft brush of his lips was dazing.

'I can't believe it. I can't believe I'm really holding you like this.'

'Did you say that to her?'

'To Eleanor? Certainly not!'

'What about all the others?'

'What others?'

'Tell me about them. All girls? Or other boys?'

'Not many boys.'

'Dozens of girls, though.'

'Yes. Sorry.' And for a moment he was wretchedly sorry; but Donnie was laughing against his throat, knuckling gently into his back.

'You feel strong! Not all ribs and backbone like me.'

Relaxed, his body was surprisingly light and fragile. Prejudging it from his wiry stamina, Alan had not expected to find him such a small armful. He cradled him now protectively, stroking the injured flesh of his right side, mouthing the hair back from his brow, which still bore the faint scar of Crabbit's fist. 'You're beautiful. You look

337

like yourself again now you're happy.'

'Me? I'm not worth looking at!' He sounded utterly astonished.

Alan gazed into his lovely eyes, too stunned to offer any denial, or to say anything at all, except 'Oh, Donnie!'.

Some incoherent hours later, Donnie fell asleep in his arms, clasping him so tightly it was almost impossible to breathe. His sleeping response to any edging or shifting was to hang on tighter. Alan spent most of the night awake, in extreme discomfort, inconceivably happy. He suppressed the clock before it could ring at five, to wake him by gentler means.

'I don't want to go!' There was a sob in his voice.

Alan was dismayed. 'You don't have to, love. I'll go and see them later – anything you like, don't worry.'

'No, I must go. It's all right, I was half asleep, that's all.'

'You're frightened. What's wrong? Is it just about telling them?'

'I'm not telling anything, except that I'm going with you when you leave. They can't stop me. They don't want me there anyway.'

'But Eleanor will guess, is that it?'

'I don't care! Don't worry about me, Alan. Only help me to find my clothes, or I'll never get home at all. Where's the light switch, anyway?'

It was damp and chill walking back, with the cries of curlews bubbling through the wind, cold as spring water. Alan held the boy to his side, worried by his trembling; but his face in the uncertain grey of dawn was serenely happy.

'Don't come any further. The dogs will be barking at a stranger,' he said, at the croft gate.

Alan held him tighter, hating to think of him afraid and under attack. It was Donnie who pulled away at last.

'I'll come soon as I can after church.'

Mairi was awake with the bedside light on, reading a magazine. She slept badly because of her pregnancy.

'Where you been, boy? I was getting worried, thought you'd drowned yourself.'

'No.' Donnie looked round the room dreamily.

'What you been up to? You been at the bottle like big brother?'

He shook his head, smiling.

She sat up. 'Oh, the row there was all day! You'll be the

one will catch it in the morning, I'm telling you – not home by midnight! Better get your excuses lined up, my lad, whatever they are.' She took up the magazine with token modesty while he undressed, but dropped it again. 'Who's been biting you? You been having an orgy over there?'

He gave a startled gasp, then began to laugh and dived into bed. She was out after him at once. 'Come on, you tell me what's been going on!'

'Nothing! Go away Mairi, stop tickling!'

'Got very ticklish, haven't you? Who else has been tickling you? You'd better not make a noise or they'll hear. Better tell before I torture you.'

He writhed and giggled and winced with pain. 'Mind my back!'

'Where've you been?'

'Alan's.'

'Who else was there?'

'No one. Honest!'

'Oh, a likely story! What's cheered you up so much, then?'

'Alan.'

'Oh, come on! Who was biting you? That wasn't Alan!'

There was a giggly sort of silence. Mairi stopped in mid-shake. '*Was* it?'

He turned over, smiling, blissfully happy. 'Yes.'

'Oh, well, honestly!' She stifled a squeal. 'Oh, you make me laugh! Is that right? Is it really? Is that what you were on about last night?'

To all of which he replied joyfully, 'Yes.'

'You ought to be ashamed of yourself! What you going to do if Murdo finds out? He'll skin you! He'll go wild!' She bounced on his bed with glee.

'I won't be here long. You don't say anything, that's all. We'll all just keep quiet.' They both started at a slight noise from the next room. 'Better be quiet now,' he whispered.

Mairi got up from his bed to go back to her own, pulling a face in the general direction of Murdo.

'Mairi—' he caught her arm. 'See, I don't care what anyone else thinks. But you don't – you're not put off, are you? It's not like people say – it's – I always wanted him.'

She looked at him rather wistfully, with her arm pressed above the big bulge. 'Lucky he'd have you, then. I hope he'll be good to you.' Her eyes flickered over the red marks on his shoulder and lit with laughter again. 'Och, you were always daft about him. You were always daft! Trust you to do something like this.'

He was bright-eyed, eager with new anticipations. 'You can come and see us, Mairi. I don't know where we'll be yet — sailing for the summer anyway, but after that I don't know. You'd come, would you?'

'Ay.' She settled herself and picked up her copy of *True Romances*, smiling slightly.

'I'll write to you.'

'You write? That'll be the day!'

'I will, honestly. You can come with the baby, make a holiday for you.'

'If you're not back home by then.'

He was silent for a moment, with his chin in his hands. 'I'll never be back home again.'

'What if he dumps you? You haven't thought of that, have you?'

'He won't! It's for good.'

She scanned her page intently. 'Everybody thinks that. I thought that, look at me now. Least he can't do that to you.'

'Oh, Mairi!' His happiness foundered in her trouble.

She sniffed once or twice and put down *True Romances*. She had cried most of her tears long before. 'It'd be nice to have a place to go, away from here — not with Alex Angus or Effie, pair of stuck-up snobs they are. I'd like to come and see you. Now shut up, you, I'm putting the light out on you. Not a hope in hell of keeping this a secret, rate you're going.'

'How did they take it?' Alan wanted to know later.

'Mum was all right really, except she's on about me getting drowned. Murdo isn't saying anything.' He hid his face so that he wouldn't have to elaborate on the quality of Murdo's silence.

'I'll go to see your mother and tell her I'm going to look after you.'

Donnie tensed.

'I haven't been to your house since your father's funeral. I'd have to see her anyway.'

'Wait till Eleanor's out, then.'

'Why? What difference does it make?'

'She'll not be in tomorrow afternoon.' He had noticed an appointment card for the clinic on the mantelpiece.

Alan was perturbed by his anxiety. He had no wish to see Eleanor; he could imagine she would have a nasty look in her eye for him. But the thought of her turning it on Donnie instead was much worse. 'It might help if I talked to her, you know.' At one time they had been able to talk to each other. It might be possible again.

'No! Don't go near her!' There was a rising of hackles.

'Why not, love? What's wrong?'

'Promise me.'

'But tell me what's so terrifying about her.'

'Promise!'

'All right, I promise, if that's what you want.'

'Yes.' He kissed hungrily, to cut out further questioning. Alan put his intensity down to some residue of jealousy, and forgot about it under the boy's searching tongue and hands.

'When can we leave?' Donnie wanted to know later, and it was a question he would not let go in the following days. The answer was problematical. The boat needed some reorganisation to accommodate both of them, and the weather showed no sign of improvement. All the equipment Alan hadn't bothered about for a solo voyage to Iceland now seemed highly desirable even to cross the Minch. He had no engine, radio or lights, let alone more sophisticated survival aids.

Donnie laughed at his worries. 'Stop fussing! The boat's seaworthy and so am I.'

'I don't want to drown you.'

'Well, we haven't any money and you can't buy any of these things here anyway, so we might as well just go.'

'There's a good chandlers in Mallaig.'

'Mallaig, that's news! I suppose we have to wait till the forecast says a month of good weather before we risk it that far?'

He wouldn't give up his job: not, he said, till they were really ready to leave. 'What we going to live on? Seaweed?'

After that Alan actually did sell the van. He was horribly embarrassed when Lal bought it; he had never sold anything in his life, except for his previous vehicle, and that to a salesman so sub-humanly mendacious he scarcely counted. But Sandy, against all expectations, had passed his driving test and could now act as family chauffeur.

While Donnie was at work, Alan chafed at the weather. When it moderated at all, he was out, testing Selena as far as possible in the short intervals between one gale and the next. He was still unhappy about the heavy boom. Running in the confused swells beyond Langasker, it dipped with an ominous hint of inexorability. He altered the internal ballast, but without improvement, and eventually removed the offending spar to lighten it. Donnie was anguished, as the operations of dismantling, hollowing and refastening would take several successive days. Alan was uneasy about it too; he was afraid of weakening it so much that it would not carry the required weight of wet sail in windy conditions. The charm of authenticity began to look faint beside the virtues of light alloy.

As Donnie had pointed out, he was fussing. He was not used to doing so. On his own, he would happily have sailed a sieve, as an interesting exercise in technique; but on Donnie's account his imagination was beset by risks he had never thought of, highly coloured by the very novelty of thinking of them at all. Every danger between hypothermia and collision with a tanker presented itself: Donnie might be swept overboard in darkness, storm, fog; might be left as sole survivor after an accident; might simply pine for home, and have no home left to return to. The lurking guilt of the past still played odd tricks. The boy was frighteningly young, a lamb to the slaughter; watching him sometimes unobserved, smooth-browed in sleep or whistling at ducks-and-drakes by the stream, Alan sweated with fear for him. There were reasons enough, which he recounted to himself soberly: alienation from family and community, exposure to ridicule, denial of reproductive capacity; the spoiling of a life, in the world's terms. But these conscientious phrases had little meaning for Alan, drowning in reciprocated love, and none at all for Donnie, who would wake or turn feeling his eyes on him, and seeing him pensive, would hurl himself into his arms: 'I love you!' He was breathless with how much he meant it, frantic. Unthinkable then to call that life spoiled, life which quivered in him as intensely true to its nature as it did in the chimney-fall starlings Alan sometimes rescued from

342

the dingy parlour, when they surged in his hand to the sweet air of the opening window.

So Alan, with such misgivings daily weakening, yet finding it still impossible not to fear for him, fretted instead about the perils of their voyage: Donnie succumbing to concussion, appendicitis, exposure; decapitated, drowned, mangled. And Donnie arrived every evening healthy and impatient, demanding to know what he was fussing about now. Alan had just enough sense not to tell him; at least, only to tell him about the latest weather forecast, rather than the attack by killer whales or the dropped-off rudder. Even Donnie could not deny the unrelenting viciousness of the weather.

In spite of imagined disasters, he shared Donnie's anxiety to be away. They were too much apart. The pretext of getting the boat ready helped most evenings: since Mairi Anna raised no objection, Eleanor's efforts were less than they had been. Nevertheless, Donnie nearly always went after a few hours, and every parting cast him down. He came smiling and brilliant-eyed, and left cowed and pale, with the hollows showing in his cheeks. Alan asked him what was going on at home, speculating uncomfortably about Eleanor's persecution.

'No, she's laying off me a bit. Hasn't said anything to Mum, anyway.'

Not saying anything to Mum was of supreme importance: how important, it was difficult for Alan to grasp. 'Can't you tell her? Or just say you're moving in with me and leave her to work it out as she likes? After all, when Mairi has the baby there won't even be room for you at home.'

He shook his head. 'I can't tell her. It would kill her if I told her that.'

'I don't like making you live a lie.'

'I don't like acting as if I'm ashamed.' He was torn. 'It's not that I am. You know that, don't you?'

'But your mother would be. Well, mine wasn't too keen on this sort of thing either.' But the deceit of it troubled him. 'Wouldn't she get over it, though? After all, everyone was furious with Mairi when she got pregnant – and with Johane, I dare say. Not to mention Murdo's binges. But no one seems to mind afterwards: I've always thought people are exceptionally tolerant here.'

Donnie shook his head again. 'It's different.'

'Why? Just another kind of sin, isn't it? There are so many in Mr MacNeil's book, surely everyone's committing two or three.'

'No, it's different.' He grew agitated, and wouldn't or couldn't explain. It was nearly time for him to go. 'I just hope to God we get away soon.'

'As soon as it gets down to about force 5 for more than half an hour.' It had been blowing hard for the whole week, swinging from south to north-west and back in wild arcs.

No one had told Mairi Anna, and no one ever would, but everyone else soon knew.

'How?' Alan wondered. He would have been amused, though the look in Roddy's eyes and Sandy's hurt too, if it hadn't been another burden for Donnie. He pretended to take it lightly, but Alan could guess the teasing or worse he suffered at work.

'Murdo got drunk with Shonny that Friday. He'll have said.'

'But that was before—'

'Och, you should have been hearing what he was calling me before that.'

'What was he calling you?'

'I'm not telling you.'

And he wouldn't. Alan began to think they might settle for force 6 or 7.

Mercifully, Johane had arranged to take her mother off to spend a few weeks with Effie, to give her a change of scene. They planned to be back in time for Mairi's baby, otherwise the rough seas might have postponed their departure longer; like most island women, they were poor sailors. Donnie came to Alan as soon as they had gone.

'That's home finished with,' he said, as he walked in. He was smiling, though a shadow of grief haunted his eyes. That seemed natural enough. Alan hugged him in silence, humbled by his willing sacrifice, but Donnie was matter-of-fact. 'I'll go back and see Mairi some time, and Murdo will need a hand at the end of the week, they'll be bringing them in for lambing. But I'm here to stay now.' He looked into Alan's eyes steadfastly, struggling against the welling sadness, till his own eyes lost their truth and clarity, and became as they had been in the time of misery.

'Oh, don't!' Alan was dismayed. 'I know you're sad, don't

344

try to hide it. You couldn't be anything else. It's goodbye to everything, isn't it?'

'To everything I can do without. I'm happy.'

'Come on, little liar, I wish you'd cry and get it over with.'

'I won't cry.'

His look was proud and intense. Alan shivered in it. 'What are you seeing?'

'You.'

'What do you see in me?'

'Everything. The whole world.' His eyes cleared and gentled as the raw memory of Murdo's insults faded. What he had said about Alan was seared into him, but he hid it; he would not speak or even think the blasphemy. Alan saw only the change in his face and did not guess the cause. If he had, he might perhaps have teased it away.

'Thou shalt not lie with mankind as with womankind. It is *abomination*,' wailed Mr MacNeil. 'Leviticus chapter 18, verse 22,' he added parenthetically, polishing his glasses.

The reference was hardly necessary: his congregation had all studied it carefully already. The sermon had been much looked forward to, and the mission house was full. Mairi Anna's departure the previous day had made the subject matter a certainty, and Lal had been unofficially instructed to warn her erring son to stay away, though in fact he had been too embarrassed to pass the message on. Now the elders in their pen and the handful of the elect in the front pews crouched over their bibles, shading their eyes from the abominable sin, while the unregenerate majority sat back comfortably with folded arms, sucking pan drops.

Mr MacNeil launched forth into the fog of peppermint and stale best clothes: 'This, my friends, is the immutable law of God: a law against unnatural lust, against the sin of Sodom – not to be thought of without the utmost abhorrence! Oh, that ever there should have been an occasion for the making of such a law, it is a reproach and a scandal to human nature. *But* – how much more of a scandal –' (he goggled, scandalised, at his stolid flock) '*how much more of a scandal*, that since this law was first made, it should ever have been broken by sinful human beings!'

345

'Amen!' shouted Uncle Kenny.

'Shush, Dad,' Marion whispered, mortified.

Mr MacNeil waited politely till the little altercation was over. 'Oooh!' he groaned, warming up again. 'It is known to many among you – I would venture to say, it is known to all of you here today – that there is dwelling in our midst a young man who has not scrupled to break this law – yes! Even the Holy Law of God – to defile himself with these abominations, to walk in the ways of Sodom and Gomorrah!'

Kirsty began to giggle. Dina had pointed out in an undertone that walking wasn't the way it was done. Mr MacNeil's anguish mounted. 'Oh, children, it is no laughing matter! This sin is such that it can scarcely be named among us. It is such that – I read to you from the Holy Word of God – it is such that "the souls that commit them shall be cut off". Oh, what a terrible thing is that, for the soul of that poor sinful young man to be cut off, to be cast into the uttermost darkness! Oh, yes –' he scanned his audience through steamy glasses. '*Oh yes!* Be not mistaken, friends. The penalty for this abomination is the pains of Hell – brimstone and fire such as the Lord rained down on the cities of the plain! Yes . . . "and the smoke of the country went up as the smoke of a furnace" – Genesis chapter 19, verse 28. Take heed – *take heed*;' – his voice was so earnest that even Kirsty sat up heedfully – "The land is defiled wherein such abominations are practised. Therefore says the Lord, I do visit the iniquity thereof upon it and the land itself vomiteth out her inhabitants." The land is defiled. Yes!' He nodded his head slowly right, left and centre. '*Defiled!*'

'Ay!' yelled Uncle Kenny, gleefully.

'The land where such abominations are practised is defiled. Oh, my friends, think what is the meaning of this, to each and every one of us. The land is defiled – polluted – cursed! It will no longer produce crops—'

'That's right!' Uncle Kenny staggered to his feet, but was suppressed by Marion.

Mr MacNeil, thus encouraged, howled with grief. 'The crops will be blasted. The beasts will not thrive. Men and women will sicken and die. Oh, friends, be warned! It is no coincidence – no coincidence, my friends – that in this very place, this very island, crops have failed and beasts are not thriving and men and women are so sick that even the doctor cannot cure them. Oh, we know from what our fathers are telling us, it was not so in the old days, in the days when our forefathers walked in the ways of the Lord and kept his laws. Then families were growing all that they needed on this land – on this same land!' He raised a significant arm. 'Oh brothers and sisters, there can be no doubt about it – no doubt! This is what is meant by the defiling of the land. This is the judgement of which the Lord has spoken to us, which in his mercy he is warning us of, that it will befall us if we do not heed his laws. "Ye shall therefore keep my statutes and my judgements, and shall not commit any of these abominations, that the land spew not you out also when ye defile it, as it spewed out the nations that were before you." *That the land spew not you out!* It will spew out those that defile it!' An enlarging bubble of saliva trembled at the corner of Mr McNeil's lips. 'They shall be cut off from among their people! Cut off – spewed out –' His voice rose to a wail of despair; he rocked in agony, eyes closed behind his misty glasses. Mairi began to sob. Some of the women leant pityingly towards her under cover of their hats. Mr MacNeil became aware of it, and blinked uncomfortably. 'Oh well well!' he said sadly, before continuing. 'Pray, my friends! Pray for the land that is defiled by our sins. Pray for this young man among us who has fallen into sin.'

'Is he no going to pray for Alan too?' whispered Dina. Kirsty kicked her ankle and looked prim. Mairi sobbed helplessly. Mr MacNeil snatched off his glasses and screwed his eyes up tight so that he would not have to see her distress.

'Pray that the gates of mercy be not closed against him and against each and every one of us. Oh, there is a way – oh yes! there is a way of healing for all sinners, and we are all sinners: make no mistake, brothers and sisters, we are all sinners! There is a fountain open to take away sin and uncleanliness, even such uncleanliness as we have read about, such as we have heard about with grief today. The pure blood of Christ is that fountain, that blood which was shed for the forgiveness of sins, for as many as will repent and turn to God with all their heart. Oh, let us turn again unto Him, my friends. Let us turn unto Him this very day, and repent. Amen!'

'Amen!' agreed Uncle Kenny, fervently.

Mr MacNeil shook hands at the door: patted Mairi's shoulder, told Murdo it was a terrible thing, asked Eleanor solicitously how she was keeping. The women looked at the two girls with concern, but the men for the most part were grim. It was raining again, sleet in a dour grey wind in the second week of April. The grass was slimy underfoot, lacking new growth; with less than a fortnight to go till lambing, prospects were poor. Uncle Kenny muttered imprecations and waved one of his sticks at Murdo, not behind his back either, but before his eyes in open insult. Murdo's face had the tinge of lead.

The defiler of the land was hanging precariously by one arm from a half-dead scrub rowan, trying to reach an early lamb stuck on one of the ledges above the croft he had blasted.

'You'd think the mother would have had more sense. What a place to choose! Maybe she fell, though.'

The ewe had sprung from the ledge to a lower one at their approach, and stood weaving her head anxiously to and fro for the scent of her lamb. It staggered on rickety legs, in a bleating frenzy of loss and fear.

'Be careful!' Alan, scrambling up from below, averted his eyes from the cracked stump of dead wood. He caught the little creature by throwing his jacket over it, and passed it across to Donnie. They dropped down beside the ewe. Donnie let her sniff the lamb, and she followed as they picked their way downhill.

Alan took his hand above Johane's croft. 'Do you remember that evening?'

He smiled, a look almost as shy as it had been then, his strong fine wrist as tender across the little animal's frail chest. Alan kissed his neck, nuzzling into the scent of lamb and the scent of Donnie.

'You don't start that with the church bus coming along the road any minute!' The old life still had enough power to make him jump aside, laughing, but shamefaced. 'I'll have to go down with this lamb, it needs an extra feed soon as possible.'

'I'll come with you.'

'No you won't!'

'I wish you would let me. I don't like skulking.'

'No.' As usual whenever the subject was raised, he was on edge.

Alan let him go, watching his slight figure down the hill with the ewe at heel, half aware of spring birdsong between the sleety squalls, half dreaming in the sunlight of that earlier evening; the two instances one, bridged by a cobweb thread, diamond-dancing in a shift of light, showing this spray of heather and that whorl of lichen related; as if that past incident had revealed the present as limpidly in its pattern as the present held the past clear in memory: Donnie strange and rare, yet utterly familiar, then as now. But I didn't know, he thought, mocking his own alarming solemnity, about the mole on the inside of his thigh, or that he loathes marmalade. Immediately faith protested, I knew! Solmenity fell on him, knowing. He ceased to think then.

Donnie warmed milk for the lamb, and crouched with it at the back door. It sucked weakly, letting the teat fall away, and dribbling. 'Hurry up!' he begged, huddling it against his chest. It was too weak to hurry, though. They were back before it had taken half the bottle. Eleanor stalked past him, withering by her presence. Mairi tried to smile, but she had been crying. Murdo stopped in front of him. He was in his decent Sunday suit and polished shoes and his language would have to be fairly decent too.

'You were preached against.'

He had known it would be that day. He stood up slowly, still holding the lamb to his breast. The weight of his brother's hatred battered on him so that he ached with weariness. 'It once happened to you too, Murdo.'

His face darkened and twisted. 'You stinking little poof. The disgrace you brought on this family, you and your filthy—'

'You'll say nothing more against Alan. Call me what you like. If you put any names on him, I'll smash your face in.'

The lamb and bottle were down and his fists up. Murdo, conscious of the Sabbath, hesitated, just long enough for Eleanor to call furiously. 'Murdo! Come in.' Donnie was past him and down the path, and the wind was too blustering for him to catch the foul names flung after him. They were quietly voiced anyway, because it was Sunday.

Alan had the radio on when he got back. 'Palm Sunday,' he said. Some sort of religious music was coming and going between atmospheric crackle. 'Seems incredible. It'll be cherry blossom and hyacinths down there. Sleeting again, is it?' He switched off as a wave of interference overwhelmed the singing.

'No, leave it on.' Donnie was entranced by the calm sweet voices and the idea of cherry blossom. He wanted very much to know if they preached against people in the churches where Alan came from, but had to hide it. 'What's Palm Sunday?' he asked, obliquely.

'Popish idolatry, you ask Mr MacNeil. You're freezing cold, love.'

It wasn't much of an answer, but with Alan smiling and warming him in his arms, it was good enough.

Chapter 34

'Malin, Hebrides, Minches. Force 6 to 7, increasing gale 8 later. North-west backing west later. Wintry showers. Moderate, locally poor in showers. Faeroes, Fair Isle. Force 7 to gale 8, increasing severe gale 9 in places later. West. Scattered showers. Moderate to good.'

The click of the switch roused Alan from sleepy non-comprehension. 'Time to get up already?' he muttered.

'No, go back to sleep. I'm not going to work. I've had enough.' Donnie settled beside him again, warm and angular. 'We've got to get away,' he said, half to himself.

Alan woke up sufficiently to ask, 'What was the general synopsis?' but the only reply was a drowsy grunt. He was more than ready to agree that Donnie had had enough of breaking his back on the coal lorry; less sure, lying warmly in bed listening to the hailstones rattling on the roof, that they need be in a hurry to confine life to a small boat in bad weather. Curving a protective hand round Donnie's head, he reflected upon its obduracy.

'Burn the house over them,' Shonny suggested, almost genially. He was enjoying himself. His nose for trouble had brought him to the Ardbuie road
end with a carry-out the evening after Mr MacNeil's sermon.

'Too good for them.' Murdo curled his lip, but his mouth watered. The imagination was pleasant: trapped screams and the smell of burnt flesh.

'Beat that bastard up anyway, eh?' Shonny drank reflectively. 'You never know, I might just join in the fun.'

Murdo eyed him, pondering. Shonny didn't look much, slack face and the start of a beer gut, but there were stories about him, some he told himself and others only whispered around. After a minute he shook his head: if the whispers were true he'd be boasting about it, for sure. No chance there. 'You can't touch these people.' He wasn't drunk enough to have become unreasonable in his reasoning. 'Friends on the mainland, family's wealthy – you'd be in court if you would lay a finger on anyone like that. You'd no get off, either.'

'If you were found out.'

'You would be found out all right.'

'At night? It's quiet down there – really nice and quiet.'

'It's no going to be quiet with my wee brother squealing, is it?'

'Fuckin' hell, he's just a kid. He'll shut up if he's told what'll happen to him if he splits on you.'

'Not him.'

'Look, Murdo, I'm no scared of your brother – or of his boyfriend.'

In the latter case this was not strictly true: Shonny disliked an opponent with a longer reach than his own. Murdo knew it. His eyes narrowed in suspicion of a gratuitous jibe at his family's shame. They had talked for half an hour in careful avoidance of the nature of his brother's abominable sin; the term, 'boyfriend' was deliberate indelicacy.

Shonny caught the look and tactfully passed the bottle. 'You got to watch yourself with them fucking Englishmen right enough.' He intended to watch himself, but not to the extent of forgoing mischief altogether. 'What you going to do with the kid?' he asked encouragingly.

'Which kid?' Murdo was becoming slightly confused. A sequence of grudges had led him through Shonny's relationship to Mairi's, and thence to the paternity of Eleanor's.

'Your brother. Disgracin' the family like that. Can't let him off with it.'

'No.' He breathed hard and took a long pull at the bottle. The thought of what Eleanor would have to say about it made it work more urgently. The blood surged into his temples. 'I'll kill him,' he said, with hoarse satisfaction.

'Uh huh?'

'Would if I could get off with it, I'm telling you. What that devil's done to us down here – I can't hold my head up. Everyone laughing at me.'

'Teach him a lesson, eh?'

'You bet!'

They drank in silence, considering it.

'Better go,' muttered Murdo. He was still not thoroughly drunk.

'Well, Murdo lad, best of luck.' Shonny chucked the cans in the ditch and turned to clap him on the shoulder. 'You know where to find me. I'll stand by you.'

They stared at each other intently. Shonny passed the last of the bottle and Murdo drained it. There was another silence.

'Gathering this week, later this week. You could give us a hand.' He turned a slatey look on Shonny. 'Cash in the pocket.'

'You not usually got much of that, boy.'

'I got some all right.'

'Where'd it come from?'

Murdo mumbled a curse, and made his face blank.

Shonny nodded understandingly. 'Oh ay, ay, Dad was keeping some out of sight, eh? Good on you, Murdo. Say nothing to anyone, that's my motto – ay, all right, I could do with cash.'

'I got cash. All right then?'

Shonny smiled blandly. 'Ay. Good enough.'

Murdo got out of the car, closing the door carefully. Shonny sat back, still smiling. 'Oh Jesus! Good enough!' he repeated to himself before starting up.

Eleanor was on her own, crocheting in front of the fire. 'You've been drinking again,' she said, without looking up.

He flung himself down on the sofa. 'Not much wonder, Eleanor. Not much bloody wonder.'

'No.' She pulled the shawl out over her knee, picking at the fine stitches. 'Not much bloody wonder.'

He watched her sideways, waiting for the explosion, but she

stared silently into the fire, with tightening nostrils. She put both hands up to push back her hair. 'What are you going to do about it?' she asked, in a low voice.

Murdo sat up slowly. 'Do about it? What do you mean?'

'You know what I mean.' She tugged at the border of the shawl. 'That boy.' Her eyes glittered with sudden angry tears, and her voice rose. 'You may have forgotten yesterday, but I haven't. I never will as long as I live, Murdo. I've never felt so humiliated in my life.'

Murdo eyed her thoughtfully. She was working herself up into a rage, he could see, but not at him. He pondered this strange new thing and guessed some, but not all. He pulled out his secret half-bottle from his inside pocket. 'Have a dram, Eleanor.'

'I'm not drinking just now. You know that.'

'Have one tonight, just a wee one. You need it.'

He fetched two glasses from the kitchen. She gulped hers, and stared at him. He sat down on the arm of her chair with his elbow on her shoulder. He was less drunk than he had been. 'Can't do much, Eleanor.' She looked fixedly at the fire, without answering. Her hair on end tickled his chin. 'Can I, now?'

She was silent for a minute. 'I don't know what you can do,' she said tonelessly at last.

'Don't know myself.'

There was another silence, longer. Suddenly, she sprang up facing him with clenched fists and open mouth, sobbing, 'Oh, oh, I hate them! You must do something, Murdo, you must, you must! I'll never forget it, never!'

He caught hold of her arms, scanning her fire-flecked eyes and wet red lips. 'You hate them, do you?'

'Yes!'

'Both of them?'

'Yes!'

'My brother Donnie – your lover Alan?'

'Yes – oh, Murdo, after what he's done to me!'

He pulled her close and she sobbed against his chest, pounding his shoulders with her fists. 'I hate him, I hate him!'

'Good girl. You're my girl, Eleanor, aren't you?'

'Yes.'

He got his hand under her chin, to look into her face. 'Eleanor, tell me now, you tell me right this time – is it my baby?'

She pushèd him away violently, with a howl of anguish. 'Shut up, damn you! Damn you, Murdo – I don't know!'

She rushed out of the room and upstairs, slamming doors. He sat down slowly and gazed at the half-bottle on the mantelpiece, with the clouded puzzlement of a long-penned bull.

Donnie was determined. He listened to every weather forecast, relevant and irrelevant, day and night.

'It's getting better,' he announced, after Wednesday evening's instalment.

'I don't know how you work that out, with gales not only here but Shannon and Rockall, and a strong south-westerly airstream.'

Donnie looked very stubborn. 'The ordinary forecast for the weekend is good: "warmer more settled weather spreading every-where by Friday".'

'"– except the extreme north-west of the country."'

'That's supposed to clear later too.'

'How much later? I'd say it sounds as if might be feasible by Monday.'

'Ay, or Sunday.'

'Well, perhaps. I forgot Sunday was even a possibility; I've lived here too long.'

As he said it, it dawned on him how much of his life was Boreray, and that leaving was painful. And Donnie: he had scarcely known anything else. Every stone and tussock of his home ground, the pro-files of the hills and windings of the coast, were mapped in his bones. Alan wondered, not for the first time, if he knew what he was doing. 'I'm afraid it's going to be wretched for you when we do leave,' he said, rather nervously, because similar remarks had provoked anger and even tears; but it was a recurrent worry to him.

'I can't wait. It's you keeps making excuses.'

'Donnie, they're not excuses! The weather's been dreadful, and I don't know the boat that well yet. And anyway, I'm responsible for you. You'll have to put up with that, I'm sorry.'

He was scowling, and ducked his head away from Alan's hand.

Alan paced round the room, much distressed; it was the nearest they had come to falling out.

'Look, I have to be the one to take decisions as far as sailing's concerned. You said you did what I told you in a boat, remember?'

'I always have, haven't I?' He was furious, but immediately penitent when he saw Alan's hurt look. He made it up with his usual dog-like affection, pressing close with speaking eyes and wordless caresses. If he had insisted then that they had to set out at once on that or any other suicidal enterprise, Alan would have been incapable of denying him; but with customary humility he did not exercise his power. It was when Alan was occupied with charts and tide-tables again that he said, 'Please, we must get away from here.'

'Yes. Sunday, if the weather's improving.'

Donnie did not look, on Thursday morning, as if he liked the thought of the gathering. Alan walked with him part of the way, on the pretext of settling up the rent with Roddy.

'Let me come with you,' he tried as usual.

'No.'

'Why not? Look, I'm sure everyone's laughing at us anyway. Why should you have to stick it on your own? It worries me that you take it to heart so much.'

'No, just keep away. I don't want trouble.'

'What sort of trouble?'

He clenched his jaw and made no answer.

'It's Murdo, I suppose.' Alan felt and looked grim. 'Why on earth are you going to help him today? Why don't you leave him to it?'

'He's my brother.'

'And how much brotherly affection has he shown you recently?'

'Oh, or ever! He hates me and I feel the same about him. But I'm not going to fall out with him now. I don't want people telling my mother I was not helping him. Everyone would be talking, it would give him something else against me, like that.' His words were reasonable enough in Borerayan terms, but his face was more strained than they warranted. 'I don't want trouble,' he said again; then uncertainly, when Alan didn't answer, 'You're not angry with me, are you?'

355

'I wish—' but looking into his pleading eyes, he dropped his reservations about pig-headedness and obstinacy. 'No. I'm angry with myself for getting you into this situation. Or for not getting you out of it sooner. We could have abandoned the boat and bolted.'

'No!'

His indignation made Alan laugh. 'It's Selena you love, not me.'

Roddy's house was imminent. Suddenly bright-eyed and mischievous, Donnie caught him tightly at the last concealed dip in the path. 'Don't forget to listen to the forecast,' he reminded, between kisses.

'You and your bloody forecast!'

He ran off up the hill, whistling. Alan leant against a boulder to recover for a minute before facing Roddy.

The encounter was wretchedly embarrassing. Roddy was in the porch, scanning the hill through binoculars. He came out, and they talked politely about weather and lambing prospects, but his eyes wandered between the hill and his own boots. He did not ask Alan in. Of course, it would not have been mannerly to accept such an invitation at the beginning of a working day, but it should have been offered. Alan realised that his presence was regarded as a pollution; he felt sadder than he had thought would be possible, after Donnie. In a few minutes he cut through the stilted chat to say, 'I'd better let you get going. Thanks for everything, and say goodbye to Chrissie and the girls for me.'

He held out his hand. Roddy hesitated. Alan's arm dropped back to his side. 'It's not infectious,' he said, faintly.

Roddy's face flamed suddenly crimson. 'Oh well, Alan, I – I don't know what to say to you,' he stammered.

'Goodbye, Roddy.' He made for the gate as he spoke.

'Alan, wait you . . .'

He waited.

'You have been a good neighbour, I'll no say not.'

Alan could say nothing at all. He wanted to say that he and Chrissie had been the best neighbours in the world, that he hadn't known the meaning of the word until he came to Boreray.

'You understand –' Roddy went on, red and sweating, 'Angus was my own cousin. My first cousin.'

Alan nodded, and managed, 'No hard feelings.' He set off again down the path, but Roddy followed.

'You will be leaving soon, I'm sure?'

'Yes, as soon as possible.'

'Ay, that will be best.' He paused, removing and replacing his bonnet. 'Tomorrow, maybe?'

The blood drained from Alan's face. 'The weather's appalling. Do you really hate us that much?'

'Oh no, no – not at all!' Distress showed in every line of his features. 'But – I am telling you, Alan, it would be better to get the lad out of here. It would be better for him.'

'Yes, I know.'

Roddy appeared relieved. He shook hands then, civilly if not warmly, and went back into the house.

It seemed treacherous to feel miserable. When his mind turned to Donnie for forgiveness, he felt considerably worse, wondering who was working with him and what ill looks he was suffering, if anyone would talk to him, if he would get anything to eat. These questions nagged all day, causing him to scrub the table with water he had already used on the floor, and to wash the windows with one of Donnie's tee-shirts. He applied himself as concertedly as possible to making the house decent before leaving it. He had already sent most of his possessions off to Harold's address, and there was not much left, except for an alarmingly large pile of sailing gear. He put it all in one corner and cleaned round it, then regarded it with growing consternation. The volume of it looked about twice that of Selena's tiny cabin. In the afternoon he ferried some of the more waterproof items out and stowed them, but the operation was not encouraging: the little dory was almost swamped even crossing the bay, the lockers seemed full in no time, and the heap on the kitchen floor looked undiminished. He moved on to distracted contemplation of the sitting room, which he never used. The problem, as usual, was mice. They had eaten the undersides of the fat shiny cushions, then turned to the upholstery beneath; they were undoubtedly nesting in the springs. There seemed to be no way of persuading them to come out. He considered the soft mushrooms of white flock sprouting from every chair with paralysed indecision. Eventually he replaced the cushions carefully, intact side up, hoping Chrissie wouldn't persecute the inhabitants. He cleaned the room with great thoroughness so that she might pass it by, but he had doubts: she was houseproud.

He almost missed the shipping forecast: a stationary depression in the North Atlantic, force 6 locally gale 8, south to south-west, rain clearing later. The picture for nose-to-tail Englishmen on motorways seemed rosier, 'a warm sunny bank holiday in most parts of the country—'

'— except for the extreme north-west corner,' finished Donnie, as he walked in the door.

He was dripping wet and smelt of sheep.

'A day without you is unbearable,' Alan said smoothing water out of his hair. 'How was Murdo?'

'Not so bad, really. I saved him some running, after all. I've got to go out again, though.'

'What, tonight?'

He nodded, and began to pull off wet boots and clothes. 'We didn't get the far end here done. Tess run off, we were looking for her most of the morning. Didn't find her, though. It's bad that, there's been a dog worrying sheep beyond Ardbuie out on the common grazing there, she could have joined up with it. Someone will shoot her if they see her near sheep.'

Alan dropped an armful of dry clothing beside him. 'Poor Tess. When did she disappear?'

'Tuesday night.'

'She hasn't run off before, has she?'

'Ay, when she's on heat, and she is. She might just have a boyfriend.' He grinned, wriggling into dry jeans. 'Does funny things to dogs, too.' He elbowed Alan off, laughing. 'Get away! Shonny will be here for me in a minute.'

'Shonny? What's he doing down here?'

'Working for Murdo a couple of days. It's good, it means I won't have to go out tomorrow.'

'Great! I've just thought of something. There was a dog barking on the hill when I was out at the boat this afternoon. I wonder if she could be stuck up there?'

Donnie looked doubtful. 'Probably one that was out with us. Lal's Dileas is awful for barking.'

'I'll go up and have a look when you're out, anyway. Here comes Shonny.'

Shonny greeted Alan obsequiously, with an unpleasing smirk.

358

Alan took it as calmly as possible, not to make Donnie's evening worse than necessary; but his responses dwindled to monosyllables as Shonny leant at ease on Uncle Ewan's propane pen, blocking the doorway while he expatiated on the foulness of the weather.

'Holding you two back, I suppose. Too much wind, eh? Even for a grand sailor like yourself, Alan.'

'Yes.'

'Och well, might be better in a day or two. I'll say a wee prayer for you, how's that?'

'Thanks.'

Donnie scowled and said nothing.

'Murdo's wanting you over there,' Shonny told him, after he had dealt fulsomely with the weather. 'He's got word of the dog out back of the hill. Eachan Mackinnon Achmore seen two dogs there at his sheep this afternoon. He lost a few, too. Big bill for Murdo if that's her. Eachan's a hard one.'

'What's he need me for?'

'It's a big area that, they could be anywhere between Achmore common grazing and Càrn Bàn. Do a side each and meet at Neilie's, Murdo's thinking. He'll need to get her tonight, if she's at that game.'

'Poor Tess.' Donnie stole an undercover glance at Alan. 'Bullet for her, then.'

'I'll come with you.' He expected the usual rebuff, but this time Donnie's eyes assented.

'Well,' Shonny looked from one to the other, 'if you wouldn't mind me asking, Alan – I'll need a hand to get them in from Traìgh Mhór. I've got no dog, see. I thought Roddy might come out, but he's no well. Gone down with a sudden stomach upset. He was fine earlier, too.'

Donnie's eyes were lowered. He half nodded for Alan to agree. He did so, reluctantly; it sounded like a long grim night for Donnie.

'I mightn't be back tonight at all,' he said, in a miserable undertone, as they donned coats and boots. 'There's a moon later. Murdo won't give up till he gets her, not when he's paying for every beast she pulls down.'

'Oh God! I wish he'd leave you in peace. Can't anyone else go?'

'She'll not come but to Murdo or me. Then it's the gun between the eyes.' He drew in an audibly wavering breath, touched hands, and went out into the rain.

'This is very good of you, Alan,' Shonny assured him as they set off.

'Not at all.' Alan was desperately polite; he could never meet Shonny without an intense desire to put as much space between them as possible.

'Och, but indeed it is. After all you've been through, you and Donnie – all the unpleasantness there's been.'

'No one's been unpleasant to me. Where do we start?' Involuntarily, he was almost at shouting distance. He forced himself to close the gap.

The evening was crawlingly distasteful. Alan kept reminding himself that the man was trying to be friendly. He could have no ulterior motive for heavy insinuations about the narrow-mindedness of locals who had never been away, or about the world which he, Shonny, had seen a lot of outside Boreray, or even for remarking (several times) that Donnie was a nice-looking lad. Alan became exaggeratedly civil, even to the extent of agreeing, at the third opportunity, that Donnie was indeed extremely good-looking. By the time they reached the Tràigh Mhór machair, his stomach seemed to be tangling with his lungs, and he had never been so near punching anyone's nose. He was glad of the running and chasing that followed. There was plenty of it for Alan: Shonny was surprisingly unathletic, in spite of his early training. At every critical moment he seemed to be too far away, or doubled up with a stitch, or tripping in a rabbit hole, while the little knots of wily ewes hurtled for the gaps. As they were near lambing, it was important not to drive them too hard; there were long detours and uphill sprints to take them by surprise. It was sunset by the time they had the flock together, and keeping it that way without a dog made the homeward journey energetic.

'Couldn't Roddy have let you have Spot?' Alan wondered, as he loped round the complaining herd for the twentieth time. His bad knee throbbed violently.

'Och, I didn't think, now, wasn't that silly?' Shonny was bland. He hadn't done much running. 'You're fit, man,' he continued, affably. 'You must be in good shape.'

Alan didn't manage a reply.

It was long after dark by the time they turned the flock on to Johane's croft. Alan lashed the gate by feel: one of those ramshackle Boreray gates, dropped on its hinges and bedded in mud, fastened with frayed ends of rope salvaged from the shore. The air was full of bleating, as the ewes got their bearings and found their friends, some voices anguished and others relieved. He had always liked the end of a drive when the beasts were let onto fresh pasture, but that night he heard terror and grief in the bleak gusty darkness, animal, disquieting because terror and grief are always animal, because there is no better answer to violence and loss. Poor old half-witted sheep, harried by human wolves: no comfort for them in the will of the Lord. Comfort maybe for wolves, no better answer than that. Jumbled thoughts of pogroms and autos-da-fé interfered with the knots. He wished reunion to the white woolly bodies invisible in the darkness, and quiet grazing.

Shonny clapped his shoulder. 'We'll just catch the pub before closing time. Come for a dram, eh?'

'No thanks, Shonny. I think I'll get home.'

'I'll run you along.'

'No, I'll walk. You'd better hurry or the pub will be closed. Goodnight.'

'If you're sure, then. So long, Alan.'

Alan bounded shorewards with his shoulders contracting in an involuntary shudder. He felt guilty: Shonny had made such efforts to be friendly, which was certainly more than anyone else had done of late, but he inspired loathing. An unclean presence; that's me too, thought Alan, passing Roddy's house, with a memory of the morning. There was still a distant miserable bleat in the air, between drumming gusts of wind. Someone had been separated from her daughter or her dam, and cried for loss. A few might have strayed in the darkness coming along the road. Alan stumbled now and again, wrenching his knee and cursing. He thought about Donnie, tramping all day, and then all night as well. It was a good fifteen miles to Achmore and back through the boggy interior, if they had to make the whole journey. At least the rain had stopped. The sky was clearing, with Orion bright over Skalanish Island; but an overcast sky would have been more likely to bring Donnie home early. Alan suffered a pang of disappointment seeing the house in darkness, though he had known he was unlikely to be back so soon.

The sensation of Shonny's unwelcome hand was still on his shoulder, and he grieved inwardly over his cowardly compliance towards the remarks about Donnie. He wanted to tell about it and say he was sorry at once; and knew that whatever social and ethical constraints had been observed, he would have had more peace with himself if Shonny's nose had been thoroughly flattened. He had a bath and felt cleaner, and managed to stay awake long enough to listen to the shipping forecast.

'Fastnet, Shannon, Rockall. Force 3 to 4, 6 to north of area at first. South veering south-west. Fair. Good. Malin, Hebrides, Minches. Force 7 to 8, decreasing 5 later. South-west veering west. Fair. Good.'

It definitely sounded better. Even Saturday might be possible. Alan buried his face in Donnie's pillow and slept.

Donnie turned one of the dead ewes over. The underside was flat and wet, the empty eye-sockets black in the moonlight.

'But these have been dead two or three days. She won't still be here – if it was her. When were you hearing from Eachan?'

'Today.' Murdo sat down on a boulder with the gun over his knee. He took out his half-bottle. He had had more than a drop at Neilie's earlier, too.

Donnie was deathly tired. 'It's no good. I searched all that over to the west already, and you've done this bit. If she'd have been here, she'd have come to you then, if she was going to. We might as well go home.'

Murdo sucked on his bottle, wiped it slowly and screwed the cap back on. 'Tired are you? Ready for bed?'

There was a sneering emphasis on the last word. Donnie rejected its implication with a fierce effort of will. He would not let Alan's image or even his name into his mind in Murdo's presence: he chilled with fear for him whenever his guard slipped. 'I'm just thinking it's useless,' he said evenly. 'I'll go on if you want to, though.'

Murdo hunched dark against the moon, fumbling the bottle back into his pocket. 'We'll try the ridge.'

'The coffin road?'

362

'No scared, are you?'

'No. I was thinking that was the way you would have come earlier, that's all.'

'I was on the main road most of the time.'

They climbed the landward slope in silence. The coffin road, banked above the surrounding bog and peat-pools, clung to its own winding shadow in the moonlight. The resting cairns stood up pale and still in the stream of the wind, intent and full with the count of the dead who had passed there, like fishing herons in the flood tide. There was a movement up and down the ridge, a monotonous restlessness, sometimes the fading echo of a voice. Donnie knew Tess would not have come that way, because animals fear the human dead and the ill thing in them that doesn't die, as sheep or birds die, sinking away into the peat and the new season's grass. He pitied them, whispering up and down there, greedy and lamenting and not letting go, but he was not afraid, except of Murdo walking behind him. Facing him, he could fight him down with his eyes, keeping Alan covered; but he had not eyes in the back of his head, and he felt his brother's look on his buttocks and thighs, prying into what they did in bed, gloating and loathing at the same time. Twice he fell back to Murdo's side, but he lurched as he walked, sticking out his elbows on the narrow path, and making room for the gun.

Where the coffin road curved round to Ardbuie, Murdo halted and took out his bottle again. 'Where now?' he said. 'Maybe over the top.'

Donnie waited silently, leaning against a cairn. He remembered then about the barking Alan had heard in the afternoon. 'Who was at the top today?' he asked. 'She might be stuck in a gully up there.'

'Shonny cleared that.'

'I wouldn't trust him to notice.'

'Well, maybe not, right enough.' Murdo looked at him thoughtfully, and drank again. 'Will you have a dram yourself?'

'No, thanks.' He was faint with exhaustion, but he couldn't risk slackening his grip. His fear was growing; he would not dull it, or Alan would be alone.

'We'll go over the top then.'

As they reached the summit, the south-westerly wind swooped up the steep seaward face, battering their breath away, keening in

363

the crazy old fence which separated bare rock from bare rock.

'Listen!' Donnie cocked his head. There was a whimper in the wind, a small weak sound that hadn't come out of the heaving surges betwen the moon and Langasker. He pushed against the weight of the gale to the end of the fence, and dropped down.

'She's here!' She was tangled in a cruel trap of old wire, looped round and round her hindquarters. He kissed and fondled her and she licked his face, whining with relief. He set to work on her legs, murmuring to her.

There was a stunning blast at his ear. Tess arched and jerked, without a sound. Donnie staggered to his feet, staring at the shining ooze of blood welling out over her soft tongue. The thump of Murdo's descent roused him.

'Why did you do that?'

'Dog's no use. It's finished.' He spoke thickly, swaying against the rock face.

'You devil!' A sob rose in Donnie's throat. He turned for Alan and home, thrusting blindly past Murdo. The butt of the gun thudded into his crotch.

Chapter 35

The house shuddered with the scream. Alan's outflung arm in Donnie's place encountered emptiness, and terror that it was his presence which was the dream, that loss was infinite and eternal. He woke crying out in fear. Tess was on the fringes of consciousness somewhere, trapped and frantic-eyed.

The clock registered 4.00, and Donnie wasn't back. Alan lay down again, sweating and trembling. The scream lingered, shivering his flesh. His rigid muscles would not let him lie; he sat up, blinking at the brilliant patch of moonlight on the floor of the adjoining room. Donnie should be home. He had said he might not be, but Alan, still half under the nightmare, didn't believe it. He was afraid for him, afraid in bones and blood, listening, straining to hear, hearing nothing but the wind on the roof and the oystercatchers calling along the shore. He switched the light on, and off again at once. He could hear better without it: but there was nothing to hear.

The momentary mundane yellow glow over the familiar untidy room had brought back some of the motions of common sense. He got up and dressed, telling himself he might as well go out and see what the weather was doing, since he was awake. He could guess that the wind had veered and dropped from the tune it played in the loose gutter above the bedroom window.

Outside, the moon-luminous sky vibrated and hummed. Dapples of white light broke and scattered the outlines of the old clachan. Without intending it, he held his breath, focussing eyes and ears beyond the splintering moonlight and the confused voices of wind and water. He leapt the stream and ran up the slope, turning around and back. *Where?* he questioned, silently. The voices were urgent, out of hearing. His name formed; but it was only wind and water. A woman laughed, a long way away.

'Eleanor.'

He jumped, startled at his own voice, and shook himself. He made himself stand still, frowning at the pulsing sky and tumbling walls till they too stood still and empty, categorised as moonlight, which did not move or make a noise, and wind, which did. His behaviour was ridiculous. He half shrugged at it: a bad dream not fully shaken off. Donnie would still be searching for Tess, or if not, he was probably curled up asleep in a chair at Neilie's, or perhaps he had gone home with Murdo: that would be a mile or so less to walk after a long hard day. Thinking of it, Alan was already racing down the path. He pulled himself up, forcing reason; though Donnie might well be at home, he couldn't barge into the house at that time of morning. He hesitated, but did not turn back. Eleanor lodged in his mind. He would reach the place and find her in bed: in Murdo's bed, which would be strange. She would be dreadfully scandalised at his intrusion, and furious at being wakened up, and she would make nonsense of his fear. He began to run again, desperate for her sarcastic assurance, for her brisk common sense and snappy ill-temper, clearing absurdities and forebodings like a scythe through grass. Matter-of-fact Eleanor, who was never absent-minded and never got carried away, who diagnosed 'flu rather than a rare tropical disease, who could keep a dozen toddlers happy and Murdo under her thumb: she would know.

He slowed, but the wind was behind him, thrusting inexorably, and soon he was running again. 'She hates my guts,' Donnie said; but Eleanor's hate was a mood, a passing fancy. She had said she hated Murdo, Murdo miserable as sin, and had turned round and married him. Donnie was immaturely sensitive and jealous, that was all. But afraid. 'We must get away,' he had said that so often: that was why, but he had never spoken of it, never confessed what he was afraid of. His fear crept into Alan: fear of Eleanor, fear of Murdo. At Roddy's croft gate he jolted to a halt, fighting against the flood of dread in his veins. 'You would be better to get the lad out of here.' He turned, incredulous, staring back at the dip in the path where Donnie had kissed him the previous morning, and run off to the hill with everyday cheerfulness. There could be nothing wrong. But Roddy's strained face: 'It would be better for him.' He stood frozen. Out of jumbled anxieties and reassurances, certain things fell with fatal weight. 'Angus was my first cousin,' 'What could anybody do? They were neighbours,' and from a long way back, icily clear, 'There's a murderer living in Garve.'

At the Morrisons' door he stopped, sobbing for breath and sanity. It couldn't be that. Murdo was his brother. He had the rifle. For Tess. Not for Donnie. Eleanor would know. He pushed the door open; the house was in darkness, everyone was asleep. Nothing could be wrong.

She was in the dark, waiting. She had risen thinking it was Murdo, her face half hidden in the dark, half white and ghastly in the window square of moonlight. Reasoning and sense shattered and fell away from Alan. She thought it was Murdo, and that it was over. She hated. It took a long time to reach her, a terrible effort to touch her flesh. Her hatred paralysed. He got hold of her wrists at last, labouring to speak. 'Where is he?'

'What do you think you're doing here?' Her tone was sharply indignant, normal. He no longer noticed it.

'Where's Donnie?'

'How should I know? He's not my business. Let me go at once!'

He moved his hands up her arms, shaking her violently, though he was unaware of it, or of anything except her hatred and Donnie's fear. She scratched and struggled then.

'You're mad! Leave me alone!'

'Where?'

He had her off the ground, raising her to throw her down. She twisted and shrieked, her mouth a black hole in her moonlight-white face.

'Alan, be careful, Alan! It's your child, it's yours!'

He hurled her to the floor, and himself on top of her. 'Tell me!'

She screamed as he caught her throat. 'I don't know, I don't know! Don't hurt it!'

'Alan!'

There was a sudden yellow light, and Mairi, sobbing and dragging at him, then he was outside, casting this way and that, the hill, the shore. Mairi shouted behind him. He turned, desperate, without direction. She was floundering and falling in her long nightdress. He ran to her and jerked her to her feet. She had a rifle under her. She thrust it at him. 'Go on!' she sobbed, and doubled over with a hoarse scream, clutching his arm. He held her up, frenzied between her pain and Donnie's danger. She pushed him away as the spasm passed. 'No – go on, it's loaded. Up the hill. Oh God, it's too late, I heard a shot!'

The sheep in the wire, long ago. The scream, shuddering the night. He was blind, deaf, unaware that the gasping breath was his own, that he was choosing footholds, keeping direction, checking the gun, running over the forgotten lessons of school rifle-practice.

'It's yours.'

He had said it many times before. Murdo pressed the gun into his throat. 'You're lying.' He was trying to look at his watch in the moonlight, without taking his eyes off Donnie, or moving the gun. He was unsteady. He cursed the bottle he had finished. Four forty-five, he saw at last. Five thirty was Shonny's time. There was the thing Shonny didn't know about. 'Why not get them both together?' Shonny said. Shonny didn't know what he had to find out first.

'Is it his?'

'No.'

He nudged his chin up with the barrel, to get the moonlight on his face; but it gave nothing away. 'It's his. You know, he'll have told you.'

'No, it's yours.'

'Ah, damn you!' He jabbed the gun in hard, making him choke and clutch. 'Keep your hands down or I'll kill you!'

It surprised and exhilarated him that he intended to kill his own brother, whether he kept his hands down or not. Squinting with drink, he glared at the boy. He hadn't reacted much. Maybe he didn't believe it, because they were brothers.

'I'll kill you!' he repeated, indignantly.

Better be careful, though. Have to find out first. Time was getting short. Shonny would do it on the dot and then scarper, no waiting around for him. If he did it at all. He was hard up anyway, there was money in it for him. He might do it. He'd done it before, he said. He seemed to know about it, anyway.

'Hurry up, I haven't got all night. Tell me what you know.' If Shonny didn't do it, he'd have that to do himself too.

'It's yours.'

'I'll kill you if you don't tell.'

'It's yours.'

He cursed, a stream of soft filthy abuse. He was perplexed. He would have liked to make him scream again. A bullet or a blow here or there. The barrel dipped, but he jerked it back again, warily. One wrong move, he'd be off. Shouldn't have drunk so much, unsteady hands. Eleanor was quite right. He tried kicking, but he staggered dangerously and there wasn't much of an impact. 'Bloody drink,' he muttered. 'Never again!' he promised Eleanor, solemnly.

Donnie's eyes were closed. He gave another jerk under his chin, so that his skull cracked against the rock. He did that a few more times, leaning forward cautiously to help with his left hand pushed into his face, watching out for him biting, he always used to bite. But he didn't want to get too close. Safer with both hands on the gun.

'Come on. Tell. I'll let you go.'

He waited a decent time for an answer. There was none. Indignation swelled in his temples. 'You're no good. You're disgusting. A disgrace to the family.' He enunciated it with dignified clarity, picking his way carefully through the whisky. 'You filth! You should be wiped out. You don't deserve to live.' He emphasised with a jab at each word. 'Don't deserve to live, after what you've done.' Eleanor said that. She didn't know, but she'd be pleased afterwards. 'I'm going to kill you. But first I'm going to tell you what's going to happen to your Alan.'

The boy cried out, a sharp wail of anguish. Murdo took time to look at his watch, holding the gun firm. 'What's going to happen in thirty-five minutes from now. Will you like that, eh?'

'Alan, Alan.' He whispered the name then, over and over. That was good, and the tears pouring down his cheeks and the shudders passing through his body. Murdo watched him for a bit, then remembered the other thing.

'You tell. I'll let you both go.'

'It's his. I know looking at her, she wanted it. Alan doesn't know, leave him alone!'

That was hell. It was triumph. He breathed great gusts of power. He had it all now. 'Leave him alone to go sneaking on me? No fucking likely. No chance. First you, then him.' He paused, the ecstasy of blood thumping in his ears, relishing the despairing face. He stroked the trigger, not in a hurry: but time was passing too. 'I'm going to kill you. But by God, I'll make a mess of you first.'

Shakily, because of the drink and his hammering pulse, he edged the gun down. Careful; not too many bullets. Shonny said, don't leave them in him. Better not. He raised the barrel regretfully, wondering what to do instead. It would be a pity not to do anything. 'Pity I didn't do it long ago,' he said. He peered down at the crown of his brother's head, where the gash had been. 'I tried,' he added proudly.

There was a splintering crack, knifing his face. He howled, lurched, fired. The blast was in his own ear, and he was falling.

Alan knew the place. He fired as soon as he could distinguish the spike of fence on the summit, and again at the head and upflung arm with the gun. Murdo arched and fell, roaring. Alan dodged his fall mechanically, without understanding. He clawed upwards and threw himself on the inert body.

From his bedroom window on the point at Ardbuie, Uncle Kenny

369

glowered out towards Skalanish. He often glared in that direction; he had hated his brother-in-law cordially, and in the past week he had acquired an additional malevolent interest in the place. '"For which things the wrath of God cometh upon the children of disobedience,"' he muttered, longingly. His customary loud 'Amen!' was stopped in his throat by distant gunfire. He thrust his head forward, listening, his ears were still good.

'Marion!' he shouted, angrily.

She came in yawning, carrying her father's first cup of tea of the day. He had had her out of bed even earlier than usual. He had been restless all week, reading the bible half the night and getting himself all worked up.

'Who's that shooting?'

'It would be Angus Gnipadale's boys, Dad. I was hearing they're out after a dog tonight.'

The old man's hand trembled with rage, rattling the spoon on the rim of the cup. She steadied it for him.

'A household of sinners!' He shook his free fist in her face. 'You'll not mention that family under my roof!' He began to fumble through the bible at his side. '"For whosoever shall commit any of these abominations, even the souls that commit them shall be cut off from among the people,"' he proclaimed, jabbing with his bent old finger till the thin paper crumpled. 'Children of disobedience!'

'It's only one of them, Dad,' Marion said gently. 'Just wee Donnie. Murdo is a good steady lad if he would keep away from the drink.'

'Ach, be quiet woman! "The land is defiled: therefore I do visit the iniquity thereof upon it,"' he intoned, with relish.

She was quiet. She was wondering who the ambulance was for. She had seen it racing down the main road when she was pouring the tea in the kitchen. It would be for old Johane or Angus's Mairi.

'"There shall be no whore of the daughters of Israel nor sodomite of the sons of Israel!"' He waved the bible at her vigorously.

'Ay, Dad.' It made her uneasy to see the sacred pages flapping like that. 'Calm down now, Dad. Were you taking your pills today yet?'

'The Lord giveth and the Lord taketh away. Pills no bloody use to me.'

She sighed. She was hoping, God willing, that the next sermon would not be like the last one. It had got him too excited. He'd be having a turn like the time he found the tourist girl bathing with not a stitch on her.

Kenny mumbled a grace, slurped his tea in one noisy draught, and banged the cup down tetchily. 'What's that bloody fool at, shooting a bloody dog? It's his brother he should be shooting. "If a man also lie with mankind, they shall surely be put to death: their blood shall be upon them!" Amen!'

'Oh well, right enough, Dad.' Marion took his cup. 'Poor lad,' she added to herself as she refilled it in the kitchen.

Shonny heard the shots. Two. He raised his eyes to heaven. Bloody fool, one would have done. He wasn't leaving himself much time to clean up, either. People would be near enough waking up, hearing and seeing this and that. It was too dangerous to wait, the light was beginning to grow. He let off the handbrake and coasted down the hill, smirking at his own legs clad in Murdo's boiler suit and boots: he had found them convenient in Murdo's car when he had borrowed it quietly for the occasion. 'Just in case,' he explained to the boots.

Roddy heard the shots too, and sweated where he lay, cowering under the compelling weight of centuries.

'Murdo,' said Donnie at last. 'Where is he?'

Alan's heart chilled. 'I shot him.'

'Dead?'

'I don't know. I meant to.' Had meant to kill. He was trembling uncontrollably. His arms tightened round Donnie, alive.

'Let's look.' Donnie reached for the gun. They slithered down, clinging to each other. Alan turned the body over. The face was masked in blood, open-mouthed. Alan was shaking too much to feel breath or heartbeat. Donnie crouched at the head for a moment, pushing it from side to side. 'Not dead,' he said. 'You got half his ear, that's all. Drunk and dazed.'

'Thank God!'

'You want him to live? Why?'

Alan looked at his white face in the moonlight, the weary sag of his body, the dark trickles of blood on his neck. Murdo had done that, had tormented him, would have killed him in cold blood. 'I don't know,' he whispered.

'Did you see Tess?'

'Yes.'

'He'll be the death of plenty more like that. I'd put a bullet through his brain now.'

He had the gun cocked and pointed. 'Why not? Why not, Alan?'

He shook his head, not knowing: why life, even that life, destroying and hating, should live, unjustly, undeservedly. Donnie by right could do it: could do what his brother would have done, what justice demanded, what pity for future victims demanded.

'Will you stop me?'

'No.' There was no innocence. He choked with grief. He dropped on his knees, sobbing with his arms over his face.

The rifle clattered on the rock. 'Alan, oh my love.'

Donnie's arms sheltered him, his slight bruised body a shield, his love the only truth. 'Come away,' he whispered, pulling Alan to his feet. He bent again for the gun, and as they went down tossed it into the dark gulley below them. 'I follow your ways now,' he said, smiling. 'No more guns.'

Behind his tilted head Alan saw a sudden nimbus of orange flaring on the silver moor. Even the dull shock in the air did not fill the gap of incomprehension, till Donnie slumped against him, shuddering violently.

'That was for you.'

They held each other tightly. There was nothing else left.

Marion huddled by the stove, yawning and dozing, lulled by the monotonous grumbling from the next room. She glanced at the clock from time to time, wondering when would be the earliest she could ring Chrissie to find out about the ambulance. Not before seven thirty, anyway: well, maybe the quarter past. It had gone back up the road very quick. It must be Mairi, surely, it would have taken them longer than that to move the old woman. She wasn't due, but she was big enough with it, poor wee soul.

She started up, suddenly aware that the familiar muttering and groaning in her father's room had stopped. 'Dad, are you all right?'

There was no answer.

She hurried through. 'Dad, what's wrong?'

He was motionless at the window, with his two arms up and his two sticks pointing in the air. His jaw sagged and his eyes were fixed.

'Dad!'

He flailed the curtains with his sticks, roaring in triumph. 'Brimstone and fire from the Lord out of Heaven! Hallelujah! Oh, great stuff, man!'

'What now?' Alan knew the answer, but it was at odds with his education.

'Get out. That's all they want. Come on, the day is good anyway.'

They went down in the two-edged light of the moon and dawn, slithering and lurching against each other, unwilling to lose hold.

'Why?' Alan asked, when the ground was more level.

'Hate.'

'But why?'

'No why! Why do you love?'

He rememberd with a gush of pity that he had heard the like before. 'Eleanor.' She was lost, swallowed in her own abyss. She had loved him in her way, and he had never known, had not recognised the disnatured thing she bred from it. 'Donnie – she says it's my child.'

'Yes, that's what Murdo thought.'

He turned him face to, searching his eyes in the faint light. 'Is it?'

There was fear in his face, bitter fear of the truth; but truth it would be. He looked inward, with unfocussed eyes.

'No!' he said at last. 'Och no, it's none of yours, Alan. It's Murdo's all right. Black as the devil!' He flung his arms round Alan, laughing and then crying.

He knew then what had gone unsaid for terror. 'Oh Donnie! Why didn't you tell me?'

'Black as the devil!' he repeated, rubbing his own dark head against Alan's cheek. 'Now let's get going.'

They came down above Roddy's sleeping house, among dew-wet sheep still vocal in their new pasture, over the stile, and for the last time up the pass. The air was bright before sunrise, the sky delicate as violets, feathered with dove grey. The moor was waking with peewits and larks. Selena bobbed in the bay, misting and clearing in the long plume of smoke driving over the ridge. The ugly stink of it violated the sweet morning smell of mosses and seaweed. Alan grieved for the mice, and hugged Donnie closer.

'Fladday, then, till the sea goes down.' He bent over the wet knots tying down the dory.

Donnie snorted. 'No friends to us on Fladday. It's got to be Rona. There's food in the house there and we'll get water.'

'Rona? Not in this, Donnie.' The wind was due west, and pushing the inflowing swells into great shining whalebacks through the narrows, sucking in and out of every fang and skerry. 'I daren't risk running down there.'

'We daren't not risk it.' Donnie heaved the dory over. His eyes were ice-bleak, fighting weariness and desperation. 'Go to Fladday or stay here, we'll be up for attempted murder and arson. Have you thought of that?'

He hadn't, of course.

'Our word against everyone else's, Alan. We're unclean, remember. We'd better go quietly.'

'Oh, but surely—' He stopped. Very little was sure.

Donnie took his hands, smiling. 'You've got a lot of brains, but no sense.'

'Oh, none at all! Rona, then.'

Past the end of Vatasgeir the violent three-directional swells eased.

'It's getting better,' said Donnie, still pumping. It was some minutes since they had shipped any water.

At the last moment before the shoals inshore of Vatasgeir, they turned across seas, but out of the current. Donnie scrambled up as the wind came strongly on the beam. 'It's great!' he said, through chattering teeth. He was drenched.

Alan grovelled to a few more swells before he could agree. Rona's treacherous wind-tossing cliffs loomed ahead, but with flat water under them. He chanced a smile at Donnie between surges. 'I think we might make it after all.'

'Och, yes, in time for breakfast. Christ, it's cold!' He began to sing, laughing at the shivers in his own voice. With new mast and white sails, Selena going like a roe deer: and so she was. The song rang out strongly as the sea-roar of the great swells on Vatasgeir faded behind them. The last verses were different from usual.

'What have you done to that song?'

'It was not the girl going round the cattle that you saw.' His eyes brimmed with laughter. 'It was the boy going round the sheep.'